MISERY LOVES COMPANY

J'merlia opened his mouth to protest again and found that he could not speak. Could not breathe. Could not *think.* He was being dismembered—no, dis*minded,* in exquisite torture.

The entry of the seedship into the outskirts of the amorphous singularity had been painful, but that had been *physical* pain, twisting and tearing and stretching. This was far worse. J'merlia's soul was being *fractionated,* his mind splitting into pieces, his consciousness spinning away along many divergent worldlines.

He tried to scream. And when he at last succeeded, he heard a new sound: a dozen beings, all of them J'merlia, crying their agony across the universe.

By Charles Sheffield
Published by Ballantine Books:

PROTEUS UNBOUND

SIGHT OF PROTEUS

TRADER'S WORLD

THE WEB BETWEEN THE WORLDS

The Heritage Universe
Book One: SUMMERTIDE
Book Two: DIVERGENCE
Book Three: TRANSCENDENCE

TRANSCENDENCE

Book Three of
The Heritage Universe

Charles Sheffield

A Del Rey Book
BALLANTINE BOOKS • NEW YORK

A Del Rey Book
Published by Ballantine Books

 Published in the United States by Ballantine Books, a division of Random House, Inc., New York, and simultaneously in Canada by Random House of Canada Limited, Toronto.

Library of Congress Catalog Card Number: 91-47012

ISBN 0-345-36982-3

Manufactured in the United States of America

First Hardcover Edition: May 1992
First Mass Market Edition: April 1993

For Ann, Kit, Rose, and Toria,
and all other bi-modal distributions.

CHAPTER 1

Sentinel Gate

THE BUILDER ARTIFACT known as Paradox *lies deep in Fourth Alliance territory (Bose Access Node, G-232). The fact that Paradox contains a Lotus field has been known for almost three thousand years, since the Ruttledge expedition of E.1379 (Reference: Parzen, E.1383). Although such a field destroys both organic and inorganic memories, it does not invariably inhibit the passage of electrical signals along a neural cable conductor. At least one counter-example is known. (Reference: . . .*

Reference?

Darya Lang's hands hovered over the input coder, while she stared at the display in total frustration. What could she write next? It was a point of pride with her that the entries in the *Lang Universal Artifact Catalog* (Fifth Edition) be as accurate and up-to-date as possible. It was not her fault that some of her recent proposed entries were being criticized because of the ignorance of other editors. She *knew,* even if they did not, that in certain circumstances an electrical signal could travel along a neural cable from inside a Lotus field to a computer outside. Although she had not seen it herself, she had the word of the councilor who had observed it, and councilors did not lie.

Not to mention the word of the embodied computer, E. Crimson Tally, to whom it had actually happened.

She chewed at her bottom lip, and at last made the entry.

Reference: private communication, Councilor Julius Graves.

It was the best that she could do, a far cry from the usual form of academic references that Professor Merada would consider satisfactory. But in this case, the less said, the better. If Darya were to add that the cited incident with the Lotus field had taken place on an artificial planetoid known as Glister, just before Graves and Tally and Darya herself had been thrown thirty thousand light-years out of the spiral arm by a Builder transportation system, to a location where they had encountered . . . well, don't go any further. Merada would just lose his mind. Or more likely tell Darya that she was losing hers.

Maybe she was—but not for that reason.

It was late in the evening, and Darya had been working outside in the quiet of a little leafy bower. The calm air of Sentinel Gate was filled with the perfume of the planet's night-scented flowers and the faint cooing of nesting birds. Now she stood up from the terminal and moved to push the vines aside.

She knew exactly where to look: east, to where Sentinel itself was rising. Two hundred million kilometers away and almost a million across, that shining and striated sphere dominated the moonless night sky. Since childhood, it and the mystery of the Builder artifacts had also dominated Darya's thinking. She would be the first to admit that it had shaped her whole life.

And the artifacts shaped her life still—but in a quite different way. Darya stared at Sentinel, as she had stared at it a thousand times before, and marveled at how much she had changed in so short a time. One year ago she had been a dedicated research scientist who asked nothing more than her library and her work, cataloging and analyzing data on the thousand-plus Builder artifacts scattered around the spiral arm. The discovery of a statistical anomaly involving *all* the artifacts had persuaded her to leave her quiet study on Sentinel Gate, and travel from the civilized region of the Fourth Alliance to the rough outpost worlds of Quake and Opal.

There she had found her anomaly—and more. She had found danger, excitement, despair, terror, pain, exhilaration, and companionship. Half-a-dozen times she had been close to death. And returning at last to Sentinel Gate, the place she had longed for so hard and so long, she had found something else. She had found herself to be—to be—

Darya stared at Sentinel, and struggled to admit the truth.

To be *bored.*

Incredible, but that was the only word for it. The life of a successful archeo-scientist, once so rich and satisfying, was no longer enough.

It was easy to see why. The disappearance of the Builders from the spiral arm five million years ago had provided for Darya the most fascinating mystery imaginable. She could think of nothing more interesting than exploring the artifacts left behind by the long-vanished race, seeking to understand them and perhaps to learn where the Builders had gone, and why.

Nothing more interesting, that is, so long as the Builders *remained* vanished. But once one had met constructs who explained that they were the Builders' own representatives, who still served the Builders' interests . . . why, then the past became irrelevant. What mattered was the present and the future, with the possibility of encountering and studying the Builders *themselves.* Even the most interesting parts of her old life, including her cherished catalog of artifacts, could not compete.

Darya's communication terminal was sending a soft piping sound in her direction. She walked back to it in no particular hurry. It was going to be Professor Merada—these days it was *always* Professor Merada, at any hour of the day or night.

His serious, heavy-browed face had already appeared on the screen, overwriting her catalog inputs.

"Professor Lang." He began to speak as soon as she came into his field of view. "Concerning the proposed entry on the Phages."

"Yes?" Darya had an idea what was coming.

"It states here—I quote—'although Phages are generally considered to be slow-moving free-space forms, shunning all forms of gravity field, there are exceptions. In certain circumstances Phages may be induced to move *into* a gravity field, and move with considerable speed.' Professor Lang, I assume that you wrote those words."

"Correct. I wrote them."

"Then what is your *authority* for the statement? You quote none."

Darya swore at herself. Even when she had made that addition to the Phage entry, she had known it would cause trouble. It was the old problem: Should she parrot conventional wisdom on the Phages and the Builder artifacts? Or should she tell what she knew to be the truth, even though it could not be supported by anything but her own word and that of a few other people in her party? She had *seen* Phages, moving far faster than any Phage was supposed to be able to move, dive-bombing the ship that she herself rode in. Others had seen those same Phages—supposedly indestructible—smashed into fragments on the surface of a high-field planetoid.

She felt angry with Merada, and knew she had no right to. He was doing exactly what a conscientious and first-rate scientist should do—what Darya herself would have done one year ago: ruling out hearsay and shoddy research, by insisting on complete documentation.

"I will send you a reference, as soon as I have approval to release it."

"Make it soon, Professor Lang. The official closing date for changes to the catalog is already past. Are you sure that you will be able to obtain approval?"

"I'll do my best." Darya nodded to indicate that the conversation was over and moved away from the terminal. Merada assumed that the approval she referred to was no more than the consent of another researcher to make known a preliminary finding, perhaps in advance of official publication. The truth was insanely more complex. Approval for this information would have to come from the whole interclade Council.

She had moved no more than half-a-dozen steps when the communications terminal issued another soft whistle. Darya sighed and turned back. Persistence was a prime virtue in any research worker; but sometimes Merada took it to extremes.

"Yes, Professor?" She spoke without looking at the screen.

"Darya?" a faint voice queried. "Is that you?"

Darya gasped and stared at the terminal, but all it offered was the white-noise display of a sound-only link.

"Hans? Hans Rebka? Where are you? Are you on Miranda?"

"Not any more." The voice was faint and distorted, but even so the bitterness could be heard in it. "There was no point in staying. The Council wouldn't even *listen*. I'm at the final Bosc Network Node before Sentinel Gate. I can't talk now. Expect me on Sentinel Gate in half a day."

The space-thinned voice faded and the connection was abruptly broken. Darya walked forward to the easy chair in front of the terminal and collapsed into it. She sat staring at nothing.

The Council did not believe them. Incredible. That meant that it had rejected the sworn statements of one of its own Council members; and of the embodied computer, E. C. Tally, who did not know how to lie; and of Hans Rebka, recognized as one of the most experienced and canny troubleshooters in the whole spiral arm.

Darya roused herself. She ought to call Professor Merada and tell him that many of the references that she wanted to cite had been dismissed by the highest authority in the spiral arm. What the Council did not accept, no one else would consider reliable. But she did not move. The Council rejection was certainly bad news, since it meant that *nothing* that she, or anyone else in their party, said about the events of the past year would have credibility.

But what the rejection implied was far worse, the worst news of all: Zardalu were at large in the spiral arm—and no one in authority believed it.

CHAPTER 2

"ALLOW ME TO introduce Captain Hans Rebka."

Darya had steeled herself for the looks she would receive when Hans was ushered into the Institute's dining room. Even so, they were hard to take.

"Captain Rebka is a native of Teufel, in the Phemus Circle," she went on, "although most recently he has been on Miranda."

The score of research workers sitting at the long table were doing their best not to stare—and failing. Darya could easily put herself in their shoes. They saw a small, thin man in his late thirties, dressed in a patched and dingy uniform. His head appeared a fraction too big for his body, and his bony face was disfigured by a dozen scars, the most noticeable of them running in a double line from his left temple to the point of his jaw.

Darya knew how her colleagues were feeling. She had experienced an identical reaction when she first met Hans Rebka. Courage and skill were invisible; it took time to learn that he had both.

She glanced down the table. Professor Merada had made one of his rare excursions from the den of his study to the senior dining room, while across from him at the far end Carmina Gold sat peering thoughtfully at her fingernails. Darya knew both of them well, and fully appreciated what they could do. If someone was needed to perform an excruciatingly detailed and encyclopedic survey of any element of spiral arm history, flagging every tiny inconsistency of data or missing reference, then the thoughtful, humorless Merada could not be surpassed; if someone was needed who could follow and tease out the most convoluted train of logic, simplify it to essentials, and present it so that a child —or a councilor!—could grasp it, then Carmina Gold, moody and childish herself, was the absolute best.

But if you found yourself in deep trouble, without any hope of escape and so close to Death that you could smell his breath in your own terrified sweat . . . well, then you closed your eyes tight and prayed for Hans Rebka.

But none of that *showed.* To the eye of anyone from a rich world of the Fourth Alliance, the newcomer was nothing but an ill-dressed hick from the back of nowhere. He fitted not at all into the genteel, leisurely, and cultured frame of an Institute dinner.

The others at the table were at least making an effort at politeness.

"You were recently on Miranda?" the woman next to Rebka said as he sat down. She was Glenna Omar, one of the senior information-systems specialists and in Darya's view quite unnecessarily beautiful. "I've never been there, although I suppose that I should have, since it's the headquarters for the Fourth Alliance. What did you think of Miranda, Captain?"

Rebka stared blank-faced down at his plate while Darya, sitting opposite him, waited anxiously. If he was going to be rude or sullen or outrageous, here in her own home . . . there had been no time to brief him, only to give him a hug and a hurried greeting, after he had been decanted from the subluminal delivery craft and before the Immigration officials were ushering them into the dining room to meet her colleagues.

"Paradise," Rebka said suddenly. He turned to Glenna Omar and gave her an admiring smile packed with sexual overtones. "I'm from Teufel, of course, where the best road you can find is said to be any road that takes you somewhere else; so some might argue that I'm easily impressed. But I thought that Miranda was wonderful, my idea of paradise —until I landed here on Sentinel Gate, and learned that I was wrong. *This* has to be the most beautiful planet in the whole Fourth Alliance—in the whole spiral arm."

Darya took a deep breath and relaxed—for half a second. Hans was on his best behavior, but Glenna Omar's response was a good deal too warm.

"Oh, you're just being nice to us, Captain," she was saying. "Of course, I've never been to any of the worlds of your Phemus Circle, either. How would you describe *them* to me?"

Dingy, dirty, dismal, and dangerous, Darya thought. Remote, impoverished, brutish, backward, and barbaric. And all the men are sex-mad.

"I haven't been to *all* the worlds of the Phemus Circle," Rebka was replying. "But I can tell you what they say in the Circle about my home world, Teufel: 'What sins must a man commit, in how many past lives, to be born on Teufel?' "

"Oh, come now. It can't really be that bad."

"It's worse."

"The most awful planet in the whole Phemus Circle?"

"I never said that. Scaldworld is probably as bad, and people from Styx say that they go to Teufel for vacations."

"Now I'm *sure* you're joking. If the whole Phemus Circle is as horrible as you say, no one would stay there. What job do you have, when you're back home?"

"I guess you could call me a traveling troubleshooter. One thing the Phemus Circle is never short of, that's trouble. That's how Professor Lang"—he nodded to Darya—"and I met. We ran into a spot of bother together on Quake, one component of a double planet in the Mandel system."

"And she brought you back here, to the Fourth Alliance? Wise Darya." But Glenna did not take her eyes off Rebka.

"Not right away." Rebka paused, with an expression on his face that Darya recognized. He was about to take some major step. "We did a few other things first. We and a few others—humans and aliens, plus an Alliance councilor and an embodied computer—went to one of the Mandel system's gas-giant planets, Gargantua, where we found an artificial planetoid. We flew through a bunch of wild Phages to get there, and rescued some of us from a Lotus field. Then a sentient Builder construct put our party through a Builder transportation system, thirty thousand light-years out of the spiral arm, to a free-space extragalactic Builder facility called Serenity. When we arrived there, Professor Lang and I—"

He was going to tell it all! *Everything!* All the facts that the whole party had agreed must remain dead secret until a high-level approval to discuss them had been granted. Darya tried to kick Rebka's leg under the table and hit nothing but empty air.

"We found a small group of Zardalu—" He was grinding on.

"You mean, you found people from the territory of the Zardalu Communion?" Glenna Omar was smiling with delight. Darya was sure that she thought Rebka was making up the whole thing for her benefit.

"No. I mean what I said. We found *Zardalu,* the original land-cephalopods."

"But they've been extinct for ten thousand years!"

"Most have. But we found fourteen living ones—"

"Eleven thousand years." Merada's high-pitched voice from the end of the table told Darya that everyone in the dining room was listening.

Bang went a lifetime's reputation for serious and sober research work! Darya kicked again at Rebka's leg under the table, only to be rewarded with a pained and outraged cry from Glenna Omar.

"Or rather more than eleven thousand," Merada went on. "As nearly as I can judge, it has been eleven thousand four hundred and—"

"—Zardalu who had been held in a stasis field since the time of the Great Rising, when the rest of the species were killed off. But the ones we met were very much alive, and *nasty—*"

"But this is disgraceful!" Carmina Gold had awakened from her dormouse trance and was scowling down the table at Darya. "You must know the fearsome reputation of the Zardalu—"

"Not just the reputation." Darya gave up the attempt to stay out of it. "I know them from *personal experience.* They're worse than their reputation."

"—we managed to send them back to the spiral arm." Rebka had his hand on Glenna Omar's elbow and seemed to be ignoring the uproar rising from all parts of the long table. "And later we returned from Serenity ourselves, except for a Cecropian, Atvar H'sial, and an augmented Karelian human from the Zardalu Communion, Louis Nenda, who remained there to—"

"—a dating based on admittedly incomplete, subjective, and unreliable reference sources," Merada said loudly, "such as Hymenopt race memories, and the files of—"

"—living Zardalu should *certainly* have been reported to the Alliance Council!" Carmina Gold was standing up. "At once. I will do it now, even if you will not."

"We already did that!" Darya stood up, too. Everyone seemed to be saying "Zardalu!" at once, and the group sounded like a swarm of angry bees. She did not think that Carmina Gold could even hear her. "What do you think that Captain Rebka was doing on Miranda before he came here?" she shouted along the table. "Sunbathing?"

"—about four meters tall." Rebka had his head close to Glenna Omar's. "An adult specimen, standing erect, with a midnight-blue torso supported on thick blue tentacles—"

"—*living* Zardalu—"

"My *God*!" Merada's piercing tenor cut through the hubbub. His worries over the dating of Zardalu extinctions had apparently been replaced by a much more urgent one. He turned to Darya. "Wild Phages, and an Alliance councilor, and an embodied computer. Professor Lang, those entries for the fifth edition of the catalog, the ones for which you promised to provide the references. *Are you telling me that the only reference sources you will offer me are—*"

There was a loud crash. Carmina Gold, hurrying out of the dining room but turning to glare back at Darya, had collided with a squat robot carrying a big tureen of hot soup. Scalding liquid jetted across the room and splashed onto the back of Glenna Omar's graceful bare neck. She screamed like a mortally wounded pig.

Darya sat down again and closed her eyes. With or without soup, it was unlikely to be one of the Institute's most relaxing dinners.

"I thought I handled things rather well." Hans Rebka was lying flat on the thick carpet in the living room of Darya's private quarters. He claimed that it was softer than his bed on Teufel. "You have to understand, Darya, I said all those things about the Builders and the Zardalu *on purpose.*"

"I'm sure you did—after we all agreed to reveal absolutely nothing to anyone about them! *You* agreed to it, yourself."

"I did. Graves proposed it, but we all agreed we should keep everything to ourselves until the formal briefing to the Council. The last thing we wanted was to throw the spiral arm into a panic because there are live Zardalu on the loose."

"And a panic is just what you started at dinner. Why did you all of a sudden do the exact opposite of what we said we'd do?"

"I told you, the briefing to the Council was an absolute *fiasco.* We *need* to get people worked up about the Zardalu now. Not one Council member would believe a word of what we had to say!"

"But Julius Graves *is* a Council member—he's one of them, an insider."

"He is, and yet he isn't. *He* was elected one of them, but

of course his interior mnemonic twin, *Steven* Graves, as someone pointed out early in the hearing, was never elected to *anything.* No one expected a simple memory extension device to develop self-awareness, and that happened *after* Julius was elected to the Council. The integration of the personalities of Julius and Steven seems to be complete now —the composite calls himself *Julian,* and gets upset if you forget and still call him Julius or Steven. But there were more than a few hints by other councilors that the development of Steven had sent Julius off his head while the integration was going on. You can see their point: although councilors do not lie or fabricate events, *Julian* Graves is not, and never was, a councilor."

"But what about E. C. Tally? A computer, even an embodied computer, can't lie. He should have had more to say than anyone—his original body was torn to bits by the Zardalu."

"Try and prove that, when you don't have one tangible scrap of evidence that all the Zardalu didn't become extinct eleven thousand years ago, and stay extinct. A computer can't lie, true enough—but it can sure as hell be reprogrammed with a false set of memories."

"Why would anyone want to do that?"

"That's not the Council's worry. And old E.C. didn't help *his* case at all. Halfway through his testimony he started to lecture the Council about the inadequacies of the Fourth Alliance central data banks, and the nonsense that had been pumped into him from those banks about the other clades of the spiral arm before he was sent to the Phemus Circle. The Council data specialist interrupted E.C. to say that was ridiculous, her data banks contained nothing but accurate data. She insisted on doing a high-level correlation between E.C.'s brain and what's in the central banks. That's what convinced the Council that Tally's brain had been tampered with. His memory bank shows that Cecropians believe themselves superior to humans and all other species, and that a Lo'tfian interpreter for a Cecropian can when necessary operate quite independently of his Cecropian dominatrix. It shows that Hymenopts are intelligent, too—probably more intelligent than humans. It shows that there exist sentient Builder constructs, millions of years old but able to communicate with humans. It shows that instantaneous travel is possible, even without the use of the Bose Network."

"But that's true—we did it, when we traveled to Serenity. It's *all* true. Every one of the statements you just made is accurate!"

"Not according to your great and wonderful Alliance Council." Rebka's voice was bitter. "According to them, Serenity doesn't even exist, because it's not in their data banks. The information there is holy writ, something you just don't argue with, and what's not there isn't knowledge. It's the same problem I've suffered all my life: somebody a hundred or a thousand light-years from the problem thinks they can have better facts than the workers on the spot. But they can't, and they don't."

"But didn't you *say* all that to them?"

"Me say it? Who am I? According to the Alliance Council, I'm a nobody, from a nowhere little region called the Phemus Circle, not big or important enough to have clout with either the human or the interspecies Council. They took less notice of me than they did of E. C. Tally. I began to describe the Zardalu's physical strength, and their phenomenal breeding rate. Do you know what they said? They explained to me that the Zardalu are long-extinct, because if that were not the case, then certainly their presence would have been reported *somewhere,* in the Fourth Alliance, or the Cecropia Federation, or the Zardalu Communion. Then they mentioned that the Fourth Alliance has evolved techniques unknown in the Phemus Circle 'for dealing with mental disorders,' and if I behaved myself they might be able to arrange for some kind of treatment. That's when Graves lost his temper."

"I can't believe it. He *never* loses his temper—he doesn't know how to."

"He does now. *Julian* Graves is different from Julius or

Steven. He told the Council that they are a bunch of irresponsible apes—Senior Councilor Knudsen does look just like a gorilla, I noticed that myself—who are too closed-minded to recognize a danger to the spiral arm when it's staring them in the face. And then he quit."

"He left the Chamber?"

"No. He *resigned from the Council*—something no one has ever done before. He told them that the next time they saw him, he would make them all eat their words. And *then* he left the Chamber, and took E. C. Tally with him."

"Where did he go?"

"He hasn't gone anywhere—yet. But he's going to, as soon as he can get his hands on a ship and recruit the crew he needs. Meanwhile, he's going to tell anyone who will listen about the Zardalu, and about how dangerous they are. And then he's going to look for the Zardalu. He and E. C. Tally feel sure that if the Zardalu came back anywhere in the spiral arm, they will have tried to return to their cladeworld, Genizee."

"But no one has any idea where Genizee is. The location was lost in the Great Rising."

"So we're going to have to look for it."

"We? You mean that *you'll* be going with Graves and E. C. Tally?"

"Yes." Rebka sat upright. "I'm going. In fact, I'll have to leave in just a few hours. I want to make the Council eat their words as much as Graves does. But more than that, I don't want the Zardalu to breed themselves back to power. I don't frighten easily, but they *scare* me. If they're anywhere in the spiral arm, I want to find them."

Darya stood up abruptly and moved across to the open window. "So you're leaving." It was a warm, breezy night, and the sound of rustling palm leaves blurred the hurt in her words. "You travel four days and nine light-years to get here, you've been with me only a couple of hours, and already you want to say good-bye."

"If that's all I can say." Hans Rebka had risen quietly to his feet and moved silently across the thick pile of the carpet.

"And if that's all you can say, too." He put his arms around Darya's waist. "But that's not my first choice. I'm not just visiting, love. I'm recruiting. Julian Graves and I are going a long way; no one knows how far, and no one knows if we'll make it back. Can you come with us? *Will* you come with us?"

Darya glanced across to her terminal, where the remaining entries for the fifth edition were awaiting their final proofreading; and at her diary on the desk, with its heading Important Events—seminars and colloquia, publication due dates and the arrival of visiting academics, birthdays and vacations and picnics and galas and dinner parties. She went across to her desk, switched off the terminal, and closed her diary.

"When do we leave?"

CHAPTER 3

Miranda

THE WAITING ROOMS of Miranda Spaceport were Downside, in the ninth passenger ring twenty-six miles from the foot of the Stalk. Cleanup and maintenance was the job of the service robots, but ever since the incident when the Doradan Colubrid ambassador had accidentally been left to sit and patiently starve to death while robots dutifully dusted and mopped and polished around and over her, human supervisors had made occasional routine inspections.

One of those supervisors had been hovering around waiting room 7872, where a silent figure occupied and overflowed a couch in the room's center. Supervisor Garnoff had three times approached, and three times retreated.

He knew the life-form well enough. It was an adult Cecropian, one of the giant blind arthropods who dominated the Cecropia Federation. This one was strange in two ways. First, she was alone. The Lo'tfian slave-translator who invariably accompanied a Cecropian was absent. And second, the Cecropian had an indefinably dusty and battered look. The six jointed legs were sprawled anyhow around the carapace, rather than being tucked neatly beneath in the conventional rest position. The end of the thin proboscis, instead of being folded into a pouch on the bottom of the pleated chin, was drooping out and down onto the dark-red segmented chest.

The big question was, was she alive and well? The Cecropian had not moved since Garnoff first came on duty five hours earlier. He came to stand in front of her. The white, eyeless head did not move.

"Are you all right?"

He did not expect a spoken answer, although the Cecropian, if she was alive, undoubtedly heard him with the yellow open horns set in the middle of her head. Since all Cecropians "saw" by echolocation, sending high-frequency sonic pulses from the pleated resonator on the chin, she had sensitive hearing all through and far beyond the human frequency range.

On the other hand, she could not speak to him in any language that he would understand. With hearing usurped for vision, Cecropians "spoke" to each other chemically, with a full and rich language, through the emission and receipt of pheromones. The pair of fernlike antennas on top of the great blind head could detect and identify single molecules of the many thousands of different airborne odors generated by the apocrine ducts on the Cecropian's thorax.

But if she was alive, she must know that he was talking to her; and she should at least register his presence.

There was no reaction. The yellow horns did not turn in his direction; the long antennas remained furled.

"I said, are you all right?" He spoke more loudly. "Is there anything you need? Can you hear me?"

"She sure can," said a human voice behind him. "And she thinks you're a pain in the ass. So bug off and leave her alone."

Garnoff turned. Standing right in front of him was a short, swarthy man in a ragged shirt and dirty trousers. He needed a shave, and his eyes were tired and bloodshot. But there was plenty of energy in his stance.

"And who the devil might *you* be?" It was not the supervisor's approved form of address to Mirandan visitors, but the newcomer's strut encouraged it.

"My name's Louis Nenda. I'm a Karelian, though I don't see how that's any of your damn business."

"I'm a supervisor here. My business is making sure everything's going all right in the waiting rooms. And *she*"—Garnoff pointed—"don't look too hot to me."

"She's not. She's tired. *I'm* tired. We've come a long way. So leave us alone."

"Oh? Since when did you learn to read Cecropian thoughts? You don't know how she feels. Seems to me she might be in trouble."

The squat stranger began to stretch to his full height, then changed his mind and sat down, squeezing onto the couch next to the Cecropian. "What the hell. I got too much to do to hassle on this. Atvar H'sial's my partner. I understand her, she understands me. Here, take a look at this place from ten feet up."

He sat silent for a second, frowning at nothing. Suddenly the Cecropian at his side moved. Two of the jointed forearms reached out to grip Garnoff by the waist. Before the supervisor could do more than shout, he was lifted into the air, high above the Cecropian's great white head, and held there wriggling.

"All right, At, that's enough. Put him down easy." Louis Nenda nodded as the Cecropian gently lowered Garnoff to the floor. "Happy now? Or do you need a full-scale demo?"

But Garnoff was already backing away, out of reach of the long jointed limbs. "You can both stay here and rot, far as I'm concerned." When he was at a safe distance he paused. "How the hell did you *do* that? Talk to her, I mean. I thought no human could communicate with a Cecropian without an interpreter."

Louis Nenda shrugged without looking at Garnoff. "Got me an augment, back on Karelia. Send and receive. Cost a lot, but it's been worth it. Now, you go an' give us a bit of peace."

He waited until Garnoff was at the entrance to the waiting

room, forty meters away. "You were right, At." The silent and invisible pheromonal message diffused across to the Cecropian's receptors. "They're here on Miranda, staying over in Delbruck. Both of 'em, J'merlia and Kallik."

There was a slow, satisfied nodding of the blind white head. "So I surmised." Atvar H'sial vibrated her wing cases, as though shaking off the dust of weeks of travel. "That is satisfactory. Did you establish communication?"

"Not from here. Too dangerous. We don't call 'em, see, till we know we can get to 'em in person. That way nobody can talk them out of it."

"No one will talk my J'merlia out of anything, once he knows that I am alive and present again in the spiral arm. But I accept that personal contact is preferable . . . if it can be accomplished. How do you propose that we proceed?"

"Well . . ." Louis Nenda reached into his pocket and pulled out a wafer-thin card. "That last jump pushed us down to the bottom of our credit. How far to Delbruck?"

"Two thousand four hundred kilometers, by direct flight."

"We can't afford that. What about overland?"

"How are the mighty fallen." Atvar H'sial sat crouched for a moment in calculation. "Three thousand eight hundred kilometers over land, if we avoid crossing any water body."

"Okay." It was Nenda's turn to calculate. "Three days by ground transport. Just enough for the trip, with nothing left at the end. Not even for food on the way. What you think?"

"I do not think." The pheromones were touched with resignation. "When there is no choice, I act."

The great Cecropian untucked her six limbs. She stood erect to tower four feet above Louis Nenda. "Come. As we say in my species, *Delay is the deadliest form of denial.* To Delbruck."

It was a transformed Louis Nenda who led Atvar H'sial off the bus in Delbruck three days later. He was clean-shaven and wearing a smart new outfit of royal blue.

"Well, that worked out real nice." The pheromones grinned at Atvar H'sial while Nenda waved a serious good-bye to four gloomy passengers. He hailed a local cab sized to accommodate large aliens.

The Cecropian nodded. "It worked. But it will not work twice, Louis Nenda."

"Sure it'll work. 'One born every minute' needs updating. One born every *second* is more like it. The arm's full of 'em."

"They were becoming suspicious."

"Of what? They checked the shoe to make sure there was no way anyone could see into it."

"At some point one of them would wonder if the shoe were equally opaque to sound." Atvar H'sial sprawled luxuriantly across the back of the cab and opened her black wing cases to soak up the sun. The delicate vestigial wings within were marked by red and white elongated eyespots.

"What if they did? They made you sit over in the back, where you were out of sight of me."

"Perhaps. But at some point one of them would have begun to wonder about pheromones, and nonverbal and nonvisual signals. I tell you, I will not repeat that exercise."

"Hey, don't start feeling *sorry* for them. They work for the Alliance government. They'll chisel it back. All it means is another microcent on the taxes."

"You misunderstand my motives." The yellow horns quivered. "I am of a race destined to build worlds, to light new suns, to rule whole galaxies. I will not again sink to such trivia. It is beneath the dignity of a Cecropian."

"Sure, At. Beneath mine, too. *And* you might get caught." Nenda peered up to the top of the building where the cab had halted. He turned to the driver. "You real sure of this address?"

"Positive. Fortieth floor and up, air-breathing aliens only. Just like the bug here." The cabbie stared down his nose at Atvar H'sial and drove off.

Nenda glared after the cab, shrugged, and led the way inside.

The air in the building was filled with a stench of rotting

seaweed. It made Nenda's nose wrinkle as they entered the thirty-foot cube of the elevator. "Air-breathers! Smells more like Karelian mud-divers to me." But Atvar H'sial was nodding happily. "It is indeed the right place." The antennas on top of her eyeless white head partially unfurled. "I can detect traces of J'merlia. He has been inside this structure within the past few hours. Let us proceed higher."

Even with his augment, Nenda lacked the Cecropian's infinitely refined sensitivity to odors. He took them up floor by floor in the elevator, until Atvar H'sial finally nodded.

"This one." But now the pheromones carried a hint of concern.

"What's wrong, At?"

"In addition to traces of my J'merlia, and to your Hymenopt, Kallik . . ." She was moving along a broad corridor, and at last paused before a door tall and wide enough to admit something twice her size. "I seem to detect—wait!"

It was too late. Nenda had pressed the side plate and the great door was already sliding open. The Cecropian and the Karelian human found themselves on the threshold of a domed and cavernous chamber, forty meters across.

Nenda peered in through the gloom. "You were wrong, At. There's nobody in here."

But the Cecropian had reared up to her full height and was pointing off to the side where two figures were bent over a low table. They looked up as the door opened. There was a gasp of mutual recognition. Instead of seeing the stick-thin figure of a Lo'tfian and the tubby round body of the Hymenopt, Louis Nenda and Atvar H'sial were facing the human forms of Alliance Councilor Graves and embodied computer, E. C. Tally.

"We were dumped off in the middle of nowhere . . ."

There had been half a minute of surprised and unproductive reaction—"What are you two doing here? You're supposed to be off chasing Zardalu . . ." "More to the point, what are *you* doing here? You're supposed to be thirty thousand light-years away, out on Serenity and fighting each other . . ." After a little of that, Louis Nenda had been given the floor. His pheromonal aside to Atvar H'sial—*Don't worry. Trust me!*—went unnoticed by the other two.

". . . dumped with just the clothes we were wearing, and no warning that anything funny was going to happen. One minute we were standing in one of the main chambers, the same one where we rolled the Zardalu into the transition vortex—"—*and where we had the biggest pile of loot pulled together that you'd see in a dozen lifetimes. I know, At, I'm not going to say that. But it's hard—fifty new bits of Builder technology, each one priceless and ready to grab. Two and a half months' work, all down the tubes. Well, no good crying over what might have been—*

And may yet be, Louis. Surrender wins no wars.

Mebbe. It's still hard.

Graves and E. C. Tally were staring at Nenda, puzzled by his sudden silence. He returned to human speech: "Sorry. Started thinkin' about it again. Anyway, all of a sudden Speaker-Between, that know-it-all Builder construct, popped up right behind us, quiet like, so we didn't know he was there. He said, 'This is not what was agreed to. It is *unacceptable.*' And the next minute—"

"May I speak?" E. C. Tally's voice was loud and off-putting.

Nenda turned to Julian Graves. "Couldn't you stop him doing that when you gave him a new body copy? What's wrong now, E.C.?"

"It was reported to me by Councilor Graves that you and Atvar H'sial were left behind on Serenity not to *cooperate,* but to *engage in single combat.* That is not at all the way that you are now describing matters."

"Ah, well, that was somethin' me and At worked out after you lot had left. Better to cooperate *at first,* see, until we understood the environment on Serenity, an' *after* that we'd have plenty of time to fight it out between us—"

—as indeed we would have fought, Louis, once we were home in the spiral arm with substantial booty. For there are

limits to cooperation, and the Builder treasures are vast. But pray continue . . .

If anyone will let me, I will. Shut up, At, so I can talk.

"—so Atvar H'sial and I had been working together, trying to figure out where the Zardalu were likely to have gone after they left Serenity—" *And making sure we didn't finish up anywhere near them when* we *left Serenity ourselves.*

"—because, you see, there was this little baby Zardalu who had been left behind when all the others went ass-over-tentacle down the chute—"

"Excuse me." Julian Graves's great bald, radiation-scarred head nodded forward on its pipestem neck. "This is of extreme importance. Are you saying that there was a Zardalu *left behind* on Serenity?"

"That's exactly what I said. You have a problem with that, Councilor?"

"On the contrary. And by the way, it is now *ex*-councilor. I resigned from the Council over this very issue. The Alliance Council listened—perfunctorily, in my opinion—and rejected our concerns in their totality! They do not believe that we traveled together to Serenity. They do not believe that we encountered Builder sentient artifacts. Worst of all, *they deny that we encountered living, breathing Zardalu.* They claim we imagined all of it. So if you have with you a specimen, an infant or a dead body, or even the smallest end sucker of a tentacle—"

"Sorry. I hear you, but we don't have even a sniff. It's Speaker-Between's dumb fault again. He accused me and Atvar H'sial of *cooperating,* instead of feuding; and before we could tell him that he was full of it, he made one of those hissing teakettle noises like he was boiling over, and another one of them vortices swirled up right next to us. It threw us into the Builder transportation system. Just before the vortex got us it grabbed the little Zardalu. He went God-knows-where. We haven't seen him since. Atvar H'sial and I come out together in the ass end of the Zardalu Communion, on a little rathole of a planet called Peppermill. But my ship was still on Glister, along with all our major credit. It took our last sou to get us to Miranda. And here we are."

"May I speak?" But this time Tally did not wait for permission. "You are here. I see that. But *why* are you here? I mean, why did you come to Miranda, where neither you nor Atvar H'sial are at home? Why did you not go to some other and more familiar region of the spiral arm?"

Careful! Councilor Graves, whether he be Julius, Steven, or Julian, can read more truth than you think. Atvar H'sial's comment to Louis Nenda was more a command than a warning.

Relax, At! This is the time to tell the truth. "Because until we can return to the planetoid Glister and to my ship, the *Have-It-All,* Atvar H'sial and I are flat broke. The only valuable things that either of us own"—Nenda reached into his pants pocket, pulled out two little squares of recorder plastic, and squeezed them—"are these."

Under the pressure of his fingers, the squares began to intone simultaneously: "This is the ownership certificate of the Lo'tfian, J'merlia, ID 1013653, with all rights assigned to the Cecropian dominatrix, Atvar H'sial." "This is the ownership certificate of the Hymenopt, Kallik WSG, ID 265358979, with all rights assigned to the Karelian human, Louis Nenda." And to repeat: "This is the ownership certificate of the Lo'tfian, J'merlia, ID—"

"That'll do." Nenda pressed the edge of the plastic wafers, and they fell silent. "The slaves J'merlia and Kallik are the only assets we got left, but we own 'em free and clear, as you know and as these documents prove."

Nenda paused for breath. The hard bit was coming right now.

"So we've come here to claim 'em and take 'em back to Miranda Port, and rent 'em out so we'll have enough credit to travel back to Glister and get the *Have-It-All.*" He glared at Graves. "And it's no good you gettin' mad and tellin' us that J'merlia and Kallik are free agents because we let 'em go free back on Serenity, because none of that's documented, and these"—he waved the squares—"prove otherwise. So don't give me any of that. Just tell me, where are they?"

Graves was going to give him a big argument, Nenda just knew it. He faced the councilor, waiting for the outburst.

It never came. Multiple expressions were running across Graves's face, but not one of them looked like anger. There was satisfaction and irony, and even what might be a certain amount of sympathy in those mad and misty gray eyes.

"I cannot deliver J'merlia and Kallik to you, Louis Nenda," he said, "even if I would. For one very good reason. They are not here. Both of them left Delbruck just two hours ago—on a high-speed transit to Miranda Port."

MIRANDA PORT

"If you wait long enough in the Miranda Spaceport, you'll run into everyone worth meeting in the whole spiral arm."

There's a typical bit of Fourth Alliance thinking for you. Pure flummery. The humans of the Alliance are a cocky lot—no surprise in that, all the senior clade species think they're God's gift to the Universe, with an inflated view of the importance of their own headquarters world and its spaceport.

But I'm telling you, the first time you visit Miranda Port, you think for a while that the Alliance puffery might be right.

I've seen a thousand ports in my time, from the miniship jet points of the Berceuse Chute to the free-space Ark Launch Complex. I've been as close as any human dare go to the Builder Synapse, where the test ships shimmer and sparkle and disappear, and no one has ever figured out where those poor bugger "volunteers" inside them go, or why the lucky ones come back.

And Miranda Port? Right up there with the best of them, when it comes to pure boggle-factor.

Visualize a circular plain on a planetary surface, two hundred miles across—and I mean a *plain,* absolutely level, not part of the surface of the globe. The whole Downside of Miranda Port is flat to the millimeter, so the center of the circle is a mile and a half closer to the middle of the planet than the level of the outer edge.

Now imagine that you start driving in from that outer edge toward the middle, across a uniform flat blackness like polished glass. It's hot, and the atmosphere of Miranda is muggy and a bit hazy. At ten miles in you pass the first ring of buildings—warehouses and storage areas, thousand after thousand of them, thirty stories high and extending that far and more under the surface. You keep going, past the second and third and fourth storage areas, and into the first and second passenger arrival zones. You see humans in all shapes and sizes, plus Cecropians and Varnians and Lo'tfians and Hymenopts and giggling empty-headed Ditrons, and you wonder if it's all going on forever. But as you clear the second passenger ring, you notice two things. First, there's a thin vertical line dead ahead, just becoming visible on the horizon. And second, it's midday but it's getting darker.

You stare at that vertical line for maybe a couple of seconds. You know it must be the bottom of the Stalk, running from the center of Miranda Port right up to stationary orbit, and it's no big deal—nothing compared to the forty-eight Basal Stalks that connect Cocoon to the planetary surface of Savalle.

But it's still getting darker, so you look up. And then you catch your first sight of the Shroud, the edge of it starting to intersect the sun's disk. There's the Upside of Miranda Port, the mushroom cap of the Stalk. The Shroud is nine thousand miles across. That's where the real business is done—the only place in the spiral arm where a Bose Access Node lies so close to a planet.

You stop the car, and your mind starts running. There's a million starships warehoused and netted up there on the edge of the Shroud, some of 'em going for a song. You know that in half an hour you could be ascending the Stalk; in less than a day you'd be up there on the Shroud, picking out some neat little vessel. And a few hours after that you could be whomping through a Transition on the Bose Network, off to another access node a dozen or a hundred or even a thousand light-years away . . .

And if you're an old traveler like me, there's the real magic of Miranda Port; the way you can sit flat on the surface of a planet, like any dead-dog stay-at-home Downsider, and know that you're only a day away from the whole spiral arm. Before you know it you're itching for another look at the million-mile lightning bolts playing among the friction rings of Culmain, or wondering what worlds the Tristan free-space Manticore is dreaming these days, or what new lies and boasts old Dulcimer, the Chism Polypheme, is telling in the spaceport bar on Bridle Gap. And suddenly you want to watch the universe turn into a kaleidoscope again, out on the edge of the Torvil Anfract in far Communion territory, where space-time knots and snarls and turns around itself like an old man's memories . . .

And then you know that the space-tides are running strong in your blood, and it's time to raise anchor, and kiss the lady good-bye, and hit the space-lanes again for one last trip around the Arm.

—from *Hot Rocks, Warm Beer, Cold Comfort: Jetting Alone Around the Galaxy;* being the personal and unadorned reminiscences of Captain Alonzo Wilberforce Sloane (Retired). (Published by Wideawake Press, March E.4125; remaindered, May E.4125; available only in the Rare Publications Department of the Cam H'ptiar/Emserin Library.)

CHAPTER 4

MONEY AND CREDIT meant little to an interspecies Council member. To serve the prestigious needs of a Council project, any planet in the spiral arm would readily turn over the best of its resources; and should there ever be any hesitation, a councilor had final authority to commandeer exactly who and what was needed.

But for an *ex*-councilor, one who had resigned in protest . . .

After a lifetime in which costs were irrelevant, Julian Graves was suddenly exposed to the real world. He looked on his new credit, and found it wanting.

"The ship we can afford won't be very big, and it doesn't have to be brand-new." He offered to J'merlia the authorization to draw on his private funds. "But make sure that it has defensive weapons. When we track down the Zardalu, we cannot assume that they will be friendly."

The Lo'tfian was too polite to comment. But J'merlia's pale-lemon eyes rolled on their short eyestalks and swiveled to glance at E. C. Tally and Kallik. *They* were not likely to assume that the Zardalu would be friendly. The last time that the four of them had encountered Zardalu, E. C. Tally's body had been torn to pieces and the little Hymenopt, Kallik, had had one leg pulled off. Julian Graves himself had been blinded and had required a new pair of eyes. He seemed to have forgotten all about that.

"But range and drive capability are even more important," Graves went on. "We have no idea how far we will have to go, or how many Bose Transitions we will be obliged to make."

J'merlia was nodding, while at his side Kallik was bobbing up and down on her eight springy legs. The Hymenopt had found the endless formal proceedings of the Council hearing dull and hard to endure. She was itching for action. When Graves held out his credit authorization she grabbed it with a whistle of satisfaction.

The same urge to be up and doing had dictated the actions of Kallik and J'merlia when they flew out of Delbruck and came to Miranda Port. Catalogs of every vessel in the Shroud moorings were held in the Downside catalogs, and a prospective buyer could call up specifications on any of the ships. She could even conjure a 3-D holographic reconstruction that allowed her to wander vicariously through the interior, listen to the engines, and inspect passenger accommodations. Without ever leaving Downside she could do everything but stroke the polished trim, press the control button, and smell the Bose Drive's ozone.

But that was exactly what Kallik was keen to do. At her urging, she and J'merlia headed at once to the base of the Stalk. In the very moment when Louis Nenda and Atvar H'sial were entering Delbruck, their former slaves were lifting for free-fall, the Shroud, and the Upside Sales Center.

It was not practical to make a physical inspection of more than a tiny fraction of the ships. With an inventory of almost a million vessels scattered through a hundred million cubic miles of space, and with ships of every age, size, and condition, even Kallik admitted that the selection had to begin with a computer search. And that meant the central office of Upside Sales.

It was the tail end of a busy period when they arrived, and the manager eyed the two newcomers with no enthusiasm.

She was tired, her feet were hurting, and she did not feel she was looking at sales potential. There were funny-looking aliens aplenty running around Miranda Port, but mostly they didn't buy ships. *Humans* bought ships.

The skinny one was a Lo'tfian, and like all Lo'tfians he seemed mostly a tangle of arms and legs. The eight black articulated limbs were attached to a long, pipestem torso, and his narrow head was dominated by the big, lemon-colored compound eyes. In the experience of the sales manager, Lo'tfians did not have money, or make purchase decisions. They did not even speak for themselves. They accompanied Cecropians as translators and servants, and they never offered a word of their own.

The Lo'tfian's companion was even worse. There were eight legs again, but these sprang from a short, stubby torso covered with fine black fur, and the small, smooth head was entirely surrounded by multiple pairs of bright, black eyes. It had to be a Hymenopt, a rarity outside the worlds of the Zardalu Communion—and a dangerous being, if reputation was anything to go by. Hymenopts had superfast reactions, and the end of the rotund body concealed a deadly sting.

Could the pair even *talk*? The only sound that the aliens were making was an odd series of clicks and whistles.

"Patience, Kallik." The skinny Lo'tfian switched to human speech as he turned to the sales manager. He held out a bank chit. "Greetings. I am J'merlia, and this is Kallik. We are here to buy a ship."

So at least one of them could talk human. *And* he had credit. That was a surprise. The manager's first reaction—*don't waste five seconds on these two*—was overridden by long training. She took the chit that the Lo'tfian was holding out to her and performed an automatic check on it.

She sniffed.

Two dozen eyes blinked at her. "Are we in luck?" the Hymenopt asked.

So they could both speak.

"You're lucky in at least one way. The choice won't be

too difficult. You won't have to worry about ninety-nine percent of our inventory."

"Why not?" Kallik's circular ring of black eyes was taking in the holograms of a dozen ships at once.

"Because you don't have enough credit to buy them. For instance, you can't have any of the ones that you're looking at right now. Can you give me a summary of your requirements?"

"Range," J'merlia said. "Weapons. Enough accommodation for us and at least four humans, but also plenty of interior cargo space."

"What kind of cargo?"

"Living cargo. We might need room to carry a group of Zardalu."

"I see." The manager gave him a tight-lipped smile. *Zardalu.* Why not say dinosaurs and have done with it? If a customer did not want to admit what they would be carrying in the ship—and many didn't—it was better to say so outright. *She* didn't care what the ships were used for after they were sold, but she hated it when people tried to play games with her.

Well, she had her own games.

"All right, now I know what you need we can look at a few. How about this? It's in your price range."

The vessel she called onto the 3-D display was a stunted blue cylinder with three stalklike landing braces. It had a drunken and lopsided look, as though it was hung over after some major party. "Lots of power. Great on-board computer—Karlan emotional circuits and all. What do you think?"

She could not read the expressions of the aliens, but their chitters and whistles sounded subdued.

"I'm not sure I like the idea of an emotional on-board computer," J'merlia said at last. "How big is it inside?"

"Ah. Good point. You could fit half-a-dozen people in easily enough, but it's low on cargo space. It wouldn't do for you. But this one"—she switched the display—"has all the interior space you'll ever need. *And* power to spare."

The vessel that appeared on the screen was mostly open space, like a widespread bunch of rotting grapes loosely connected to each other by frayed lengths of string.

"Of course, it only looks saggy like this when the drive is off and it's docked," the manager added after a long silence. "When it's in flight there's electromagnetic coupling of the components, and it all tightens up."

"Weapons?" Kallik asked feebly.

"Weapons!" The manager snapped her fingers. "Good point. That's this ship's one weak spot. It *has* weapons, but they're in a self-contained pod, so you have to switch the drive right off before you can get to them and activate them. Not too convenient.

"All right, let me try again. I know I've got just what you need, I just have to find it. Interior space, good power and range, good weapons system . . ." She bent for a few seconds over her catalog, entering search parameters. "I knew it!" She looked up, smiling. "I'm a dummy. I forgot all about the *Erebus.* A supership! Just what you want! Look at this!"

She threw the hologram of a vast, black-hulled craft onto the 3-D display. Its exterior was a rough ovoid, the dark outer surface disfigured by gleaming studs and warts and irregular cavities.

"More than big enough, power to spare—and see those weapons systems!"

"How big is it?" J'merlia asked.

"The *Erebus* is four hundred meters long, three hundred and twenty wide. There's accommodation for hundreds of passengers—thousands if you want to convert some of the cargo space—and you could fit most interstellar vessels easily inside the primary hold. You want weapons? See those surface nodules—every one of them is a self-contained facility powerful enough to vaporize a decent-sized asteroid. You want to talk range, and power? There's enough in this ship's drive to take you ten times round the spiral arm!"

The display was moving in through one of the ports and showing the interior appointments of the ship. A human figure led the way to provide an idea of scale. Every fixture was substantial and solid, and the drive drew a whistle of approval from Kallik.

"Do we really have enough credit to purchase this?" she asked, after they had examined the vast interior cargo volume, a spherical open space two hundred and fifty meters across.

"Just enough." The manager pushed the sales entry pad across to J'merlia. "Right here, where I've marked it, and then at the bottom. And once you've signed, I'll throw in a special option that ends today. The ship will be scrubbed clean for you, inside and out. I definitely recommend that you add this option—it's been a little while since the *Erebus* was in regular use."

Neither J'merlia nor Kallik possessed external ears, so nothing was burning as they completed their purchase of the *Erebus* and gloated over its size and capabilities. But back in Delbruck they were the focus of an increasingly loud argument.

"I can't believe it. You let Kallik and J'merlia go off to *buy a ship*—just the two of them, with no help from anyone?" Louis Nenda was hunched over a chair back, glowering at Julian Graves, while Atvar H'sial and E. C. Tally silently looked on.

"I did." Graves nodded. "For I recognize what you, in your attempts to impose slavery on J'merlia and Kallik, are all too willing to forget: these are mature, adult forms of highly intelligent species. It would be quite wrong to treat them like children. Give them responsibility, and they will respond to it."

"Don't kid yourself."

"But you surely admit that they are highly intelligent."

"Sure. What's that got to do with it? Smart, and adults, but until a few months ago they had somebody else making all their decisions for them. They're missin' *experience*. If you need somebody to calculate an orbit, or reduce a set of observations, I'd trust Kallik over anyone in the spiral arm.

But when it comes to *negotiating,* they're like babies. You should have gone with 'em. They have no more idea how to cut a deal without gettin' gypped than E. C. Tally here, or than—oh, my Lord."

Nenda had seen the flicker of discomfort cross Julian Graves's scarred face.

"No more idea than *you* do." Nenda slapped the back of the chair in his frustration. "Come on, Graves, admit it. You never had to bargain for anything in your whole life—councilors get whatever they need, handed to them on a plate."

Graves squirmed in his seat. "It is true that my duties seldom called for—*purchases* of any kind, or even for discussion of material needs. But if you think that J'merlia and Kallik may be at a disadvantage—"

"Disadvantage? Get a good sales type up there, they'll be eaten alive. Can you call 'em—let me talk before they go too far?"

"If you believe that you can, by conversation with Kallik—"

"I'm not gonna get into the slavery bit, I promise. I'll keep it to the negotiation, get in the middle of it if I can, that and nothing else."

"I gave them no specific itinerary, but I *may* be able to reach them. Give me a few moments." Graves hurried across to the communications complex on the other side of the room. After a few moments, E. C. Tally trailed after him.

"May I speak?" he whispered as Graves set to work at the terminal. "I do not deny, Councilor, that Louis Nenda and Atvar H'sial sometimes favor deceit. But recall our experiences on Serenity—it was precisely those elements of deceit that permitted us to overcome the Zardalu. And soon we will be facing Zardalu *again.*"

"What is your point?" Graves was only half listening. In his search for J'merlia and Kallik he was being bounced randomly from one signal center to another, first on Downside, then on Upside.

"That they may again be of value. Unlike most others in the spiral arm, Nenda and Atvar H'sial are fully convinced of the existence of the Zardalu. They know as much as anyone of Zardalu behavior patterns—more, perhaps, after their interaction with the immature form. They are also widely traveled, and at home in scores of planetary environments. You yourself have said that you expect our ship may have to explore fifty alien worlds, before we locate the hiding place of the Zardalu. Finally, we know that Louis Nenda and Atvar H'sial are brave and resourceful. Would it not therefore be logical to cease to argue with them, and instead *recruit them to our cause*?"

Graves paused in his frustrating struggle with the communications unit. "Why would they ever agree? They made it clear that all they want is to return to Glister and take possession of Nenda's ship, the *Have-It-All.*"

"Like you, I am unfamiliar with the process that Louis Nenda terms *cutting a deal.* But it occurs to me that a mutually beneficial arrangement might be possible. It will surely be as difficult to return to Glister as it was to reach it originally. Nenda and Atvar H'sial know that. Suppose therefore that they help us now. And suppose that you in return offer the assistance and resources of our whole party in recovering the *Have-It-All,* as soon as our own goal has been accomplished. I know that Nenda has a high regard for Professor Lang. If we were to mention to him that she, too, will be part of our group . . ."

At the other side of the room, Nenda was deep in explanation to Atvar H'sial. He had been too busy arguing with Graves to maintain parallel pheromonal translation for the Cecropian's benefit.

"I know you just want to get out of here, At, and not waste time talking with these turkeys. But a few minutes ago I had a thought. Here I am and here you are, stuck on Miranda without a credit to scratch your pedicel with. Now, why did we come here in the first place?"

"To claim possession of J'merlia and Kallik."

"Sure. And why did we do *that*?"

"J'merlia is mine by right. I have been his dominatrix since he was first postlarval."

"True—but we didn't come here just to *claim* 'em, did we? We came to claim 'em and *rent* 'em to others, so we could get the use of a ship. Now, suppose we keep pushing the fact that we own 'em. You know we'll get into a big hassle with Graves—an' we might *lose*. Where would that leave us?"

"I will tear off his ugly bald head."

"Fine. And for an encore? Even if you don't get scragged for it, we'll still be stuck up Miranda Creek, without a paddle. You see, what we need, same thing that made us come here in the first place, is a *ship*. And that's what J'merlia and Kallik are off buying, right now. So suppose they get one. And suppose instead of acting all bent out of shape about who owns who, we smile and say everything is just fine. And we go along with 'em on their ship, to help out —because you can bet they'll need help, with whatever old piece of junk they get saddled with, or it won't fly at all. So sooner or later there comes a time when most people are off doing something else, and there's just you and me, or maybe you and me and J'merlia and Kallik, on board the ship—"

"Say no more." Atvar H'sial's blind white head was nodding. "I am persuaded. I have remarked before, Louis Nenda, that you are the most capable partner that I have ever had. So much so, I fear to trust you myself. But for the moment, we have few choices. Therefore I agree: we will proceed as you suggest—*if* our servants procure a ship." The yellow horns turned to point across the room, to where E. C. Tally was hurrying toward them. "And that we may soon know."

"Does he have 'em on the line?" Nenda asked as Tally came close.

The embodied computer shook his head. "Councilor Graves tracked J'merlia and Kallik to their last stop, but they had already left the sales center. They bought a ship, the *Erebus*, and now they are heading back here. They are reportedly highly excited and delighted with their purchase. Councilor Graves requested full specifications. They will be arriving shortly through his terminal."

"Keep your fingers and claws crossed." Nenda and Atvar H'sial followed Tally over to the communications unit. "The Miranda sales force has quite a reputation. Let's hope what J'merlia and Kallik bought is a ship, and not a Builder bathtub. Here it comes. External dimensions . . ."

As the vessel's physical parameters and performance characteristics began to unroll across the screen, Nenda summarized and commented on each section for Atvar H'sial's benefit.

"Main cargo hold, eight point two million cubic meters. That's more open cargo space than a superfreighter, plus there's two big subsidiary holds. You could stow fifty million tons of metal in the *Erebus*—and you could haul it halfway across the galaxy. Listen to these engine power figures." The pheromonal message revealed Nenda's surprise at what he was seeing. "And if you ever have main engine problems," he went on, "there's an auxiliary Bose Drive good for at least a dozen transitions. Here's the ratings . . ."

Atvar H'sial was crouched close to the floor, her head nodding as the listing of internal and external dimensions and performance ratings went on. After ten minutes the Cecropian began to sit up straight, towering over the humans.

"Weapons?" The single word to Nenda carried an overtone of speculation.

"We're just getting to 'em. You'll love this, At, it's the cream on the cake. Fifteen weapons centers in the main control room. Forty-four turrets, all around the ship and all fully independent. Each one has as much kick as a Lascelles complex—any one would beat what I had on the *Have-It-All.* Plus you can make a Dalton synthesis combining all turrets—"

"A question, Louis Nenda, for you to ask Julian Graves. How much did J'merlia and Kallik pay for the *Erebus*?"

"I don't need to ask—it's shown right here. One hundred and thirty-two thousand. Damnation, I see what you mean. That's *way* too cheap."

"Perhaps not, Louis. I would like the answer to one further question. How *old* is this ship?"

"That's not shown on the listing." Nenda turned to Julian Graves. "Can you interrupt the display for a query? Atvar H'sial is asking about the age of the *Erebus.*"

"No problem." Graves had been leaning back in his chair, watching with huge satisfaction as the statistics rolled past. He entered Nenda's query, then turned to face the Karelian. "I hope that this gives you increased faith in my methods, Mr. Nenda. I sent J'merlia and Kallik to negotiate for purchase of a ship. They have bought a ship—and what a ship! And at a most reasonable price. I ask you, do you believe that you, or Atvar H'sial, or anyone, could have found a better bargain? The moral of this is—"

He paused and goggled at the screen. "Is that the date it was put into service? It can't be. Let me check again."

"Three thousand nine hundred years, At," Nenda said softly. "That's the listed age of the *Erebus.*" He continued silently, using only pheromonal communication. "What's going on? You must know, or you'd never have asked the question."

"I will tell you, though you may prefer to allow Councilor Graves to learn what I have to say for himself, rather than from you. The information is not likely to bring joy to his heart. Your description of the *Erebus*—especially of its weapons system—sounded familiar. It reminded me of the Larmeer ships used in the long-ago battles between the Fourth Alliance and the Zardalu Communion. Those ships were commissioned by the Alliance, but they were manufactured by my people, in the Cecropia Federation, in the free-space weapons shop of H'larmeer. J'merlia and Kallik have purchased something with the carrying capacity of a freighter, the firepower of a battleship, and the internal life-support systems and personnel accommodations of a colony ship. But it is none of these. It is a Tantalus orbital fort."

"And it's four thousand years old. Will it still work?"

"Assuredly. The orbital forts were created for multimillennial working lifetimes, with negligible maintenance. There will be a problem recognizing the *purpose* of some of the on-board devices, since the common day-to-day knowledge of one generation lies unused and forgotten in a later one, to the point of incomprehensibility. To quote an old Cecropian proverb: *Any sufficiently antique technology is indistinguishable from magic.* However, I would expect little or no degradation in ship performance."

"So Graves got a really good deal. He's going to be crowing over us for months."

"I regard that as unlikely. Councilor Graves has already told us that it may be necessary to visit dozens of different worlds before he finds the Zardalu."

"He can do it. The *Erebus* has ample power. And if the Zardalu get pesky, the ship has plenty of weapons."

"It does indeed. But still I suspect that Councilor Graves will shortly become less satisfied with his purchase."

"Huh?"

"Less satisfied, indeed." Atvar H'sial paused for dramatic effect. "*Much* less satisfied, as soon as he realizes that what he has purchased is an *orbital* fort—a device which can never make a landing, ever, on any planet."

CHAPTER 5

Sentinel Gate

DARYA LANG SAT in the main control room of the *Erebus,* staring at the list of locations that she had generated and swiveling her chair impatiently from side to side.

Stalemate.

The way that Hans Rebka had described the plan, it sounded almost too easy: acquire the use of a ship and recruit a crew; seek out the refuge of the escaped Zardalu, with adequate firepower to assure their own safety; and return to Miranda with unarguable proof of Zardalu existence.

They had the ship, they had the weapons, and they had the crew. But there was one gigantic snag. The Zardalu had not left a forwarding address. They could be anywhere in the spiral arm, on thousands of habitable planets scattered through thousands of light-years. Neither Hans Rebka nor Julian Graves had offered a persuasive method of narrowing that search, and no one else on board had been able to do any better. To examine all the possibilities, the *Erebus* would have to fly in a thousand directions at once.

As soon as Darya and Hans Rebka arrived on board the whole group had met; and argued; and dispersed. And now the ship sat in lumbering orbit around Sentinel Gate, while the Zardalu—somewhere—were relentlessly breeding.

Everything in the *Erebus* had been built in a multiply redundant and durable style. The control room was no exception. Fifteen separate consoles, each with its own weapons center, ran floor-to-ceiling around the circular room. General information centers were fitted into niches between them. Darya sat in one of those, and across from her on the other side of the chamber Atvar H'sial was crouched over another, manipulating controls with a delicate combination of four clawed limbs.

The flat screens could not provide images "visible" to the Cecropian's sonic sight—so how could she be obtaining useful feedback of information? Darya wished that Louis Nenda or J'merlia were there to act as interpreter, but they had headed off with Hans Rebka to the auxiliary engine room of the ship, where Graves claimed to have found "a fascinating device."

Kallik was sitting in the niche next to Atvar H'sial, deeply immersed in her own analysis of data. Without examining the outputs, Darya had a good idea what the Hymenopt was doing—she would be sifting the data banks for rumors, speculation, and old legends concerning the Zardalu, and pondering their most likely present location. Darya had been doing the same thing herself. She had reached definite conclusions that she wanted to share with the others—if only the rest would come back from their excursion to the engine room. What was keeping them so long?

It occurred to her that there was something deeply significant in what was happening. She, Atvar H'sial, and Kallik—the females in the party—were working on the urgent problem of Zardalu location, analyzing and reanalyzing available data. Meanwhile all the males had gone off to play with a dumb gadget, a toy that had sat on the *Erebus* for millennia and could easily wait another few years before anyone played with it.

Darya's peevish thoughts were interrupted by a startling sound from the middle of the control chamber. She turned, and the skin on her arms and the back of her neck tightened into goose bumps.

A dozen hulking figures stood no more than a dozen paces from her. Towering four meters tall on splayed tentacles of pale aquamarine, the thick cylindrical bodies were topped by bulbous heads of midnight blue, a meter wide. At the base of the head, below the long slit of a mouth, the breeding pouches formed a ring of round-mouthed openings. While Darya looked on in horror, lidded eyes, each as big across as her stretched hand, surveyed the chamber then turned to look down on her. Cruel hooked beaks below the broad-spaced eyes opened wide, and a series of high-pitched chittering sounds emerged.

Once seen, never forgotten. *Zardalu.*

Darya jumped to her feet and backed up to the wall of the chamber. Then she realized that Kallik, across from her, had left her seat and was moving *toward* the looming figures. The little alien could understand Zardalu speech.

"Kallik! What are they—" But at that moment the Hymenopt walked right *through* one of the standing Zardalu, then stood calmly inspecting it with her rear-facing eyes.

"Remarkable," Kallik said. She moved to Darya's side. "More accurate than I would have believed possible. My sincere congratulations."

She was talking not to Darya, but to someone who had been sitting tucked out of sight in a niche on the side of the control room. As that figure came into view, Darya saw that it was E. C. Tally. A neural connect cable ran from the base of the skull of the embodied computer, back into the booth.

"Thank you," E. C. Tally said. "I must say, I like it myself. But it is not *quite* right." He inspected the Zardalu critically, and as Darya watched, the aquamarine tentacles of the land-cephalopods darkened a shade and the ring of breeding pouches moved a fraction lower on the torso.

"Though congratulations are due more to this ship's image restoration and display facilities," the embodied computer went on. He circled the group of Zardalu, trailing shiny neural cable along the floor behind him. "All I did was feed it my memories. If something as good as this had been available on Miranda, perhaps I would have had more success in persuading the Council. Do you think that it is a plausible reconstruction, Professor Lang? Or is more work needed before it can mimic reality?"

Darya was saved from answering by the sound of voices from the control-room entrance. Louis Nenda and Hans Rebka appeared between two of the massive support columns, talking animatedly. They glanced at the Zardalu standing in the middle of the room, then marched across to Darya and Kallik.

"Nice job, E.C.," Nenda said casually. "Put it on video and audio when you're done." He turned from the embodied computer and the menacing Zardalu, and grinned at Darya. "Professor, we got it. We agree on everything. But me and Rebka gotta have your help persuading Graves and J'merlia."

"You've got what?" Darya was still feeling like a fool, but she could not help returning Nenda's grin. Villainous or not, his presence was always so *reassuring*. She had been unreasonably delighted to see him at their first meeting on the *Erebus,* and she found herself smiling now.

"We figured out how to track down the Zardalu." Hans Rebka flopped down into the chair where Darya had been sitting.

"Damn right." But Nenda was turning to face the crouched figure of Atvar H'sial. "Hold on a minute, At's sending to me. She's been working the computer. I'll be back."

If Nenda and Rebka agreed on anything, that was a first. It seemed to Darya that they had been snarling at each other since the moment when the *Erebus* picked up Darya and Hans Rebka and made its subluminal departure from Sentinel Gate. It did not help to be told by Julian Graves that Darya herself was the hidden reason for the argument.

She watched as Nenda moved to crouch below the carapace of the Cecropian, where pheromonal messages were most easily sent and received, and remained there in silence for half a minute.

"I don't see how Atvar H'sial can interface with the computer at all," Darya said. "The screen is blank, and even if it weren't, she couldn't get anything from it."

"She does not employ the screen." Kallik pointed one wiry limb to where Atvar H'sial was now rising to her full height. "She obtains information feedback aurally. She has reprogrammed the oscillators to give audible responses at high frequencies. I hear only the lower end of the range. J'merlia would catch the whole thing, but all of it is too high for human ears."

Nenda returned, followed by Atvar H'sial. He was frowning.

"So now we got *three* ideas," he said. He stared at Darya and Kallik. "I hope that neither of you two think you know where the Zardalu are."

"I do," Darya said.

"Then we got problems. So does At."

"And I also have suggestions." Kallik spoke softly and diffidently. Since they had been reunited, Darya had noticed a strange change in the relationship between Louis Nenda and Atvar H'sial, and their former—or was it current?—slaves. Kallik and J'merlia had greeted their sometime owners with huge and unconcealed joy, and those owners were clearly delighted to see them. But no one was sure how to behave. The Lo'tfian and the Hymenopt were ready and eager to take orders, but the Cecropian and the Karelian human were not giving them. Nenda in particular was on his absolute best behavior—which was not very good, in terms of social graces. If Darya had been forced to introduce *him* to the research staff of the Institute, Professor Merada would have had a fit. But Glenna Omar, with her appetite for anything rough and male, would more than likely have been all over him.

She pushed away that last thought as unworthy as Nenda scratched thoughtfully at his backside, sniffed, and dropped into a chair next to Hans Rebka.

"We gotta sort all this out quick," he said. "We sit here jerking ourselves off, while new little Zardalu must be poppin' out of the pouches every five minutes."

"We must proceed," Rebka said. He and Nenda were having their usual silent tussle as to who was in charge, something they did whenever Julian Graves was not around. "We can't afford to wait for the other two to show up. It seems that we all have ideas, so who wants to go first?"

Darya realized that Kallik was glancing deferentially in her direction.

"I guess that I do," she said. "What I have to say won't take long. I'll start with two facts: First, when the Builder transportation system returned us from Serenity, it landed us in different parts of the spiral arm. But in every case, we came out on or next door to the location of a Builder artifact. Second, no one has reported the sighting of any live Zardalu—and you can bet that would make news everywhere. So I deduce two things. First, the Zardalu would almost certainly have arrived close to an artifact, too. And second, that artifact cannot be in Fourth Alliance territory, or in the Cecropia Federation, or even in the Phemus Circle. It has to be where you might expect Zardalu to be sent—to a location somewhere in the territories of the Zardalu Communion. That makes sense for two reasons: the Zardalu were originally picked up there; and the Communion still has a lot of unexplored territory. If you *wanted* to disappear, and remain hidden, that's the first place in the spiral arm that you'd pick."

She stared around at five silent and expressionless faces. "Any comment?"

"Go on," Rebka said. "No quarrels so far. Where do you go from here?"

"I know the locations of all the Builder artifacts. Three hundred and seventy-seven of them lie within the Zardalu Communion territory. A hundred and forty-nine of those lie in fairly remote territory, where a Zardalu appearance might not be spotted at once. More than that, if you go along with my assumption that the Zardalu had to land someplace close to one of those artifacts, then I can narrow the field a lot further. You see, for many artifacts there's just no planet within many light-years where an air-breathing life-form can survive. Throw in that requirement, and you have my final list."

She turned to the console and touched three keys. "And here it is, along with my calculations."

"Sixty-one planets, around thirty-three different stars." Louis Nenda was frowning. "I can rule out a couple of those —I know 'em. Don't forget Kallik and me are from the Communion. But it's still too many. Hold on a minute, while I pass your list to At."

The others waited impatiently during the transfer. Nenda was still in silent dialogue with the Cecropian when Julian Graves and J'merlia arrived in the control room. Rebka gestured to Darya's list, still on the screen. "Candidate places we might find Zardalu. Too many."

"And while I have no wish to complicate matters"—Kallik was busy at the console—"here are the results of my analysis, quite independently evolved although with a similar guiding logic."

Another substantial list was appearing on the screen, next to Darya's. "Seventy-two planets," Kallik said apologetically, "around forty-one different stars. And only twenty-three planets in common with Professor Lang."

"And it's getting worse," Nenda said. "Atvar H'sial did *her* own analysis, with a logic similar to Darya's. But she didn't prepare it for visual output. She's doing that now."

The Cecropian was back at her console. Within a few seconds, a third long list and a series of equations began to appear on the displays. Julian Graves groaned as it went on and on. "Worse and worse."

"Eighty-four planets," E. C. Tally said. "Around forty-five stars." The embodied computer's internal processing unit, with a clock rate of eighteen attoseconds, could query the ship's data bank through the attached neural cable and perform a full statistical analysis while the humans were still trying to read the list. "Twenty-nine planets," he went on, "in common with Professor Lang, thirty in common with Kallik, and eleven planets common to all three. There is a sixty-two percent probability that the planet sought is one of the eleven, and a fifteen percent chance that it is not any one of the one hundred and forty-six in the combined list."

"Which says you got too many places, and lousy odds." Nenda turned to Hans Rebka. "So I guess it's our turn in the barrel. You want to tell it? People tend to get sort of excited when I say things."

Rebka shrugged. He moved to sit closer to Darya. "Nenda and I did our own talking when we were in the engine room. What you three did was interesting, a nice, *abstract* analysis; but we think you're missing a basic point.

"You said, hey, nobody reported Zardalu in the Fourth Alliance or the Cecropia Federation or the Phemus Circle, so that means they can't be there. But you know the Zardalu as well as we do. Don't you think it's more likely that they didn't get reported because there was nobody *left* to report them? If you want to find Zardalu, you look for evidence of *violence*. Better yet, you look for evidence of *disappearances* somewhere close to a Builder artifact. If the Zardalu arrived in the spiral arm and took a ship to get them back to their home planet, they'd have made sure there were no survivors to talk about it. Nenda and I took a look at recent shipping records for spiral arm travel, close to Builder artifacts, to see how many interstellar ships just *vanished* and never showed up again. We found two hundred and forty of them, all in the past year. Forty-three of them look like real mysteries—no unusual space conditions at time of disappearance, no debris, no distress messages. Here they are."

He pulled a listing from his pocket and handed it to E. C. Tally, who said at once, "Not much correlation with the earlier tabulations. *And* scattered all over the spiral arm."

"Sure. Given a ship, the Zardalu could have gone to a world a long way from the artifact where they first arrived."

"Except that if they went through many Bose Transitions, they *would* have been observed." Darya stood up, heard her voice rising, and knew she was doing what she insisted that a scientist should never do: allowing passion and the defense of personal theories to interfere with logical analysis. She sat down sharply. "Perhaps you're right, Hans. But don't you think they *have* to be within one or two transitions of where they first arrived in the spiral arm?"

"I'd like to think so. But I still favor our analysis over yours. What you said was reasonable, in a reasonable world, but violence plays a bigger part in the universe than reason —especially when it comes to the Zardalu."

"And psychology and fixed behavior patterns play a larger part than either." It was Julian Graves, who had so far remained a silent observer. "They are factors which have so far been omitted from consideration, but I am convinced they are central to the solution of our problem."

"Psychology!" Nenda spat out the word like an oath. "Don't gimme any of that stuff. If you're gonna question our search logic, you better have something a lot better than *psychology* to support it."

"Psychology *and* behavior patterns. What do you think it is that decides what you, or a Zardalu, or any other intelligent being, will do, if it is *not* psychology? J'merlia and I discussed this problem, after you and Captain Rebka left, and we were able to take our ideas quite a long way. On one point, we agree with you completely: the Zardalu would *not* be content to stay near an artifact, although they probably arrived there. They would leave quickly, if for no other reason than their own safety. There is too much activity around the artifacts. They would seek a planet, preferably a planet where they would be safe from discovery and able to hide away and breed freely. So where do you think that they would go?"

Nenda glowered. "Hell, don't ask me. There could be a thousand places—a million."

"If you ignore psychology, there could be. But put yourself in their position. The Zardalu will do just what you would do. If *you* wanted to hide away, where would you go?"

"Me? I'd go to Karelia, or someplace near it. But I'm damned sure the *Zardalu* wouldn't go there."

"Of course not. Because they are not *Karelians*. But the analogy still holds. The Zardalu will do just what you would do—they would try to *go home*. That means they would head for Genizee, the homeworld of the Zardalu clade."

"But the location of Genizee has never been determined," Darya protested. "It has been lost since the time of the Great Rising."

"It has." Graves sighed. "Lost *to us*. But assuredly not lost to the Zardalu. And although they do not know it, it is the safest of all possible places for them—a world that, in eleven thousand years of searching, none of the vengeful subject races enslaved by the Zardalu has ever succeeded in finding. The ultimate, perfect hiding place."

"Perfect, except for one little detail," Rebka said. "It's ideal *for them*, but it's sure as hell not perfect for *us*. We have to find them! I don't agree with the approach that Darya Lang and Atvar H'sial and Kallik propose, but even if it's wrong it at least tells us what places to *look*. So does the approach that Louis Nenda and I favor, and I'm convinced that it's the right approach. But you and J'merlia are telling us to go look for a place that *no one has ever found*, in eleven millennia of trying. And you have no suggestions as to how we ought to start looking. Aren't you just telling us that the job is *hopeless*?"

"No." Julian Graves was rubbing at his bulging skull in a perplexed fashion. "I am telling you something much worse than that. I am saying that although the task *appears* hopeless and the problem insoluble, we absolutely *must* solve it. Or the Zardalu will breed back to strength. And our failure will place in jeopardy the whole spiral arm."

The tension in the great control chamber had been rising, minute by minute. Individuals were listening to the arguments presented by others, at the same time as they prepared to defend their own theories, regardless of merit.

Darya had seen it happen a hundred times in Institute

faculty meetings, and much as she hated and despised the process, she was not immune to it. You proposed a theory. Even in your own mind, it began as no more than tentative. Then it was questioned, or criticized—and as soon as it was attacked, emotion took over. You prepared to defend it to the death.

It had needed those ominous words of Julian Graves, calmly delivered, to make her and the others forget their pet theories. The emotional heat in the chamber suddenly dropped fifty degrees.

This isn't a stupid argument over tenure or publication precedence or budgets, thought Darya. This is *important.* What's at stake here is the *future,* of every species in this region of the galaxy.

An uncomfortable silence blanketed the chamber, suggesting that others were sharing her revelation. It was broken at last by E. C. Tally. The embodied computer was still wearing the neural cable plugged into the base of his skull. Like a gigantic shiny pigtail, it ran twenty yards back to the information-center attachment.

"May I speak?"

For once in E. C. Tally's life, no one objected as he went on: "We have heard three distinct theories regarding the present location of the Zardalu. At least one of those theories exists in three different variants. Might I, with all due respect, advance the notion that all the theories are wrong in part?"

"Wonderful." Julian Graves stared gloomily at the embodied computer. "Is that your only message, that none of us knows what we're talking about?"

"No. My message, if I had only one message, would be to suggest the power of synthesis, after many minds work separately on a problem. I could never have *originated* the thinking that you provided, but I can *analyze* what you jointly produce. I said you are all wrong in part, but more important, you are all *correct* in part. And your thoughts provide the prescription that points us to the location of the Zardalu.

"There are components on which you all agree: the Zardalu, no matter where they *first arrived* in the spiral arm, would seek to return to familiar territory. Councilor Graves and J'merlia take that a little further, by suggesting the most familiar territory of all—the Zardalu homeworld of Genizee, the origin of the Zardalu clade. Let us accept the plausibility of that added proposal.

"Now, Professor Lang, Atvar H'sial, and Kallik point out that each of *us* was returned from Serenity close to the place from which we started."

There was a snort from Louis Nenda. "Don't try that on At and me. We were dumped off in the middle of *nowhere.*"

"With respect: you are *from* the middle of nowhere. You speak with disdain of the planet Peppermill, where you and Atvar H'sial arrived after transit through the Builder transportation system. But the planet of Peppermill is, galactically speaking, no more than a stone's throw from your own homeworld of Karelia." E. C. Tally paused. "Karelia, which could certainly be said to be in the middle of nowhere—and to which, oddly enough, you did not seek to go although it was close-by."

"Let's not get into that. I got reasons."

"I will not ask them. I will continue. It seems reasonable to assume that the Zardalu, too, were returned close to their point of origin, which would place them in the territories of the Zardalu Communion, rather than within the Alliance, Cecropia Federation, or Phemus Circle regions. Let us accept that they arrived close to an *artifact* in Communion territory. As Professor Lang and others have pointed out, *we* all arrived close to artifacts. It seems unlikely, however, that the Zardalu would have arrived *exactly* where they wished to be. So let us also accept the validity of Captain Rebka and Louis Nenda's logic, that the Zardalu would have found it necessary to *acquire a ship,* and destroy all evidence of such acquisition.

"Let us agree with Professor Lang, that if such a ship were required to make more than one or two jumps through the Bose Network, that would have been noticed.

"Finally, let us agree that Genizee, wherever it is, cannot be in a location that is fully explored, and settled, and familiar. Preferably, the location ought to be difficult to reach, or even dangerous. Otherwise, the Zardalu homeworld would have been discovered long ago.

"Put all this information together, and we are left with a well-defined problem. We want a place satisfying these criteria:

"One: it should be a planet within the territories of the Zardalu Communion.

"Two: it should occupy a blank spot on the galactic map, little-explored and preferably hard to reach.

"Three: it should be within one or two Bose Transitions of a Builder artifact.

"Four: the only Builder artifacts that need to be considered are ones where an unexplained ship disappearance has taken place since the return of the Zardalu to the spiral arm.

"That leaves a substantial computational problem, but each of you already performed part of the work. And fortunately, I was designed to tackle just such combinatorial and search problems. Look."

The lights in the chamber dimmed, and as they did so the figures of the Zardalu simulation vanished from the central display region. In their place was total darkness. Gradually, a faint orange glow filled an irregular three-dimensional volume. Within it twinkled a thousand blue points of light.

"The region of the Zardalu Communion," E. C. Tally said, "and the Builder artifacts that lie within it. And now, the Bose Access Nodes."

A set of yellow lights appeared, scattered among the blue points.

"Eliminating the artifacts where there were no unexplained ship disappearances"—two-thirds of the blue lights vanished—"and considering only little-explored regions within two Bose Transitions, we find this."

The single orange region began to shrink and divide, finally leaving a score of isolated glowing islands.

"These remain as candidate regions for consideration.

There are too many. However, the display does not show what I could also compute: the *probability* associated with each of the remaining regions. When that is included, only one serious contender remains. Here it is. It satisfies all our requirements, at the ninety-eight-percent probability level."

All but one of the lights blinked out, leaving a shape like a twisted orange hand glowing off to one side of the display.

"Reference stars!" It was Julian Graves's voice. "Give us reference stars—we need the location."

A dozen supergiants, the standard beacon stars for the Zardalu Communion portion of the spiral arm, blinked on within the display volume. Darya, trying to orient herself in an unfamiliar stellar region, heard the surprised grunt of Louis Nenda and the hiss of Kallik. They must have been three steps ahead of her.

"I have the location." E. C. Tally's voice was quiet. "That was no problem. But what the ship's data banks do not contain, surprisingly, is navigation information. I have also not yet found image data of this region. However, it has a name. It is known as—"

"It's the Torvil Anfract." That was Nenda's flat growl in the darkness. "And you'll never get image data, not if you wait till I grow feathers and fly."

"You know the region already?" E. C. Tally asked. "That is excellent news. Perhaps you have even been there, and can provide our navigation?"

"I know the place—but only by its reputation." There was a tone in Nenda's voice that Darya Lang had never heard before. "An' if you're talking about me takin' you into the Torvil Anfract, forget it. You can have my ticket, even if it's free. As my old daddy used to say, I ain't never been *there,* and I ain't never *ever* going back."

THE TORVIL ANFRACT

I wish that I understood Time, with a capital T. It's no consolation to realize that no one else does, either. Every book you ever read talks about the "Arrow of Time," the thing that points from the past into the future. They all say that the arrow's arranged so things never run backward.

I'm not convinced. How do we *know* that there was never a connection that ran the other way? Or maybe sometimes Time runs crosswise, and cause and effect have nothing to do with each other.

The thing that got me going this way was thinking again about the Torvil Anfract, and about Medusa. You remember Medusa? She was the lady with the fatal face—one eyeful of her and you turned to stone. Miggie Wang-Ho, who ran the Cheapside Bar on the upside edge of Tucker's Tooth, was a bit like that. One mention of credit, and she froze you solid, and what she did to Blister Gans doesn't bear thinking about. But I guess that's a story for someplace else, because right now I want to talk about the Anfract.

The spiral arm is full of strange sights, but most of them you can *creep up on.* What I mean is, the big jumps are all made through the Bose Network, and after that you're subluminal, plodding along at less than light-speed. So if there's a big spectacle, well, you see it first from far off, and then gradually you get closer. And while you're doing that, you have a chance to get used to it, so it never hits you all of a piece.

Except for the Anfract. You approach *that* subluminal, but for a long time you don't see it at all. There's just *nothing,* no distortion of the star field, no peculiar optical effects like you get near Lens. Nothing.

And then, all of a sudden, this great *thingie* comes blazing out at you, a twisting, writhing bundle of filaments ranging across half the sky.

The Torvil Anfract. The first time I saw it, I couldn't have moved a muscle to save my ship. See, I knew very well that it was all a natural phenomenon, a place where creation happened to take space-time and whop it with a two-by-four until it got so chaotic and multiply-connected that it didn't know which way was up. That didn't make any difference. I was frozen, stuck to the spot like a Sproatley smart oyster, and about as capable of intelligent decision-making.

Now, do you think it's possible that somebody else saw that wriggling snake's-nest of tendrils, and was frozen to the spot like me? And they gave the Anfract a different name—like, maybe, Medusa. And then they went *backward* ten thousand years, and because they couldn't get it out of their mind, they talked about what they'd seen to the folks in a little Earth bar on the tideless shore of the wine-dark Aegean?

That's theory, or if you prefer it, daydreaming. It's fair to ask, what's *fact* about the Anfract?

Surprisingly little. All the texts tell you is that ships avoid the area, because the local space-time structure possesses "dangerous natural dislocations and multiple connectivity." What they never mention is that even the *size* of the region is undefined. Ask how much mass is contained within the region, and no one can tell you. Every measurement gives a different answer. Measure the dimension by light-speed crossing, and it's half a light-year. Fly all around it, a light-year out, and it's a little over a six-light-year trip, which is fine; but fly around it *half* a light-year out, and it's only a one-light-year journey. That would suggest that near the Anfract, $\pi = 1$ (which doesn't appeal too much to the mathematicians).

I didn't make any measurements, and I hardly know how to spell multiple connectivity. All I can tell is what I saw when I got close to the Anfract, flew around it, and tried to stare inside it.

I say *tried*. The Anfract won't let you look at anything directly. There's planets inside there—you can sometimes see them, because now and again there's a magnifying-lens effect in space that brings you in so close you can watch the clouds move downside and on a clear day you can count the mountains on the surface. Then that same planet, while you're watching, will dwindle to a little circle of light, and then split, so you find that you're looking at a dozen or a hundred of them, swimming in space in regular formation.

You'll read about that in most books. But there's another effect, too, one that you don't often see and never read about. After you've encountered it, it burns in your mind for the rest of your life and tells you to return to the Anfract again, for one more look.

I call it God's Necklace.

You stare at the Anfract long enough, and a black spot begins to form in the center, a spot so dark that your eyes want to reject its existence. It grows as you watch, like a black cloud over the face of the Anfract (except that you know it must be *inside,* and part of the structure). Finally it obscures two-thirds and more of the whole area, leaving just a thin annulus of bright tendrils outside it.

And then the first bead of the Necklace appears in that dark circle. It's a planet, just as it would appear from a few planetary radii out; and it's a spectacularly beautiful world, misty and glowing. At first you think that it must be one of the planets inside the Anfract—except that as the image sharpens and moves you in closer, you realize that it's *familiar,* a world that you've seen before somewhere on your travels. You once lived there, and loved it. But before you can quite identify the place it begins to move off sideways, and another world is being pulled in, a second bead on the Necklace. You stare at that, and it's just as familiar, and even more beautiful than the first one; a luscious, fertile world whose fragrant air you'd swear you can smell from way outside its atmosphere.

While you're still savoring that planet and trying to remember its name, it, too, begins to move off, pulled out of sight along the Necklace. No matter. The world that it draws in after it is even better, the world of your dreams. You once lived there, and loved there, and now you realize that you never should have left. You slaver over it, wanting to fly down to it *now,* and never leave.

But before you can do so, it, too, is sliding out of the field of view. And what replaces it makes the last planet seem nothing but a pale shadow world . . .

It goes on and on, as long as you can bear to watch. And at the end, you realize something dreadful. You never, in your whole life, visited any one of those paradise worlds. And surely you never will, because you have no idea where they are, or *when* they are.

You pull yourself together and start your ship moving. You decide that you'll go to Persephone, or Styx, or Savalle, or Pelican's Wake. You tell yourself that you'll forget all about the Anfract and God's Necklace.

Except that you won't, no matter how you try. For in the late night hours, when you lie tight in the dark prison of your own thoughts, and your heart beats slow, and all of life feels short and pointless, that's when you'll remember, and yearn for one more drink at the fountain of the Torvil Anfract.

Your worst fear is that you'll never get to make the trip; and that's when you lie sleepless forever, aching for first light and the noisy distractions of morning.

—from *Hot Rocks, Warm Beer, Cold Comfort: Jetting Alone Around the Galaxy;* by Captain Alonzo Wilberforce Sloane (Retired).

CHAPTER 6

Bridle Gap

THE *EREBUS* WAS a monster, more like a whole world than a standard interstellar ship. Unfortunately, its appetite for power matched its huge size.

Darya sat in one of the information niches off the main control room, her eyes fixed on two of several hundred displays.

The first showed the total available energy in the vessel's central storage units.

Down, down, down.

Even when nothing seemed to be happening, the routine operation and maintenance of the ship sent the stored power creeping toward zero.

But normal operation was nothing compared to the power demands of a Bose Transition. For something as massive as the *Erebus,* each transition *guzzled* energy. They had been through one jump already. Darya had watched in horror as the transition was initiated and the on-board power readout flickered to half its value.

Now they were sucking in energy from the external Bose Network, in preparation for another transition. And that energy supply was far from free. Darya switched her attention to the second readout, one specially programmed to show *finance,* not engineering. It displayed Darya's total credit—and it was swooping down as fast as the on-board power of the *Erebus* went up. Three or four jumps like the last one, and she would be as flat broke as the rest of the group.

She brooded over the falling readout. It was a pretty desperate situation, when a poor professor at a research institute turned out to be the *richest* person on board. If she had been of a more paranoid turn of mind, she might have suspected that she had been invited along on this trip mainly to bankroll it. Julian Graves had used all his credit to buy the *Erebus.* E. C. Tally was a computer, albeit an embodied one, and owned nothing. J'merlia and Kallik had been penniless slaves, while Hans Rebka came from the Phemus Circle, the most miserably poor region of the whole spiral arm. The exceptions should have been Louis Nenda and Atvar H'sial; but although they *talked* about their wealth, every bit of it was on Nenda's ship, the *Have-It-All,* inaccessible on far-off Glister. At the moment they were as poor as everyone else.

Darya glanced across to the main control console, where Louis Nenda was all set to take them into their second jump. They were just one Bose Transition away from the region of the Torvil Anfract; one jump would leave them with comfortably enough power for the return journey.

Except that they were not going to make the jump! Louis Nenda had been adamant.

"Not with me on board, you don't." He glared around the circle. "Sure, we been through a lot together, and sure, we always muddle through. That don't mean we take chances with this one. This is the *Anfract.* It's *dangerous,* not some rinky-dink ratbag planet like Quake or Opal."

Which came close to killing all of us, Darya thought. But she did not speak, because Julian Graves was slapping his hands on his knees in frustration.

"But we *have* to go into the Anfract. You heard E. C. Tally's analysis, and I thought you were in agreement with it. There is an excellent chance that the Zardalu cladeworld is hidden within the Torvil Anfract, with living Zardalu upon it."

"I know all that. All I'm saying is we don't go charging in. People have been pokin' around the Anfract for thousands of years—an' most who went in never came out. We need *help.*"

"What sort of help?"

"We need an expert. A pilot. Somebody who's been around this part of the arm for a long time and knows it like the back of his chelicera."

"Do you have a candidate?"

"Sure I got one. Why'd you think I'm talking? His name's Dulcimer—an' I'm warning you now, he's a Chism Polypheme. But he knows the arm cold, and he probably needs work. If we want him, we have to go looking. One thing for sure, you won't find him around the Anfract."

"Where will we find him?" Darya had not understood Nenda's warning about Chism Polyphemes, but figured they'd better take one problem at a time.

"Unless he's changed, he'll be sittin' around and soaking up the hot stuff in the Sun Bar on Bridle Gap."

"Can you take us there?"

"Sure." Louis Nenda moved to the main control console. "Bridle Gap, no sweat. Only one jump. If Dulcimer still hangs around in the same place, and if he's broke enough to need work, and if he still has a brain left in his pop-eyed head after he's been frying it for more years than I like to think—well, we should be able to hire him. And then we can all go off together an' get wiped out in the Anfract."

Chism Polypheme.

As soon as the Bose jump was complete and the *Erebus* had embarked on its subluminal flight to Bridle Gap, Darya consulted the *Universal Species Catalog* (Subclass: Sapients) in the ship's data banks.

And found nothing.

She went to see Louis Nenda, lounging in the ship's auxiliary engine room. He was watching Atvar H'sial as she ran a dozen supply lines to a glossy chestnut-brown ellipsoid about three feet long.

"It don't surprise me," Nenda said in answer to Darya's question. "Lot more things in the spiral arm than there is in the data banks—an' half of what's in there is wrong. That's why E. C. Tally's so screwed up—he only knows what the data banks dumped into him. You won't find the Polyphemes in the Species Catalog, because they're not local. Their homeworld's way outside the Periphery, some godawful place in the Sagittarius arm on the other side of the Gap. What you want to know about Dulcimer?"

"Why did you say 'I'm warning you now, he's a Chism Polypheme'?"

"Because he's a Chism Polypheme. That means he's sly, and servile, and conceited, and unreliable, an' he tells lies as his first preference. He tells the truth when there's no other option. Like they say, 'There's liars, and damn liars, and Chism Polyphemes.' There's another reason the Polyphemes aren't in your data bank—no one could get the same story from 'em twice running, to find out what they are."

"So why are you willing to deal with him, if he's such an awful person?"

Nenda gave her the all-admiring, half-pitying glance that so annoyed Hans Rebka, and stroked her upper arm. "First, sweetie, because you know where you stand with a guaranteed liar. An' second, because we got no option. Who else would be crazy enough to fly into the Anfract? *And* be good enough to get us there. You only use a Polypheme when you're desperate, but they're mebbe the galaxy's best pilots, and Dulcimer's top of the lot. He usually needs work, too, 'cause he has this little problem that needs feedin'. Last of all, we want Dulcimer because he's a *survivor*. He claims he's fifteen thousand years old. I think he's lying—that would mean he was around before the Great Rising, when the Zardalu ruled the Communion—but the records on Bridle Gap show he's been droppin' into the Sun Bar there for over three thousand years. That's a survivor. I like to go with survivors."

Because you are one, yourself, Darya thought. And *you're* a liar, too—*and* you're self-serving. So why do I like you? And speaking of lying . . .

"Louis, when you told us how you and Atvar H'sial left Serenity, you said something I don't understand."

"We didn't just *leave*—we were thrown out, by that dumb Builder construct, Speaker-Between."

"I know that. But you said something else about Speaker-Between. You said that you thought it was lying about the Builders themselves."

"I never said it was *lying.* I said I thought it was *wrong.* Big difference. Speaker-Between believes what it told us. It's been sittin' on Serenity for four or five million years, convinced that the Builders are just waitin' in stasis until Speaker-Between and The-One-Who-Waits an' who knows how many other constructs have selected the right species to help the Builders. An' then the Builders will pop back out of stasis, and everything will be fine, and Speaker-Between and his lot will live happy ever after.

"Except that's all bunk. Speaker-Between's dodderin' along, doing what it *thinks* it was told to do. But I don't believe that's what it was *really* told by the Builders. You can get things screwed up pretty bad in five million years. Atvar H'sial agrees with me—the constructs are conscientious, an' real impressive when you first meet 'em. An' they got lots of power, too. But they're not very *smart.*"

"If that's true, where are the Builders? And what do they *really* want the constructs to do?"

"Beats me. That's more your line than mine. An' right now I don't much care. We got other worries." Nenda turned, to where Atvar H'sial had finished connecting the supply lines. "Like how we land on Bridle Gap. We'll be there in two days. The *Erebus* can't go down, because J'merlia and Kallik were dumb enough to buy us a Flying Dutchman. An' we don't have credit to rent a downside shuttle. So you better cross your fingers."

Atvar H'sial was turning spigots, and the pipes leading to the brown ovoid were filling with cloudy liquid. Darya followed Louis Nenda and bent to stare at the shiny surface of the egg.

"What is it?"

"That's the question of the moment. This is the gizmo that Julian Graves found when he was pokin' around the other day. No one could identify it, but yesterday At took a peek at its inside with ultrasonics. She thinks it might be a ship-seed. The *Erebus* is a Tantalus orbital fort, so it never expected to land anywhere. But there would be times when people on board needed to escape. There were a dozen of these eggs, stacked away close to the main hatch. In a few hours we'll know what we've got. 'Scuse me. At says I hafta get busy."

He hurried away from Darya to crouch by the spigots and control their flow. Fluids were moving faster through the supply lines, and the glossy surface of the ellipsoid was beginning to swell ominously. A soft, throbbing tone came from its interior.

"Don't get too close," Nenda called.

The warning was unnecessary. As the egg began to quiver, Darya turned and headed out through the exit of the auxiliary engine room. Nenda had given her a lot to think about.

Atvar H'sial watched until Darya was out of sight. "That departure is not before time, Louis Nenda." The pheromonal message carried a reproving overtone. "As I have remarked before, the human female provides an undesirable distraction for you."

"Relax, At. She don't care about *me,* an' I don't care about her. All she's worried about is the Builders, and where they are."

"I am not persuaded; nor, I suspect, is Captain Rebka."

"Who can go stick it up his nose. And so can you." Louis Nenda spoke in irritated tones—but he did not provide his final comment in pheromonal translation.

* * *

The world of Bridle Gap had never been settled by humans.

The reason for that was obvious to the crew of the *Erebus* long before they arrived there. The parent star, Cavesson, was a tiny fierce point of violet-blue at the limit of the visible spectrum, sitting within a widespread shell of glowing gas. The stellar collapse and shrugging off of outer layers that had turned Cavesson into a neutron star forty thousand years earlier would have vaporized Bridle Gap—if that world had been close-by at the time. Even today, the outpouring of X rays and hard ultraviolet from Cavesson created an ionized shroud at the outer edge of Bridle Gap's atmosphere. Enough ultraviolet came blazing through to the surface to fry an unshielded human in minutes.

"It must have been a rogue planet," said Julian Graves. The *Erebus* had sat in parking orbit for a couple of hours, while the ship's scopes revealed as much surface detail as possible. Now it was time for action.

"It was on a close-approach trajectory to Cavesson," he went on, "and if the star hadn't blown up, Bridle Gap would have swung right on by. But the ejecta from Cavesson smacked into it and transferred enough momentum to shove it to a capture orbit."

"And if you believe that," Hans Rebka said softly to E. C. Tally, "you'll believe anything."

"But you reject that explanation?" The embodied computer was standing between Rebka and Darya Lang, waiting for Atvar H'sial's signal from within the seedship that the interior was thoroughly hardened and the little vessel ready to board.

Rebka gestured to the blazing point-image of Cavesson. "See for yourself, E.C. You take a look at the spectrum of that, then tell me what sort of life could develop on a void-cold rogue world, far from any star, but adapt fast enough to survive the sleet of radiation from Cavesson."

"Then what is your explanation for the existence of Bridle Gap?"

"Nothing to make you feel comfortable. Bridle Gap was

moved here by the Zardalu, when they controlled this whole region. The Zardalu had great powers when humans were still swinging in the trees—just another reason to worry about them now." He began to move forward. "Wherever it came from, the planet must have had natural high-radiation life-forms. You'll see them for yourself in a couple of hours, because it looks like we're ready to go."

Louis Nenda had appeared from within the seedship's hatch. "Tight squeeze," he said. "And goin' to be rough when we get down there. Sure one of you don't want to stay with the rest?"

Rebka ignored the invitation to remain behind and pushed E. C. Tally on ahead of him into the seedship's interior. With Atvar H'sial already inside, it was a tight fit. The seed, full-grown, was a disappointment. The hope had been for a sizable lifeboat, capable of carrying a substantial fraction of the *Erebus*'s total passenger capacity. Instead the final seedship proved to be a midget: puny engines, no Bose Drive, and only enough room to squeeze in four or five people. The landing party had been whittled down: Louis Nenda and Atvar H'sial, most familiar with Zardalu Communion territory and customs; E. C. Tally, to provide an exact visual and sound record of what happened on the surface, to be played back for the others who stayed on board the *Erebus;* and finally Hans Rebka, for the good—but unmentioned—reason that somebody less naive than E. C. Tally was needed to keep an eye on Nenda and Atvar H'sial.

The group remaining on the *Erebus* had been assigned one unrewarding but necessary task: to learn all that could be learned about the Torvil Anfract.

The planet that the seedship drifted down to was at its best from a distance. Two hundred miles up, the surface was a smoky palette of soft purple and gray. By two thousand feet that soft, airbrushed texture had resolved to a jumbled wilderness of broken, steep-sided cliffs, their faces covered with spiky gray trees and shrubs. The landing port for Bridle

Gap occupied half of an isolated long, flat gash on the surface, with a dark body of water at its lower end. Louis Nenda took the ship down with total confidence and landed at the water's edge.

"That'll do. Cross your fingers and claws. We'll know in another five minutes if Dulcimer's here." He was already smearing thick yellow cream over his face and hands.

"Five minutes?" E. C. Tally said. "But what about the time it takes to clear Customs and Immigration?"

Nenda gave him one incredulous stare and continued applying the cream. "Better get coated, too, 'less you wanna crisp out there in two seconds." He went to the hatch, cracked it open and sniffed, then fitted improvised goggles into position. "Not bad. I'm goin'. Follow me as soon as you're ready."

Hans Rebka was right behind as Nenda stepped out onto the surface. He gazed all around and made his own evaluation. He had never been to this particular planet, but he had seen a dozen that rivaled it. Bridle Gap was bad, and one would never go outside at noon, but it was no worse than his birthworld of Teufel, where no one who wanted to live went out while the *Remouleur* dawn wind blew.

He looked east through his goggles, to where Cavesson's morning rays were barely clearing the jagged upthrust fingers of the cliffs. The sun's bright point was diffused by the atmosphere, and the breeze on his face was actually chilly. He knew better than to be misled by either of those. Even thinned by dust and cloud and ozone, Cavesson was delivering to the surface of Bridle Gap a hundred times as much UV as a human's eyes and skin could tolerate. The air smelled like a continuous electrical discharge. The flowers on the vegetation at water's edge confirmed the deadly surroundings. Drab gray and sable to Rebka's vision, they would glow and dazzle out in the ultraviolet, where the tiny winged pollinators of Bridle Gap saw most clearly.

It was also a low-gravity world, well-suited to Atvar H'sial's physiology. While Rebka was still staring around, the Cecropian floated past him in a gliding leap that carried her to Louis Nenda's side. He had reached a long, low building built partly on the spaceport's rocky surface and partly in the black water beyond it. Together, the Cecropian and the Karelian human waded through shallow water to reach the entrance to the Sun Bar.

Hans Rebka took a quick glance back at the seedship. There was still no sign of E. C. Tally, but it would be a mistake to let Nenda and Atvar H'sial begin a meeting alone. Rebka had heard their explanation of what they had been doing on Serenity that led to their expulsion and return to the spiral arm. He did not believe a word of it.

He splashed forward, entered a dark doorway of solid obsidian, and took off his goggles to find himself confronted by a waist-high circle of bright black eyes.

The neurotoxic sting of a Hymenopt was deadly, and the chance that this one understood human speech was small. Rebka pointed to the backs of Nenda and Atvar H'sial, visible through another stone doorway, and walked steadily that way without speaking. He followed them through three more interior rooms, then set his goggles in position again as he emerged into a chamber that was open to the glaring sky, with a ledge of rock across its full width, ending at oily black water.

A dozen creatures of all shapes and sizes lay on the ledge, soaking in Cavesson's lethal rays. Louis Nenda advanced to speak to one of them. After a few seconds it rose to balance on its thick tail and came wriggling back into the covered part of the room.

"Hello there." The voice was a croaking growl. The blubbery green lips of a broad mouth pursed into an awful imitation of a human smile. "Honored to meet you, sirs. Excuse my bare condition, but I was just having myself a bit of a wallowbake. Dulcimer, Master Pilot, at your service."

Rebka had never met a Chism Polypheme, but he had seen too many aliens to consider this one as anything more than a variation on a theme, one who happened to lack both radial and bilateral symmetry. The alien was a nine-foot helical cylinder, a corkscrew of smooth muscle covered with rubbery green skin and topped by a head the same width as the body. A huge eye of slaty gray, shifty and bulging, leered out from under a scaly browridge. The lidded ocular was half as wide as the head itself. Between that and the pouting mouth, the tiny gold-rimmed pea of a scanning eye continuously flickered across the scene. As Rebka watched, five flexible three-fingered limbs, all on one side of the pliant body and each just long enough to reach across it, picked up a corsetlike pink garment from the ledge, wrapped it around the Polypheme's middle, and hooked it in place. The five arms poked through five holes, to lodge comfortably into broad lateral slings on the corset. The alien tightened its corkscrew body and crouched lower onto the massive, coiled tail to match Rebka's height.

"At your service," the creaking voice repeated. The scanning eye on its short eyestalk roved the room, then returned to stare uneasily at the towering blind form of Atvar H'sial, twice the size of the humans. "Cecropian, eh. Don't see too many of you in these parts. You're needing a top pilot, do you say?"

Atvar H'sial did not move a millimeter. "We are," Rebka said.

"Then you need look no farther." The main eye turned to Rebka. "I've guided ten thousand missions, every one a success. I know the galaxy better than any living being, probably better than any dead one, too. Though I say it myself, you couldn't have better luck than getting me as your pilot."

"That's what we've heard. You're the best." And the only one crazy enough to take the job, Rebka thought. But flattery cost nothing.

"I am, sir, the very best. No use denying it, Dulcimer is the finest there is. And your own name, sir, if I might ask it?"

"I am Captain Hans Rebka, from the Phemus Circle. This is Louis Nenda, a Karelian human, and our Cecropian friend is Atvar H'sial."

Dulcimer did not speak, but the great eye blinked.

A silent message passed from Atvar H'sial to Louis Nenda: *This being seems unaware of his own pheromones. I can read him. He recognizes you, and Rebka was a fool to mention that you are in his party. This may cost us.*

"And now, Captain," said Dulcimer, "might I be asking where it is that you want to be taken?"

"To the Torvil Anfract."

The great eye blinked again and rolled toward Louis Nenda. "The Anfract! Ah, sir, that's a bit different from what I was given to suppose. Now, if you'd told me at the first that you were wanting to visit the *Anfract*—"

"You don't know the region?" Rebka asked.

"Ah, and did I say that, Captain?" The scaly head nodded in reproof. "I've been there dozens of times, I know it like I know the end of my own tail. But it's a dangerous place, sir. Great walloping space anomalies, naked singularities, Planck's-constant changes, and warps and woofs that have space-time ringing like a bell, or twisted and running cross-ways . . ." The Polypheme shivered, with a spiraling ripple of muscle that ran from the tip of his tail up to the top of his head. "Why would you ever want to go to a place like the Anfract, Captain?"

"We have to." Rebka glanced at Louis Nenda, who was standing with an unreadable expression. They had not discussed just how much the Polypheme would be told. "We have to go there because there are living Zardalu in the spiral arm. And we think they must be hiding deep within the Anfract."

"Zardalu!" The croak rose an octave. "Zardalu in the Anfract! If you'd excuse old Dulcimer, sirs, for just one minute, while I check something . . ."

The middle arm was reaching into the pink corset, pulling out a little octahedron and holding it up to the bulging gray eye. There was a long silence while the Polypheme peered into its depths, then he sighed and shivered again, this time from head to tail.

"I'm sorry, sirs, but I don't know as I can help. Not in the

Anfract. Not if there might be Zardalu there. I see great danger—and there's death in the crystal."

He is lying, Atvar H'sial told Nenda silently. *He shivers, but there is no emanation of fear.*

Louis Nenda moved closer to the Cecropian. *Rebka's telling him about the Zardalu,* he replied.

Then Dulcimer does not believe it. He is convinced that the Zardalu are long-gone from the spiral arm.

"But see for yourself, in the Vision Crystal." The Polypheme was holding the green octahedron out to Hans Rebka. "Behold violence, sir, and death."

The inside of the crystal had turned from a uniform translucent green to a turbulent cloud of black. As it cleared, a scene grew within it. A tiny Dulcimer facsimile was struggling in the middle of a dozen looming attackers, each one too dark and rapidly-moving to reveal any details as to identities.

"Well, if you can't help us, I guess that's that." Rebka nodded casually, handed the octahedron back to the Polypheme, and began to turn away. "I'm afraid we'll have to look elsewhere for a pilot. It's a pity, because I'm sure you're the best. But when you can't get the best, you have to settle for second best."

"Now, just a second, Captain." The five little arms jerked out of their slings all at once, and the Polypheme bobbed taller on his coiled tail. "Don't misunderstand me. I didn't say as how I *couldn't* be your pilot, or even as I *wouldn't* be your pilot. All I'm saying is, I see exceptional danger in the Anfract. And danger calls for something different from your usual run-of-the-arm contract."

"What do you have in mind?" Rebka was still as casual as could be.

"Well, surely not just a flat fee, Captain. Not for something that shows danger . . . and destruction . . . and death." The great eye fixed unblinking on Rebka, but the tiny bead of the scanning eye below it flickered across to Louis Nenda and rapidly back. "So I was thinking, to make up for the danger, there should be something like a fee, *plus* a *percent-*

age. Something maybe like fifteen percent . . . of whatever your party gets in the Anfract."

"Fifteen percent of what we get in the Anfract." Rebka frowned at Louis Nenda, then looked back at the Polypheme. "I'll need to discuss this with my colleagues. If you'd wait here for a minute." He led the way back to an inner room and removed his goggles. "What do you think?" He waited for Nenda to relay the question to Atvar H'sial.

"At and I think the same." Nenda did not hesitate. "Dulcimer recognized me and he knows my reputation—I'm pretty well known in this part of the Communion—so he assumes we're off on a treasure hunt. He's greedy, and he wants his cut. But since what we're likely to get in the Anfract is a cartload of trouble, and that's about all, so far as I'm concerned Dulcimer can have fifteen percent of my share of that any time he likes."

"So we take his offer?"

"Not straight off—he'll be suspicious. We go back in and tell him five percent, then let him haggle us up to ten." Louis Nenda stared at Rebka curiously. "Mind telling me something? I had At prompting me, 'cause she could read Dulcimer pretty good. But *you* saw through him without that. How'd you do it?"

"At first I didn't. He should never have brought out that dumb 'Vision Crystal.' Back in the Phemus Circle the con men used to peddle the same thing as the 'Eye of the Manticore,' and claim they had been stolen by explorers from the Tristan free-space Manticore. All nonsense, of course. They're nothing but preprogrammed piezoelectric crystals, responding to finger pressure. They let you look at maybe two hundred different scenes, depending where and how you squeeze. A kid's toy."

Atvar H'sial nodded as Rebka's words were translated for him. *He is smart, your Captain Rebka,* she said to Nenda. *Too smart. Smart enough to endanger our own plans. We must be careful, Louis. And tell this to the captain: Although the Polypheme is sly and self-serving, his pretenses are not all false. My own instincts tell me that we will meet danger in the Anfract; and perhaps we will also meet death there.*

The negotiations with Dulcimer took hours longer than expected. Hans Rebka, aware that the *Erebus* was huge and powerful but ungainly and restricted to a space environment, while the seedship though nimble was small and unarmed, insisted that the Chism Polypheme should include the use of his own armed scoutship, the *Indulgence,* as part of the deal. Dulcimer agreed, but only if his share of whatever was recovered from the Anfract was increased to twelve percent.

A binding contract was signed in the Sun Bar's offices, where half the space business on Bridle Gap was conducted. When Nenda, Rebka, and Atvar H'sial finally left they found E. C. Tally at the entrance. He was addressing in fluent Varnian the Hymenopt who guarded the door, politely requesting permission to enter.

The Hymenopt was unresponsive. To Hans Rebka's eyes, she seemed fast asleep.

E. C. Tally explained that it was the hundred and thirty-fifth spiral arm language that he had tried, without success. The embodied computer was pointing out that his chance of eventual communication was excellent, since he had a hundred and sixty-two more languages at his command, plus four hundred and ninety dialects, when the others dragged him away to the seedship.

CHAPTER 7

The Torvil Anfract

OLD HABITS DID not just die *hard.* They refused to die at all.

Darya Lang, sitting alone in an observation bubblc stuck like a glassy pimple on the dark bulk of the *Erebus,* gazed on the Torvil Anfract and felt vaguely unsatisfied. As soon as the seedship had left for Bridle Gap, she had started work.

Reluctantly. She would have much preferred to be down on the planet, sampling whatever strangeness it had to offer. But once she got going on her research—well, then it was another matter.

She did not stop. She *could not* stop.

Back in school on Sentinel Gate, some of her teachers had accused her of being "slow and dreamy." Darya knew that was unfair. Her mind was fast, and it was accurate. She took a long time to feel her way into a problem; but once she was immersed, she had the devil's own mental muscles. It took an act of God to pull her out. If she had been a runner, she would have specialized in supermarathons.

Even the return of the landing party from Bridle Gap and the arrival on board of the no-legged, five-armed oddity of the Chism Polypheme, bobbing and smirking and croaking while he was introduced to her, his scanning eye roaming over everyone and everything on the *Erebus* as if he were pricing them . . . all that had been unable to distract Darya for even a few minutes.

She had decided that the Anfract was more than interesting. It was *unique,* in a way that she could not yet express.

She had tried to explain its fascination to Hans Rebka when he first returned with the Polypheme.

"Darya, everything in the universe is unique." He cut her off in a moment, hardly listening. "But we're on our way. Dulcimer says he can have us there in two days. We'll need the most detailed data you can give us."

"It's not just the data that matters, it's the *patterns*—"

But he was heading for the cargo holds, and she was talking to herself.

And now the Anfract was shimmering beyond the observation port—and Darya was still plodding along on what to Hans Rebka was no more than unproductive analysis. Hard-copy output surrounded her and overflowed every flat surface of the observation bubble. There was no shortage of data about the Torvil Anfract. Hundreds of ships had scouted its outer regions. Fifty or more had gone deeper, and a quarter of those had returned to tell about it. But their data had never been combined and *integrated.* Reading the earlier reports and analyzing their measurements and observations made Darya feel that the Anfract was like a gigantic Rorschach test. All observers saw their own version of reality, rather than a physical object.

There was unanimity on maybe half-a-dozen facts. The Anfract's location within Zardalu Communion territory was not in question. It lay completely within a region two light-years across, and it possessed thirty-seven major lobes. Each lobe had its own characteristic identity, but the components of any pair of lobes were likely to *interchange,* instantaneously and randomly. Ships that had traveled inside the Anfract confirmed that the interchange was real, not just an optical effect. Two vessels had even entered the Anfract at one point, become involved in a switch of two lobes, and emerged elsewhere. They agreed that the transition took no time and produced no noticeable changes in ship or crew. All researchers believed that this phenomenon showed the Anfract to possess *macroscopic* quantum states, of unprecedented size.

And there the agreements ended. Some ships reported that the subluminal approach to the Anfract from the nearest Bose Access Node, one light-year away, had taken five ship-years at relativistic speeds. Others found themselves at the edge of the Anfract after just two or three days' travel.

Darya had her own explanation for that anomaly. Massive space-time distortion was the rule, near and within the Anfract. Certain pathways would lengthen or shorten the distance between the same two points. "Fast" approach routes to the edge of the Anfract could be mapped, though no one had ever done it. The two-day approach route that the *Erebus* had followed was discovered empirically by an earlier ship, and others had followed it without understanding why it worked.

Darya had begun to map the external geometry of the Anfract. She began to have a better appreciation of why it had never been done before. The continuum of the region was enormously complex. It was a long, long job, but it did not require all her attention. While she was organizing the calculation, Darya felt a faint sense of uneasiness. There was something missing. She was overlooking some major factor, something basic and important.

She had learned not to ignore that vague itch in the base of the brain. The best way to bring it closer to the surface was to explain to someone else what she was doing, clarifying her thoughts for herself as she did so. She found Louis Nenda in the main control cabin and started to explain her work.

He interrupted her within thirty seconds. "Don't make no difference to me, sweetheart. I don't give squat about the structure of the Anfract. We still gotta go in there, find the Zardalu, an' get out in one piece. Get your head goin' on *that*." He had left her, still talking, and wandered off to the main hold to make sure that Dulcimer's ship, the *Indulgence,* was safely stowed and the seedship was again ready for use.

Barbarian, Darya thought.

He was no better than Hans Rebka. No use telling *them* that knowing was necessary, that knowledge was good for its own sake, that understanding *mattered.* That learning new things was *important,* and that it was only abstract knowledge, no matter what Nenda or Rebka or anyone else on board might say, that separated humans from animals.

She went angrily back to work on the Anfract's external geometry. Could other variations reported by earlier ships also be explained in geometric terms? All approaching observers agreed that the Anfract popped into being suddenly. One moment there was nothing to see, the next it was just *there,* close up. But to half the approaching ships, the Anfract was a glowing bundle of tendrils grouped into thirty-seven complex knots. Others saw thirty-seven spherical regions of light, like diffuse multicolored suns. Half-a-dozen observers reported that the only external evidence of the Anfract was *holes* in space, thirty-seven dark occlusions of the stellar background. And two Cecropian ships, their occupants blind to electromagnetic radiation and relying on instruments to render the Anfract visible in terms of sonic echolocation, "saw" the Anfract, too—as thirty-seven distorted balls of furry velvet.

Darya believed that she could explain it all in terms of geometry. Space-time distortion in and around the Anfract affected more than approach distances. It changed the properties of emitted light bundles. Depending on the path taken, some were smoothed, others cancelled by phase interference. She happened to be seeing the pattern of glowing white-worm tendrils, but if the *Erebus* had followed a different approach route she would have seen something different. And her geometric mapping of the Anfract's exterior could be continued to its *interior,* based on light-travel properties.

Darya set up the new calculations. While they were running, she brooded over the vast inconstant vista beyond the observation bubble. Her mood seemed as changeable and uncontrollable as the Anfract itself. She felt annoyed, exhilarated, guilty, and *superior* in turn.

A major mystery was hovering just beyond her mental horizon. She was sure of that. It was infuriating that she could not see it for herself, and just as maddening that the others would not let her *explain* the evidence to them. That was her favorite way of making things clear in her own mind. Meanwhile, the itch inside was getting worse.

The arrival of Kallik in the observation bubble was both an unwelcome interruption and a reminder to Darya that there were other formidable intelligences on board the *Erebus.*

The little Hymenopt came drifting in, to stand diffidently by Darya's side. Darya raised her eyebrows.

"One has heard," began Kallik. She had learned to interpret human gestures, far better than Darya had learned to read hers. "One has heard that you have been able to perform a systematic mapping of Anfract geometry."

Darya nodded. "How do you know that?"

"Master Nenda said that you spoke of it to him."

"Pearls before swine."

"Indeed?" Kallik bobbed her black head politely. "But the statement is true, is it? Because if so, a discovery of my own may have relevance." She settled down on the floor next to Darya, eight legs splayed.

Darya stopped glooming. The unscratched itch in her brain started to fade, and she began to pay serious attention to Kallik. It was the Hymenopt, after all, who had—quite independently of Darya—solved the riddle of artifact spheres of change which had led them to Quake at Summertide.

"I, too, have been studying the Anfract," Kallik went on. "Perhaps from a different perspective than yours. I decided that, although the geometric structure of the Anfract itself is interesting, our focus should be on *planets* within it. They, surely, are the only places where Zardalu could reasonably be living. It might seem well established from outside observation that there are many, many planets within the Anfract —the famous phenomenon known as the Beads, or String of Pearls, would seem to prove it: scores of beautiful planets, observed by scores of ships. Proved, except for this curious fact: the explorers who succeed in reaching the *interior* of the Anfract, and returning from it, report *no planets* around the handful of suns that they visited. They say that planets in the Anfract must certainly be a rarity, and perhaps even nonexistent. Who, then, is right?"

"The ones who went inside." Darya did not hesitate. "Remote viewing is no substitute for direct approach."

"My conclusion also. So the Beads, and the String of Pearls, must be illusions. They are the result of an odd lens effect that focuses planets from far away, perhaps outside the spiral arm or in another galaxy entirely, and makes them visible in the neighborhood of the Anfract. Very well. I therefore eliminated all the *multiple* planetary sightings of the Beads, and of String of Pearls. That left only a handful of isolated planet sightings within the Anfract. If our earlier analyses are correct, one of them will be Genizee. I have locations from which they were viewed, and their directions at the time. But I did not know how to propagate through the Anfract's complex geometry to the interior—"

"I do!" Darya was cursing herself. She had worked alone because she usually worked alone, but it was clear now that she should have been collaborating with Kallik. "I needed to do those calculations so I could derive lightlike trajectories across the Anfract."

"As I surmised and hoped." Kallik moved to the terminal that tied the observation bubble to the central computer of the *Erebus.* "So if I provide you with my locations and directions, and you continue their vectors along Anfract geodesics—"

"—we'll have your planet locations." The mental itch was almost gone. Darya felt a vague sense of loss, but action overrode it. "Give me a few minutes, and I'll crank out all your answers."

* * *

Darya was tempted to call it a law of nature.

Lang's Law: Everything always takes longer.

It was not a few minutes. It was six hours before she could collate her results and seek out Hans Rebka and Louis Nenda. She found them with Julian Graves in the main control room of the *Erebus.* Dulcimer was nowhere to be seen, but three-dimensional displays of the Anfract, ported over from the Polypheme's data banks on the *Indulgence,* filled the center of the room.

She stood in silence for a few seconds, savoring the moment and waiting to be noticed. Then she realized that might take a long time. They were deep in discussion.

She stepped forward to stand right between Nenda and Rebka, where she could not be ignored.

"Kallik and I know how to find the Zardalu!" A touch of sensationalism, maybe even a little smugness—but no more than their discovery deserved. "If Dulcimer will take us into the Anfract, we know where we should go."

Nenda and Rebka moved, but only so that they could still see each other and talk around her. It was Julian Graves who turned to face her, with a ringing, "Then I wish that you would bring it to *their* attention." He gestured at Nenda and Rebka. "Because the conversation here is certainly going nowhere."

At that moment Darya became aware of the level of tension in the room. If she had not been so full of herself, she would have read it from the postures. The air was charged with emotion, as invisible and as lethal as superheated steam.

"What's wrong?" But she was already guessing. Louis Nenda and Hans Rebka were close to blows. Atvar H'sial hovered close-by, rearing up menacingly on her two hindmost limbs.

"It's him." Rebka stabbed an accusing finger an inch short of Nenda's chest. "Tells us he'll take us to somebody who can pilot us in, then wastes our energy and money and days of our time getting to Bridle Gap and arguing with that lying corkscrew. And then *that*'s what we get for our Anfract approach routes."

He was pointing at the big display. Darya stared at it in perplexity. It was not the Anfract she had been studying. In addition to the usual features, the 3-D image was filled with yellow lines snaking into the center of the anomaly. "What's wrong with it?"

"Take a close look, and you'll see for yourself. Like to fly that one?" He pointed to a wriggling trajectory that abruptly terminated in a tiny sphere of darkness. "See where it *ends*? Follow it, and you'll run yourself right into the middle of a singularity. No more *Erebus,* no more crew."

"You're dumb as a Ditron." Nedra stepped closer to Rebka, pushing Darya aside as though she did not exist. "If you'd just listen to me for a minute—"

"Now wait a second!" The days when Darya would let herself be ignored were over. She pushed back and grabbed Rebka's arm. "Hans, how do you *know* that the Polypheme suggests those as approach paths? For heaven's sake, why don't you *ask* him what he's proposing to do?"

"Exactly!" Nenda said, but Rebka roared him down.

"Ask him! Don't you think I *want* to ask him? He's on board, we know that, but that's all we know. He's vanished! That brain-burned bum, as soon as we started to talk about Anfract approach routes, and safety factors, and time-varying fields, he excused himself for a minute. No one has seen him since."

"And it's your damned fault!" Nenda was as loud as Rebka, pushing Darya to one side again and glaring at him eyeball-to-eyeball. "Didn't I tell you not to let Tally do that stupid data download from the *Indulgence*? I warned you *all.*"

Two long, jointed limbs came swooping down, grasped Nenda and Rebka by the back of their shirts, and drew them easily apart. Julian Graves nodded gratefully to Atvar H'sial. "Thank you." He turned to Rebka. "Louis Nenda indeed warned you."

"Warned him of *what*?" Darya was tired of this.

Nenda shook himself free of Atvar H'sial's grasp and slumped into a seat. "Of the obvious thing." His voice was exasperated. "Dulcimer makes his *living* as a pilot. But he's a Chism Polypheme, so that means he's paranoid and expects people to try to rob him. His stored displays are exactly how I'd expect them to be—totally useless! He has all the real stuff hidden in his head, where no one can steal it. There's nothing but lies in the data bank. Pilfer from him and use that to fly with, and you're a dead duck."

"With respect, Atvar H'sial would like to make a statement," J'merlia put in. He had been translating the argument for the Cecropian. "Dulcimer is a liar, says Atvar H'sial, but he also has low cunning. We must assume that he made himself absent not by accident at this time, but by *design.*"

"Why?" Graves asked. He bit back the urge to order J'merlia to stop acting like a slave to Atvar H'sial. J'merlia was a free being now—even if he didn't *want* to be.

"In order to divide our group against itself," the Lo'tfian translator went on, "as it has just been divided by the fighting of Louis Nenda and Captain Rebka. Dulcimer's influence is maximized when we are not united. Also, he wished us to realize what we seem to be proving for ourselves, by our substitution of emotion for thought: without the Polypheme, we have no idea how to penetrate the Anfract. You have been playing Dulcimer's game." Atvar H'sial's blind white head swung to survey the whole group. "If this battle does not cease, Dulcimer will surely return—to gloat over our disarray."

Atvar H'sial was getting through—Darya knew it, because Louis Nenda and Hans Rebka would not look at each other.

"Hell, we weren't fightin'," Nenda muttered. "We were just havin' a discussion about where we want to go."

"That's right," Rebka added. "We wouldn't know what to tell Dulcimer, even if he was here."

"Yes, we would!" It had taken a long time, but Darya could finally make her point. "If Dulcimer can get us to the

Anfract, Kallik and I can give him a destination inside it."

At last she had their attention. "If you'll sit still for a few minutes, without fighting, I'll show you the whole thing. Or Kallik will—it was really her idea." She glanced at Kallik, but the little Hymenopt sank to the floor, while her ring of black eyes flickered in the signal of negation. "All right, if you don't want to, I'll do it. And I can use this same display."

Darya took over the control console, while the others moved to sit where they could easily see. They watched silently as she outlined her own analysis of geodesics around the Anfract, mated it with Kallik's sifting of planetary sightings within the complex, and carried on to provide a summary of computed locations.

"Five or six possibles," she finished. "But luckily previous expeditions have provided good-quality images of each one. Kallik and I reviewed them all. We agree on just one prime candidate. This one."

She was zooming into the Anfract display along one of her computed light-paths, a dizzying, contorted trajectory with no apparent logic to it. A star became visible, and then, as Darya changed the display scale and the apparent speed of approach, the field of view veered away from the swelling disk of the sun. A bright dot appeared.

"Planet," Julian Graves whispered. "If you are right, we are looking at something lost for more than eleven millennia: Genizee, the Zardalu cladeworld."

A planet, and yet not a planet. They were closing still, and the point of light was splitting.

"Not just one world," Darya said. "More of a doublet, like Opal and Quake."

"Not too like either one, I hope." The anger had gone out of Hans Rebka and he was staring at the display with total concentration. As the world images drew closer he could see that there were differences. Quake and Opal had been fraternal twins, the same size though grossly dissimilar in appearance. The Anfract doublet was more like a planet and its single huge moon, the one blue-white and with a surface hazily visible between swirls of cloud cover, the other, just as bright though only half the size, glittering like burnished steel. Darya's display in accelerated time showed the gleaming moon, tiny even at highest magnification, whirling around the planet at dizzying speed, against a fixed backdrop of steady points of light. Rebka peered at the planet and its moon, not sure what it was that forced him to such intense examination.

"And now we need Dulcimer, more than ever," Louis Nenda added, breaking Rebka's trance. Nenda, too, had been sitting quietly through Darya's presentation, but during the approach trajectory he had twisted and writhed in his seat as though matching its contortions.

"Why?" Darya felt hurt. "I just *showed* you the way to go into the Anfract."

"Not for any vessel I ever heard of." Nenda shook his dark head. "There's not a ship in the arm could follow that path an' stay in one piece. Not even this monster. We gotta find an easier way in. That means we need Dulcimer. We gotta have him."

"Quite right," said a croaking voice at the entrance to the control chamber. "*Everybody* needs Dulcimer."

They all turned. The Chism Polypheme was there, sagging on his coiled tail against the chamber wall. The dark green of his skin had faded and lightened to the shade of an unripe apple. While all had been intent on Darya's presentation, no one had noticed his entry or knew how long he had been slumped there.

Atvar H'sial had predicted that the Chism Polypheme would return to gloat. She had been wrong. He had returned, but from the look of him he was far from gloating. While they watched, Dulcimer's tail wobbled from under him and he slid lower down the wall. Louis Nenda swore and hurried to his side. The scanning eye on its short eyestalk had withdrawn completely into the Polypheme's head, but the master eye above it remained wide open, vague and blissful as it peered up at the stocky Karelian human. Nenda bent and placed his hand on Dulcimer's upper body.

He cursed. "I knew it. Look at the green on him. He's *sizzlin'*. Without a radiation source! How the blazes could he get so hot, without even leavin' the *Erebus*?"

"Not hot," Dulcimer murmured. "Little bit warm, that's all. No problem." He lay face down on the floor and seemed to sag into its curved surface.

"A power kernel!" Nenda said. "It has to be. I didn't know there were any on this ship."

"At least four," E. C. Tally informed them.

"But shielded, surely, every one of 'em." Nenda stared suspiciously at the embodied computer. "Aren't they?"

"Yes. But when the Chism Polypheme first came on board the *Erebus*—" Tally paused at Nenda's expression. He was programmed to answer questions—but he was also programmed to protect himself from physical damage.

"Go on." Nenda was glowering. "Amaze me."

"He asked me to show him any kernels that might be on board. Naturally, I did so. And then he wondered aloud if there might be any way that a shield could be lowered in just one place, to permit a radiation beam to be emitted from the kernel interior to a selected site outside it. It was not a standard request, but I contain information on such a procedure in my files. So naturally, I—"

"Naturally, you." Nenda swore again and prodded Dulcimer with his foot. "Naturally, you showed him just how to cook himself. What junk did they put in that head of yours, Tally, after they pushed the On button? Look at him now, grilled both sides. If you don't know enough to keep a Polypheme away from hard radiation . . . I've never seen the skin color so light. He's really smoking."

"Nice and toasty," Dulcimer corrected from floor level. "Just nice and toasty."

"How long before he'll be back to normal?" Darya asked. She had moved to stand closer to the Polypheme. He did not seem to see her.

"Hell, I dunno. Three days, four days—depends how big a radiation slug he took. A whopper, from the looks of it."

"But we need him right now. He has to steer us to the

Anfract." She had run off a copy of the computed coordinates of Genizee, and she waved it in Nenda's face. "It's so *frustrating,* when we finally know where we have to go to find the Zardalu . . ."

"Zardalu!" said the slurred and croaking voice. The bulging high-resolution eye went rolling from side to side, following the movement of the sheet that Darya was holding. Dulcimer seemed to see her for the first time. His head lifted a little, to move the thick-lipped mouth farther away from the floor. "Zardalu, bardalu. If you want me to fly you to the location listed on what you're holding there . . ."

"We do—or we would, if you were in any shape to do it. But you are—"

"A trifle warm, 's all." The Polypheme made a huge effort and managed to stand upright on his coiled tail, long enough for his top arm to reach out and snatch the coordinate sheet from Darya's hand. He slumped back, lifted the page to within two inches of his master eye, and stared at it vacantly. "Aha! Thirty-third lobe, Quisten-Dwell branch. Know a *really* good way to get there. Do it in my sleep."

Darya stepped back as he collapsed again on the floor in front of her. In his sleep? It seemed about the only way that Dulcimer could do it. But from somewhere the Polypheme was finding new reserves of coordination and energy. He wriggled his powerful tail and began to inch single-mindedly toward the main control chair.

"Wait a minute." Darya hurried to stand behind him as he pulled himself up into the seat. "You're not proposing to fly the *Erebus* now."

"Certainly am." The five arms were flying over the keyboards seemingly at random, pressing and flipping and pulling. "Have us inside the Anfract in half a minute."

"But you're *hot*—you admit it yourself."

"Little bit hot." The head turned to stare at Darya. The great slate-gray eye held hers for a second, then turned upward to fix its gaze solidly and vacantly on the featureless ceiling. The five hands moved in a blur across the board.

"Just a little bit. When you're hot, you're hot. Little bit, little bit, little bit."

"Somebody stop that lunatic!" Julian Graves cried. "Look at him! He's not fit to fly a kite."

"*Better* if I'm hot, you see," Dulcimer said, throwing a final set of switches before Rebka and Nenda could get to him. " 'Cause this's a real bad trip we're taking, 'n I wouldn't dare do it 'f I was cold." The *Erebus* was moving, jerking into motion. *"Littlebitlittlebitlittlebitlittle."* Dulcimer went into a fit of the giggles, as the ship began a desperate all-over shaking. "Whooo-oo-ee. Here we go! All ab-b-oard, shipmates, and you all b-b-better hold on real t-t-t-t-t—"

CHAPTER 8

WHEN DARYA LANG was a three-year-old child growing up on the garden world of Sentinel Gate, a robin made its nest on the outside ledge of her bedroom window. Darya told no one about it, but she looked each day at the three blue eggs, admiring their color, wishing she could touch their smooth shells, not quite realizing what they were . . .

. . . until the magical morning when, while she was watching, the eggs hatched, all three of them. She sat frozen as the uniform blue ellipsoids, silent and featureless, gradually cracked open to reveal their fantastic contents. Three downy chicks struggled out, fluffy feathers drying and tiny beaks gaping. And at last Darya could move. She ran downstairs, bubbling over with the need to tell someone about the miracle she had just witnessed.

Her house-uncle Matra had pointed out to her the importance of what she had experienced: one could not judge something from its external appearance alone. That was as true for people as it was for things.

And it also applied, apparently, to the Torvil Anfract.

The references spoke of thirty-seven lobes. From outside, the eye and instruments confirmed them. But as the *Erebus* entered the Anfract and Darya's first panic subsided, she began to recognize a more complex interior, the filigree of detail superimposed on the gross externals.

Dulcimer knew it already, or he had sensed it with some pilot's instinct denied to Darya. They had penetrated the Anfract along a spiraling path, down the center of a dark, starless tube of empty space. But then, when to Darya's eyes the path ahead lay most easy and open to them, the Polypheme slowed the ship to a cautious crawl.

"Getting granular," said the croaking voice from the pilot's seat. "Easy does it."

Easy did not do it. The ship was moving through vacuum, far from any material body, but it jerked and shuddered like a small boat on a choppy sea. Darya's first thought—that they were flying through a sea of small space-time singularities—made no sense. Impact with a singularity of any size would destroy the *Erebus* totally.

She turned to Rebka, secured in the seat next to her. "What is it, Hans? I can't see anything."

"Planck scale change—a big one. We're hitting the quantum level of the local continuum. If macroscopic quantum effects are common in the Anfract we're due for all sorts of trouble. Quantum phenomena in everyday life. Don't know what that would do." He was staring at the screens and shaking his head. "But how in heaven did Dulcimer *know it was coming*? I have to admit it, Nenda was right—that Polypheme's the best, hot or cold. I'd hate to have to fly through this mess. And what the hell is *that*?"

There was a curious groaning sound. The jerking had ended and the ship was speeding up again, rotating around its main axis like a rifle bullet. The groaning continued. It was the Chism Polypheme in the pilot's chair, singing to himself as he accelerated the *Erebus*—straight for the heart of a blazing blue-white star.

Closer and closer. They could never turn in time. Darya screamed and grabbed for Hans Rebka. She tightened her arms around him. Dulcimer had killed them all.

They were near enough to see the flaming hydrogen

prominences and speckled faculae on the boiling surface. Nearer. One second more and they would enter the photosphere. Plunging—

The sun vanished. The *Erebus* was in a dark void.

Dulcimer crowed with triumph. "Multiply-connected! Riemann sheet of the fifth order—only one in the whole spiral arm. Love it! Wheeee! Here we go again."

The blue-white star had popped into existence behind them and was rapidly shrinking in size, while they went spinning along another narrowing tube of darkness. There was a rapid series of stomach-wrenching turns and twists, and then all lights and power in the *Erebus* had gone and they were in free-fall. "Oops!" said the croaking voice in the darkness. "Hiatus. Sorry, folks—just when we were nearly there, too. This is a new one on me. I don't know how big it is. We just have to wait it out."

There was a total silence within the ship. *Was* it no more than a simple hiatus? Darya wondered. Suppose it went on forever? She could not help thinking about the stories of the Croquemort Timc-well. The earlier twisting and spinning had affected her balance centers and her stomach, and now the free-fall and the darkness were making it worse. If it went on for much longer she felt sure that she would throw up. But to her relief it was only a couple of minutes before the screens flashed back to life, to show the *Erebus* moving quietly in orbit around a translucent and faintly glowing sphere. Wraiths of colored lights flickered and swirled within it. Occasionally they would vanish for brief moments and leave transparency; at other times the sphere became totally opaque.

"And here we are," Dulcimer announced. "Right on schedule."

Darya stared again at the displays. She was certainly not seeing the planet and moon that she and Kallik had proposed as Genizee, the Zardalu homeworld.

"Here we are? Then *where* we are?" Louis Nenda said, asking Darya's question. He was in a seat behind her.

"At our destination." The roller coaster through the

twisted structure of the Anfract had done Dulcimer good. The Chism Polypheme sounded cheerful and proud and was no longer sagging in his seat. "There." He pointed with his middle arm to the main display. "That's it."

"But that's not where we want to go," Darya protested.

The great slaty eye rolled in her direction. "It may not be where you *want* to go, but it's the coordinates that you gave me. They lie right in the middle of that. Since I am opposed to all forms of danger, this is as close as I will take the ship."

"But what is it?" Julian Graves asked.

"What it looks like." Dulcimer sounded puzzled. "A set of annular singularities. Isn't that what you were all expecting?"

It was not what anyone had been expecting. But now its existence made perfect sense.

"The Anfract is tough to enter and hard to navigate around," Hans Rebka said. "But it has been done, many times, and ships came back to prove it. Yet not one of them reported finding a world like the sightings of Genizee made with high-powered equipment from *outside* the Anfract. So it stands to reason there has to be some *other* barrier that stops ships from finding and exploring Genizee. And a set of shielding singularities like this would do it. Enough to scare most people off."

"Including us," Darya said. Space travel Rule #1: avoid major singularities; Rule #2: avoid *all* singularities.

"No chance," Louis Nenda said. "Not after we dragged all this way."

Darya stared at him. It was occurring to her, at the least convenient moment, that the reason why Hans Rebka and Louis Nenda got on so badly was not that they were fundamentally different. It was that they were fundamentally *the same.* Cocky, and competent, and convinced of their own immortality. "But if all those other ships came here and couldn't get in," she said, "then why should we be any different?"

"Because we know something they didn't know," Rebka

said. He and Nenda apparently enjoyed one other thing in common: cast-iron stomachs. The flight into the Anfract that had left Darya weak and nauseated had affected neither one of them.

"The earlier ships didn't have a good reason to spend a lot of time here," he went on. "They didn't expect to find anything special inside, so they didn't do a systematic search for a way in. But we *know* there's something in there."

"And if it's the Zardalu cladeworld," Louis Nenda added, "we also know there has to be a way in *and* a way out, and it can't be a too difficult way. All we have to do is find it."

All we have to do.

Sure. All we have to do is something no exploring ship ever did before. Darya added another item to the list of common characteristics of Rebka and Nenda: irrational optimism. But it made no difference what she thought—already they were getting down to details.

"Can't take the *Erebus,*" Rebka was saying. "That's our lifeline home."

"*And* it can't even land," Nenda added. His glance at Julian Graves could not be missed.

"On the first look that's no problem," Rebka said. "Let's agree on one thing, before we go any further: whatever and whoever goes, *no one* even thinks of landing. If there's planets down there, you take a good look from a safe distance. Then you come back here and report. As for whether the ship we use is the *Indulgence* or the seedship, I vote seedship—it's smaller and more agile." He paused. "And more expendable."

"And talking of lifelines," Nenda added, "Atvar H'sial points out that even the *Erebus* is not much use without Dulcimer to pilot it. He ought to stay outside, too—"

"He certainly ought," Dulcimer said. The Polypheme was rolling his eye nervously at the flickering sphere outside. He apparently did not like the look of it.

"—so who flies the seedship and looks for a way in past the singularities?" Nenda finished.

"I do," said Rebka.

"But I am most *expendable.*" J'merlia spoke for the first time since they entered the Anfract.

"Kallik and I know the Anfract internal geometry best," Darya said.

"But I can maintain the most detailed record of events," said E. C. Tally.

Deadlock. Everyone except Dulcimer seemed determined to be on the seedship, which held, at a squeeze, four or five. The argument went on until Julian Graves, who had so far said nothing, shouted everyone down in his hoarse, cracking bass. "Quiet! I will make the assignment. Let me remind all of you that the *Erebus* is my ship, and that I organized this expedition."

It's *my* bat, Darya thought. And it's *my* ball, and if you don't go along with *my* rules you can't play. My god, that's what it is to them. They're all crazy, and to them it's just a *game.*

"Captain Rebka, Louis Nenda, Atvar H'sial, J'merlia, and Kallik will fly on the seedship," Graves went on. He glared the group to silence. "And Dulcimer, Professor Lang, and E. C. Tally will stay on the *Erebus.*" He paused. "And I—I must stay here also."

There was a curious diffidence and uneasiness in his last words.

"But I think—" Darya began.

"I know you do." Graves cut her off. "You want to go. But someone has to stay."

That had not been Darya's point. She was going to say that it was asking for trouble, putting Rebka and Nenda together in one group. She glanced across at the two men, but Rebka was distracted, staring in puzzlement at Graves. Julian Graves himself, with the uncanny empathy of a councilor, somehow picked up Darya's thought and read it correctly.

"We may need several individuals oriented to fast action on the seedship," he said. "However, to avoid potential conflicts let it be clear that Captain Rebka will lead that group unless he becomes incapacitated. In which case Louis Nenda will take over."

Darya half expected Nenda to flare up, but all he did was shrug and say thoughtfully, "Good thinkin'. It's about time the action group had somethin' to do. Keep the academic types all together back here, an' mebbe the rest of us—"

"*Academic* types! Of all the nerve . . ." After the last year, Darya found such a description of herself totally ludicrous. And then she saw that Nenda was grinning at the way she had taken the bait.

"You may get your chance anyway, Darya," Hans Rebka said. "Once we know the way in we'll relay it back to you. Keep the *Indulgence* ready in case we have problems and need you to come through and collect us. But don't start worrying until you haven't heard from us in three days. We may need that long before we can send you a drone."

He started to lead the seedship group out of the control chamber. "One other thing." He turned back as he reached the exit. "Keep the *Erebus* engines powered up, too, all the time, and be ready to leave. And if you get a call from us and we tell you to run for it, don't try to argue with us or wait to hear details. *Go.* Get out of the Anfract and into free-space, as fast as you can."

Dulcimer was coiled in the seat next to Darya. He turned his slate-gray monocular to her. "Fly away and *leave* them? I can see that there may be perils for the seedship in passing through the singularities—especially without the services of the spiral arm's master pilot. But what can they be expecting to find *within* the singularities, dangerous to us back here on the *Erebus*?"

"Zardalu." Darya returned the stare. "You still don't believe they're real, do you, even after everything we've told you? They are, though. Cheer up, Dulcimer. Once we find them, according to your contract you're entitled to twelve percent."

The great lidded orb blinked. If Darya had known how to read his expressions she would have recognized a scowl on the Polypheme's face. Zardalu, indeed! *And* she had referred to his twelve percent far too glibly. She was taunting him! How would he know what they found on Genizee—or how much they would stow away, to recover when he was no longer around to claim his share—if he was not with them?

Dulcimer knew when someone was trying to pull something over on him. Darya Lang could say what she liked about living Zardalu, the original bogeymen of the spiral arm, but he was sure that was all nonsense. The Zardalu had been wiped out to the last land-cephalopod, eleven thousand years before.

Dulcimer realized how he'd been had. They all *talked* dangers, and being ready to fly for your life, just so that Dulcimer would not want to go into the singularities.

And it had worked! They had caught him.

Well, you fool me once, shame on you. You fool me *twice,* shame on me. They would not trick him so easily again. The next time anyone went looking for Genizee—or Zardalu! Dulcimer sniggered to himself—he certainly intended to be with them.

CHAPTER 9

Genizee

THE SEEDSHIP WAS making progress.

Slow progress. It had penetrated the sphere of the first singularity through a narrow line vortex that shimmered threateningly on all sides, and now it was creeping along the outer shell of the second, cautious as bureaucracy.

Hans Rebka sat in the pilot's seat, deep in thought, and watched the ghostly traces of distorted space-time revealed on the displays. There was little else to look at. Whatever might be hidden within the shroud of singularities, its nature could not be discerned from their present position. It had not been his decision as to who would travel on the seedship, but he realized he was glad that neither Darya Lang nor Julian Graves was aboard. They would be going mad at the slow pace, chafing at the delays, pointing out the absence of apparent danger, pushing him to speed up.

He would have refused, of course. If Hans Rebka had been asked for his basic philosophy, he would have denied that he had any. But the nearest thing to it was his profound conviction that the secret to everything was *timing.*

Sometimes one acted instantly, so fast that there seemed no time for any thought at all. On other occasions one took forever, hesitating for no apparent reason, pondering even the most seemingly trivial decision. Picking the right pace was the secret of survival.

Now he was crawling. He did not know why, but it did not occur to him to speed up. There had been no blue-egged robin's nests in Rebka's childhood, no idyllic years of maturing on a garden planet. His homeworld of Teufel offered no birthright but hardship. He and Darya Lang could not have been more different. And yet they shared one thing: the hidden voice that sometimes spoke from deep within the brain, asserting that things were not what they seemed, that something important was being overlooked.

The voice was whispering to Rebka now. He had learned from experience that he could not afford to ignore it.

As the seedship crept along a spiral path that promised to lead through the shell of another singularity, he probed for the source of his worry.

The composition of the seedship's crew?

No. He did not trust Nenda or Atvar H'sial, but he did not doubt their competence—or their survival instincts. J'merlia and Kallik's desire to be given orders, rather than acting independently, was a nuisance more than a threat. It would have been better if Dulcimer could have been on board and flying the seedship—Rebka knew he could not compete with the Chism Polypheme on the instinctual level where a great master pilot could operate. But it was even more important to have Dulcimer back on the *Erebus*, to take it out of the Anfract.

Rebka had learned not to expect optimal solutions for anything. They existed in Darya Lang's clean, austere world of intellectual problems, but reality was a lot messier. So he did not have the ideal seedship crew. Very well. One took the crew available and did with it what one had to do.

But that was not the problem that nagged at his subconscious. It did not have the right feel to it.

Was the world inside the shell of singularities actually Genizee, and would the Zardalu be found there?

He considered that question as the adaptive control system sensed a way through the next singularity and delicately began to guide them toward it. Rebka could override if he saw danger, but he had no information to prompt such action. His warning flags were all internal.

It might be the planet Genizee inside there, or it might not. Either way, they were going in. Once you were committed to a course of action, you didn't waste your time looking back and second-guessing the decision, because every action in life was taken on the basis of incomplete information. You looked at what you had, and you did all you could to improve the odds; but at some point you had to roll the dice —and live or die with whatever you had thrown.

So his worry had to be arising from somewhere else. Something unusual that he had noticed, and lost when he was interrupted. Something . . .

Rebka finally gave up the struggle. Whatever was troubling him refused to show itself. Experience told him that it was more likely to return if he stopped thinking about it for a while, and now there were other things to worry about. The ship had turned again and was crawling along a path that to Rebka's eyes led only into a white, glowing wall. He tensed as they came closer. They were heading straight for that barrier of light.

Should he override? If only human senses included a direct sensitivity to gravity waves . . .

He forced himself to trust the ship's sensors. They reached the wall of light. There was a faint shiver through the seedship's structure, as though an invisible tide had swept along it, and then they were through.

Right through. The innermost shell singularity was behind them. The front of the ship was suddenly illuminated by the marigold light of a dwarf star.

Louis Nenda had been crowded into the rear of the seedship, deep in pheromonal conversation with Atvar H'sial. He squeezed quickly forward past the sixteen sprawled legs of J'merlia and Kallik, to stand crouched behind Rebka.

"Planet!"

Rebka shrugged. "We'll know if there's one in a few minutes." Then he would release a tiny drone ship, designed to retrace their path from the *Erebus* and provide information of their arrival to the others waiting outside. Whatever happened, Julian Graves and Darya should be told that the singularities were navigable. Rebka ordered the on-board sensors to begin their scan of space around the orange-yellow sun, masking out the light of the star itself.

"I wasn't *askin'*, I was tellin'." Nenda jerked his thumb to the display that showed the region behind the ship. "You can *see* the damn thing, naked eye, outa' the rear port."

Rebka twisted in his seat. It was impossible—but it was true. The rear port showed the same blue-white world with its big companion moon that Darya Lang and Kallik had displayed, back on the *Erebus*. They were both in half-moon phase, no more than a few hundred thousand kilometers away. Large landmasses were already visible. Rebka turned on the high-resolution sensors to provide a close-up view.

"Do you know the odds against this?" he asked. "We fly through that whole mess of singularities, we emerge at least a hundred and fifty million kilometers away from a star—and there's a planet sitting right next to us, close enough to spit on."

"I know a good bit about odds." Nenda's voice was an expressionless growl. "This just don't happen."

"You know what it means?"

"It means we found Genizee. An' it means you oughta get us the hell out of here. Fast. I hate welcomes."

Rebka was ahead of him. He had taken the controls of the seedship even before Louis Nenda spoke, to send them farther away from the planet. As the ship responded to Rebka's command, high-resolution images of both planet and moon filled the screen.

"Habitable." Nenda's curiosity was competing with his uneasiness. He was flanked by Kallik and J'merlia. Only Atvar H'sial, unable to see any of the displays, remained at the rear of the ship. "Five-thousand-kilometer radius. Spectrometers say plenty of oxygen, classifiers say eighteen percent land cover, forty percent water, forty-two percent swamps, imagers say three main continents, four mountain ranges but nothin' higher than a kilometer, no polar caps. Wet world, warm world, flat world, plenty of vegetation. Looks like it could be rich." His acquisitive instincts were awakening. "Wonder what it's like down there."

Hans Rebka did not reply. For some reason his attention had been drawn not to the parent planet, but to the images of its captive moon. The view that Darya Lang and Kallik had provided on the *Erebus* was from a long distance, so that all he had seen then was a small round ball, gleaming like a matte sphere of pitted steel. Now that same ball filled the screen.

His mind flew back to focus on Darya's accelerated-time display, with the moon whirling around and the planet steady against a fixed background. And he realized what had been puzzling him then, below his threshold of awareness: *any* two freely-moving bodies—binary stars, or planet and moon, or anything else—revolved around their common center of gravity. For so large a satellite as this, that center of gravity would lie well outside the planet. So *both* bodies should have been moving against the more distant background, unless the moon had negligible mass, which would have to mean—

He stared at the image filling the screen, and now he could see that the pits and nodules on its surface were regularly spaced, its curvature perfectly uniform.

"Artificial! And negligible mass. Must be *hollow*!" The words burst out of him, though he knew that they would be meaningless to the others.

No matter. Soon they would learn it for themselves. Part of the moon's surface was beginning to open. A saffron beam of light speared from it to illuminate the seedship. Suddenly their direction of motion was changing.

"What the hell's going on here?" Nenda was pushing forward, grabbing at the controls.

Hans Rebka did not bother to stop him. It would make no difference. The ship's drive was already at its maximum setting, and still they were going in the wrong direction. He stared out of the rear port. Instead of moving away from the moon and planet, they were being drawn toward it. And soon it was clear that this was more than a simple tractor beam, drawing them in to a rendezvous with the gleaming moon. Instead their trajectory was turning, under the combined force vector of the beam and the drive, taking them to a different direction in space.

Rebka looked and extrapolated, with the unconscious skill of a longtime pilot. There was no doubt about the result.

Wonder what it's like down there, Louis Nenda had said. They were going to find out, and very soon. Like it or not, the seedship was heading for a rendezvous with Genizee. All they could do was sit tight and pray for the long shot of a soft landing.

Soft landing, or good-bye, life.

He thought of Darya Lang and felt sorrow. If he had known that this was coming, he would have said a decent farewell to her before he left the *Erebus.*

While Hans Rebka was remembering Darya and imagining their last good-bye, she was thinking of him and Louis Nenda in much less favorable terms.

They were self-centered, overbearing bastards, both of them. She had tried to tell them that she might be on the brink of a major discovery. And what had they done? Brushed her aside as though she were nothing, then at the first chance dashed off in search of Genizee—which she and Kallik had found for them—leaving her behind to fester on the *Erebus* and endure the babbling of E. C. Tally and the groveling of Dulcimer.

The Chism Polypheme was desperate to have another go at the power kernel. Julian Graves had ordered E. C. Tally not to release another radiation beam, so Darya was Dulcimer's only hope. He pestered her constantly, ogling and smirking and offering her the unimaginable sexual delights that according to him only a mature Chism Polypheme could provide. If she would just crack open a kernel for him and let him soak in the beam for a few hours—a few minutes . . .

Darya retreated to the observation bubble and locked herself in. All she sought was solitude, but once that was achieved her old instincts took over. She went back to her interrupted study of the Anfract.

And once started, again she could not stop. With no Kallik to interrupt her work, she entered her own version of Dulcimer's radiation high.

Call it research addiction.

There was nothing else remotely like it in the whole universe. The first long hours of learning, all apparently futile and unproductive. Then the inexplicable conviction that there was *something* hidden away in what you were studying, some unperceived reality just beyond reach. Then the creeping-skin sensation at the back of the neck—the lightning flash as a thousand isolated facts flew to arrange themselves into a pattern—the coherent picture that sprang into sharp focus. The bone-deep pleasure of other ideas, apparently unrelated, hurrying into position and becoming parts of the same whole.

She had felt that satisfaction a dozen times in as many years, in her work on the ancient Builder artifacts. One year earlier she had lost touch with that life, consumed by the excitement of pursuing evidence of the Builders themselves across the spiral arm and beyond. And less than a month ago, sure that her cerebral contentment was gone forever, she had gladly agreed to go with Hans Rebka.

Well, she had been wrong. Once a research worker, always a research worker. She didn't have a hundredth the interest in the Zardalu that she was finding in the study of the Torvil Anfract. It was the most fascinating object in the universe.

And then, the paradox: as Darya tried to focus harder and harder on the Anfract, she found her mind turning *away* from it, again and again, back to her old studies of the Builders. It seemed like a lack of control, an irritating mental foible. The Builders were a distraction, just when she did not need one.

And then it hit her. The revelation.

The Anfract was a Builder artifact.

It was of a scale that dwarfed any other artificial structure in the spiral arm. The Anfract was a bigger project than the reconstruction of the Mandel system, bigger than the Builders' out-of-galaxy creation of Serenity itself. Improbably big, impossibly big.

But the analogies with other artifacts, once seen, became undeniable. The light-focusing properties of Lens were here. So was the multiply-connected nature of Paradox. She recalled the Builder-made singularity in the Winch of the Dobelle Umbilical, and the knotted topology of Sentinel. They all had a correspondence with the structure of the Anfract.

And that meant—

Darya's mind made the intuitive leap that reached beyond hard evidence. If the Anfract was a Builder construct, then the "natural" set of nested singularities around which the *Erebus* was orbiting was surely an artifact, too. But within it, according to Darya's own analysis, lay the original Zardalu homeworld. If that was true, it could not be coincidence. There must be a far closer relationship than anyone had ever realized between the vanished Builders and the hated Zardalu.

A connection, between the Builders and the Zardalu.

But *what* connection? Darya was tempted to reject her own logic. The time scales were so incompatible. The Builders had disappeared millions of years ago. The Zardalu had been exterminated from the spiral arm only eleven thousand years ago.

The link: it had to be the sentient Builder constructs. The only surviving specimens of the Zardalu had been captured by the constructs during the Great Rising and preserved in stasis on Serenity far out of the galactic plane. Now it seemed that the world of Genizee had itself been shielded from outside contact, by barriers designed to discourage—or destroy—approaching expeditions. And only the Builders, or more likely their sentient creations, could have constructed those guarding walls.

Darya thought again of Hans Rebka, but now in very different terms. If only he were there. She desperately needed someone to talk to, someone who could listen with a cool head and demolish logical flaws or wishful thinking. But instead Hans was—

Dear God! She was jerked out of her intellectual trance by a dreadful thought. The seedship party was flying into something more complex and potentially dangerous than anyone on board had imagined. They believed that they were entering a set of natural singularities, with a natural planet inside. Instead they were entering an artifact, a lion's den of uncertainty, filled with who-knew-what deliberate booby traps. There could be other barriers, designed to frustrate or destroy all would-be explorers of the region inside the singularities.

They had to be warned.

Darya waded out through the mess in the observation bubble—the floor was littered with her hard-copy outputs—and ran back to find Julian Graves. There was no sign of him in the control room, the galley, the sleeping quarters, or anywhere that he would normally be.

Darya cursed the huge size of the *Erebus,* with its hundreds of chambers of all sizes, and ran on along the main corridor that led to the cargo holds and the engine rooms.

She did not find Graves, but along the way she encountered E. C. Tally. The embodied computer was standing by the shield that surrounded one of the power kernels.

"Councilor Graves expressed a desire for privacy," he said. "I think he wished to avoid further conversation."

So Darya was not the only one who found Tally and Dulcimer's yammering intolerable. "Where did he go?"

"He did not tell me."

Any more than Darya had. He did not *want* them to know. "We have to find him. Has there been any word from the seedship?"

"Nothing."

"Come on, then. We'll need Dulcimer, too, to do some tricky flying. He should be thoroughly cooled off by now. But first I must see Julian Graves. We'll search the whole ship if we have to." She started back toward the engines, examining every chamber. E. C. Tally trailed vaguely along behind.

"You take the rooms along that side of the corridor." Darya pointed. "I'll handle these."

"May I speak?"

Gabble, gabble, gabble. "Do you have to? What is it now, E.C.?"

"I merely wish to point out that if you wish to *talk to* Julian Graves, there is a much easier method than the one you are employing. Of course, if as you said, you wish to *see* him, with your own eyes, or if it is also necessary that *he* talk to *you* . . ."

Darya paused with a doorlatch in her hand. "Let's stop it right there. I want to talk to him."

"Then might I suggest the use of the public-address system? Its message is carried to every part of the *Erebus.*"

"I didn't even know there *was* a public-address system. How did you find out about it?"

"It is part of the general schematics of the *Erebus,* which naturally I transferred from the ship's data bank to my own memory."

"Take me to an input point. We can talk to Dulcimer, too, and find out where he is."

"That will not be necessary. I already know where Dulcimer is. He is back at the power kernel, where you found me."

"What's he doing there? Didn't Graves tell you to keep him *away* from the kernels?"

"No. He told me not to release another radiation beam from within a kernel. I have not done so. But as Dulcimer pointed out, no one said that he was not to be allowed inside the kernel shield itself." Tally looked thoughtful. "I think he should be ready to come out by now."

WHAT HAPPENED TO THE BUILDERS?

I don't think I'll ever understand Downsiders, though I've spent enough time with them. The pattern never changes. As soon as they learn that I've done a deal of space-wandering, they'll sit and talk to me quiet enough, but you can see there's only one thing on their minds. And finally they ask me, every one of them: You must have visited a lot of Builder artifacts, Captain. What do you think *happened* to them? Where did the Builders *go*?

It's a fair question. You've got a species that was all over the spiral arm for fifty million years or more, scattering their constructs over a couple of thousand locations and a few thousand light-years, all of them huge and indestructible and three-quarters of them still working fine—I've seen scores, close up, ranging from the practical and useful, like the Dobelle Umbilical, to the half-understandable, like Elephant and Lens, and on to the absolutely incomprehensible, like Succubus and Paradox and Flambeau and Juggernaut.

Builders, and Artifacts. And then, bingo, about five million years ago, the Builders vanish. No sign of them after that. No final messages. In fact, no messages of any kind. Either the Builders never discovered writing, or they were even worse than programmers at documentation.

Maybe they did leave records, but we've not yet found out how to decipher them—some say that the black pyramid in the middle of Sentinel is a Builder library. But who can tell?

Anyway, I claim that the Downsiders don't really *care* what happened to the Builders, because nothing that the Builders left behind makes much difference to planet-grubbers. I've watched a man on Terminus cut a Builder flat fabricator—something priceless, something we still don't come close to understanding—in two, to patch a window. I've seen a woman on Darien use a section of a Builder control device, packed with sentient circuits, as a *hammer*. A lot of Downsiders think of Builder artifacts just the same way they think of a brick or a stone or any other ancient material: in terms of what they can be used for today.

So I don't answer the Downsiders, not directly. Usually I ask them a question or two of my own. What happened to the Zardalu, I say?

Oh, the Great Rising wiped them out, they say, when the slave races rebelled.

Then what happened to the dinosaurs, back on Earth?

Oh, that was the March of the Mitochondria. It killed them all off—everyone knows that.

The answers always come pat and fast. You see, what the Downsiders want isn't an *explanation;* it's a catchphrase they can use *instead* of an explanation.

And suppose you tell them, as I used to tell them until I got fed up, that there were once other theories? Before the paleomicrobiologists discovered the Cretaceous mitochondrial mutation that slowed and weakened every land animal over seventy pounds to the point where it didn't have the strength to carry its own weight, there were explanations of dinosaur extinction ranging from drought to long-period solar companion stars to big meteors to nearby supernovas. Suppose you tell them all that? Why, then they look at you as though you're crazy.

Now the odd thing is, I *do* have the explanation for what happened to the Builders. It's based on my own observations of species all around the arm. It's logical, it's simple, and no one but me seems to believe it.

It's this:

There's a simple biological fact, true of every life-form ever discovered: although a single-celled organism, like an amoeba or one of the other Protista, can live forever, any complex multicelled organism will die of old age if nothing else gets it.

Any species, humans or Cecropians or Varnians or Polyphemes (or Builders!), is just a large number of individuals, and you can think of that assembly as a single multicelled organism. In some cases, like the Hymenopts and the Decantil Myrmecons, the single nature is a lot more obvious than it is for humans or Cecropians—though humans seem like a swarm when you've seen as many worlds as I have from space, with cities and road nets and superstructures spreading over the surface like mold on a ripe fruit.

Anyway, *species are organisms,* and here's my simple syllogism:

Any species is a single, multicelled organism. Every multicelled organism will over the course of time grow old and die. *Therefore,* any species will at last grow old and die.

That's what happened to the superorganism known as the Builders. It lived a long time. Then it got old. And then it died.

Convincing? If so, you shouldn't expect anything better for humans. I certainly don't.

—from *Hot Rocks, Warm Beer, Cold Comfort: Jetting Alone Around the Galaxy;* by Captain Alonzo Wilberforce Sloane (Retired).

CHAPTER 10

HANS REBKA'S JOB as a Phemus Circle troubleshooter had taken him to a hundred planets. He had made thousands of planetary landings; and because by the nature of things his job took him only to places where there were already problems, scores of those landings had been made in desperate circumstances.

The first thought after a hard impact was always the same: *Alive! I'm alive.* The questions came crowding in after that: Am I in good enough shape to function? Are my companions alive and well? Is the ship in one piece? Is it airtight? Is it intact enough to allow us to take off again?

And finally, the questions that made the condition of the ship and the crew so important: *Where are we?* What is it like *outside*?

By Rebka's standards, the seedship had made a soft landing—which is to say, it had been brought down at a speed that did not burn it up as it entered the atmosphere and the impact had not killed outright every being on board. But it had not made a *comfortable* landing. The ship had driven obliquely into the surface with force enough to make the tough hull shiver and scream in protest. Hans Rebka had felt his teeth rattle in his head while a sudden force of many gravities rammed him down into the padded seat.

He had blacked out for a few seconds. When he swam back to consciousness his eyes were not working properly. There was a shifting flicker of bright lights, interspersed with moments of total darkness.

He shook his head and squeezed his eyes shut. If sight failed, he would have to make do with other senses. The key questions still had to be asked and answered.

Concentrate. Make your brain work, even though it doesn't want to.

Hearing. He listened to the noises around him. First answer: some of the others on board had survived the crash. He could hear cursing and groaning, and the clicks and whistles of conversation between Kallik and J'merlia. The groans had to be Louis Nenda. And anything that had left humans alive was unlikely to have harmed a Lo'tfian, still less a Hymenopt. Atvar H'sial, most massive of the ship's occupants, might be in the worst shape. But that fear was eased when Rebka felt a soft proboscis touching his face, and heard Nenda's voice: "Is he alive? Lift him up, At, let me get a look at him."

Smell. The ship had fared less well. Rebka could smell an unfamiliar and unpleasant odor, like cloying damp mold. The integrity of the hull had been breached, and they were breathing the planet's air. That disposed of any idea of testing the atmosphere before exposing themselves to it. Either it would kill them, or it wouldn't.

Touch. Someone was poking his chest and belly, hard enough to hurt. Rebka grunted and opened his eyes again, experimentally. The flicker was fading, reduced to a background shimmer. His head ached horribly. Louis Nenda had finished his abdominal poking and was moving Rebka's arms and legs, feeling the bones and working the joints.

"Don't need to do that." Rebka took a deep, shuddering breath and sat up. "I'm good as new. The ship . . ."

"Should probably fly atmospheric with no problem. But we can't leave for space till that's fixed." Nenda was pointing forward. Hans Rebka saw a spray of black mud right in front of his seat, squirted in through a caved section of the seedship's hull. "Atvar H'sial and J'merlia are checking it out, seein' how big a job we got before we'd be ready for a space run."

"If we're *allowed* to leave." Rebka was trying to stand and finding that his legs did not want to cooperate. It did not help that the floor of the seedship remained at ten degrees to the horizontal. Rebka came upright in the cramped space and leaned on the wall. He noticed a deep bleeding gash on Nenda's muscular left arm. The Karelian was calmly suturing it with a needle and thick thread—and, of course, without anesthetic.

Rebka registered that without comment. Whatever Nenda's defects, he was tough and he was not a whiner. A good man to have at your back in a fight—but watch your own back, afterward, he thought.

"We didn't have any control coming in," Rebka said. "If we leave, that same beam could drop us right back—less gently next time."

"Yeah. We were lucky," Nenda mumbled through clenched teeth. He had finished his stitching and was biting through the coarse thread. He finally spat out the loose end, went to the open hatch, and peered out. "Soft mud. If you have to hit, best possible stuff to land on. Kallik!" he called outside, adding a click and a loud whistle. "Damn that Hymenopt. I said to take a peek outside, but I don't see her nowhere. Where's she got to now?"

With the ship tilted as it was, the bottom of the open hatch was five feet above the ground. Rebka followed Louis Nenda as the Karelian sat on the sloping floor and swung himself out of the hatch to drop onto the surface of the planet. The two men found themselves standing on a flat, gray-green moss that gave an inch or two beneath their weight. The skidding arrival of the seedship had gouged a straight black furrow, a few hundred yards long, in that level surface.

"Lucky," Nenda said. "We could have landed in *that.*"

He pointed to the ship's rear. Half a mile away the flat ground gave way to a patchwork of tall ferns and cycads, from which twisted fingers of dark rock were projecting. Their serried tops were sharp as dragons' teeth. "Or in *that*."

Nenda turned and pointed the other way, ahead of the ship. The gray-green moss on which they were standing formed a shoreline, a flat between the jutting rocks and a silent, blue-gray sea. "If we'd flown one mile farther, right now we'd be trying to breathe water. Lucky again. Except I don't believe it was luck."

"We were *brought* here," Rebka agreed. The two men moved farther from the crippled ship, searching the surface from horizon to horizon. There was an unspoken thought in both their heads. Every planet carried its own life-forms and its own potential dangers. But if this world was in fact Genizee, there was a formidable *known* danger to worry about: the Zardalu.

Rebka was cursing the decision—*his* decision, he made himself admit—to penetrate the singularities using the nimble but unarmed seedship. They could not have brought the *Erebus*, bristling with weapons, without risking the loss of the whole party if the ship was unable to negotiate the encircling singularities; but they could have brought Dulcimer's ship, the *Indulgence*, well-armed enough to allow adequate self-defense. With only the seedship, they were reduced to fighting with their bare hands—and they knew how hopeless that was against the Zardalu. True enough, they had never *intended* to land; but Rebka would not excuse his error.

"I don't see 'em," Nenda offered. He did not need to specify *what* he did not see.

"And we don't want to. Maybe we can repair the ship and take off for orbit before they know we're here. This is a whole planet. We're seeing maybe a millionth of the whole surface."

"Don't bet on whether anyone knows we're here. *We* didn't pick where we landed—something else did. Mebbe we're about to find out *who.*" Nenda pointed to the straggling rocks, curving away in a half circle beyond the ship. "Here comes Kallik—an' in a hurry."

Rebka stared at the dark, distant blur with a good deal of curiosity. He had never seen a Hymenopt at full stretch. The rotund, barrel-shaped body with its short, soft fur and eight sprawling legs looked too pudgy and clumsy for speed. But Kallik's nervous system had a reaction speed ten times as fast as any human's. The wiry limbs could carry her a hundred meters in less than two seconds.

They were doing it now, each leg moving too fast to be visible. All that Rebka could see was the central speeding blur of the black body. Kallik skidded to a halt at their side in less than ten seconds. Her coat was covered with wet brown mud.

"Trouble?" Nenda asked.

"I think so." The Hymenopt was not even out of breath. "There are structures along the shoreline about three kilometers away, hidden by the rocks. I approached them and went briefly inside two of them. It was too dark to see much within, but it is clear that they are artificial. However, there was no sign of the inhabitants."

"Could they be Zardalu dwellings?"

"I believe they are." Kallik hesitated, while Rebka reflected on the little Hymenopt's courage. Thousands of years had passed since her species had been slaves of the Zardalu, but the images of the land-cephalopods were still strong in Kallik's race memory. On her last encounter with the Zardalu they had torn one of her limbs off, casually, to make a point to humans. Yet she had entered those unknown structures alone, knowing there might be Zardalu inside.

"For several reasons," Kallik continued, "not least of which is my conviction that this planet is indeed Genizee. Look at this."

Before Rebka or Nenda could object she was off again, racing down to the water's edge and continuing into it. The beach fell away steeply, and within a few feet Kallik vanished beneath the surface. When she reappeared she was holding a wriggling object in her two front claws and blurring back toward them.

Hans Rebka could not see her prize clearly until she was again at his side. When she held it out to him he took a step backward. Irrational fear and alarm began to eat at the base of his brain. He stopped breathing.

The two-foot-long creature that Kallik grasped so casually was a millennia-old nightmare in miniature. Multiply its size by ten times, and the tentacled cephalopod became a Zardalu, seven deadly meters of midnight-blue muscle and intelligent ferocity.

"A precursor form, surely," Kallik was saying. "Already this is amphibious, able to function on both land and water. Observe." She placed the creature on the ground. It rose onto splayed tentacles and blinked around it with big lidded eyes.

"Allow evolution to proceed," Kallik went on, "and from this form a land cephalopod would be quite a natural result. With emergence onto land, a substantial increase in size and intelligence would also not be surprising." The creature at her feet made a sudden snatch at her with its cruel hooked beak. She swatted it casually before it made contact. It flew ten meters to land on the soft moss, and scuttled off for the safety of the water. Its speed on land was surprising.

"Another reason I'm glad we didn't land in the water a mile further on," Nenda said cheerfully. "How'd you like a dozen of *them* chewing your butt when you're tryin' to swim?"

But he was not as cheerful and relaxed as he tried to appear. Rebka had not been the only one to step away instinctively when that Zardalu-in-miniature had been dropped at their feet.

"We need to go to those buildings," Rebka said. "And if—"

Before he could complete his thought, there was a clattering sound from inside the seedship. J'merlia stood at the edge of the hatch. His compound eyes swiveled from the soaking-wet Kallik to Hans Rebka.

"With respect, Captain Rebka, but Atvar H'sial has bad news."

"The ship is past repairing?"

"Not at all. The drive is intact. With a few hours' work the hull can be sealed adequately and the ship readied for space takeoff. I am prepared to begin that work at once. The bad news is that this is the only surviving drone, and even it will need repair before it can be used." He lifted a small and buckled cylinder, covered with black mud. "The rest were crushed on impact. If we wish to send a warning message back to the *Erebus,* this single unit is our only hope. And it cannot be launched until the seedship itself is again in space."

Rebka nodded. As soon as he had seen the little drone, the question of a message to Darya and the others had come again to his mind. But *what* message? The more he thought about their situation, the more difficult it became to know what should be said. What did they *know*?

"J'merlia, ask Atvar H'sial to come outside. We need to brainstorm for a few minutes."

"She is already on the way."

The Cecropian was squeezing through the hatch, to drop lightly onto the soft moss. The great white head with its sonic generator and yellow receiving horns scanned the shoreline and the inland tangle of rocks and vegetation. She stretched to her full height, and the six-foot-long cephalic antennas unfurled.

"You sure, At?" Nenda asked. He was picking up her pheromonal message before J'merlia could translate for the others.

The blind head nodded.

"Zardalu," J'merlia said.

"She can smell 'em," added Nenda. "Long way off, and faint, but they're here. That settles that."

"Part of it," Rebka said. He waited until Atvar H'sial had turned back to face him and J'merlia had moved for easy communication into the shelter of the Cecropian's carapace. "Even if we could send the drone this minute, I've still got real problems about what we ought to say."

"Like what problems?" Nenda had picked up a shred of moss and was nibbling it thoughtfully.

"Like, we know *we're* not in charge here. Somebody else brought us down. But who's doing what? What should we tell Darya and the others? My first thoughts for a message were probably the same as yours: We got through the singularities all right, this planet is Genizee, and there are live Zardalu here though we haven't seen them yet. We can't get back, because somebody forced our ship to make a crash landing on Genizee and we have to fix it.

"So *who* forced us down? We were shaken up a bit when we hit, but we're in fair shape and so is our ship. Now, you know the Zardalu. If *they* were in charge, they'd have blasted us right out of the sky—no way we'd have survived a landing if they were running the show.

"But let's be ridiculous and suppose they *did* want us to land in one piece, because they had other plans for us."

"Like eating us." Nenda spat out the bit of moss that he was chewing and made a face. "They'd like us better than this stuff. I've not forgotten their ideas from last time. They like their meat superfresh."

"Whatever they want to do with us, it would only make sense for them to bring us to a landing place *where they are.* So where are they?"

"Maybe they're worried about our weapons," Nenda offered. "Maybe they want to have a look at us from a distance. *They* wouldn't think we were dumb enough to fly here in a ship that didn't have weapons."

"Then why not land us hard enough to make sure that all our weapons were put out of action?" Rebka ignored Nenda's crack about coming weaponless, but he stored it up for future reprisal. "It doesn't make sense, soft-landing us and then *leaving us alone.*"

"With respect," J'merlia said softly. "Atvar H'sial would like to suggest that the source of your perplexity is in one of your implicit assumptions. She agrees that we were surely landed here by design, although her own senses did not allow her to detect the presence of the beam that tore the seedship from its trajectory and deposited it at its present location. But according to what you have told her, the beam came from the *moon*—that hollow, artificial moon of which you spoke—not from Genizee itself. What does that suggest? Simply this: the unwarranted assumption that you are making is that the Zardalu who are here also *brought* us here."

J'merlia paused. There was a long silence, broken only by the ominous sigh of strong wind across gray moss. It was close to sunset, and with the slow approach of twilight the weather was no longer the flat calm that had greeted their arrival.

"That don't help us at all," Louis Nenda said at last. "If the Zardalu didn't grab our ship and bring us here, then who the blazes did?"

"Atvar H'sial does not know," J'merlia translated. "However, she suggests that what you are asking is a quite different—though admittedly highly significant—question."

The seedship's computational powers had not been affected by impact with the surface of Genizee. From the planet's size, mass, orbital parameters, and visible features, the computer readily provided an overview of surface conditions.

Genizee rotated slowly, with a forty-two-hour day, about an axis almost normal to its orbital plane. The atmospheric circulation was correspondingly gentle, with little change of seasons and few high winds. The artificial moon, circling just a couple of hundred thousand kilometers away, looked huge from Genizee's surface, but its mass was so tiny that the planet's tides came only from the effects of its sun; again, the slow rotation rate decreased their force.

The climate of mid-latitude Genizee was equable, with no extremes of freezing or baking temperatures. Surface gravity was small, at half standard human. As a result the geological formations were sharp and angled, sustaining steeper rock structures than would be possible in a stronger field; but the overall effect of those delicate spires and arches was more aesthetic than threatening, as abundant vegetation softened their profiles. The final computer summary suggested a delicate and peaceful world, a cozy environment where native animals needed little effort to survive. There should be nothing to fear from the easygoing native fauna.

"Which proves just how dumb a computer can be," Louis Nenda said. "If Zardalu are easygoing and laid back, I'll—I'll invest everything I have in Ditron securities."

He and Atvar H'sial had lagged behind Rebka and Kallik as they walked along the shore. With three hours to go to planetary nightfall, Hans Rebka had decreed that before they could rest easy they needed to take a close look at the structures that Kallik had found. He was particularly keen to have Atvar H'sial's reaction. Given her different suite of sensory apparatus, she might perceive something where others did not.

J'merlia had been left behind in the seedship. He had already begun work on the repair of the hull and the message drone, and he had insisted that the work would go fastest with least interference. If they stayed away for three hours or more, he said, he would have the ship ready for takeoff to orbit.

"Investment in securities of any kind begins to appear as an attractive alternative to our own recent efforts for the acquisition of wealth." The pheromonal message diffused across from Atvar H'sial, who was crouching low to the ground and reducing her speed to a crawl to match Nenda's pace. "It is never easy to be objective about one's own actions and one's accomplishments, but it occurs to me that our recent history has not been one of uninterrupted triumph."

"What you mean?"

"You and I chose to remain on Serenity to acquire an unprecedented and priceless treasure of Builder technology.

When we were returned to the spiral arm by the Builders' constructs—for whatever reason—our new objective became the planetoid of Glister, for the purpose of the acquisition of Builder technology *there,* and the repossession of your ship, the *Have-It-All.* To that end, we agreed that we would need the use of some other ship, and we set out for Miranda with that in mind. But see where our fine strategy has taken us. We find ourselves deep in the middle of one of the spiral arm's least understood and most dangerous regions, on a world we believe to be native to the arm's most ferocious species, with a ship that is presently incapable of taking us to orbit. One wonders if our record is much superior to a suggested Ditron investment."

"You're too negative, At. Did you ever see a big snake like a python swallow a big fat pig?"

"That event, I am happy to say, has not been part of my life experience."

"Well, the thing about it is this: once it starts, it can't stop. Its teeth curve backward, so it has to open its mouth wider an' wider an' swallow an' swallow an' swallow until it downs the whole thing. See, it *can't* give up in the middle."

"How very unedifying. But a question appears to be in order. Do you see us in the role of the python, or of the pig?"

"At, none of that. Stop puttin' me on."

Atvar H'sial's pheromones were in fact filled with sly self-satisfaction as they walked the last quarter mile to the structures along the shoreline. It took a lot to shake a Cecropian's invincible self-satisfaction and conviction of superiority.

There were five buildings, each made of a fine-grained material like cemented gray sand. The shore of the blue-gray sea jutted out at that point into a long, spoon-shaped peninsula, four hundred yards long, with the beach falling away steeply on each side of it. The buildings, each sixty feet tall, sat together in a cluster within the bowl of the spoon, with water lapping up to within thirty yards of their walls. Although the tides of Genizee were small and the winds usually mild, it was easy to imagine that the water sometimes came up to and even inside all of the buildings.

Kallik and Hans Rebka had walked out along the long handle of the spoon and already made a circuit of each building by the time Nenda and Atvar H'sial reached them.

"Not a window in sight." Rebka advanced to an elliptical doorway, three times as tall as he was and at least six feet across. "Atvar H'sial, you'll see a lot more than the rest of us in there, even with the lights we've got. Lead the way, would you, and pass word through Nenda about what you're seeing."

When Nenda had translated, the Cecropian nodded and shuffled forward into the first of the buildings. The pleated resonator below her chin was vibrating, while the yellow horns on each side of her head were turned to the dark interior. Louis Nenda followed right behind her, then Kallik. Rebka stayed at the entrance. He was their watchdog, dividing his attention between the activity inside and the deserted shore. As the light faded, the interior of the building became increasingly hard to see. Squinting west, Rebka estimated that sunset was less than an hour away.

"Three steps up, then four down. Watch how you go," Nenda translated. "At's standing where the inside divides into two, into a couple of big rooms that split the whole interior in half. One's nearly empty—a bedroom, she'd guess. Wet floor, though—whatever sleeps there likes everything real damp. The other room's more interesting. It has furnishings: long tables, various heights, no chairs, and a wet floor, too. There's a lot of weird growing stuff, all different shapes an' sizes, where you might expect equipment. At's not sure what most of it is. She thinks it shows the Zardalu preference for fancy biological science and technology, where we and the Cecropians would use machines. That's what the race memories and old legends about the Zardalu say—they could make biology stand on its head, do with natural growth what we still can't get near yet. Nothin' looks dangerous, but it might be. Long tunnel in the middle of the room, spiraling down farther than At can see—way underground, she'd guess from the echoes. Impossible to know how far it might go. And there's more equipment by the tunnel's edge. Hold on, she's changing sonic frequencies. Wants to see if she can get an inside look without goin' too close."

There were a few seconds of silence, followed by a startled grunt from Nenda.

"What is it?" Rebka was edging his way farther into the building, propelled by curiosity.

"Somethin' really impenetrable, At says. Her echolocation is bouncing off it right at the surface. Hold on. She's going to have a feel."

There was a longer pause, even harder to take, then Rebka heard a rapid shuffle of movement a few yards away in the darkness. "What's happening?" he asked. As he spoke, Kallik and Nenda popped into sight, with Atvar H'sial just behind.

"See that!" Nenda said as they emerged into the fading light. He was pointing at something that the Cecropian was cradling in her front legs. "An' you thought we had a mystery *before* we went in."

Atvar H'sial extended the object that she was holding out toward Rebka. He stared at it, too surprised and baffled to speak. It was a small black icosahedron about six inches across, as familiar and unmistakable as it was mysterious. He had seen hundreds like it, scattered on free-space structures all around the spiral arm. He had seen them on planets, too, used for every possible purpose—studied in science laboratories, worshiped and feared, used as talismans and royal sigils and doorstops and paperweights.

No one knew how to penetrate one of those objects without causing the interior to melt to an uninformative gray mass. No one knew their purpose, though there were hundreds of suggestions. No one knew how old they were, or how they had reached the places where they were found.

Most workers believed that the black icosahedrons were related to the Builders, although they were on a scale far smaller than the usual artifacts. Analysts had amassed powerful arguments and statistical evidence to support those claims. A few researchers, equally adamant, denied any Builder connection. They argued with some validity for another vanished race, as old as or older than the Builders.

Rebka reached out to take the little regular solid from Atvar H'sial. As he did so there was an urgent whistle of warning from Kallik and a cry of "Behind!"

Rebka spun around. For the past few minutes he had been neglecting his self-imposed task as lookout. The sun was on the horizon, setting in a final glow of pink and gold. It cast four gigantic elongated shadows along the spit of land on which he and the others were standing. And those shadows were *moving,* as the objects that were throwing them emerged from the water and reared up to their full heights. Behind them, swarming up from the deep offshore, came at least a dozen others.

Zardalu. The light was poor, but those black shapes against the dying sun could be mistaken for nothing else. They were boiling up from the sea, more and more of them, threshing the water with the force of their movements. Within seconds they were ashore.

And ready for action. There was no place to hide as they came gliding forward on splayed tentacles, straight toward Hans Rebka and his three companions.

Back at the seedship, J'merlia had watched the others go with mixed feelings. He certainly wanted to be with his dominatrix, Atvar H'sial, and he certainly was curious to know more about the structures on the shoreline that Kallik had seen. But at the same time he wanted to be left in peace to repair the seedship. It was something that he could do faster and better than anyone else in the group, and their presence would only slow his progress.

He watched them leave, nodding at Rebka's final order: "If anything happens to us, don't try heroics. Don't even think that way. Get the ship up to space where it's safe, and send that drone back to the *Erebus.* We'll look after ourselves."

Their departure confirmed J'merlia's conviction that repairs would go faster without them. He had told Rebka and Atvar H'sial that the seedship and drone fixes would be about three hours' work, but in less than two the drone was ready to fly, the seedship hull patch was in position, the seal perfect, and everything was ready for space. J'merlia tidied up, peered at the sun, and wondered how long it would take them to walk back.

Then it occurred to him that they did not have to walk. The seedship was ready to go to orbit, but it was just as capable of making atmospheric flights, short or long, around the surface of Genizee. In fact, a minimal hop over to the structures that Kallik had described would serve a dual purpose. It would save the others a walk, and it would provide a proof—though he knew that none was needed—that the seedship was back to full working condition.

The ship lifted easily at his command. He took it to ten thousand feet and held it there for half a minute. Perfect. Completely airtight. J'merlia descended to two hundred feet and sent the ship cruising west at a soundless and leisurely twenty miles an hour. Soon he could see the buildings, looming above the flat, sandy promontory. And there, unless he was mistaken, were Kallik and Captain Rebka and Louis Nenda and his beloved dominatrix, Atvar H'sial, standing by the entrance to one of the buildings.

J'merlia was fifty yards from the spit of land, all set to descend and looking forward to their surprise when they saw the carefully repaired and functioning seedship, when the nightmare began: he saw Zardalu, dozens of them, seething up from the dark water. They were onshore—standing upright—advancing fast on Atvar H'sial and the others. And his master and companions had nowhere to go! The Zardalu were in front of them; the steep-sided beach and deep water were on all sides. J'merlia watched in horror as Atvar H'sial turned and led the trapped group into the dark interior of one of the buildings.

They were only thirty or forty paces ahead of the Zardalu. The land-cephalopods came gliding with ghostly speed on their powerful tentacles, rippling across the dark sand. Within a few seconds they, too, had crowded into the first of the buildings.

J'merlia lowered the ship to thirty feet and waited, hypnotized with horror. No one emerged. No sound rose up to his straining ears. The buildings and the sandy promontory remained empty and lifeless, while the sun fell its last few degrees in the darkening sky.

And then there was nothing but darkness. J'merlia wanted to land, but Rebka's instructions had been quite specific.

Get the ship up to space, where it's safe. And get that drone back to the Erebus.

A Lo'tfian found it almost impossible to disobey direct orders. J'merlia miserably initiated the ascent command to take the seedship up into orbit, away from the surface of Genizee. He stared down at the world that was fast diminishing beneath him to a tiny disk of light, and wondered what was happening to the four he had left behind. Were they fighting? Captured? Already dead? He felt terrible about leaving.

He launched the little drone without adding to its message, and sat slumped at the seedship control console. What now? Rebka had given no further instructions. He had only told J'merlia what *not* to do: *Don't try heroics.* But J'merlia *had* to go back and try to rescue Atvar H'sial—except that was in conflict with Rebka's command.

J'merlia sat locked in an agony of indecision. He longed for the good old days, when all he had had to do was to follow Atvar H'sial's orders. Why did Julian Graves and the others keep pushing freedom on him, when all it did was make him miserable?

He scarcely noticed when the seedship raced past the artificial moon of Genizee. He was only vaguely aware of Genizee's sun, off to one side, and the all-around glow of the annular singularities that surrounded the system. And he did not see at all the great swirl of light in space, its vortex moving into position directly ahead of the trajectory of his speeding ship. The first that J'merlia knew of the shifting whirlpool was an unpleasant shearing sensation through his whole body.

Singularity. No time for thought, no time for action. His body flexed, twisted in an impossible direction, turned to smoke.

Isolated essential singularity. Amorphous, physically divergent. J'merlia felt himself stretching, expanding, dissociating. His problems were over now. He would obey Rebka's command . . . because the decision had been made for him . . . because return to Genizee was no longer an option . . . because he was . . .

. . . *because he was . . . dead.* With that thought, J'merlia popped out of existence.

THE ZARDALU

You'd think that the spiral arm would have dangers and horrors enough, God knows, without people having to go on and *invent* new ones. But human (and inhuman) nature being what it is, we're not satisfied with natural bogeymen, so every world you go, you hear the local tales of terror: of free-space vampires, ship-eaters that suck every living essence from a vessel as it goes by and leave an empty mechanical shell flying on through the void; of computerworlds, where every organic being that ever approaches them is destroyed; of the Malgaians, baleful sentient planets who so hate large-scale development that when the surface changes become large enough, the Malgaian modifies its environment to kill off the intruders; of the Croquemort Time-well, where a ship can fall in and stay there in stasis until the end of the universe, when planets and stars and galaxies are all gone and everything has decayed to a uniform heat-bath; of the Twistors, shadowy forces that live in the strange nonspace occupied by ships and people when they undergo a Bose Transition, performing their Twistor distortions in ways so subtle that you never realize that the "you" going in on one end of a transition and the "you" coming out at the destination are quite different beings.

And then, in a class by themselves, there are the Zardalu.

I say in a class by themselves, for one good reason: unlike all the others, there's no doubt that the Zardalu are *real*.

Or rather, they *were* real. The reference texts tell you that the last Zardalu perished about eleven thousand years ago, when a handful of subject races of their thousand-world empire rose up against them and exterminated them.

That's the references. But there's a rumor you'll find all around the spiral arm, as widespread as greed and as persistent as sin, and it says otherwise. It says: not every Zardalu perished. Somewhere, in some hidden backwater of the arm, you may find them still. And if you do, you'll live (but not long) to regret it.

Now, I'm not a man who can resist a temptation like that.

I've been bouncing all over the arm for over a century, poking into all the little backwater worlds. Why not gather the scraps of information from all over the arm? I said to myself. Then make a patchwork quilt out of them, and see if it looks like a map with a big X saying "Here be Zardalu."

I did just that. But I'll spare you the suspense, right now, and say I never found them. I'm not saying they're not there; only that I never ran them down. But in the course of searching, I found out a lot of mixed facts and rumors about what they were—or are—like.

And I got scared. Forget their appearance. They were supposed to be huge, tentacled creatures, but so are the Pro'sotvians, and a gentler, milder life-form is hard to imagine. Forget their legendary breeding rates, too. Humans can give them a run for their money, in *intention* and devotion to the job at hand, if not in speed of results. And even forget the fact that they ruled over so many worlds. The Cecropians call it the Cecropia Federation, not Empire, but they control almost as many worlds as the Zardalu did at their peak.

No. You have to look at what the Zardalu *did.*

It's not easy to see that. If you've ever gone on a fossil hunt for invertebrate forms, you'll know that you never find one. They decay and vanish. All you ever find is an *inverse,* an imprint in the rock where the life-form once sat in the mud. It's a bit like having to look at a photographic negative, with the photograph itself never available.

The Zardalu were supposed to be invertebrates, and in searching for their deeds you have to examine their imprint: what is *missing* on the worlds that they ruled.

Even that takes an indirect approach. We don't know where the Zardalu homeworld was, but it is reasonable to assume that they spread outward through a roughly spherical region, because that's the way that every other clade has spread. So it is very plausible to assume that the *edges* of the region of the Zardalu Communion were the most recently conquered, while places a bit farther in were conquered earlier. On hundreds of worlds around the Zardalu Communion, we find evidence of wonderful civilizations—the arts and sciences of intelligent species, but all long-vanished. And if you look at the age when those cultures disappeared, you find that the *closer* to the middle of the Zardalu Communion territory the planet lies, the *longer ago* its civilization vanished.

The obvious conclusion is not terribly alarming: when the Zardalu conquered, they insisted that the subject races abandon their own culture in favor of that of the Zardalu. There are precedents for that in human and Cecropian history.

It's two *other* facts that frighten: first, there are marginally intelligent species on most worlds of the Zardalu Communion, but there are *far fewer* true intelligences than you would expect, based on the statistics for the rest of the spiral arm. And second, all the evidence suggests that the Zardalu were highly advanced in the biological sciences.

And this is what they did: They conquered other worlds. And as they did so they *reduced the intelligence of the inhabitants,* bringing them down to a level where a being was just smart enough to make a good slave. No capacity for abstract thought, so no ability to plan a revolt, or cause trouble. And, of course, no art or science.

The Great Rising, from species still undegraded, saved more than their own worlds. If the Zardalu had gone on spreading, their sphere of domination would long ago have swallowed up Earth. And I might be sitting naked and mindless in the ruins of some old Earth monument, not smart enough to come in out of the rain, chewing on raw turnip, and waiting to be given my next order.

And at that point in my thinking, I reach my main conclusion about the Zardalu: If they *are* extinct, then thank Heaven for it. The whole spiral arm can sleep better at night.

—from *Hot Rocks, Warm Beer, Cold Comfort: Jetting Alone Around the Galaxy*; by Captain Alonzo Wilberforce Sloane (Retired).

CHAPTER 11

DARYA FOUND THE logic of her thought processes so compelling that it never occurred to her that others might have a different reaction. But they did.

"No, no, and absolutely no," Julian Graves said. He had reappeared in response to Darya's call over the ship's address system, but he had offered no reason for his absence. He looked exhausted and worried. "Even if what you say is true, it changes nothing. So what if the Anfract and the nested singularities are Builder creations? We cannot afford to risk the *Erebus* and additional members of our party."

"Captain Rebka and his team are in more danger than we realized."

"More danger than *what*? None of us had any idea at all of the degree of danger to the seedship when they left. And we all agreed that until three days had passed we would do nothing."

Darya began to argue, claiming that she had never agreed to any such thing. She called on Dulcimer to support her, but the Polypheme was too far gone, a long unwound corkscrew of apple-green giggling on the hard floor. She tried E. C. Tally. The embodied computer played his visual record of the actual event through the display system of the

Erebus, only to prove that Darya had nodded agreement along with everyone else.

"Case closed," Graves said. He sat there blinking, his hands cradling his bald head as though it ached almost too badly to touch.

Darya sat and fumed. Julian Graves was so damned obstinate. And so logical—except when it came to understanding the complicated train of her own analysis of the Anfract. Then he didn't want to be logical at all.

She was getting nowhere. It took the unexpected arrival of the message drone to change the mind of the former Alliance councilor. Graves opened it carefully, lifted out the capsule, and hooked it into the *Erebus*'s computer.

The result was disappointing. There was a continuous record showing the path that the seedship had taken through the uncharted region of the annular singularities, a trip which had been accomplished in less than twenty-four hours. But then there was nothing, an inexplicable ten-hour gap in the recording with no information about the ship's movements or the activities of its crew.

"So you see, Professor Lang," Julian Graves said. "Still we have no evidence of problems."

"There's no evidence of *anything.*" Darya watched as the capsule ran to its uninformative end. "Surely that in itself is disturbing."

"If you are hoping to persuade me that the *absence* of evidence of a problem itself constitutes evidence of a problem—" Graves began. But he was interrupted.

"Mud," said a vague, croaking voice. "Urr. Dirty black mud."

When the message capsule had been removed, the useless outer casing of the drone had been discarded on the control-room floor. It had rolled to rest a couple of feet in front of the open, staring eye of the Chism Polypheme. Now Dulcimer was reaching out with his topmost arm, scratching the side of the drone with a flexible and scaly finger.

"What's he mumbling about?" Graves asked.

But Darya was crouched down at the side of the Polypheme, taking her first close look at the casing of the drone. All they had been interested in when it had reached the *Erebus* had been the messages it was carrying. The drone itself had seemed irrelevant.

"Dulcimer's right," she said. "And so am I!"

She lifted the cylinder and carried it across to Julian Graves. He stared at it blankly. "Well?"

"Look at it. *Touch* it. When the seedship left the *Erebus,* all its equipment was clean and in good working order—have Tally run the record, if you don't believe me. Now look at the antenna and drone casing joints. They're filthy, and there has been repair work done on them. That's a replacement cable. And see here? That's *mud.* It was vacuum-dried, on its flight back, but before that the whole drone plunged into wet soil. Hans and the others not only found a planet—they *landed* there."

"They agreed, before they left, that they would not do that." Graves shook his bald and bulging head reprovingly, then winced. "Coating material can occur anywhere, even in open space. Anyway, why cover a drone with mud?"

"Because they had no choice. If the drone was battered and muddied like this in landing, the ship must have been damaged."

"You are constructing a case from nothing."

"So let me make you one from *something.* Sterile coating material picked up in space is quite different from planetary mud. I'll bet if I dig some of this dirt from the drone's joints and run an analysis, I'll find microorganisms that don't exist in any of our data banks. If I do, will you accept *that* as proof that the seedship landed—and on an unfamiliar world?"

"*If.* And it is a big if." But Julian Graves was taking the drone wearily from Darya, and handing it to E. C. Tally.

Darya saw, and understood the significance of that data point. She had won! She moved on at once to the next problem: how to make sure that she was not, for any reason, left behind on the *Erebus* when others went through the singularities to seek Hans Rebka and his party.

In parallel, Darya's mind took satisfaction in quite a different thought: She had changed an awful lot in one year. Twelve months before in faculty meetings at the Institute, she would have wasted an hour at that point, presenting more and more evidence to buttress her arguments; and then the subject would have been debated endlessly, on and on, until everyone in the meeting was either at the screaming point or mad with boredom.

Not anymore, though, at least for Darya. Somehow, without ever discussing such things, Hans Rebka and Louis Nenda had taught her a great truth: *Once you win, shut up. More talk only makes other people want to argue back.*

There was a corollary to that, too: *If you save time in an argument, don't waste it. Start work on the next problem.*

Darya admired her own new acuity as she left the control room and headed for the cargo bay that housed the *Indulgence.* It was time for work. When E. C. Tally returned with an analysis of that soil sample and Graves made up his mind what to do, Darya wanted to be second only to Dulcimer himself in knowledge of the Polypheme's ship.

Before she even reached the cargo bay, Julian Graves was calling her back. He had already made up his mind. He knew what had to be done: Darya would fly into the nested singularities. E. C. Tally would accompany her, with Dulcimer as pilot of the *Indulgence.* Julian Graves would remain on the *Erebus.* Alone.

Baffling. But say it again: *Once you win, shut up.*

She grabbed Tally and Dulcimer, hustled them onto the *Indulgence,* and was heading the ship out of the cargo bay of the *Erebus*—before Julian Graves had a chance to change his mind.

In her eagerness to leave, Darya did not apply another of Hans Rebka's survival rules: *If you win too easy, better ask what's going on that you don't know about.*

Hans Rebka might have guessed it at once: Julian Graves *needed* to be alone, for some compelling reason of his own. But Hans was not there to observe Graves, or to warn

Darya of something else. He had observed her over the past year, and he would have agreed with her: there *had* been big changes in Darya Lang. But those changes were incomplete. Darya was too self-confident. Now she knew just enough to be dangerous to herself and to everyone around her.

Rebka would have offered a different corollary to her Great Truth: *Don't waste time solving the wrong problems.*

Darya Lang was intellectually very smart, up at genius level. But no one, no matter how intelligent, could make good inferences from bad data. That was where Darya's troubles began. In Hans's terms, when she lacked the right data she still did not know how to acquire it.

That was not her fault. Most of Darya's life had been spent evaluating information collected by other people, of far-off events, times, and places. Data were printouts and articles and tables and images. Success was defined by an ability to digest a huge amount of information from all sources, and then devise a way to impose order and logic on it. Progress was often slow. The path to success might be decades long. No matter. *Speed* was not an issue. *Persistence* was far more important.

Hans Rebka was a graduate of a different school of life. Data were *events,* usually happening in real time and seldom written out for inspection. They could be anything from an odd instrument reading, to a sudden change in the wind, to a scowl that became a smile on a person's face. Success was measured by *survival.* The road to success might remain open only for a fraction of a second.

Rebka had noticed the anomaly when Julian Graves first announced who would go down in the seedship to look for Genizee, and who would remain on the *Erebus:* Graves would not go, although it was *Graves* who had felt most strongly the need to seek out the Zardalu—Graves who had resigned from the Council, Graves who had organized the expedition, Graves who had bought the ship. And then, with Genizee identified and the Zardalu hidden only by the shroud of singularities, Julian Graves had suddenly declined to pursue them. *"I must stay here."*

Now Graves had again refused to leave the *Erebus.* Unfortunately, Hans Rebka had not been around to warn Darya Lang that this second refusal must be regarded as far more significant.

To penetrate the nested singularities for the first time had been an episode of tension, of cautious probing, of calculated risk. For the *Indulgence,* following the path of the seedship less than two days later, the journey was routine. The information returned with the drone had provided a description of branch points and local space-time anomalies in such detail that Dulcimer took one look at the list, sniffed, and set the *Indulgence* to autopilot.

"It's an insult to my profession," he said to E. C. Tally. The Chism Polypheme was lounging in his pilot's chair, a lopsided device arranged so that his spiral tail fitted into it and all his arms had access to the control panel. He was cool again, his skin returned to its dark cucumber green, but as the heat faded from him he became increasingly irritable and haughty. "It's a slur on my Chism-hood."

Tally nodded, but did not understand. "Why is it an insult and a slur?"

"Because I'm a Polypheme! I need challenges, perils, problems worthy of my talents. There is *nothing* to this piloting job, no difficult decisions to make, no close calls—a Ditron could do it."

Tally nodded again. What Dulcimer seemed to be saying was that a Chism Polypheme found work unsatisfying unless there was substantial risk attached to it. It was an illogical attitude, but who was to say that Polyphemes were logical? There was no information about them in Tally's data bank.

"You mean you thrive on difficulty—on danger?"

"You better believe it!" Dulcimer leaned back and expanded his body, stretching to full length. "We Polyphemes—specially me—are the bravest, most fearless beings in the Galaxy. Show us danger, we eat it up."

"Indeed." Tally took a microsecond to mull over that odd statement. "You have often experienced danger?"

"Me? Danger?" Dulcimer swiveled his chair to face Tally. An embodied computer was not much of an audience, but there was nothing else available. "Let me tell you about the time that I beat the Rumbleside scad merchants at their own game, and came *this* close"—he held up his top two hands, a fraction of an inch apart—"to being killed along the way. Me and the scad merchants had been having a little disagreement, see, about a radiation shipment I made that shrunk on the way—nothing to do with me, as I explained to them. They said not to worry, things like that can happen to anyone, and anyway they had another job for me. I was to go to Polytope, fill up my cargo hold with local ice, and bring it back to Rumbleside. Water-ice? I said. That's right, they said. There's a lot of water-ice on Polytope? I said. There sure is, they said, any amount. But we want just *Polytope* water-ice, no other. And we want big penalties if you don't deliver on time.

"I should have known something was a bit funny when I read the agreement, because the penalties for nondelivery included my arms and my scanning eye. But I've shipped water-ice a thousand times, with never a problem. So we shook tongues on it like civilized beings, and I headed the *Indulgence* for Polytope.

"Only thing is, they hadn't mentioned to me that Polytope is a world that the Tristan free-space Manticore dreamed on one of its off days. On Polytope, you see, water *decreases* in volume as it turns to ice instead of expanding as it does everywhere else. And it was a cold world, too, below freezing point most of the year. So the oceans never froze over, but when the water at the top got cold enough to turn to ice, that ice just sank down to the bottom and stayed there.

"There was certainly plenty of water-ice on Polytope, and a shipment of it would sure be valuable—but it was all down under five kilometers of water. I checked the land surface. Polytope had plenty of that, too, but no water-ice on it. I needed a submersible. But the nearest world where I could rent one big enough was so far away, I'd have blown my contract deadline before I could get there and back. What to do, Mr. Tally. What to do?"

"Well,"—Tally's pause for thought was imperceptible in human terms—"if I were placed in such a position—"

"I know you have no idea, sir, so I'll tell you. There was a mining world less than a day's jump away. I flew there, rented land-mining equipment, flew back, and put the *Indulgence* down by the side of the ocean. I dug a slanting tunnel, thirty kilometers long—very scary, I was worried all the way about the roof collapsing on me—down under the ocean bed. And then I dug *upward* until I reached the water-ice sitting on the seabed. I mined it from the *bottom,* you see, then pulled it along the tunnel to my ship. I took off, and got back to Rumbleside with the shipment and with two minutes to spare before my deadline. You should have seen the disappointed faces of those scad merchants when I arrived! They were already sharpening their knives for me." Dulcimer leaned back expansively in his chair. "Now, tell me true, sir, did you ever have an experience to match that?"

E. C. Tally considered experiences and matching algorithms. "Not exactly *equivalent.* But perhaps *comparable.* Involving the Zardalu."

"Zardalu! You met Zardalu, did you? Oh yes." Dulcimer put on the facial expression that to a thousand worlds in the spiral arm indicated a Chism Polypheme at its most sneering and insulting. To E. C. Tally it suggested that Dulcimer was suffering badly from stomach gas.

"Zardalu. Well, Mr. Tally." The Polypheme inclined to indulgence, as the name of his ship pointed out. He nodded. "Since we've nothing better to do, sir, I suppose you may as well tell me about it. Go ahead."

Dulcimer lolled back in his chair, prepared to be thoroughly skeptical and bored.

The *Indulgence* had negotiated the final annular singularity. They were inside, and Darya could see the planet of

Genizee, surely no more than half-a-million kilometers away. She did a quick scan of the surface for the seedship beacon, whose signal should have been easily detected from this distance.

There was no sign of it. She was not worried. There was no chance that the beacon could have been destroyed, no matter how fast the atmospheric entry or how hard the impact with the surface. The beacon was meant to withstand temperatures of thousands of degrees, and decelerations of many hundreds of gravities.

The seedship must be on the other side of the planet, with its signal shielded by Genizee's bulk. The planet was amazingly close. Darya decided that Dulcimer had done an outstanding job. Who had said that the Polypheme was only a good pilot when he was radiation-hot? Well, they were quite wrong.

She headed from the observation bubble of the *Indulgence* to the control room, intending to congratulate Dulcimer. He was sitting in the pilot's chair, but his corkscrew body was coiled so tightly that he was no more than three feet long. His scanning eye was withdrawn, his master eye focused on infinity. E. C. Tally was sitting next to him.

"We've arrived, E.C. That planet outside is Genizee." She bent to peer at Dulcimer. "What's wrong with him? He hasn't been soaking up hard radiation again, has he?"

"Not one photon." Tally moved his shoulders in the accepted human gesture of puzzlement. "I have no idea what has happened to him. All we have done is talk."

"Just talk?" Darya noticed that Tally had a neural cable attached to the back of his skull. "Are you sure?"

"Talk—and show a few visuals. Dulcimer told me of one of his numerous dangerous experiences. Nothing comparable has ever happened to me, but I in return explained our encounter with the Zardalu, back on Serenity. I fed some of my recollections into the display system of the *Indulgence,* though I chose to do so from the point of view of an uninvolved third party, rather than from my own perspective."

"Oh, my lord. Louis Nenda warned us—Dulcimer is easily excited. Run it again, E.C. Let me see what you showed him."

"Very little, really."

The three-dimensional display in the center of the control room came alive. The chamber filled with a dozen hulking Zardalu, advancing on a small group of humans who were vainly trying to hold them off with flashburn weapons that did little more than sting them. In the center of the group, noticeably less nimble than the others, stood E. C. Tally. He hopped clumsily from side to side, then closed with one of the Zardalu to provide a maximum-intensity burn. He was too slow jumping clear. Four tentacled arms, as thick as human thighs, seized and lifted him.

"Tally! Stop it there."

"I explained to Dulcimer," E. C. Tally said defensively. "I told him that although I am sensitive to my body's condition, I do not feel pain in any human or Polypheme sense. It is curious, but I have the impression that when I began to talk he did not really believe that we had encountered the Zardalu. Certainly his manner suggested skepticism. I think it was at this point that he became convinced."

The display was still running. The Zardalu, filled with rage and bloodlust, had started to pull E. C. Tally apart. Both arms were plucked free, then the legs, one by one. Finally the bloody stump of the torso was hurled away, to smash against a wall. The top of Tally's skull was ripped loose. It flew free and was cracked like an eggshell by a questing Zardalu tentacle.

"Tally, will you for God's sake *stop it*!" Darya reached for the arm of the embodied computer, just as the display flickered and vanished.

"That is exactly where I did stop it." Tally reached behind his head and unplugged the neural connect cable. "And when I looked again at Dulcimer, he was already in this condition. Is he unconscious?"

"He might as well be." Darya moved her hand up and down in front of the Polypheme's eye. It did not move. "He's petrified."

"But I do not understand it. Polyphemes thrive on danger. Dulcimer *enjoys* it—he told me so himself."

"Well, he seems to have enjoyed more of it than he can stand." Darya leaned down and grabbed the Polypheme by the tail. "Come on, E.C., give me a hand. We need him in working order if we're going to orbit Genizee and locate Captain Rebka and his party."

"What are you going to do with him?"

"Take him down to the reactor. It's the only thing that might bring him out of this in a hurry. We'll let him have some of his favorite radiation." Darya began to lift the Polypheme, then paused. "That's very strange. Did Dulcimer program an approach orbit before you scared him half to death?"

"He did no programming of any kind. We came in through the singularities on autopilot."

"Well, we're in a capture orbit now. Look." The display screen above the control board in front of Darya showed Genizee, much closer than when they had emerged from the innermost spherical singularity.

Tally shook his head. The embodied computer could do his own trajectory computations almost instantaneously. "That is not a capture orbit."

"Are you sure? It certainly looks like one."

"But it is not." Tally released his hold on Dulcimer and straightened up. "With respect, Professor Lang, I suggest that there may be more urgent matters than providing Dulcimer with radiation. Or with anything else." He nodded at the display of Genizee, growing fast on the screen. "What we are flying is not a capture orbit. It is an *impact* orbit. If we do not change our velocity vector, the *Indulgence* will intersect the surface of Genizee. Hard. In seventeen minutes."

CHAPTER 12

LIKE MOST RATIONAL beings in the spiral arm given any opportunity to do so, J'merlia had read the description of his own species in the *Universal Species Catalog* (Subclass: Sapients). And like most rational beings, he had found his species' entry most puzzling.

The physical description of an adult male Lo'tfian was not a matter of dispute. J'merlia could look at himself in a mirror, and agree with it point by point: pipestem body, eight articulated legs, lidless yellow compound eyes. Fine. No argument about that. Great gift for languages. No doubt about it. What he found mystifying was the description of male Lo'tfian mental processes: "Confronted by a Lo'tfian female, the reasoning ability of a male Lo'tfian apparently switches off. The same mechanism is believed to be at work to a lesser extent when a Lo'tfian male encounters Cecropians or other intelligences."

Could it be true? J'merlia had felt no evidence of it—but if it *was* true, would he even know it? Was it possible that his own intelligence changed according to his company? When he was in the presence of Atvar H'sial, what could be more right and natural than that he should subdue his own thought processes and desires in favor of hers? She was his very own dominatrix! And had been, since he was first post-larval.

Yet what he could not deny was the change in his level of activity when he was left *alone,* without instructions from anyone. He became nervous and worried, his body moved in jerks, his thoughts jumped and skittered in a dozen random directions, his mind was ten times as active as comfort permitted.

Like now.

He was dead. He had to be dead. No one could fly smack into the middle of an unstructured singularity and live. And yet he *couldn't* be dead. His mind was still working, chasing a hundred thoughts at once. Where was he, *why* was he, what had happened to the seedship? Would the others survive? Would they ever learn what had happened to him? How could any mind pursue so many thoughts *in parallel*? Could even a dead mind do that, operating in limbo?

It was an academic question. He was certainly in free-fall, but certainly not in limbo. For one thing, he was breathing. For another, he *hurt.* He had been pulled apart, and now he could feel his body re-forming, settling back into place atom by atom. His sight was returning, too. As the whirlpool of rainbow colors around him subsided, J'merlia found himself hovering in the middle of an empty enclosure. He was surrounded by a million points of sparkling orange, randomly scattered in space. He stared in every direction and found nothing to provide a sense of scale. The glittering points could be feet away, or miles—or light-years. He moved his head from side to side, trying for parallax. Nothing. The lights were all at the same distance, or they were all very remote.

So he would hang there in the middle of nothing, until he starved to death.

J'merlia pulled his limbs in close to his body, retracted his eyestalks, and slowly rotated in space. As he did so he noticed a just-perceptible change in his surroundings. A small part of the orange glitter had been obscured by a tiny circle of more uniform orange light. Staring, he watched the occulting disk grow steadily in size.

It was coming toward him. And it was not small. As it came closer he realized that it must be many times as big as he was. By the time it stopped, it was obscuring a third of the field of orange spangles. Its surface was a uniform silver, a soft burnished matte that diffused the light of the orange sparkles falling on it.

There was a sighing whistle, like a gentle escape of steam. Undulations grew on the surface of the sphere, ripples on a great ball of quicksilver. It changed shape, to become a distorted ellipsoid. As J'merlia watched he saw a frond of silver grow upward from the top, slowly developing into a five-petaled flower that turned to face him. Open pentagonal disks extruded from the front of the ball, and a long, thin tail grew downward. In a couple of minutes the featureless sphere had become a horned and tailed devil, with a flower-like head that looked directly at J'merlia.

He felt a sense of relief for the first time since the seedship had flown into the heart of the singularity. He might not know where he was, or how he had come here, or what would happen to him. But he knew the nature of the entity that had just arrived, and he had a pretty good idea what to do next.

He was facing a sentient Builder construct, similar to The-One-Who-Waits, on Glister, or Speaker-Between, on Serenity. It might take a while to communicate with it—the other two had been out of action for three million years, and a little rusty—but given time they had both understood speech. They had just needed a few samples, to get the ball rolling. J'merlia's concentration and will had weakened when the other being had first approached. Now, as he realized that he was dealing with no more than an intelligent machine, his own intelligence seemed to rise to a higher level.

"My name is J'merlia." He spoke in standard human. He could have used Lo'tfian or Hymenopt, or a pheromonal language, but human had worked well with the Builder constructs before.

There was a soft hissing, like a kettle coming to the boil. The flower-head quivered. It seemed to be waiting for more.

"I came to this system with a group of my fellow beings, from far away in the spiral arm." Was that even true? J'merlia was not sure what "this system" was—for all he knew he had been thrown ten million light-years, or into a completely different universe. Except that the air around him was certainly breathable, and his body was unchanged. The being in front of him still seemed to be waiting. "My ship encountered a singularity. I do not understand why that event did not kill me. But I am alive and well. Where am I? Who are you?"

"Amm-m-m I . . . am-m I . . . am I," a wheezing voice said. "Where am I? Who am I?"

J'merlia waited. The sentient Builder constructs took a while to warm up. Some long-dormant language-analysis capability had to be retrieved and used.

"J'merlia?" the hoarse voice said at last.

"I am he. My name is J'merlia, and I am a Lo'tfian, from the planet Lo'tfi."

"A Lo'tfian. Is that a . . . a live intelligence? Are you a . . . sentient *organic* form?"

"Yes."

"Then that is the reason for your preservation. The singularity that sought you out and captured you is part of the system under my care. It functions automatically, but it was not designed to kill organic intelligence. To confine, yes, but not to kill. It therefore transferred you here, to Hollow-World."

Language contained so many subtleties. Just when J'merlia was convinced that they had established clear communication, the other came up with something baffling. *To confine, but not to kill.* Was Hollow-World the artificial moon of Genizee?

"How big is the system under your care? Does it include the planet from which I just came?"

"It does. True-Home is in my care. Had you not entered the singularity, you would have been returned there, as all ships bearing organic intelligence and seeking to leave this region are returned to True-Home. That is part of my responsibility. You ask, who am I? I tell you, I am *Guardian.*"

"Guardian—of what?"

"Of *True-Home,* the world within the singularities. The closed world that will—one day—become the true home of my designers and makers; the home of the Builders."

J'merlia felt dizzy, and not only because of the wrenchings of his passage to Hollow-World. According to Guardian, Genizee was to become the home of the Builders. But *Serenity,* the great artifact thirty thousand light-years out of the galactic plane, was also destined to become the home of the Builders, if Speaker-Between could be believed. And even little Quake, back in the Mandel system, was supposed to be the home of the Builders, too—despite the fact that Darya Lang, who knew more about the Builders than anyone J'merlia had ever met, insisted that they must have developed on a gas-giant planet like Gargantua and would live only there or in free-space.

"I sense an anomaly," Guardian continued, while quicksilver ripples crisscrossed its body. "You say that you are from the planet Lo'tfi. Are you telling me that you did *not* originate on True-Home? That you came from elsewhere?"

"I did—we did, my whole party. I told you, we are from outside the Anfract, from far away in another part of the spiral arm."

"Tell me more. I sense a possible misunderstanding, although I am not persuaded without more direct evidence. Tell me all that has happened."

It was a direct command, but one that J'merlia felt poorly equipped to obey. Where was he supposed to begin? With his own birth, with his assignment to Atvar H'sial as his dominatrix, with their trip to Quake? Whatever he told Guardian, would the other being really understand him? Like the other sentient Builder constructs, Guardian must have been in standby mode for millions of years.

J'merlia sighed and began to talk. He told of the original home planet of each member of the party; of their convergence on the twin worlds of Opal and Quake, for Summertide Maximum; of their move to the gas-giant planet Gargantua and their passage through the Eye of Gargantua and a Builder transportation system to Serenity; of their successful fight with the surviving Zardalu, who had been set free from stasis fields by the Builder construct Speaker-Between; and then of how the Zardalu had returned to the spiral arm and to the planet Genizee—True-Home, as it was known to Guardian.

J'merlia and some of his companions had followed, seeking the surviving Zardalu. And at that point their ship had been plucked from the sky and deposited against their will on the surface of True-Home.

"Naturally," Guardian said when J'merlia was finally silent. "The system in operation about True-Home assumes that any ship within the nested singularities is seeking to *leave,* and that is forbidden unless the organic intelligences within it have passed the tests. True-Home is a quarantined planet, under my stewardship. It was not anticipated that organic intelligences would *arrive* here through the protecting singularities, seek to explore within, and then hope to leave."

"But my companions are there now. They are in danger, or even dead."

"If what you have told me is true, and if certain other criteria are satisfied, then I will admit the possibility of a misunderstanding. Do you wish this situation to be corrected, and your companions assisted in their attempt to leave True-Home?"

"I do." Even someone as naturally subservient as J'merlia had trouble giving a restrained answer to something as obvious as that. "Of *course* I do."

"Then we can begin at once. There must be direct verification. Are you ready?"

"Me!" J'merlia was suddenly aware of his own insignificance and ineptitude. He was the idiot whose brain-frozen incompetence had allowed the seedship to be caught by the amorphous singularity, while he sat and did nothing. He was the fool who had launched the battered drone back to the *Erebus*—without even mentioning in its message the fate of Captain Rebka and the others. He was a male Lo'tfian, a natural slave who was happiest taking orders from others. He was inadequate.

"I can't help. I'm nothing. I'm *nobody.*"

"You are *all* that can help. You are organic intelligence. You are not nothing. You are manything. You are manybody. You have many components. You must use them."

"I can't do it. I know I can't."

But Guardian was not listening. An oval opening had formed in the middle of the fat silver body, and J'merlia was being drawn into it along a green beam of light. He opened his mouth to protest again and found that he could not speak. Could not breathe. Could not *think.* He was being dismembered—no, dis*minded,* in exquisite torture.

The entry of the seedship into the outskirts of the amorphous singularity had been painful, but that had been *physical* pain, physical disruption, twisting and tearing and stretching. This was far worse, something he had never experienced before or heard described. J'merlia's soul was being *fractionated,* his mind splitting into pieces, his consciousness spinning away along many divergent world lines.

He tried to scream. And when he at last succeeded, he heard a new sound: a dozen beings, all of them J'merlia, crying their agony across the universe.

CHAPTER 13

THE ZARDALU HAD been breeding—fast.

The original group released from the stasis field on Serenity had consisted of just fourteen individuals. Now Hans Rebka, retreating into the building after Atvar H'sial, Louis Nenda, and Kallik, could see scores of them already on land. Hundreds more were rising from the sea. And these were only the larger specimens. There must be thousand after thousand of babies and immature forms, hidden away in breeding areas.

Escape along the spit of land that led to the seedship?

Impossible. It was blocked by Zardalu, with more of them arriving ashore every second.

Then escape to sea?

Even more hopeless. The Zardalu had always been described as land-cephalopods, and they were fast and efficient there; but it was clear that they had not lost mastery of their original ocean environment. They were *land-and-sea*-cephalopods.

Add *that* fact to the descriptions in the *Universal Species Catalog*—if you're lucky enough to live so long, thought Rebka. He grabbed the back of Louis Nenda's shirt and stepped across the threshold. The sun outside had almost set, and the building they were entering was unlit. Ten paces inside, and Rebka could see nothing. He blindly followed Nenda, who was presumably holding on to Atvar H'sial and Kallik. The Cecropian was the only one who could still see. She provided the sonic bursts used by her own echolocation system, and she was as much at home in total darkness as in bright sunlight.

But how much time could she really buy before the Zardalu brought lights inside and followed them? This was a Zardalu building; they would know every hiding place. Wouldn't it be better to agree on the place for a last stand?

"Nenda!" He spoke softly into the darkness. "Where are we going? Does Atvar H'sial know what she's doing?"

There was a grunt ahead of him. "Hold on a second." And then, after a pause for pheromonal exchange, "At says she don't actually know what she's doing, but she prefers it to bein' pulled to bits. She don't see no end to this stupid tunnel"—they had been descending for half a minute in a steady spiral—"but she's ready to go down for as long as it does. We've passed five levels of chambers and rooms. There were signs that the Zardalu lived on the first three; now she's not seeing so much evidence of 'em. She thinks we're mebbe gettin' down below the main Zardalu levels. If only this damn staircase would branch a few times, we might make a few tricky moves and get 'em off our track. That's At's plan. She says she knows it's not much, but have you any other ideas?"

Rebka did not reply. He did have other ideas, but they were not likely to be helpful ones. If the Zardalu used only the first few belowground levels, then why did lower ones exist? Were they even the work of the Zardalu? This would not be the first planet with a dominant aboveground species and a different dominant belowground species, interacting only at one or two levels. If Genizee had spawned a subterranean species powerful enough to stop Zardalu access, what would they do to a blind and defenseless group of strangers?

Rebka, still clutching the back of Louis Nenda's shirt,

tried to estimate a rate of descent. They must have come through a score of levels, into darkness so total and final that it made his straining eyes ache. He itched for a look around, but he was reluctant to show a light. The huge eyes of the Zardalu were highly sensitive, designed by evolution to pick up the faintest underwater gleam.

"Time to take a peek an' see what we got here." Louis Nenda had halted, and his whisper came from just in front. "At can't hear or smell anythin' coming down behind us, so she thinks we're deep enough to risk a bit of light. Let's take a look-see."

The space in front of Rebka filled with pale white light. Louis Nenda was holding a flat illumination disk between finger and thumb, rotating it to allow the center of the beam to scan in all directions.

They were standing on a descending sideless pathway like a spiral staircase with no central shaft or guardrail, looking out onto a high-ceilinged chamber. Nenda played the beam in silence on the fittings and distant walls for a few seconds, then he whistled. "Sorry, Professor Lang, wherever you are. You were right, and we should have listened."

Hans Rebka heard Nenda and was baffled. They were at least three hundred feet underground. All evidence of Zardalu existence had vanished, and the surroundings that replaced the furnishings of the upper levels were totally unfamiliar. He stared again, at a great arch that rose at forty-five degrees, swept up close to the ceiling, then curved gracefully back down all the way to the floor.

Almost. *Almost* to the floor. The far end stopped, just a foot short. The abrupt termination made so little sense that the eye insisted on trying to continue it to meet the level surface. But there was a space at the end. Forty centimeters of nothing. Rebka wanted to walk across and sweep his hand through the gap to prove it was real. The stresses on the support at this end must be huge. Everything else in the chamber was equally strange and unfamiliar. Wasn't it?

His subconscious mind was at work while his conscious mind seemed to be giving up. One area where organic intelligence still beat inorganic intelligence, and by a wide margin, was in the subtlest problems of pattern recognition. E. C. Tally, with his eighteenattosecond memory cycle, could compute trillions of twenty-digit multiplications in the time of a human eye-blink. If he had been present in the chamber he might have made the correct association in five minutes. Louis Nenda and Atvar H'sial had done it in a few seconds, aided by their weeks of examining—and pricing for future sale—the masses of new Builder technology on Glister and Serenity. Kallik, with the advantage of her long study of the Builder artifacts, was almost as quick. It was left for Hans Rebka, least familiar with Builder attributes, to stand baffled for half a minute. At the end of that time his brain finally connected—and he felt furious at his own stupidity and slowness.

His anger was typical, but unjustified. The evidence of Builder influence was indirect, absence more than presence, style more than substance. There were no constructs obviously of Builder origin. It was more a subtle lack of the up-and-down sense that permeated all lives and thinking controlled by gravitational fields. The chamber stretched off into the distance, its airy ceiling unsupported by pillars, arches, or walls. It should have collapsed long since. And the objects on the floor lacked a defined top and bottom, sitting uneasily as though never designed for planetary use. Now that Rebka examined his surroundings more closely, he saw too many unfamiliar devices, too many twelve-sided prisms of unknown function.

The light went off just as he reached his conclusion. Rebka heard a soft-voiced curse from Louis Nenda: "Knew it. Too good to last! Grab hold."

"What's the problem?" Rebka reached out and again seized the shirt in front of him.

"Company. Comin' this way." Nenda was already moving. "At took a peek up the tunnel—she can see round corners some—and she finds a pack of Zardalu on our tail. May not be their usual stamping ground, but they're not gonna let us off that easy. Hang on tight and don't wander around. At says we've got a sheer drop on each side. A big one. She can't sense bottom."

Rebka stayed close, but he looked up and back. The descending ramp was not solid, it was an open filigree that looked frail but did not give a millimeter under their weights. And far above, through the grille of the stairway's open lattice, Rebka saw or imagined faint moving lights.

He crowded closer to Nenda's back. Down and down and down, in total darkness. After the first minute Rebka began to count his own steps. He was up to three thousand, and deciding that his personal hell would be to descend forever through stifling and pitchy darkness, when he felt a hand on his. It was Louis Nenda, reaching back.

"Stay right there and wait. At says don't move, she'll get you across."

Across what? Hans Rebka heard a scuffle of claws. He stood motionless. After half a minute the pale light of an illumination disk cut through the darkness. It was in Louis Nenda's hands, ten meters away and pointing down. Rebka followed the line of the beam and flinched. Between that light and his own feet was *nothing,* an open space that dropped away forever. Atvar H'sial was towering at his side. Before he could move, the Cecropian had seized him in her forelimbs, crouched, and glided away across the gulf with one easy spring.

She set Rebka down a step or two away from the far edge. He took a deep breath. Louis Nenda nodded at him casually and pointed the beam again into the abyss.

"At says she *still* can't sense bottom, an' I can't see it. You all right?"

"I'll manage. You might have kept that light off until after I was over."

"But then Kallik couldn't have seen what she was doing." Nenda nodded across the gulf, to where the Hymenopt was hanging upside down, holding on to the spiraling stairway by one leg. "She has the best eyes. Anything down there, Kallik?"

"Nothing." She swung herself onto the upper side of the

stair and launched casually across the ten-meter gap. "If there is another exit point it is at least a thousand feet down." She moved to the very edge and leaned far out to stare upward. "But there is good news. The lights of the Zardalu are no longer approaching."

Good news. Hans Rebka moved a few steps away from the sheer drop and leaned on a waist-high ledge of solid green, an obviously artificial structure. Good news was relative. Maybe they were not being pursued, but they were still thousands of feet below the surface of an alien world, without food or water. They could not return the way that they had come, without surely meeting Zardalu. They had no idea of the extent or layout of the underground chamber where they stood. And even if—unlikely event—they could somehow find another way to the surface, the chance was slim that the seedship was there to take them away from Genizee. Either J'merlia had left, as ordered, or he had been captured or killed by Zardalu.

Kallik and Nenda were still standing at the edge of the shaft. Rebka sighed and walked across to them. "Come on. It's time to do some hard thinking. What next?"

Nenda dismissed him with a downward chop of one hand and turned off the illumination disk. "In a minute." His voice was soft in the darkness. "Kallik can't see any lights up there anymore, nor can I. But At insists there's something on the path—a long way up, but coming this way. Fast."

"Zardalu?"

"No. Too small. And only one. If it was Zardalu, you'd expect a whole bunch."

"Maybe this is what we need—something that knows the layout of this place." Rebka stared up into the darkness. He was useless without light, but he imagined he could hear a rapid pattering on the hard surface of the spiraling tunnel. "Do you think Atvar H'sial could hide quietly on this side, and grab whatever it is as it comes by?"

There was a moment's silence for pheromonal contact. The scuffling above became clearer. Rebka heard a grunt of surprise from Louis Nenda, followed by a laugh. The illumination disk again lit the chamber.

"At could do that," Nenda said. He was grinning. "But I don't think she's going to. She just got a look at our visitor. Guess who's coming to dinner?"

There was no dinner—that was part of the problem. But Rebka did not need to guess. The beam from the disk in Nenda's hand was directed upward. Something was peering out over the edge of the stairway, eyestalks extended to the maximum and worried lemon-yellow eyes reflecting the light.

There was a whistle of pleasure from Kallik, and a relieved hoot in reply. The pipestem body of J'merlia came soaring across the gulf to join them.

Lo'tfians were one of the underprivileged species of the spiral arm. The use of their adult males as interpreters and slaves of Cecropians was seldom questioned, because the male Lo'tfians themselves never questioned it; they were the first to proclaim Cecropian mental and physical superiority.

Hans Rebka did not agree. He believed that male Lo'tfians, left to themselves, were as bright as any race in the arm, and he had said so loud and often.

But he was ready to question it now, on the basis of J'merlia's account of how he came to be deep inside Genizee. Even with not-so-gentle nudging from Louis Nenda and direct orders from Atvar H'sial, J'merlia didn't make much sense.

He had repaired the seedship, he said. He had flown it up to altitude, to make sure that the air seal was perfect. He had decided to bring the ship back close to the buildings that Hans Rebka and his group were exploring. He had seen them near the building. He had come lower. He had also seen Zardalu.

"Very good," Louis Nenda said. "What happened next? And where's the seedship now? That's our ticket out of here."

"And why did you come into the building yourself?"

Rebka added. "You must have known how dangerous it was, if you saw the Zardalu follow us in."

The pale-lemon eyes swiveled from one questioner to the other. J'merlia shook his head and did not speak.

"It's no use," Nenda said. "Look at him. He's bugger-all good for anything just now. I guess Zardalu can do that to people." He walked away in disgust to the edge of the great circular hole and spat over the edge. "The hell with all of 'em. What now? I could eat a dead ponker."

"Don't talk about food. It makes it worse." Rebka walked across to Nenda, leaving Atvar H'sial to question J'merlia further with pheromonal subtlety and precision, while Kallik stood as a puzzled bystander and close observer. The Cecropian could read out feelings as well as words, so maybe she and the Hymenopt would do better than the humans had.

"We have a choice," Rebka went on. "Not much of one. We can go up, and be torn apart by the Zardalu. Or we can stay here, and starve to death. Or I suppose we could plow on through this cavern, and see if there's another way up and out." He was speaking softly, almost in a whisper, his head close to Louis Nenda's.

"There must be." The cool, polite voice came from behind them. "Another way out, I mean. Logically, there must be."

Hans Rebka and Louis Nenda swung around in unison with the precision of figure skaters.

"Huh?" said Nenda. "What the hell—" He stopped in mid-oath.

Rebka said nothing, but he understood Nenda perfectly. "Huh?" and "What the hell—" meant "Hey! Lo'tfians don't eavesdrop on other people's private conversations." They didn't interrupt, either. And least of all did they stand up and walk away from their dominatrix when she was in the process of questioning them. And Nenda's sudden pause meant also that he was worried about J'merlia. Whatever the Lo'tfian had been through on his way to join them, it had apparently produced in him a serious derangement, enough to throw him far from his usual patterns of behavior.

"Look at the way you came here," J'merlia continued as though Nenda had not spoken. "Through a building by the seashore, and down a narrow shaft. And then look at the extent of these underground structures." He swept a front limb around, taking in the whole giant cavern. "It is not reasonable to believe that all this is served by such mean access, or even that this chamber itself represents a final goal. You asked, Captain Rebka, if we should go up, or stay here, or move through this cavern. The logical answer to all your questions is, no. We should do none of those things. We should go *down.* We *must* go down. In that direction, if anywhere, lies our salvation."

Rebka was ready for his own "Huh?" and "What the hell—" The voice was so clearly J'merlia's, but the clarity and firmness of opinions were a side of the Lo'tfian that Hans, at least, had never seen. Was that what researchers meant when they said a Lo'tfian's intellect was masked and shrouded by the presence of other thinking beings? Was this how J'merlia thought *all the time,* when he was on his own? If so, wasn't it a crime to let people near him? And if it was true, how come J'merlia could think so clearly *now,* with others around him?

Rebka pushed his own questions aside. They made no practical difference, not at a time when they were lost, hungry, thirsty, and desperate. The ideas expressed by J'merlia made so much sense that it did not matter how or where they had originated.

"If you have light," J'merlia went on, "I will be more than happy to lead the way."

Louis Nenda handed over the illumination disk without another word. J'merlia leaped across to the spiral stairway and started down without waiting for the others. Kallik was across, too, in a fraction of a second, but instead of following J'merlia she stood and waited as Atvar H'sial ferried first Louis Nenda and then Hans Rebka across the gap. As the

Cecropian moved on down the spiral, Kallik hung behind to position herself last in the group.

"Master Nenda." The whisper was just loud enough for the human to catch. "I am gravely concerned."

"You think J'merlia's got a few screws loose? Yeah, so do I. But he's right about one thing—we oughta go down rather than up or sideways."

"Sanity, or lack of it, is not my worry." Kallik slowed her pace further, to put more space between her and J'merlia. "Master Nenda, my species served the Zardalu for countless generations before the Great Rising. Although my race memory carries no specific data, there is instinctive knowledge of Zardalu behavior ingrained deep within me. You experienced one element of that behavior when we were on Serenity: the Zardalu love to take *hostages.* They use them as bargaining chips, or they kill them as stern examples to others."

Rebka had fallen behind, too, listening to the Hymenopt. "Don't worry, Kallik. Even if the Zardalu get us, Julian Graves and the others won't trade for us. For one good reason: I won't let them."

"That is not my concern." Kallik sounded as though the idea that anyone would consider *her* worth trading for was ridiculous. "J'merlia's behavior is so strange, I wonder if he was *already* captured by the Zardalu. And if he is now, after conditioning by them, simply carrying out their orders."

CHAPTER 14

ACCORDING TO ALLIANCE physicians, Julian Graves could not exist. He was a statistical fluke, a one-in-a-billion accidental variation on a well-proved medical technique. In other words, there was nothing anyone could do to help him.

It had begun as a simple storage problem. Every councilor needed to know the history, biology, and psychology of each intelligent and potentially intelligent species in the spiral arm. But that data volume exceeded the capacity of any human memory, so when he was elected to the Council, Julius Graves, as he had been called then, had been given a choice: he could accept an inorganic high-density memory implant, cumbersome and heavy enough that his head and neck would need a permanent brace, or he could allow the physicians to develop within him an interior mnemonic twin, a second pair of cerebral hemispheres grown from his own brain tissue and used solely for memory storage and recall. They would fit inside his skull, posterior to the cerebral cortex, with minimal cranial expansion. The first option was the preference of many Council members, especially those with exoskeletons. Julius Graves chose the second.

The procedure was standardized and not uncommon,

though Julius Graves was warned that the initial interface with his interior mnemonic twin through an added corpus callosum was a delicate matter. He must avoid physical stimulants, and he would have to endure the difficult period of time when the interface was being developed. He had readily agreed to that.

What he had not expected—what no one had dreamed might happen—was that the interior mnemonic twin would then develop *consciousness* and self-awareness.

But it had happened. For fourteen months, Julius Graves had felt his sanity teetering on the brink, as the personality of Steven Graves developed and supplied its own thoughts to Julius in the form of *memories*—recollections by Julius of events that had never happened to him.

It had been touch and go, but at last the interface had steadied. The synthesis was complete. Both personalities had made their accommodation, until finally neither knew nor cared where a thought originated. Julius Graves and Steven Graves had fused, to become the single entity of *Julian* Graves.

Now it was hard even to remember those old problems. There had been no recent clash or confusion to suggest that in the bald and bulging skull there once resided two different people . . .

. . . until the *Erebus* entered the twisted geometry of the Torvil Anfract and flew on to orbit the shimmer of nested singularities that guarded the lost world of Genizee; and then the old problem had reemerged to shiver the mind of Julian Graves.

Conflicting thoughts warred within him. For every idea, there seemed to be another running in parallel.

Make *Hans Rebka* leader of the group who would enter the singularities, because he was a first-rate pilot and had a reputation as a troubleshooter. *No.* Make the chief of the party *Louis Nenda,* because with his augment he could communicate with humans, Cecropians, Lo'tfians, and Hymenopts, whereas Rebka could talk to Atvar H'sial only through an interpreter of pheromonal speech.

Send the seedship through the singularities—it was the most agile and versatile. *No.* Send the *Indulgence,* which was less nimble but far better armed.

Use Dulcimer as pilot—he was much better even than Hans Rebka. *No.* He had to stay on the *Erebus,* to guarantee a passage out of the bewildering geometry of the Anfract. *No.* The whole point of the expedition was to locate Genizee and search for living Zardalu. *No.* If the expedition did not *return* to report their findings, there was no point to finding anything.

They were not sequential thoughts. That would have been tolerable. They were *simultaneous* thoughts, screaming for attention, fighting for dominance.

After a few hours of internal conflict, Julius/Steven/Julian Graves could only agree on one thing: while the condition persisted, he was worse than useless—he was positively dangerous. He might make a decision, then a moment later do something to undermine or change it.

And yet he was the organizer and nominal leader of the whole expedition. He could not add to everyone's problems by making them focus on worries that should be his alone.

Let the others explore the singularities, then, and look for Genizee and the Zardalu. All his internal thoughtstreams agreed on one thing: that he could best serve the party by staying out of the way. If he remained on the *Erebus* and did not touch the controls, it was difficult to see how he could do much damage. And perhaps in a few hours or days his personal reintegration would occur, and he could be useful again.

He watched Darya Lang and the second party leave with a feeling of vast relief.

And learned, within a few hours, that he had no reason for satisfaction. Without others to distract him and to channel his thoughts to particular subjects, the split in his personality became more noticeable. He was incapable of holding any thought without another—*several* others—riding along beside it. It was worse than it had been during the first days of interface, because there were more than two thoughts jousting for dominance. His mind darted and veered and fluttered from place to random place like a startled bird, unable to find a stable resting place. And when the monitors sounded to indicate that some object was seeking rendezvous with the *Erebus,* any worry that the main ship might be vulnerable to attacking Zardalu was swamped by the knowledge that he would no longer be alone. The presence of another being—*any* other being—would help to focus his mind.

The control system of the *Erebus* indicated that the new arrival had docked at one of the medium-sized external holds. Graves set off through the ship's interior. In the final narrow corridor that led to the hold, a crouching shape rose suddenly before him.

He gasped, with surprise and then with relief. "J'merlia! Are the others with you? Did you meet Professor Lang?"

The two questions had risen in his mind in the same fraction of a second. But when the Lo'tfian shook his thin head and said, "I am alone," Graves's divided mind managed to agree on one emotion: disappointment. Of all the beings in the party, J'merlia showed the least independence of thought. He was likely to mirror Graves's own mental patterns, however confused and fragmented they might be.

"I did not meet Professor Lang," J'merlia continued. "Did she leave the *Erebus*?"

"She, and also Dulcimer and E. C. Tally. They went to seek your group. They went to learn why there was damage to the returned drone, and mud on it."

Graves put his hand to his head. He was getting worse; his voice was no more controllable than his thoughts. But J'merlia was merely nodding and turning to walk with Graves back to the control room.

"We must have passed each other on the journey through the annular singularities. I have been sent back to tell you that everything goes well. Captain Rebka and the others have landed, and confirm that the planet is the famous lost world of Genizee. It appears to be a peaceful and pleasant place, with no sign of danger."

"There are no *Zardalu*?" With a gigantic effort Graves forced his divided brain to the single question. The mental energy required to resolve alternatives and form one thought was enough to crack his skull, or so it felt.

"We are not sure. No trace of them had been discovered when I left. But Captain Rebka decided to land only when an extensive survey from space showed that it was safe to do so."

Even to the distracted thought processes of Julian Graves's split brain, there seemed something wrong with that statement. "But the message drone was damaged. How did that happen? Who launched the drone? It has to be done in space. Why was there mud on it? Why did you leave the others on Genizee without a ship and return here alone? How can they be safe, when there may still be Zardalu on the planet?"

Graves cursed himself as he flopped down at the control console of the *Erebus.* J'merlia had a linear mind; he would be hopelessly confused by a stream of questions delivered all at once. Graves was confused by them himself. Where were they all coming from?

"I will reply to your inquiries, if you do not mind, in a rather different order from that in which they were asked." J'merlia sat down without waiting for permission. He lifted six legs and began to click off answers on his claws. "First, I left Genizee under the direct orders of Captain Rebka. I launched the message drone for the same reason. He commanded me to take off from the planet and launch it. The drone itself suffered minor damage and became muddied on our landing on Genizee, as did the seedship, but it was not enough to affect performance. As to the safety or lack of it of Captain Rebka and the others, you know my relationship to Atvar H'sial. Do you imagine that I would ever leave her if I thought that she might be in danger, *except* under direct orders?"

There was something wrong with the J'merlia who gave

those answers. Graves knew it. Something odd about the answers, too. Lo'tfians did not tell lies—that was well known—but did that mean they always told the truth? Those two were logically equivalent, weren't they? But suppose that one was *ordered* to tell lies. His own condition prevented him from thinking it through. His mind was splitting into pieces. He put his hands up to rub his eyes. Even they seemed to want to provide double vision. Well, why not? The optic nerve was part of the brain.

He covered his eyes with his hands and fought to concentrate. "But why did you come back? Why didn't you send another probe here? If there are Zardalu . . ."

"The seedship is unarmed, Councilor. Even if it were still on Genizee, it could do nothing to protect the party from any Zardalu that may be encountered. I know that, quite certainly. I came back to help you to bring the *Erebus* through the singularity rings. There was no way of knowing that the probe had reached you with the information that charts the way in. We must prepare to leave at once, and bring the *Erebus* to orbit Genizee."

Graves hesitated. J'merlia was right: the seedship had been defenseless. But to take the *Erebus* inside the singularities, surely not . . .

But why not? Almost the whole party was there now, anyway. Julian Graves took his hands away from his eyes, almost ready to force his mind to a decision, and found that J'merlia had not waited for one. The Lo'tfian was already working at the control console, entering an elaborate sequence of navigational instructions.

When the program was complete, J'merlia turned flight execution over to the *Erebus* main computer and turned his thin body to face Julian Graves. "We are on our way. In a day or less, depending on the condition of stochastic elements of our path, we will be within sight of Genizee. But this raises a new question, and one that fills me with concern. Suppose that when we reach Genizee, Captain Rebka's group, or possibly Professor Lang's group, have indeed discovered that the planet is the home of the Zardalu.

What will we do then? Would it not be logical to bring our group away to safety, and employ the arsenals of the *Erebus* to exterminate the Zardalu?"

Graves considered himself lucky. He did not have to think about the last question with his poor community of a brain, because he had already thought about it long before, for days and weeks and months. The Zardalu were bloodthirsty and violent and cruel, former masters and tormentors of dozens of other intelligent races. That could not be denied. But Julius Graves had spent years working on an interspecies Council. One of the Council's prime duties was to protect any species that had borderline or even *potential* intelligence. The idea of genocide, of destroying all the surviving members of a *known*-intelligent species, made his stomach turn over.

Revulsion and anger allowed him to generate the single response. "I am not sure what we will do if Hans Rebka or Darya Lang's parties find Zardalu on Genizee. But I can tell you, J'merlia, what we will definitely *not* do: we will not contemplate deliberate mass destruction of any species that does not threaten *our* species—yours, or mine, or anyone else's—with extinction. I cannot make that point clearly enough."

He did not know how J'merlia would react. This was not the docile, obedient J'merlia that they were all used to. This was an action-oriented, clear-thinking, decisive Lo'tfian. Graves almost expected an argument, and doubted that he was clear-headed enough to manage his end of it.

But J'merlia was leaning back in the chair, his pale eyes staring intently at Graves. "You *can* make that point clear enough, Councilor," he said. "And you *have* made the point clear enough. You will not pursue, permit, or condone the extermination of intelligence. I hear you speak."

As though evaluating the final summing-up of some lengthy argument, J'merlia sat nodding to himself for a few moments. Then he was away, off his seat and scurrying out of the control room. Julian Graves remained to stare after him, to review his perplexed—and oddly multiple—impressions of the past few minutes, and to wonder if he had finally become deranged enough to have imagined the whole encounter.

Except that the *Erebus,* beyond all argument and imaginings, was entering the region of annular singularities, the region that guarded that most famous lost world of all Lost Worlds: Genizee, home of the Zardalu.

LOST WORLDS

It's no secret that a damned fool can ask more questions than the smartest being in the arm can answer. And yes, I am talking about Downsiders. And yes, I am talking about the Lost Worlds. They seem to have an obsession with them.

Captain Sloane—that's how they always start, polite as could be—you claim to have traveled a lot (but there's a little skepticism, you see, right there). Where is Genizee, the Lost World of the Zardalu?

I don't know, I say.

Well, how about Petra, or the treasure world of Jesteen, or Skyfall or Primrose or Paladin? They know damn well that my answer has to be the same, because every one of those worlds—if they were ever real places—has been lost, all traces of their locations vanished into time.

Of course, the Downsiders would never dream of going out and *looking themselves.* Much better to huddle down in the mud and wonder, then pester people who *have* been out and seen it all, or as much of it as a body can see.

People like me.

So they say, Captain (and now they're getting ruder), you're full as an egg with talk, and you waffle on to anybody who'll listen to you. But what happened to Midas, where it rains molten gold, or Rainbow Reef, where the dawn is green and the nightfall blazing scarlet and midday's all purple? Hey? What happened to *them*? Or to Shamble and Grisel and Merryman's Woe? They were *once* there, and now they're not. Where did they go? You can't answer *that* one? Shame on you.

I don't let myself get mad (though it's not easy). I burn slow, and I say, Ah, but you're forgetting the wind.

The *wind*? That always gets them.

That's right, I say, you're forgetting the Great Galactic Trade Wind. The wind that blows through the whole galaxy, taking worlds that were once close together and pushing them gradually farther and farther apart.

They look down their noses at me, if they have noses, and say, We've never heard of this *wind* of yours.

Ah, well, I say, maybe there's a lot you never heard of. Some people don't call it the Galactic Trade Wind. They call it Differential Galactic Rotation.

At that point, whoever I'm talking to usually says "Huh?" or something just as bright. And I have to explain.

The whole Galaxy is like every spiral galaxy, a great big wheel, a hundred thousand light-years across, turning in space. Most of the people I talk to at least know that much. But it's not like a Downsider wheel, with rigid spokes. It's a wheel where the spiral arms closer to the galactic center, and all the stars in them, turn at a *faster rate* than the ones farther out. So you take a star—for example, Sol. And you take another well-known object—say, the Crab Nebula in Taurus, six thousand light-years farther out toward the galactic rim. You find that Sol is moving around the galactic center about thirty-five kilometers a second *faster* than the Crab. They're separating, slow but sure, both moving under the influence of the Galactic Trade Wind. (And the wind can work both ways. If you drop behind, because you're farther out from the center, all you have to do is fly yourself in *closer* to the center, and wait. You'll start to catch up, because now you're moving faster.)

But what about the Crab Nebula? Ask some of my Downsider friends, the ones who have understood what I'm talking about. It's a *natural* object; you can't fly it around like a ship. Will it ever come back to the vicinity of Sol?

Sure it will come back, I say. But it'll take a while. The Crab will be close to Sol in another couple of billion years.

And then their eyes pop, assuming they have eyes, and they say, Two *billion*! None of us will be around then.

And I tell them, That's all right, I'm not sure I will be, either. In fact, some nights I'm not sure I'll be around next morning.

But what I *think* is, you Downsiders—as usual—are asking the wrong question. What *I'd* like to know about isn't the Lost Worlds, it's the Lost *Explorers*. What happened to Aghal H'seyrin, the crippled Cecropian who flew the disrupt loop through the eye of the Needle Singularity? We had one message from her—we know she survived the passage—but she never came back. Or where did Inigo M'tumbe go, after his last planetfall on Llandiver? He sent a message, too, about a "bright braided collar" that he was on his way to explore. No one has ever seen it or him. And what do you make of the last signal from Chinadoll Pas-farda, rolling up the black-side edge of the Coal Sack on a continuous one-gee acceleration, bound, as she said, for infinity?

There's your interesting cases: *people,* not dumb Lost Worlds. I want to know what happened to *them,* my fellow explorers.

I'll fly until I find out; someday. Someday I will know.

—from *Hot Rocks, Warm Beer, Cold Comfort: Jetting Alone Around the Galaxy;* by Captain Alonzo Wilberforce Sloane (Retired).

Commentator's Note: Shortly after completing this passage, the last in his published work, Captain Sloane embarked on a voyage to the Salinas Gulf, following the path of the legendary Inigo M'tumbe. He never returned. His final message told of a mysterious serpentine structure, fusion-bright against the stellar backdrop, gradually approaching his ship. Nothing has been heard from him since.

It is perhaps ironic that Captain Sloane himself has now become the most famous and most sought after of all Lost Explorers.

CHAPTER 15

THE *INDULGENCE* ARROWED at the surface of the planet in a suicide trajectory, held in the grip of a beam of startling yellow that controlled its movement absolutely. Nothing that Darya Lang did with the drive made a scrap of difference.

Her two companions were worse than useless. Tally reported their position and computed impact velocity every few seconds, in a loud, confident voice that made her want to scream, while Dulcimer, the "Master Pilot of the spiral arm" who claimed to thrive on danger, had screwed himself down tight into a moaning lump of shivering green. "I'm going to die," he said, over and over. "I'm going to die. Oh, no, I don't want to die."

"Seven seconds to impact," Tally said cheerfully. "Approach velocity two kilometers a second and steady. Just listen to the wind on the hull! Four seconds to impact. Three seconds. Two seconds. *One second.*"

And then the ship stopped. Instantly—just a moment before it hit the ground. They were hovering six feet up, no movement, no deceleration, no feeling of force, not even—

"Hold tight!" Darya shouted. "Free-fall."

No feeling even of *gravity.* Dulcimer's scoutship fell free in the fraction of a second until it smacked into the surface of Genizee with a force that jarred Darya's teeth. Dulcimer rolled away across the floor, a squeaking ball of green rubber.

"Approach velocity zero," E. C. Tally announced. "The *Indulgence* has landed." The embodied computer was sitting snug in the copilot's seat, neurally connected to the data bank and main computation center of the *Indulgence.* "All ship elements are reporting normal. The drive is working; the hull has not been breached."

Darya was beginning to understand why she might be ruined forever for academic life. Certainly, the world of ideas had its own pleasures and thrills. But surely there was nothing to compete with the wonderful feeling of being *alive,* after knowing without a shadow of doubt that you would be dead in one second. She took her first breath in ages and stared at the control boards. Not dead, but certainly *down,* on the surface of an alien world. A possibly hostile world. And—big mistake, Hans Rebka would have planned ahead better—not one of their weapons was at the ready.

"E.C., give us a perimeter defense. And external displays."

The screens lit. Darya had her first view of Genizee—she did not count the brief and terrifying glimpses of the surface as the ship swooped down at it faster and faster.

What she saw, after weeks of imagining, was an anticlimax. No monsters, no vast structures, no exotic scenery. The scoutship rested on a plain of dull, gray-green moss, peppered with tiny flecks of brilliant pink. Off to the left stood a broken region of fanged rocks, half hidden by cycads and tall horsetail ferns. The tops of the plants were tossing and bending in a strong wind. On the other side stretched an expanse of blue water, sparkling with the noonday lightning of sunbeams reflected from white-topped waves. Now that she could see the effects of the wind, Darya also heard it buffeting at the hull of the *Indulgence.*

There was no way of telling where the seedship had

landed. The chance that a pair of ships would arrive even within sight of each other, on a world with hundreds of millions of square kilometers of land, was negligible. But Darya reminded herself that she had not *landed*—she and the *Indulgence* had *been landed,* and the same may have been true of Hans Rebka and the seedship.

"Air breathable," Tally said. "Suits not required."

"Do you have enough information to compute where the seedship made planetfall?"

Instead of replying, E. C. Tally pointed to one of the display screens that showed an area behind the *Indulgence.* A long, shallow scar in the moss revealed an area of black mud of just the right width. But there was no evidence of the ship itself.

Darya scanned the whole horizon at high resolution. There was no sign of Hans and his party. No sign of Zardalu; no sign of any animal life bigger than a mouse. Other than the disturbed area of moss, nothing suggested that the seedship was anywhere within five thousand kilometers of the *Indulgence.* And—her brain should have been working earlier, but better late than never—the message drone could be launched only when the seedship was *in orbit.* So although the ship might have landed there, it was unlikely by this time to be anywhere close-by. Rebka and the others were probably far away. What should she do next? What would Hans Rebka or Louis Nenda do in such a situation?

"Open the hatch, E.C." She needed time to think. "I'm going to take a look outside. You stay here. Keep me covered, sound and vision, but don't shoot at anything unless you hear me shout. And don't *talk* to me unless you think there's something dangerous."

Darya stepped down onto the surface, her feet sinking an inch into soft mud covered with a dense and binding thicket of moss. Close up, the bright spots were revealed as little perfumed flowers, reaching up on hair-thin stalks of pale pink from the low ground cover of the plants. Every blossom was pointing directly at the noon sun. Darya walked forward, feeling guilty as each step crushed fragile and fragrant beauty. She walked down to the shore, where the moss ended and an onshore wind was carrying long, crested breakers onto pearly sand. She sat down above the high-water mark and stared at the moving water. A few yards in front of her feet the shore was alive with inch-long brown crustaceans, scuttling frantically up and down to try to stay level with the changing waterline. If this region was typical, Genizee was a fine world on which to live, an unlikely spawning ground for the most feared species of the spiral arm.

"Professor Lang." E. C. Tally's voice in her earpiece interrupted her thoughts. "May I speak?"

Darya sighed. The interruptions were coming before she had even started to generate ideas. "What do you want, E.C.?"

"I wish you to be aware of what this scoutship's sensors are reporting. Four organisms—very large organisms—are approaching you. Because of their location, however, I am unable to provide an image or an identification."

That did not make sense to Darya. Either the ship's sensors could see what was coming, or they could not. "Where are they, E.C.? Why can't you get an image?"

"They are in the water. About forty meters offshore from where you are sitting, and coming closer. We are unable to obtain images because the sensors are not designed for good underwater sighting. I disobeyed your instructions and spoke to you of this because although the weapons of the *Indulgence* are activated, you forbade me to shoot them without your command. But I thought you would like to know—"

"My God." Darya was on her feet and backing away from the wind-tossed water. Every random surge in the breakers became the head of a huge beast. She could hear Hans Rebka lecturing her: *Don't judge a planet by first appearances.*

"Although what you just said was not, strictly speaking, a *shout,* if you wish me to fire, I can certainly do so."

"Don't shoot at anything." Darya hurried back toward

the *Indulgence.* "Just keep watching," she added as she rounded the curve of the hull and headed for the port from which she had exited. "Watch, and I'll be back inside in—"

Something rose from its crouching position on the gray-green moss and sailed toward her in a long, gliding leap. She gasped with shock, tried to jump away, and tripped over her own feet. Then she was sprawled on the soft turf, staring at eyes that seemed as wide and startled as her own.

"Tally!" She could feel her heart pounding in her throat. "For heaven's sake, why didn't you *tell* me . . ."

"You gave specific instructions." The embodied computer was all wounded innocence. "Do not speak, you said, unless you think there is something dangerous. Well, that's just J'merlia, walking all nice and peaceful. We agree that *he's* not dangerous, don't we?"

"There was *evidence* of Zardalu presence," J'merlia said. "But when Captain Rebka and the others entered the buildings, they were all empty."

The Lo'tfian was leading the way, with E. C. Tally and Dulcimer just behind. A few minutes cuddled up next to the main reactor of the *Indulgence*, added to J'merlia's assurance that the members of the party who had landed earlier were all alive and well, had worked wonders. The Chism Polypheme was three shades lighter, his apple-green helix was less tightly coiled, and he was bobbing along jauntily on his muscular spiral tail.

Darya was walking last, uncomfortable about something she could not put a name on. Everything was fine. So why did she feel uneasy? It had to be the added sense that Hans Rebka insisted any human had the potential to develop. It was a faint voice in the inner ear, warning that *something*—don't ask what—was not right. Hans Rebka swore that this voice must never be ignored. Darya had done her best. The defense systems of the *Indulgence* were intelligent enough to recognize the difference in appearance of different life-forms. Darya had commanded the ship to allow entry of any of the types present in their party, but to remain tight-closed to anything that remotely resembled a Zardalu. J'merlia had said the buildings were empty, but who knew about the rest of the area?

As they approached the cluster of five buildings Darya realized that the structures must actually be visible from the place where the *Indulgence* had landed. It was their odd shapes, matching the natural jutting fingers of rock, that made them easy to miss. They were built of fine-grained sandy cement, the same color as the beach and the rock spurs. One had to come close to see that they rose from a level, sandy spit of land and must be buildings.

"I went into orbit with the seedship and launched the message drone that told the path through the singularities," J'merlia went on. "The others remained here."

"And they are in the buildings now?" They were halfway along the projecting point of land; still Darya could find no cause for her uneasiness.

"I certainly have not seen them emerge."

Darya decided that it must be the manner of the Lo'tfian's answers. J'merlia was usually self-effacing to the point of obsequiousness, but now he was cool, laconic, casual. Maybe it was freedom from slavery, at last asserting itself. They had all been wondering when that would happen.

J'merlia had paused by the first of the buildings. He swiveled his pale-yellow eyes on their short stalks and stabbed one forelimb at the entrance. "They went in *there*."

As though the word was a signal, a blue flicker moved in the dark recesses of the building. Darya went past Dulcimer and E. C. Tally and craned forward for a better look. As she did so, there was a scream from behind and something banged hard in her back and clung to her. She managed to keep her feet and turn. It was the Chism Polypheme, collapsing against her.

"Dulcimer! You great lout, don't *do* that."

The Polypheme was blubbering and groaning, wrapping his nine-foot length around her and clinging to her with his five little arms. Darya struggled to break loose, wondering what was wrong with him, until suddenly she could see *past* Dulcimer and E. C. Tally, along the spur of land that led back to the beach.

Zardalu.

Zardalu of all sizes, scores of them, still dripping with seawater. They blocked the return path along land, and they were rising on all sides from the sea. And now she also knew the nature of that blue flicker inside the building behind her.

Impossible to run, impossible to hide. Darya felt sympathy with Dulcimer for the first time. Blubbering and groaning was not a bad idea.

Humans, Cecropians—maybe even Zardalu—might entertain the illusion that there were things in the universe more interesting than the acquisition of information. Perhaps some of them even believed it. But E. C. Tally knew that they were wrong—knew it with the absolute certainty that only a computer *could* know.

Nothing was more fascinating than information. It was infinite in quantity, or effectively so, limited only by the total entropy of the universe; it was vastly diverse and various; it was eternal; it was available for collection, anywhere and anytime. And, perhaps best of all, E. C. Tally thought with the largest amount of self-satisfaction that his circuits permitted, *you never knew when it might come in useful.*

Here was an excellent example. Back on Miranda he had learned from Kallik the language she used to communicate with the Zardalu. It was an ancient form, employed back when the Hymenopts had been a Zardalu slave species. Most of the spiral arm would have argued that learning a dead language used only to speak to an extinct race was an idiotic waste of memory capacity.

But without it, E. C. Tally would have been unable to communicate with his captors in even the simplest terms.

The Zardalu had not, to Tally's surprise, torn their four captives apart in the first few moments of encounter. But they had certainly let everyone know who was boss. Tally, whisked off his feet and turned upside down in the grasp of two monstrous tentacles, had heard an "Oof!" from J'merlia and Darya Lang on one side, and a gargling groan from Dulcimer on the other. But those were sounds of surprise and disorientation, not of pain. Tally himself was moved in against a meter-wide torso of midnight blue, his nose squashed against rubbery ammoniac skin. Still upside down, he saw the ground flashing past him at a rare rate. A moment later, before he had time to take a breath, the Zardalu that held him was plunging under water.

Tally overrode the body's reflex that wanted to breathe. He kept his mouth closed and reflected, with some annoyance, that a few more minutes of *this,* and he would have to be embodied yet again, even though the body he was wearing was in most respects as good as new. And it was becoming more and more determined to breathe water, no matter how much he tried to block the urge. Tally cursed the designers of the computer/body interface who had left the reflexes organic, when he could certainly have handled them with ease. *Don't breathe, don't breathe, don't breathe.* He sent the order to his body with all his power.

The breathing reflex grew stronger and stronger. His lips were moving—parting—sucking in liquid. *Don't breathe!*

In midgulp he was turned rapidly through a hundred and eighty degrees and placed on his feet.

He coughed, spat out a mouthful of brackish water, and blinked his eyes clear. He glanced around. He stood at the edge of a great shallow upturned bowl, forty or fifty meters across, with a raised area and a gray circular parapet at its center. Two tentacles of the Zardalu were loosely wrapped around him. Another pair were holding Dulcimer, who was coughing and choking and seemed to have taken in a lot more water than Tally. The wall of the bubble was pale blue. Tally decided that it was transparent, they were underwater, and its color was that of the sea held at bay outside it.

Of Darya Lang and J'merlia there was no sign. Tally hoped they were all right. So far as he could tell, the treatment he had received was not intended to kill or maim—at once. But there was plenty of time for that.

And he could think of a variety of unpleasant ways that it might happen.

One of them was right in front of him. At first sight the space between Tally and the raised center of the room was a lumpy floor, an uneven carpet of pale apricot. But it was *moving*. The inside of the chamber was a sea of tiny heads, snapping with sharp beaks at anything in sight. Miniature tentacles writhed, tangling each with its neighbor.

They were in an underwater Zardalu breeding ground. A rapid scan counted more than ten thousand young—up from a total of *fourteen* just a few months earlier. Zardalu bred *fast*.

He was recording full details of the scene for possible future use by others when the Zardalu lifted him and Dulcimer and carried them effortlessly forward, on through the sea of waving orange tentacles. The little Zardalu made no attempt to get out of the way. They stood their ground and snapped aggressively at the base of the adult Zardalu as it passed. In return, the infants were swatted casually out of the way by leg-thick tentacles, with a force that sent them flying for many meters.

Tally and Dulcimer were dropped before a hulking Zardalu squatted on the waist-high parapet of the inner ring of the bowl. This alien was a real brute, far bigger than the one that had been carrying them. Tally could see a multicolored sheath of webbing around its thick midriff, marked with a pattern of red curlicues.

It looked familiar. He took a closer look at the Zardalu itself. Surprise! He *recognized* the creature. To most people, those massive midnight-blue torsos, bulging heads, and cruel beaks might have made all Zardalu identical, but Tally's storage and recall functions were of inhuman accuracy and precision.

And now, at last, that "wasted" effort of language learning back on Miranda could pay off.

"May I speak?" Tally employed the pattern of clicks and whistles that he had learned from Kallik. "This may sound odd, but I know you."

The Zardalu behind Tally at once smacked him flat to the slimy floor and muttered a warning growl, while the big one in front writhed and wriggled like a tangle of pythons.

"You *speak.*" The king-size Zardalu leaned forward, producing the whistling utterances with the slitted mouth below its vicious beak. "You speak in the old tongue of total submission. But that tongue is to be spoken by slaves only when commanded. The penalty for other use by slaves is death."

"I am not a slave. I speak when I choose."

"That is impossible. Slaves *must* speak the slave tongue, while only submissive beings *may* speak it. The penalty for other beings who speak the slave tongue is death. Do you accept total slavery? If not, the young are ready. They have large appetites."

There was a nice logical problem here on the question of nonslaves who chose to use the slave tongue, but Tally resisted the temptation to digress. The Zardalu in front of him was reaching down with a powerful tentacle. Flat in the slime next to Tally, Dulcimer was gibbering in terror. The Chism Polypheme could not understand anything that was being said, but he could see the vertical slit of a mouth, and above it the up-curved sinister beak, opening and closing and big enough to bite a human—or a Polypheme!—in two.

"Let's just agree that I can speak, and defer the slave question," Tally said. "The main thing is, *I know you.*"

"That is impossible. You dare to lie? The penalty for lying is death."

An awful lot of things in the Zardalu world seemed to require the death penalty. "It's not impossible." Tally lifted his head again, only to be pushed back down into the slime by the junior Zardalu behind him. "You were in the fight on Serenity, the big Builder construct. In fact, you were the one who grabbed hold of me and pulled me to bits."

That stopped the questing tentacle, a few inches from Tally's left arm. "I was in battle, true. And I caught one of your kind. But I killed it."

"No, you didn't. That was me. You pulled my arms off, remember, first this one, then this one." Tally held up his intact arms. "Then you pulled my legs off. And then you threw me away to smash me against the corridor wall. The top of my skull broke off, and the impact just about popped my brain out. Then that loose piece of my skull was crushed flat—but now I think of it, one of your companions did that, not you."

The tentacle withdrew. When Tally raised his head again, nothing pushed him back down.

The big Zardalu was leaning close. "You survived such drastic dismemberment?"

"Of course I did." Tally stood up and wiggled his fingers. "See? Everything as good as new."

"But the agony . . . and with your refusal to accept slave status, you risk it again. You would dare such pain a second time?"

"Well, that's a bit of a sore point with me. My kind doesn't *feel* pain, you see. But I can't help feeling that there are times when it would be better for my body if I did. Hey! Put me down."

Tentacles were reaching out and down. Tally was lifted in one pair, Dulcimer in another. The big Zardalu turned and dropped the two of them over the waist-high parapet. They fell eight feet and landed with a squelch in a smelly heap that sank beneath their weight.

"You will wait here until we return." A bulbous head peered over the edge of the parapet. A pair of huge cerulean blue eyes stared down at them. "You will be unharmed, at least until I and my companions decide your fate. If you attempt to leave, the penalty is death."

The midnight-blue head withdrew. Tally tried to stand up and reach the rim of the pit, but it was impossible to keep his balance. They had been dropped onto a mass of sea creatures, fish and squid and wriggling sea cucumbers and anemones. There was just enough water in the pit to keep everything alive.

"Dulcimer, you're a lot taller than I am when you're full-length. Can you stretch up to the edge?"

"But the Zardalu . . ." The great master eye stared fearfully at E. C. Tally.

"They left. They've gone for a consultation to decide what to do with us." Tally gave Dulcimer a summary of the whole conversation. "Strange, wasn't it," he concluded, "how their attitude changed all of a sudden?"

"Are you *sure* that they have gone?"

"If we could just reach the edge, you could see for yourself."

"Wait one moment." Dulcimer coiled his spiral downward, squatting in among the writhing fish. He suddenly straightened like a released spring and soared fifteen feet into the air, rotating as he flew.

"You are right," he said as he splashed back down. "The chamber is empty."

"Then, jump right out this time, and reach over to help me. We have to look for a way to escape."

"But we know the way out. It is underwater. We will surely drown, or be caught again."

"There must be *another* way in and out."

"How do you know?"

"Logic requires it. The air in here is fresh, so there has to be circulation with the outside atmosphere. Go on, Dulcimer, jump out of this pit."

The Polypheme was cowering again. "I am not sure that your plan is wise. They will not harm us if we accept slave status. But they said that if we try to escape, they will surely kill us. Why not agree to be slaves? An opportunity to escape *safely* will probably come along in three or four hundred years, maybe less. Meanwhile—"

"Maybe you're right. But I'm going to do my best to get out of here." Tally stared down and poked with his foot at a hideous blue crustacean with spiny legs. "I'd have more faith in the word of the Zardalu if they hadn't left us here in their larder—"

"Larder!"

"—while they're having their consultation to decide what to do with us."

But Dulcimer was too busy leaping out of the pit to hear Tally finish the sentence.

Darya had fared better—or was it worse?—than the others. She was grabbed and held, but at first the Zardalu who captured her remained near the sandstone buildings. She saw the other three taken and carried underwater, presumably to their deaths. When her turn came after ten more minutes, her intellect told her that it was better to die *quickly.* But the rest of her would have nothing to do with that idea. She took in the deepest breath that her lungs would hold as the Zardalu headed for the sea's edge. There was the shock of cold water, then the swirl of rapid movement through it. She panicked, but before her lungs could complain of lack of oxygen, the Zardalu emerged again into air.

Dry, *fresh* air.

Darya felt a stiff breeze on her wet face. She pushed hair out of her eyes and saw that she was in a great vaulted chamber, with the draft coming from an open cylinder in the middle of it. The Zardalu hurried in that direction. Darya heard the chugging rhythm of air pumps, and then she was being carried down a spiraling path.

They went on, deeper and deeper. The faint blue light of the chamber faded. Darya could see nothing, but ahead of her she heard the click and whistle of alien speech. She felt the unreasoning terror that only total darkness can produce. She strained to see, until she felt that her eyes were bleeding into the darkness. Nothing. She began to fight against the firm hold of the tentacles.

"Do not struggle." The voice, which came from a few feet away, was familiar. "It is useless, and this path is steep. If you were dropped now you would not survive the fall."

"J'merlia! Where did you come from? Can you see?"

"A little. Like Zardalu, I am more sensitive than humans to dim light. But more than that, I am able to speak to the

Zardalu who holds me. We are heading down a long stairway. In another half minute you also will be able to see."

Half a minute! Darya had known shorter weeks. The Zardalu was moving on and on, in a glide so smooth that she hardly felt the motion. But J'merlia was right. A faint gleam was visible below, and it was becoming brighter. She could see the broad back of another Zardalu a few yards ahead, whenever it intercepted the light.

The tunnel made a final turn in the opposite direction. They emerged into a room shaped like a horizontal teardrop, widening out from their point of entry. The floor was smooth-streaked glass, the dark rays within it diverging from the entrance and then converging again at the far end to meet at a horizontal set of round apertures, like the irises and pupils of four huge eyes. In front of the openings stood a long, high table. And at that table, leaning back in a sprawl of pale-blue limbs, sat four giant Zardalu. As they approached, Darya caught the throat-clutching smell of ammonia and rancid grease.

Darya was lowered to the floor next to J'merlia. The two Zardalu who had brought them turned and went back to the entrance. They were noticeably smaller than the massive four at the table, and they lacked the decorated webbing around their midsections.

The Zardalu closest to Darya leaned forward. The slit mouth opened, and she heard a series of meaningless clicks and whistles. When she did not reply, a tentacle came snaking out across the table and poised menacingly just above her head. She cowered down. She could see plate-sized suckers, with their surround of tiny claws.

"They command you to speak to them, like the others," J'merlia said. "It is not clear what that means. Wait a moment. I will seek to serve as spokesbeing for both of us."

He crawled forward, pipestem body close to the ground and eight legs splayed wide. A long exchange of clucks and clicks and soft whistles began. After a minute the menacing tentacle withdrew from above Darya's head.

"I have made it clear to them that you are not able to

speak or to understand them," J'merlia said. "I also took the liberty of describing myself to them as your slave. They therefore find it quite natural that I speak only after I have spoken to you, serving as no more than the vessel for the delivery of your words to them."

"What are they saying, J'merlia? Why didn't they kill us all at once?"

"One moment." There was another lengthy exchange before J'merlia nodded and turned again to Darya. "I understand their words, if not their motives. They know that we are members of races powerful in the spiral arm, and they were impressed by the fact that our party was able to defeat them when we were on Serenity. They appear to be suggesting an alliance."

"A *deal*! With Zardalu? That's ridiculous."

"Let me at least hear what they propose." J'merlia went back into unintelligible conversation. After a few seconds the biggest of the Zardalu made a long speech, while J'merlia did no more than nod his head. At last there was silence, and he turned again to Darya.

"It is clear enough. Genizee is the homeworld of the Zardalu, and the fourteen survivors headed here after they were expelled from Serenity and found themselves back in the spiral arm. They began to breed back to strength, as we had feared. But now, for reasons that they cannot understand, they find themselves unable to leave this planet. They saw our seedship arrive, and they saw it take off again. They know that it has not been returned to the surface, while all *their* takeoff attempts have been returned. Therefore they are sure that we know the secret to coming and going from Genizee as we please.

"They say that if we will help *them* to leave Genizee, and give them free access to space here and beyond the Torvil Anfract, they will in return offer us something that they have never offered before: we will have status as their junior *partners*. Not their equals, but more than their slaves. And if we help them to reestablish dominion over all the worlds in this part of the spiral arm, we will share great power and wealth."

"What if we say no?"

"Then there will be no chance of our survival."

"So they want us to trust the word of the Zardalu? What happens if they change their minds, as soon as they know how to get away from Genizee?" Darya reminded herself that *she* had no idea what force had carried the *Indulgence* to the surface of the planet, or how to get away.

"As proof that they will not later renege on their part of the bargain, they will agree to a number of Zardalu hostages. Even of the infant forms."

Darya recalled the behavior of the ravenous infant Zardalu. She shuddered.

"J'merlia, I will *never,* in any circumstances, do anything that might return the Zardalu to the spiral arm. Too many centuries of bloodshed and violence warn us against that. We will not help them, even if it means we all die horribly. Wait a minute!"

J'merlia was turning back to face the four Zardalu. Darya reached out and grabbed him. "Don't tell *them* I said that, for heaven's sake. Say, say . . ." What? What could she offer, what would stall them? "Say that I am very interested in this proposal, but first I require proof of their honorable intentions—if there's words for such an idea in the Zardalu language. Tell them that I want E. C. Tally and Dulcimer brought here, safe and unharmed. And Captain Rebka and the rest of the other party, too, if they are still alive."

J'merlia nodded and had another exchange with the Zardalu, this one much briefer. The biggest of the Zardalu began threshing all its tentacles in a furious fashion, flailing at the tabletop with blows that would have pulped a human body.

"They refuse?" Darya asked.

"No." J'merlia gestured at the Zardalu. "That is not anger, that is their own frustration. They would like to prove that they mean what they say, but they are unable to do so. Tally and Dulcimer will be no problem, they will bring them here. But the other group somehow *escaped,* into the deep interior of Genizee—and no Zardalu has any idea of their present location."

CHAPTER 16

TWO KILOMETERS BENEATH the surface, Genizee was an intriguing world of interlocking caves and corridors; of airspaces spanned by silver domes and paved with crystal; of ceiling-high columns that ran every which way but straight; of stardust floors, twinkling with firefly-light generators.

But five kilometers down, Genizee was more than intriguing. It was incomprehensible.

No longer was it necessary to walk or climb from place to place or floor to floor. Sheets of liquid light flashed horizontally and vertically, or curved away in long rose-red arches through tubes and tunnels of unknown termini. Kallik, touching the tip of a claw to one ruby light-stream, reported propulsive force and resistance to pressure. When she dared to sit on one sheet she was carried, quickly and smoothly, for a few hundred yards before she could climb off. She returned chirping with satisfaction—and immediately took a second ride. After her third try, everyone began to use the sheets of light instead of walking.

The usual laws for strength of materials had also been suspended inside Genizee. Papery, translucent tissues as thin and delicate as butterfly wings bore Atvar H'sial's full weight without giving a millimeter, while in other places J'merlia's puny mass pushed his thin legs deep into four-inch plates of solid metal. In one chamber the floor was covered by seven-sided tiles of a single shape that produced an aperiodic, never-repeating pattern. In another, webbed sheets of hexagonal filaments ran from the ceiling to deep pools of still water. They continued on beneath the surface, but there the lattice became oddly twisted and the eye refused to follow its submarine progress.

"But at least it's drinkable water," Louis Nenda said. He was bending with cupped hands by one of the still pools. After a few seconds of noisy gulping he straightened. "What color would you say *that* is?" He pointed to an object like an embossed circular shield hanging forty yards away.

"It's yellow." Rebka was also stooping to drink.

"Okay. Now peek at it sort of edgeways, with just your peripheral vision."

"It looks different. It's blue."

"That's what I'd say. How d'you like the idea of somethin' that turns a different color when you look at it?"

"That's impossible. You don't affect an object when you look at it. Your eyes *take in* photons—they don't shoot them out."

"I know that. But Kallik's always goin' on about how in quantum theory, the observer affects the observed system."

"That's different—that's down at the level of atoms and electrons."

"Maybe." Louis Nenda turned his head away from the shield, then as quickly turned back. "But I still see blue, an' then yellow. I guess if it's impossible, nobody told the shield. If I knew how that gadget worked I could name my own price at the Eyecatch Gallery on Scordato." He leaned over the pool again and filled his flask. "Wish we had something to go with this."

With worries over water supply out of the way, the humans' concerns were turning more and more to food. Kallik would be all right—a Hymenopt could reduce her metabolism and survive for five months without food or water.

J'merlia and Atvar H'sial could manage for a month or more. "Which just leaves me an' thee," Nenda said to Hans Rebka. "We have to stop gawping around and find a way out of here. You're the boss. Where do we go next? We could wander around forever."

That thought had been on Hans Rebka's mind for the past four hours, since the last sign of the Zardalu had vanished. "I know *what* we have to do," he replied. "But I don't know how." He waved his arm to take in the whole chamber. "If we're going to get out, we need a road map for this place. And that means we need to find whoever built it. One thing's for sure, it wasn't the Zardalu. It's nothing like the surface buildings."

"I do not know who built this, and I, too, do not know how to determine the present location of that entity." J'merlia had been quietly watching and listening, pale-yellow eyes blank and remote. "Also, we are dealing with a region of planetary dimensions—billions of cubic kilometers. However, I *can* suggest a procedure which may lead to a meeting with the beings who control and maintain this region."

Hans Rebka and Louis Nenda stared at him. Neither could get used to the new, poised J'merlia. "I thought you just said you *don't* know how to find 'em," Nenda grumbled.

"That is correct. I do not know where to go. Yet there are ways by which the controllers of the interior of Genizee may perhaps be persuaded to come to *us.* All we need to do, on a sufficiently large scale, is *this.*"

The Lo'tfian stepped across to where two spinning disks like giant glass cogwheels stood next to a set of long, dark prisms. He picked up one of the triangular cylinders and thrust it into the narrow gap where the wheels met. The walls of the whole chamber shuddered. There was a distant scream of superstrength materials stressed beyond their limits, and the disks jerked to a halt.

"Destruction," J'merlia went on. "Wholesale destruction. Much of this equipment may be self-repairing, but for damage sufficiently massive, outside service must also be needed. There should be reporting systems and repair mechanisms. Stand well clear." He moved to stand by a river of liquid light and pushed a plate of support material to block its path. Sparks flew. The river screamed, and light *splashed* like molten gold. A dozen machines around the chamber began to smoke and glow bright red. "Very good." J'merlia turned to the others. "I suggest that you either assist—or please stay out of the way."

Louis Nenda was already joining in, with a gusto and expertise that suggested much experience in violent demolition. He had found a straight bar of hardened metal and went along one wall, smashing transparent pipes filled with glowing fluid. Flashing liquid streams flew in all directions. Whatever they touched began to smoke and crumble. At the opposite wall, J'merlia jammed more locking bars into rotating machinery. Kallik and Atvar H'sial worked together in the center of the vault, tackling structural supports. They found a tilted and unsupported ramp and heaved on it in unison. The domino effect of its fall brought a whole chain of beams crashing down.

Hans Rebka stood aloof and watched for unknown dangers. He marveled at the energies that the small group was calling into action. Devices in the interior of Genizee must have been designed for normal wear and tear, but not for deliberate sabotage. They employed great forces, finely balanced. And when that delicate balance was destroyed . . .

"Look out behind!" Rebka cried. A rotating flywheel at the far end of the chamber, removed from all load, was spinning faster and faster. The whir of rotation rose to a scream, went hypersonic, and ended in a huge explosion as the wheel burst. Everyone ducked for cover until the flying debris had settled, then went back to work.

Within ten minutes the chamber was a smoking ruin. The only movement was the shuddering of rigid cogwheels and the rising of steam.

"Very good," J'merlia said calmly. "And now, we wait."

And hope that whoever owns this place doesn't get too

mad with hooligans, Hans Rebka thought. But he did not say anything. J'merlia's idea was wild, but who had a better one?

For another quarter of an hour there was nothing to see or hear but the slow settling of broken equipment. The first sign that J'merlia's strategy might be working came from an unexpected direction. The ceiling of the chamber had been crumbling, releasing a snow of small gray flakes. That fall suddenly intensified. The ceiling began to bulge downward in the middle, right above where the group was standing. They scattered to all sides. But instead of dropping failing struts and broken beams, the bulge grew. The ceiling parted, to become the bottom of a silvery, rounded sphere.

As the shape of the new arrival became visible, Hans Rebka felt surprise, relief, and disappointment. He had met sentient Builder constructs before, on Glister and on Serenity. He had not expected to find one in the interior of Genizee, but now he suspected that this meeting would not be useful. The constructs probably intended no harm to humans, but pursuit of their own perverse agendas often led to that result. Worst of all, they had been in stasis or working alone for millions of years, ever since the Builders had departed the spiral arm. Their performance was eccentric, rusty, too alien, or all three. Communication with them was a hit-or-miss affair, and Hans Rebka felt that he missed more than he hit. But better the devil one knows . . .

"We are lost and we need help. Our party came here from far away." As soon as the construct was fully visible, Rebka began to describe who they were, and how they had come to Genizee. As he spoke, the object in front of them began the familiar metamorphosis from quivering quicksilver sphere to distorted ellipsoid. A silver frond grew from the top, developing into the usual five-petaled flower. Open pentagonal disks extruded from the front of the ball, and a long, thin tail grew downward. The flower-head looked directly at Rebka.

He went on describing events, although he suspected that the *sense* of his words did not yet matter. Before communication could begin, the dormant translation system of the construct had to waken and be trained on a sufficient sample of human speech.

Rebka talked for a couple of minutes, then paused. That should be more than enough. There was the usual annoying wait, and at last a gentle hissing sound followed by a volcanic belch.

"On the boil!" Louis Nenda said. His arms and chest were covered with little blisters where droplets of corrosive fluid had spattered him. He ignored them. "But sluggish. Mebbe it needs a dose of salts—"

"One at a time during speech analysis," Rebka interrupted. "You can all talk once it settles on human patterns."

". . . lost . . . and need help." The gurgling voice sounded as if someone were talking through a pipe filled with water. ". . . coming . . . coming from . . . far away . . ."

The quivering of the surface continued in agitated ripples, as the petaled head scanned the smoking debris of the chamber. "Lost, but now here. Here, with the evil beings who committed this . . . this great *destruction* . . ."

"Now we're in trouble," Nenda said, in pheromones so weak that Atvar H'sial alone could catch his words. "Time to change the subject." And then, loudly to the construct, "Who are you, and what is your name?"

The quivering stopped. The open petals turned to face Nenda. "Name . . . name? I have no name. I need no name. I am keeper of the world."

"This world?" Nenda asked.

"The only world of consequence. This world, the future home of my creators."

"The Builders?" Rebka thought the construct sounded angry. No, not angry. *Peevish.* It needed to be distracted from its shattered surroundings. "Your creators were the Builders?"

"My creators need no name. They made me, as they made this world. My duties were to form this world to their needs, and then to preserve it against change until their return. I have done so perfectly, ever since their departure." The head turned again. "But now, the damage here—"

"—is small," said Rebka. Think positive! "It can be repaired. Perhaps we can help you to do it. But before we work we will need nourishment."

"Organic materials?"

"Particular organic materials. Food."

"There are no organics within this world. Perhaps on the surface . . ."

"That would be perfect. Can you arrange it?"

"I do not know. Follow me."

The silver body turned and began to glide away across the floor of the chamber.

"What you think?" said Nenda softly to Hans Rebka, as they hurried to keep up with the construct. "Future home of the Builders, here? Nuts."

"I know. Darya Lang says the Builders were free-space or gas-giant dwellers. This place is nothing like either. But I'll believe one thing: World-Keeper, or however it wants to call itself, has slaved away for millions of years getting this place ready. It certainly *thinks* the Builders will be coming—just like The-One-Who-Waits is sure that Quake and Glister are the places where the Builders will show up again, and Speaker-Between knows it's going to be out on Serenity. I think they're all as crazy as each other, and not one of them knows what the Builders want." He paused. "Uh-oh. Are we expected to try that?"

The construct had reached one of the broad channels of flowing golden light. Without a word, World-Keeper drifted forward to settle in the center of the stream. There was a low, whirring sound and the construct zipped away on the shining ribbon, rapidly accelerating to disappear from sight along a curved tunnel.

"Hurry up!" Rebka cried. "We're going to lose it." But he was the last to move. Kallik and J'merlia had already jumped, closely followed by Atvar H'sial and Nenda.

Hans Rebka dived forward and fell flat onto a yielding golden surface. He thought for a moment that he was going to slide right across and off the other side, but then his body stuck fast and he was dragged along.

This was no acceleration-free ride. He felt strong forces whipping him on, faster and faster, until whole chambers went flashing past in an eye-blink. Kilometers of straight corridor appeared and whizzed by before he could move a finger. Then the pathway curved upward, and centrifugal forces drained blood from his brain until he felt dizzy. His whole body was racked with many gravities. If he was thrown off the moving ribbon, or if it came to an end at a solid object . . .

The ribbon vanished. Hans Rebka was suddenly in free-fall and in darkness. He gasped and dropped many meters, until he was caught by a velocity-dependent field that held and slowed him like a bath of warm molasses.

He landed gently and on all fours, in a chamber that dwarfed anything he had seen so far on Genizee. The gleaming roof was kilometers high, the walls an hour's walk away. A bright silver pea halfway to the center of the cavern was presumably World-Keeper. Four moving dots, no bigger than flies, were scattered between Rebka and the Builder construct.

He stood up and hurried in their direction, reflecting as he did so that since they had entered the Torvil Anfract nothing had gone according to plan. Julian Graves had changed from expedition leader and organizer to passive observer and nonparticipant. The seedship had been forced to land when no landing was planned. J'merlia, as though balancing Julian Graves, had suddenly become a leader instead of a follower.

Even the forces of nature were different in the Anfract. In a region of cut-sheet space-time and granular continuum and macroscopic quantum effects, who knew what might happen next? He thought of Darya and hoped that she was all right. If only the group back on the *Erebus* had the sense to sit tight and wait, rather than trying to rush through the nested singularities on some ill-planned rescue mission . . .

Atvar H'sial and Louis Nenda at least were still predictable. Unflappable, they were staring silently at their new surroundings as Rebka approached. He was sure from their postures that they were deep in pheromonal conversation.

"Can we agree on something before we have another session with the construct? Unless we're already too late." Rebka gestured ahead, to where J'merlia and Kallik were already advancing to join World-Keeper. "Those two used to be your slaves. Can't you *control* them for a while, at least until we find a way out of here?"

"Don't I wish!" growled Nenda. If he was faking the frustration on his face, he was a superb actor. "We just been talkin' about that, me an' At. We figger it's all your fault, you an' Graves. You took two perfectly good slaves, an' you filled their heads with all sorts of nonsense about freedom an' rights an' privileges, stuff what neither of 'em wanted anythin' to do with before you come along. An' look at 'em now! Ruined. Kallik's not all that bad, but At says she can't even *talk* to J'merlia any more. He's all over this place like he owns it. Watch him now! Want to guess what that pair's sayin' to each other?"

The Lo'tfian was crouched by the Builder construct. Kallik suddenly turned and came racing to join Rebka and the other two.

"Master Nenda!" The Hymenopt skidded to a halt in front of the Karelian human. "I think it would be a good idea if you and Atvar H'sial were to come quickly. J'merlia is in *negotiation* with World-Keeper. And the conversation does not strike me as wholly rational!"

"See!" Louis Nenda said. "Let's go." His glare at Rebka was vindication, accusation, and trepidation, in equal parts.

"It is really very simple," J'merlia said. He was advancing quickly to meet the others, leaving World-Keeper lagging behind. "The Zardalu have access to the whole surface of Genizee, land and sea, as they have since they first evolved as land-cephalopods and then as intelligent beings. But they are denied access to the interior. Did you know that World-

Keeper was unaware of their spread into the spiral arm, and their subsequent near extinction from it, until I told him of it? We can be returned by World-Keeper to the surface, and to a location of our own choice. But it is clear that we will be at great risk from the Zardalu, facing death or enslavement.

"However, that is not our only option. The terminal point for a Builder transportation system exists. Here, in the interior of the planet! Riding the light-sheets we could be there within the hour. In less than a day, says World-Keeper, we can be at a selected point in Alliance Territory, or the Cecropia Federation, or the Zardalu Communion." He dropped his voice lower, although there was minimal chance that anyone more than a few feet away could hear him. "I recommend that we take the opportunity now, before World-Keeper changes its mind. I detect in its thought patterns strong evidence of irrationality, not to say insanity. After our destructive work on the chamber, it wants rid of us. We will surely be sent *somewhere* by it, whether we want to go or not—to the surface, or through the Builder transportation system, but away from here. So let us fly to safety while we can."

The temptation was alive in Hans Rebka, but only for a split second. A return now would leave Darya and the others waiting on the *Erebus,* ignorant of what had happened —perhaps making a suicidal rescue bid. He, at least, could not run away.

"I won't force anyone into more danger," he said. "If the rest of you want to leave through the Builder transport system, go ahead and do it. But I can't. I'm going back to the surface of Genizee. I'll take my chances there."

The others said nothing, but even before Rebka began to speak, the pheromonal dialogue had begun between Louis Nenda and Atvar H'sial.

"We could be back home and safe from the Zardalu in less than a day."

"Yes. That would be desirable. But reflect, Louis Nenda, on our condition should we elect to return to the spiral arm.

We would be in no better position than when we arrived on Miranda: penniless, slaveless, and shipless. Whereas if we stay here, and can somehow win a portion of these riches . . . any one of them would make our fortunes. World-Keeper may not be sane, but he makes wonderful gadgets."

"Hey, I know that, At. I'm not blind." Louis Nenda noticed that J'merlia had moved closer and was listening carefully to the conversation. The Lo'tfian had better command of pheromonal communication than Nenda's augment provided the human. J'merlia would catch every nuance. That couldn't be helped, and anyway it didn't matter. J'merlia's devotion and obedience to his Cecropian dominatrix was total, so nothing would be repeated to Rebka or the others.

"There's some amazing stuff here," Nenda went on. "It makes the loot on Glister look like Bercian gewgaws. I agree, we may be a long way from getting our hands on any, but we shouldn't give up yet. That means we hafta stick with Rebka."

"I concur." The pheromones from Atvar H'sial took on a tinge of suspicion. "However, I again detect emotional undercurrents beneath your words. I need your assurance that you are remaining from the soundest and most honorable of commercial motives, and *not* because of some perverse and animalistic interest in the human female, Darya Lang."

"Gimme a break, At." Louis Nenda scowled at his Cecropian partner. "After all we been through, you oughta know what I'm like by now."

"I do know, very well. That is the basis for my concern."

"Get *outa* here." Nenda turned to Hans Rebka. "Me an' At have been talkin' about this. We think it would be wrong to run for it, an' leave Julian Graves an' Tally an' Dulcimer an' . . . whoever else"—he glared at Atvar H'sial—"high an' dry, wondering where the hell we got to. So we've decided to stay with you and try our luck back on the surface of Genizee."

"Great. I need all the help I can get. Then that just leaves

Kallik and J'merlia." Rebka glanced at the Hymenopt and the Lo'tfian. "What do you two want to do?"

They were staring at him as if he were crazy.

"Naturally, we will go wherever Atvar H'sial and Master Nenda go," Kallik said, in the tone of one addressing a small and rather backward child. "Was there ever any doubt of it?"

"And so for all of us," said J'merlia, "it is onward—and upward. Literally, in this case. I will ask World-Keeper how and when we may be returned to the surface of Genizee."

"As close as possible to the seedship," Rebka said.

"And as *far* as possible from the Zardalu," added Louis Nenda. "Don't forget that, J'merlia. Rebka and I are gettin' pretty hungry. But we wanna *eat* dinner, not be it."

CHAPTER 17

J'MERLIA WAS CONVINCED that he was dead.

Again.

He *wanted* to be dead. Deader than the previous time.

Then he had merely been stupid enough to dive into the middle of an amorphous singularity, which no conscious being, organic or inorganic, could possibly survive.

That produced *physical* dismemberment: one's body was stretched along its length, and at the same time compressed on all sides, until one became a drawn-out filament of subnuclear particles, and finally a burst of neutrinos and a ray of pure radiation. Long before that, of course, one was dead and unconscious. It was an unpleasant end, certainly, but one well studied and well understood.

What he had dealt with next had been much worse: *mental* dismemberment. His mind had been teased apart, delicately separated piece from piece, while all the time he remained conscious and suffering. And then inside his fragmented brain everything that was mentally clear and clean had been taken away from him, dispatched on multiple mysterious and faraway tasks. What was left was a useless husk, devoid of purpose—vague, irresolute, and uncertain.

And now that poor shattered remnant was being *interrogated.*

"Tell me about the human you call Julian Graves—about the Hymenopt known as Kallik—about the Cecropian, Atvar H'sial." The probing came from the Builder construct, Guardian. J'merlia knew his tormentor, but the knowledge did not help. His mind, absent all trace of free will, had to answer.

"Tell me *everything,*" the questioner went on, "about all the members of your party. I can observe *present actions,* but I need to know the past before I can make decisions. *Tell.*"

J'merlia told. Told all. What he had become could not resist or lie.

But it was not a one-way process; for, as he told, into the vacuum of uncertainty that was now his mind there flowed a backwash of information from Guardian itself. J'merlia was not capable of analyzing or understanding what he received. All he could do was record.

How many are we? That I cannot say, although I have pondered the question since the time of my first self-awareness. I thought for one million years. And then, more than three million years ago, I sent out my probes on the Great Search; far across the spiral arm and beyond it, seeking. *Seeking first to contact, and then to know my brethren.*

I failed. I learned that we are hundreds, certainly, and perhaps thousands. But our locations make full knowledge difficult, and few of us were easy to find. Some lie in the hearts of stars, force-field–protected. Others are cocooned deep within planets, awaiting some unknown signal before they will emerge. A handful have moved so far from the spiral arm and from the galaxy itself that all contact has been lost. The most inaccessible dwell, like me, within the dislocations of space-time itself. Perhaps there are others, in places I did not even dream to look.

I do not know, for I did not complete *the Great Search. I* abandoned *it. Not because all the construct locations could not ultimately be found by extended search; rather, because the search itself was pointless. I learned that my self-appointed task could never achieve its objective.*

I had thought to find like minds, a community of constructs, united in purpose, a brethren in pursuit of the same goal of service to our creators. But what I found was worse than diversity—it was insanity.

These are beings who share my origin and my internal structure, even my external form. Communication between us should have been simple. Instead I found it impossible. Some were autistic, so withdrawn into their own world of delusion that no response could be elicited, no matter what the stimulus. Many were fixated, convinced past all persuasion of a misguided view as to their own role and the roles of the other constructs.

Finally, and reluctantly, I was forced to a frightening conclusion. I realized that I, and I alone of all the constructs, had remained sane. I alone understood the true program of my creators, the beings you know as the Builders; and I alone bore this burden, to preserve and protect True-Home for their return and eventual use.

Or rather, I and one ally would carry out that duty. For by the strangest irony I found one other construct who understands the nature of our true duties—and that construct is physically closest to me, hidden within the same set of singularities. That being, the world-keeper, guards and prepares the interior of True-Home, just as I guard the exterior.

When the Great Search was abandoned I realized that the world-keeper and I would be obliged to carry out the whole program ourselves. *There would be no assistance from any other of our fellows.*

And so, two million years ago—we began.

The two-way flow continued, beyond J'merlia's control, until his mind had no more information to offer and no more power to absorb. At the end of it came a few moments of peace.

And then arrived the time of ultimate agony and bewilderment.

The pain during the fragmenting of J'merlia's mind had seemed unbearable. He realized that it had been nothing only when the awful process of mental coalescence and *collapse* began.

CHAPTER 18

IN A SMALL, guarded chamber far beneath the uncharted surface of Genizee, surrounded by enemies any one of whom was fast enough to catch her if she ran and powerful enough to tear her apart with its smallest pair of tentacles once it had caught her, Darya Lang sat cross-legged on a soft, slimy floor and made her inventory.

Item A: One Chism Polypheme, too terrified to do more than lie on the ground, moan, and promise complete obedience to the Zardalu if only they would spare his life. Dulcimer, stone-cold and cucumber-green, was a pathetic sight. In that condition and color he would never do anything that required the least trace of courage. And he was getting worse. His master eye was closed and his spiral body was coiling down tighter and tighter.

Conclusion: Forget about help from Dulcimer.

Item B: One embodied computer, E. C. Tally. Totally fearless, but also totally logical. Since the only logical thing to do in this situation was to give up, Tally's value was debatable. The only things in his favor were his ability to talk to the Zardalu and the fact that for some reason a few of them held him in a certain respect. But until there was reason to talk to the Zardalu, forget about help from Tally.

Item C: One Lo'tfian. Darya had known J'merlia for a long time, long enough for his reactions to be predictable—except that here on Genizee his behavior had become totally out of character. Abandoning his usual self-effacing and subservient role, he had become cool and assertive. There was no telling how he would react to any new demand. At the moment he had become inert, legs and eyes tucked in close to the pipestem body. Forget about help from J'merlia.

Was there anything else? Well, for completeness she ought to add:

Item D: Darya Lang. Former (how long ago and far away!) research professor on Sentinel Gate. Specialist in Builder constructs. Inexperienced in leadership, in battle, or even in subterfuge.

Anything more to add about herself?

Yes. Darya had to admit it. She was *scared.* She did not want to be in this place. She wanted to be *rescued*; but the chance that Hans Rebka or anyone else would gallop out of the west and carry her away to freedom was too small to compute. If anything was going to be done, Darya and her three companions would have to do it for themselves.

And it would have to be done soon; for in a little while the Zardalu chiefs would return for her answer to their proposal.

She levered herself to her feet and walked around the perimeter of the chamber. The walls were smooth, glassy, and impenetrable. So was the domed ceiling. The only exit was guarded by two Zardalu—not the biggest and most senior specimens, but more than a match for her and all her party. Either one could hold the four captives and have a passel of tentacles left over. They were wide-awake, too, and following her every move with those huge blue eyes.

What right did they have to hold her prisoner and to threaten her? Darya felt the first stirring of anger. She encouraged it. Let it grow, let it feed on her frustration at not knowing where she was, or how long she had before death or defeat was forced upon her. That was something preached by Hans Rebka: *Get mad.* Anger drives out fear. If you are angry enough, you cannot also be afraid.

And when all the rules of the game say that you have already lost, do something—*anything*—that might change the rules.

She went across the room to where E. C. Tally was leaning against the wall.

"You can talk to the Zardalu, can't you?"

"I can. But not so well, perhaps, as J'merlia."

"I would rather work through you. I want you to come with me now, and explain something to those two horrors. We have to tell them that Dulcimer is dying."

"He is?" Tally stared across at the tightly coiled, now-silent form of the Chism Polypheme. "I thought that he was merely afraid."

"That's because you don't have Polyphemes in your data banks." This was no time to teach E. C. Tally the rudiments of deception and lying. "Look at the color of him, so dark and drab. If he doesn't get hard radiation, soon, he'll be dead. If he dies, it will complicate any working relationship we might have with the Zardalu. Can you explain that to them?"

"Of course."

"And while you are at it, see if you can get any information on where we are—how deep beneath the surface, what are the ways back up, that sort of thing."

"Professor Lang, I will do as you ask. But I feel certain that they will not provide such data to me."

"Do it anyway."

Darya followed Tally as the embodied computer went across to the two guarding Zardalu. He talked to them for a couple of minutes, gesturing at Dulcimer and then at Darya. At last one of the Zardalu rose on its tentacles and glided swiftly out of the chamber.

Tally turned back to Darya. "There are sources deeper in the interior, sufficient to provide Dulcimer with any level of radiation needed. They do not want Dulcimer to die, since he has already promised to be a willing slave and assistant to the Zardalu. But it is necessary that senior approval be obtained before radiation can be provided."

Deeper. It was the wrong direction. "Did you ask them about where we are?"

"I tried to do so. Without success. These Zardalu are difficult to talk to, because they are afraid."

"Of us?" Darya felt a moment of hope.

"Not at all. They know they are superior to us in speed and strength. The guards here fear the wrath of the senior Zardalu. If they make a mistake and fail to carry out their duties properly, that will be punished—"

"Don't tell me. By death."

"Precisely." Tally was staring at Darya with a puzzled expression. "Professor Lang, may I speak? Why do you wish me to ask questions of the Zardalu about ways out of here, when such inquiries will surely arouse their suspicions as to your intentions?"

Darya sighed. The embodied computer might be regarded as a big success back on Miranda, but that was not a world where mayhem and bloodshed ruled. "E.C., if we don't find a way out of here, we have only two alternatives: we make a deal with the Zardalu that sells out humans and every other race in the spiral arm; or we don't make a deal and we are pulled to pieces and fed to the Zardalu infants. Clear enough now?"

"Of course. However . . ." Tally seemed ready to say more, but he was interrupted by the return of the messenger Zardalu. The other one came to pick up Dulcimer, poked J'merlia awake with the tip of one tentacle, and gestured to Darya and Tally to move on out of the chamber. They descended a broad staircase and moved down another ramp, always penned between the Zardalu. After a few minutes of confusing turns and twists and another four dark tunnels, they emerged into a long, low room filled with equipment.

The Zardalu holding Dulcimer turned to click and whistle at Tally.

"It wants to know the setting," the embodied computer

said. "It assumes you want Dulcimer in that." He gestured to a massive item that stood close to one wall.

Darya went across and examined it. It was some kind of reactor, it had to be. The thickness of the shielding suggested that its radiation would be rapidly lethal to humans or most normal organisms. But Dulcimer was far from normal. What level could he tolerate, or even thrive on? She knew what she wanted, a dose big enough to fill him with pep and confidence, the same fearless bravado that he had shown when he flew the *Erebus* into the middle of the Torvil Anfract. Then, with his active help, the four of them might be able handle a Zardalu—not two, but one; and that would take some careful arranging, too. Finding the right-sized dose was the first step, but it was going to be a matter of purest guesswork.

There was a door set into the reactor side, just big enough for a human or a Polypheme to squeeze through. Darya cracked it open. When the Zardalu did not protest or back away she swung it wide.

The chamber inside was a kind of buffer zone, with a second closed door at its far end. It was the area where decontamination would take place, after a maintenance engineer, presumably wearing suitably heavy protection, had finished work and emerged from the interior.

She gestured to the Zardalu. "Put him in there."

The space was only just big enough for Dulcimer, tightly coiled as he was. Darya squeezed the door shut on the inert Polypheme and felt guilty. If she understood the mechanism, the fail-safe would allow the outer door to be opened only when the inner door was closed. But the inner door could be kept open from outside the whole unit. That meant that until Darya closed the interior door, Dulcimer would not be able to escape even if he wanted to.

She crossed her fingers mentally and moved the control of the inside door. Dulcimer was now exposed to whatever sleet of radiation came from inside the reactor. And since Darya knew nothing of its design, she had no idea how much that might be.

How long dare she leave him inside? A few minutes might be enough to kill. Too much would be worse than too little. The Zardalu just stood watching. They must assume that she knew what she was doing. Darya was in an agony of worry and guilt.

"May I speak?" It was E. C. Tally, interrupting at the worst possible moment. J'merlia was standing by his side, fully awake again.

"*No.* Keep quiet, E.C. I'm busy."

"With respect, Professor Lang," J'merlia said, "I think you will find it of advantage to listen to his thinking."

"I am still wondering," Tally went on without waiting for Darya's reaction, while she glared at both of them, "why you requested that I ask the Zardalu about the ways out of here."

Darya rounded on him. "Why do you think? Do you two *like* it here so much you want to stay forever? You will, you know, unless you do more than just sit around."

She knew that Tally did not deserve the outburst, but she was ready to be angry with anyone.

He nodded calmly. "I understand your desire to leave, and quickly. But that does not address my question. Your request still confuses me, since we *know* where we were taken as we came here. I have all that information recorded in memory. And thus we already know how to get to the surface, without asking anyone."

Darya had a few moments of wild hope before logic intruded. "That won't do, E.C. I believe that you remember exactly the way you came, and you could probably backtrack. But the first part of the trip was underwater—I saw you go before I did. And the sea around that whole area is swarming with Zardalu. Even if we escaped all the way back that far, we'd be caught in the water before we ever got close to land."

"True. But may I speak? I am aware that escape through water is infeasible, and I would not propose that."

"Then what the devil *do* you propose?" The collapse of

even the faintest hope made Darya angrier than ever. "Tunneling up through solid rock? *Eating* your way out?"

"I would propose that we retrace our downward path until we reach the first set of air pumps. And we then seek to follow their flow path directly to the surface."

Air pumps. Darya was angrier than ever—at herself. She had felt the breeze of dry fresh air and heard the chugging rhythm of pumps in the very first chamber that she had been taken to. There must be hundreds of others, riddled through the whole labyrinth of chambers. All logic said that the ducts must terminate on the surface of Genizee.

"Tally, I'll never say anything bad about embodied computers again. You can think rings around me. Bring that Zardalu over here, would you?—the bigger one. Quick as you can."

He hurried away, and she glanced at the closed reactor door while he was whistling at their captor. In her preoccupation with Tally and J'merlia she had forgotten all about Dulcimer. For all she knew, he could be cooked right through and dead. She was reassured by a sudden sound—a loud *Boom! Boom! Boom!* from inside. She closed the inner door, but held the outer one closed as the bigger Zardalu approached.

"Tell it, E.C.," she said. "Tell it to go right now and bring the senior Zardalu, the one that I was talking to earlier. Say I am ready to cooperate fully on the terms outlined to us, but I won't deal with anyone else. And both of you—get ready to move fast."

The hammering on the door of the reactor chamber was getting steadily louder, together with a muffled screaming sound from within. Darya held the tag closed, waiting and waiting while the Zardalu dithered around as though unable to agree to the terms that Tally was explaining to it. At last it headed for the exit, pausing on the threshold for a final whistling exchange with the guard who would be left behind. That Zardalu moved closer, to dangle three brawny tentacles menacingly above Darya, J'merlia, and E. C. Tally.

Darya waited thirty more endless seconds, until the other Zardalu should be well out of the way. Then she took a deep breath and unlocked the outer door. She was ready to swing it open, hoping that luck had been on her side and the Chism Polypheme had received the perfect dose of radiation.

"Come on out, Dulcimer."

She did not have a chance to open anything. The door was smashed out of her hands and whirled round to clang against the reactor wall.

Dulcimer came out. Or something did.

What had entered was a squat cucumber-mass, silent and sullen. What emerged was an extended nine-foot squirt of luminous apple green, screaming at the top of its single lung.

The remaining Zardalu was right in the line of flight. Dulcimer knocked it flat and did not even change direction.

"Dulcimer!" Darya cried. Talk about an overdose! "This way. Follow us—we've got to reach the air pumps. Dulcimer, can you hear me?"

"Whooo-ooo-eee!" Dulcimer hooted. He went zipping around the whole chamber, bouncing from wall to wall and propelled by mighty spasms of his spiral tail.

"Run for it!" Darya pointed E. C. Tally and J'merlia to the chamber exit and scrambled after them, her eyes still on Dulcimer. The Zardalu, groggy but still active, was back upright in a thresh of furious tentacles. It grabbed for the Polypheme as he flew by, but could not hold him. He bounced off the reactor, paused by the door for a second as though tempted to enter again, and then sprang up to the ceiling. In midair he turned upside down and went hurtling off at a different angle.

"Dulcimer!" Darya cried again. She had been dawdling, and the Zardalu was starting in her direction. She could not wait any longer. "Go to the air pumps."

"To the intake," J'merlia called, suddenly at Darya's side. "Quickly. It is farther along this tunnel."

As J'merlia spoke, Dulcimer came whizzing past them, straight as an arrow down the corridor. Darya gasped with relief and ran the same way. She came to the great nozzles of the air pumps—and then realized that Dulcimer had flown right on past them. He had vanished into another and wider air duct, far along the corridor. Darya heard the cackling scream fading away in the distance. And then she could not hear it at all.

"Inside," Tally called. He was far beyond the air-duct entrance. "If you climb a few meters farther, the tentacles will not be able to reach you. And this duct is too narrow to admit a Zardalu!"

"Wait a second. J'merlia is still back there." Darya was worming feetfirst into the straight section of pipe, raising her head as she pushed in deeper. Progress was slow, and the Zardalu was closing fast—too fast. She could never get out of range in time.

But J'merlia was between Darya and the Zardalu, and he was making no attempt to reach the air duct. Instead he ran off to the side, drawing the Zardalu after him. He disappeared from Darya's narrow field of view, ducking a swipe from a thick tentacle.

And then he was back. As Darya pushed herself farther toward safety she saw J'merlia leap into view and halt, right in front of the Zardalu.

Tentacles came down like a cage, enclosing the Lo'tfian on all sides. The suckered tips curled around the pipestem body, while a whistle of triumph and anger came from the slit mouth.

The tentacles snapped shut. And in that moment, J'merlia disappeared.

The Zardalu screamed in surprise. Darya gasped. J'merlia had not *escaped*—he had simply vanished, dissolved into nothing. But there was no time to pause and wonder about it. The Zardalu was moving forward—and Darya was still within reach.

She wriggled for her life along the narrowing tunnel. Long, prehensile tentacle-tips came groping after her, touching her hair, reaching for her head and neck. Darya was stuck too tight to move.

And then a hand was around her ankle, pulling her along. She gave one last big push, adding to E. C. Tally's helping heave, and slid along the tube the final vital jerk to safety. The Zardalu was straining for her. It remained a few inches out of reach.

Darya lay flat on the floor of the air duct, exhausted and gasping for breath. Dulcimer was gone—who knew where? But he should be safe for the moment. He was zipping through the air ducts, and anyway it would be a very speedy Zardalu who could even get near him in his condition. J'merlia had vanished, even more mysteriously, into air, in violation of every known physical law. They were still deep below ground, on a planet where the Zardalu ruled all the surface.

And yet Darya was oddly exhilarated. No matter what came next, they had taken at least one step toward freedom. And they had done it without help from anyone.

The path to the surface was both ridiculously easy and horribly difficult.

Easy, because they could not go wrong if they followed the flow of the air. The duct they had entered was an exhaust for the chamber. It must at last merge with other exhaust vents, or bring them directly to the surface of Genizee. All they had to do was keep going.

And difficult, because the layout of the duct network was unknown. The ducts had never been designed for humans to clamber through. In some spots the tubes became so narrow that there was no way to continue. Then Darya and Tally had to backtrack to a place where the pipes divided, and try the other fork. At other nodes the duct would widen into a substantial chamber, big enough for a Zardalu. That was not safe to enter, and again they would be forced to retrace their path.

Darya was sure that she would never have made it without E. C. Tally. He kept a precise record of every turn and gradient, monitoring their three-dimensional position relative to their starting point and making sure that their choice of paths did not take them too far afield laterally. It was he who assured Darya that they were, despite all false starts and doubling back, making progress upward. His internal clock was able to assure her that although they seemed to have walked and crawled and climbed forever through dim-lit passageways, it was only six hours since they had escaped from the Zardalu.

They took turns leading the way. Darya was in front, climbing carefully on hands and knees up a slope so steep and slippery that she was in constant danger of sliding back, when she caught a different glimmer of light ahead. She halted and turned back to E. C. Tally.

"We're coming to another chamber," she whispered. "I can't tell how big it is, only that the tunnel's widening and the light looks different. Probably big enough for Zardalu. Should we keep going, or head back to the last branch point?"

"If there are no actual sounds or sight of Zardalu, I would prefer to keep moving. This body is close to its point of personal exhaustion. Once we stop, it will be difficult to restart without a rest period."

Tally's words forced Darya to admit what she had been doing her best to ignore: she was ready to fall on her face and collapse. Her hands were scraped raw, her knees and shins were a mass of lacerations, and she was so thirsty and dry-lipped that speech was an effort.

"Stay here. I'll take a look." She forced herself up the last ten meters of sloping tunnel and reached the flat, hard floor of the chamber. She listened. Nothing. And nothing to see but the glowing, hemispherical bowl of the chamber's ceiling.

"It seems all right," she whispered—and then froze. A soft grating sound started, no more than ten feet away. It was followed by a sighing whisper and the movement of air past Darya, as though some huge air pump was slowly beginning operations.

Darya sat motionless on hands and knees. Finally she

raised her head, to stare straight up at the shining bowl of the ceiling. She began to laugh, softly and almost silently.

"What is wrong?" E. C. Tally whispered worriedly from back inside the air duct.

"Nothing. Not one thing." Darya stood up. "Come on out, Tally, and you can have your rest. *We made it.* We're on the surface of Genizee. Feel the wind? It's nighttime, and the glow up there is the nested singularities."

Darya had never in her whole life waited with such impatience for dawn. The forty-two-hour rotation period of Genizee stretched the end of night forever. First light bled in over the eastern horizon with glacial slowness, and it was two more hours after the initial tinge of pink before Darya was provided with a look at their surroundings.

She and E. C. Tally were half a mile or less from the sea—how even its brackish water spoke to her dry throat—on a level patch of flat rock, fifty feet high. Nothing stood between them and the waters but stunted shrubs and broken rocks. They could reach the shoreline easily. But the night wind had died, and in the dawn stillness Darya could see the sea's surface moving in swirls. She imagined the movement of Zardalu, just offshore. The scene looked peaceful, but it would be dangerous to believe it.

She and Tally waited another hour, licking drops of dew from cupped shrub leaves and from small depressions in the flat ground. As full light approached, Darya ascended to the highest nearby spire of rock and scanned the whole horizon. And there along the shoreline, so far away that it formed no more than a bright speck, she saw a flash of reflected light.

It was the *Indulgence.* It had to be. Nothing else on the surface of Genizee would provide that hard, specular reflection. But there was still the problem of how to get there.

The quick and easy way was to head for the shoreline and follow its level path to the ship. Quick, easy—and dangerous. Darya had not forgotten the last incident on the shore, when the four big sea creatures had approached her as she walked along the margin of the sea. Maybe they had not been Zardalu; but maybe there were other creatures on Genizee, just as dangerous.

"We'll go over the rocks," she told E. C. Tally. "Get ready for more climbing." She led the way across a jumble of spiny horsetails and sawtooth cycads, jutting rock spires, and crumbling rottenstone, struggling along a route that paralleled the shore while staying a rough quarter of a mile away from it. As the sun rose higher, swarms of tiny black bugs rose in clouds and stuck to their sweating faces and every square inch of exposed skin.

Tally did not complain. Darya recalled, with envy, that he had control over his discomfort circuits. If things became too unpleasant he would turn them off. If only she could do the same. She struggled on for another quarter of an hour. At last she paused, left the rutted path of broken stone that she had been following, and climbed laboriously to a higher level. She peered over the edge of a stony ridge and thought that she had never seen a more beautiful sight. The ship stood there, silent and welcoming.

"Just five more minutes," she turned and whispered down to Tally. "We can't be more than a hundred yards from the *Indulgence.* We'll go right to the edge of the flat area of moss, then we'll stay in the shrubs and take a rest. When we have our energy back, we go for the *Indulgence* at a dead run. I'll secure the hatches; you go to the ship controls and take us to space."

They stole forward, to a point where the brush ended and they would have a straight run across gray-green moss to the ship. Darya crouched low and brushed black flies from her face. At every breath, flies swarmed at her nose and mouth. She placed her hands to her face and breathed through a filter of closed fingers.

One more minute, then this slow torture would be history. Darya rose to a full standing position and turned to nod to E. C. Tally. *"Thirty seconds."* She could see it all in her mind's eye: the race across the moss, the ship's rapid start-up procedure, the roar of the engines, and then that wonderful sound of a powered lift-off to a place where bloodthirsty

Zardalu were just a bad memory. She could hear it happening now.

She *could* hear it happening now.

My God. She could hear it happening *now.*

Darya turned. She took a deep breath to shout, inhaled a few dozen minute bugs, and started to choke and wheeze. A hundred yards from her, the *Indulgence*—her only hope, the only way off this awful world—rose with a roar of controlled power and vanished into the salmon-pink morning sky of Genizee.

CHAPTER 19

HANS REBKA SAT on a rounded pyramid never designed for contact with the human posterior, and thought about luck.

There was good luck, which mostly happened to other people. And there was bad luck, which usually happened to you. Sometimes, through observation, guile, and hard work, you could avoid bad luck—even make it look like good luck, to others. But you would know the difference, even if no one else did.

Well, suppose that for a change good luck came your way. How should you greet that stranger to your house? You could argue that its arrival was inevitable, that the laws of probability insisted that good and bad must average out over long enough times and large enough samples. Then you could welcome luck in, and feel pleased that your turn had come round at last.

Or you could hear what Hans Rebka was hearing: the small, still voice breathing in his ear, telling him that this good luck was an impostor, not to be trusted.

The seedship had been dragged down to the surface of Genizee and damaged. Bad luck, if you liked to think of it that way. Lack of adequate precautions, if you thought like

Hans Rebka. Then they had been trapped by the Zardalu and forced to retreat to the interior of the planet. More bad luck? Maybe.

But then, against all odds, they had managed to escape the Zardalu by plunging deep inside the planet. They had encountered World-Keeper. And the Builder construct had agreed through J'merlia, without an argument, to return them to a safe spot on the surface of Genizee, a place from which they could easily make it back to the waiting seedship. If they preferred, they could even be transmitted all the way to friendly and familiar Alliance territory.

Good luck. *Too much* good luck. The little voice in Rebka's ear had been muttering ever since it happened. Now it was louder, asserting its own worries.

He stared around the square chamber, which was lit by the flicker of a column of blue plasma that flared upward through its center. World-Keeper had advised them not to approach that roaring, meter-wide pillar, but the warning was unnecessary. Even from twenty meters Rebka could feel fierce heat.

They had been told to wait here—but for how long? They were still without food, and this room had no water supply. The Builder constructs had waited for millions of years; they had no sense of human time. One hour had already passed. How many more?

J'merlia, Kallik, and Atvar H'sial were crouched in three separate corners of the chamber—odd, now that Rebka thought about it, since when J'merlia was not sitting in adoring silence under Atvar H'sial's carapace, he was usually engaged in companionable conversation with the Hymenopt. Louis Nenda was the only one active. He was delicately prying the top off a transparent sealed octahedron filled with wriggling black filaments. It floated unsupported a couple of feet above the floor as Nenda peered in at the contents.

Rebka walked across to him. "Busy?"

"Middlin'. Passes the time. I think they're alive in there."

Nenda stood up straight and stared at Rebka questioningly. "Well?"

Rebka did not resent the chilly tone. Neither man was one for casual conversation. "I need your help."

"Do you now. Well, that'll be a first." Nenda scratched at his arm, where droplets of corrosive liquid had raised a fine crop of blisters. "Don't see how I can give it. You know as much about this place as I do."

"I'm not talking about that. I need something different." Rebka gestured to Louis Nenda to follow him, and did not speak again until they were out of the room and far away along the corridor. Finally he halted and turned. "I want you to act as interpreter for me."

"All this way to tell me that? Sorry. I can't speak to silver teapots any better than you can."

"I don't mean World-Keeper. I want you as interpreter to Atvar H'sial."

"Use J'merlia, then, not me. Even with my augment, he speaks Cecropian a sight better than I do."

"I know. But I don't want J'merlia as interpreter. I don't want to use him for anything. You've seen him. He's been our main interface with the construct, but don't *you* think he's been acting strange?"

"Strange ain't the word for it. You heard Kallik, when J'merlia first rolled up an' joined us? She said she thought her buddy J'merlia might have been Zardalu brainwashed. Is that where you're coming from?"

"Somewhere like that." Rebka did not see it as a Zardalu brainwash, but he would have been hard put to produce an explanation of his own. All he knew was that something felt *wrong,* impossible to explain to anyone who did not already feel it for himself. "I want to know what Atvar H'sial thinks about J'merlia. He's been her slave and interpreter for years. I don't know if anyone can lie using pheromonal speech, but I'd like to know if J'merlia said anything to Atvar H'sial that sounded bizarrely different from usual."

"You *can* lie in Cecropian pheromonal speech, but only if you speak it really well. You know what the Decantil

Myrmecons say about Cecropians? 'All that matters to Cecropians are honesty, sincerity, and integrity. Once a Cecropian learns to fake those, she is ready to take her place in Federation society.' Sure you can lie in Cecropian. I just wish I were fluent enough to do it."

"Well, if anyone understands the change in J'merlia, I'm betting it's Atvar H'sial. That's what I want to ask her about."

"Hang on. I'll get her." Nenda headed for the other chamber, but he added over his shoulder, "I think I know what she'll tell you, though. She'll say she can't talk sensibly to J'merlia any more. But you should hear it for yourself. Wait here."

When the massive Cecropian arrived Nenda was already asking Rebka's question. She nodded at Hans Rebka.

"It is true, Captain," Nenda translated, "and yet it is more subtle than that. I can *talk* to J'merlia, and he speaks to me and for me in return. He speaks truth, also—at least, I do not feel that he is lying. And yet there is a feeling of *incompleteness* in his presence, as though it is not J'merlia who stands before me, but some unfamiliar simulacrum who has learned to mimic every action of the real J'merlia. And yet I know that must also be false. My echolocation might be fooled, but my sense of smell, never. This is indeed the authentic J'merlia."

"Ask Atvar H'sial why she did not tell her thoughts before, to you or me," Rebka said.

The blind white head nodded again. Wing cases lifted and lowered as the question was relayed. "Tell *what* thoughts?" Nenda translated. "Atvar H'sial says that she disdains to encourage anxiety in others, on the basis of such vague and subjective discomforts."

Rebka knew the feeling. "Tell her that I appreciate her difficulty. And also say that I want to ask Atvar H'sial's further cooperation."

"Ask." The open yellow horns focused on Rebka's mouth. He had the impression, not for the first time, that the Cecropian understood more than she would admit of human speech. The fact that she saw by echolocation did not rule out the possibility that she could also interpret some of the one-dimensional sonic patterns issued by human vocal cords.

"When World-Keeper returns, I do not want communication to proceed through J'merlia, as it did last time. Ask Atvar H'sial if she will command or persuade him, whatever it takes to get J'merlia out of the way."

Nenda held up his hand. "I'm tellin' her, but this one's from me. You expect At to trust *you* more than she trusts J'merlia? Why should she?"

"She doesn't have to. You'll be there, too. She trusts you, doesn't she?"

That earned Rebka an odd sideways glance from Nenda's bloodshot eyes. "Yeah. Sure she does. For most things. Hold on, though, At's talkin' again." He was silent for a moment, nodding at the Cecropian. "At says she'll do it. But she has another suggestion, too. We'll go back in, an' you ask any questions you like of J'merlia. Meanwhile At monitors his response an' looks for give-aways. I think she's on to somethin'. It's real tough to track your own pheromones when you're talking human. J'merlia won't find it any easier than I do."

"Let's go." Rebka led the way back into the flare-lit chamber. It might be days before World-Keeper returned—but it might be only minutes, and they needed to find out what they could about the new and strange J'merlia before anything else happened.

There had been one significant change since they left the chamber. J'merlia had moved from his corner to crouch by Kallik. He was speaking rapidly to her in her own language, which Rebka did not understand, and gesturing with four of his limbs. Atvar H'sial was close behind when Rebka walked up to the pair. J'merlia's eyes swiveled, first to the human, then on to his Cecropian dominatrix.

"J'merlia." Hans Rebka had been wondering what question might yield the quickest information. He made his decision. "J'merlia, have you been lying to us in any statement that you have made?"

If anything could produce an unplanned outpouring of emotional response, that should do it. Lo'tfians did not lie, especially with a dominatrix present. Any response but a surprised and immediate denial would be shocking.

"I have not." The words were addressed to Rebka, but the pale-lemon eyes remained fixed on Atvar H'sial. "I have not told lies."

The words were definite enough. But why was the tone so hesitant? "Then have you *concealed* anything from us, anything that we perhaps ought to know?"

J'merlia straightened his eight spindly legs and stood rigid. Louis Nenda, on instinct, moved to place himself between the Lo'tfian and the exit to the chamber. But J'merlia did not move in that direction. Instead he held out one claw toward Atvar H'sial and moaned, high in his thin throat.

And then he was off, darting straight at the flaming column in the middle of the room.

The humans and the Cecropian were far too slow. Before they could move an inch J'merlia was halfway to the wide pillar of flaring blue-white. Kallik alone was fast enough to follow. She raced after J'merlia and caught up with him just as he came to the column. As he threw himself at its blazing heart she reached out one wiry arm and grabbed a limb. He kept moving into the roaring pillar. Kallik's arm was dragged in with him. There was a flash of violet-blue. And then the Hymenopt had leaped backward fifteen meters. She was hissing in pain and shock. Half of one forelimb had been seared off in that momentary indigo flash.

Rebka was shocked, too. Not with concern for Kallik—he knew the Hymenopt's physical resilience and regeneration power. But for one second, as J'merlia leaped for the bright column, Rebka had thought that the pillar must be part of a Builder transportation system. Now Kallik, nursing her partial limb, banished any such idea. Louis Nenda was already crouched on the ground next to her, helping to cover the cauterized wound with a piece ripped off his own shirt. He was clucking and whistling to Kallik as he worked.

"I shoulda known." He straightened. "I should've realized somethin' was up when we come back an' saw J'merlia talkin' a blue streak. Kallik says he was tellin' her a whole bunch of twists an' turns an' corridors, a route up through the tunnels, an' he wouldn't say where he got it. She figures he must have learned it before, when he was with World-Keeper or even earlier. She says she's all right, she'll be good as new in a few days—but what now? J'merlia said before he killed himself that World-Keeper wouldn't be comin' back here. If that's right, we're on our own. So what do we do?"

It was phrased as a question, but Hans Rebka knew Nenda too well to treat it as one. The Karelian might be a crook, but he was as tough and smart as they came. He knew they had no options. There was nothing down here that humans could eat. If World-Keeper was not coming back, they had to try for the surface.

"You remember everything that J'merlia said to you?" At Kallik's nod, Rebka did not hesitate. "Okay. As soon as you can walk, lead the way. We're going—up."

Kallik raised herself at once onto her remaining seven legs.

"To the surface," Nenda said. He laughed. "Zardalu an' all, eh? Time to get tough."

Hans Rebka nodded. He fell in behind the Hymenopt as she stood up and started for the exit to the great square room with its flaring funeral pyre. Louis Nenda was behind him. Last of all came Atvar H'sial. Her wing cases drooped, and her proboscis was tucked tight into its chin pleat. She did not speak to Hans Rebka—she could not—but he had the conviction that she was, in her own strange way, mourning the passage of J'merlia, her devoted follower and sometime slave.

Going up, perhaps; but it was not obvious. Kallik led them *down,* through rooms connected by massive doors that slid closed behind them and sealed with a *clunk* of finality. Rebka hung back and tried one after Atvar H'sial had scrambled through. He could not budge it. He could not even see the line of the seal. Wherever this route led them, there would be no going back. He hurried after the others. After ten minutes they came to another column of blue plasma, a flow of liquid light that ran vertically away into the darkness. Kallik pointed to it. "We must ride that. Upwards. To its end."

To whose end? Rebka, remembering J'merlia's fate, was hesitant. But he felt no radiated heat from the flaming pillar, and Louis Nenda was already moving forward.

"Git away, Kallik," he muttered. "Somebody else's turn."

He fumbled a pen from his pocket, reached out at arm's length, and extended it carefully to touch the surface of the column. The pen was at once snatched out of his hand. It shot upward, so fast that the eye was not sure what it had seen.

"Lotsa drag," Nenda said. "Don't feel hot, though." This time he touched the blue pillar with his finger, and his whole arm was jerked upward. He pulled his finger back and stuck the tip in his mouth. " 'Sall right. Not hot—just a big tug. I'll tell you one thing, though, it's all or nothin'. No way you're gonna ease yourself into that. You'd get pulled in half."

He turned, but before he could move, Kallik was past him. One leap took her into the heart of the blue pillar, and she was gone. Atvar H'sial followed, her wing cases tight to her body to keep them within the width of the column of light.

Louis Nenda moved forward, but paused on the brink. "How many gravities you think that thing pulls? Acceleration kills as good as fire."

"No idea." Rebka moved to stand next to him. "I guess we're going to find out, though. Or stay here till we die." He gestured to the column, palm up. "After you."

"Yeah. Thanks." And Nenda was gone, swallowed up in a flash of blue.

Rebka took a last look around—was this his last sight of the deep interior of Genizee? his last sight of anything?—and jumped forward. There was a moment of dislocation, too brief and alien to be called pain, and then he was standing on a flat surface. He swayed, struggling to hold his balance. He was in total darkness.

He reached out, groping all around him, and felt nothing.

"Anyone there?"

"We're all here," said Louis Nenda's voice.

"Where's here? Can you see?"

"Not a thing. Black as a politician's heart. But At's echolocation's workin' fine. She says we're outside. On the surface."

As they spoke, Hans Rebka was revising his own first impression. The brilliance of the light column as he entered it had overloaded his retinas, but now they were slowly regaining their sensitivity. He looked straight up and saw the first flicker of light, a faded, shimmering pink and ghostly electric blue.

"Give it a minute," he said to Nenda. "And look up. I'm getting a glimmer from there. If it's the surface, it has to be night. All we'll see is the aurora of the nested singularities."

"Good enough. I'm gettin' it, too. At can't detect that, 'cause it's way outside the atmosphere. But she can see our surroundings. She says don't move, or else step real careful. There's rocks an' rubble an' all that crap, easy to break a leg or three."

Rebka's eyes were still adjusting, but he was seeing about as much as he was likely to see. And it was not enough. The faint glow of the singularities revealed little of the ground at his feet, just sufficient to be sure that there was no sign of the blue pillar that had carried them here. Like the doors, it had closed behind them. There would be no going back. And Rebka felt oddly isolated. Atvar H'sial could see as well by night as by day, and Kallik also had eyes far more sensitive than a human's. Both aliens could sense their environment and talk of it in their own languages to Louis Nenda. The Karelian understood both Cecropian and Hymenopt speech. If they chose, the three of them could leave Rebka out of the conversations completely.

It was ironic. The first time Hans Rebka had seen Nenda's augment for Cecropian speech, he had been revolted by the ugly pits and black molelike nodules on the other man's chest. Now he would not mind having one himself.

"Any sign of Zardalu?" he said.

"At says she can't see 'em. But she can smell 'em. They're somewhere around, not more than a mile or two from here."

"If only we knew where here was."

"At says hold tight. She's climbin' a big rock, takin' a peek all round. Kallik's goin' up behind her."

Rebka strained his eyes into the darkness. No sign of Atvar H'sial or of Kallik, although he could hear the muted click of unpadded claws on hard rock. It added to the soft rustle of wind through dry vegetation and something like a distant, low-pitched murmur, oddly familiar, that came from Rebka's right. Both sounds were obliterated by a sudden grunt from Louis Nenda.

"We made it. At says we're right near where we landed—she can see the green moss an' shoreline, right down to the water."

"The ship?" That was the only real question. Without a ship they would become Zardalu meat and might as well have stayed in Genizee's deep interior. According to J'merlia's original account, he had repaired the seedship and flown it closer to the Zardalu buildings. But then he had become totally vague and random, and everything he had said after that, to the moment of his immolation and suicide, had to be questioned.

"The seedship," Rebka repeated. "Can Atvar H'sial see it?"

"No sign of it."

Rebka's heart sank.

"But the weird thing is," Nenda continued, "she says she can see *another* ship, bigger than the seedship, sittin' in about the same place it was." He added a string of clicks and whistles in the Hymenopt language.

"Zardalu vessel?" Rebka asked.

"Dunno. We don't know what one looks like."

"With respect." It was Kallik, speaking for the first time since they had emerged on the surface. Her soft voice came from somewhere above Hans Rebka's head. "I have also looked, and listened with care to Atvar H'sial's description as it was relayed to me by Master Nenda. The ship resembles one on which I have never flown, but which I had the opportunity to examine closely on our journey to the Anfract."

"What?" That was Louis Nenda. It was nice to know that he did not understand any better than Rebka.

"The configuration is that of the *Indulgence*—Dulcimer's ship. And it is an uncommon design. I would like to suggest a theory, consistent with all the facts. Those of our party left behind on the *Erebus* must have received the message drone describing a safe path through the singularities, and decided to follow us here. They located the seedship by a remote scan of the planetary surface, and sent the *Indulgence* to land near it. But there was no sign of us, and no indication of where we had gone or when we might come back. Therefore they kept one or two individuals on Dulcimer's ship, with its heavy weapons, waiting for our possible return, and the rest returned to space in the unarmed seedship, safe from the Zardalu. If this analysis is correct, one or two members of our party now wait for us in the *Indulgence*. And the *Erebus* itself waits in orbit about Genizee."

Kallik's explanation was neat, logical, and complete. Like most such explanations, it was, in Hans Rebka's view, almost certainly wrong. That was not the way the real world operated.

But at that point theory had little role to play in what they had to do next. That would be decided by facts, and certain facts were undeniable. Day was approaching—the first hint of light was already in the sky. They dared not remain on the surface of Genizee, at least not close to the shoreline, once the sun rose and the Zardalu became active. And the most important fact of all: there was a ship just a few hundred yards away. How it got there, or who was on it, was of much less importance than its existence.

"We can all compare theories—once we're safe in space." Rebka peered around him. He could at last distinguish rock outcrops from lightening sky. In a few more minutes he and Louis Nenda would be able to walk or run without killing themselves. But by that time he wanted to be close to the ship. "I know it will be rough going across the rocks, but we have to try it even while it's still dark. I want Atvar H'sial and Kallik to guide Nenda and me. Tell us where to put our feet—set them down for us if you have to. Remember, we have to be as quiet as we can, so don't take us through any patches of rubble, or places where we might knock stones loose. But we have to get to where the moss and mud begins before it's really light."

The predawn wind was dying, and the sound of waves on the shore had vanished. Hans Rebka moved through an absolute silence, where every tiny clink of a pebble sounded like thunder and a dislodged handful of earth was like an avalanche. He had to remind himself that human ears, at least, would not detect him more than a few feet away.

And finally they were at a point where the amount of noise they made did not matter. The gray-green moss lay level before them, soft and fuzzy against the brightening sky. All that remained was a dash across it to the ship, a couple of hundred yards away.

Rebka turned to the Hymenopt, who, even with one injured leg, was four times as fast as any human. "Kallik, when you reach the hatch, you go right in, leave it open, and ready the ship for takeoff. Don't get into a discussion or an argument with anyone on board—we'll have time for that later. By the time I'm there, I want us ready to lift. All right?" The Hymenopt nodded. "Then *go.*"

Kallik was a dark moving streak against the flat mossy surface, her legs an invisible blur. Atvar H'sial, surprisingly fast for her bulk, was not far behind. The Cecropian covered the ground in a series of long, gliding leaps that took her smoothly up to and inside the hatch. Louis Nenda was third, his stocky body capable of real speed over short distances. Rebka was catching up with him on the final forty meters, but Nenda was through the hatch a couple of yards ahead.

Rebka jumped after him, turned as his foot skidded across the threshold, and slammed the hatch closed. "All in," he shouted. "Kallik, take us up."

He swung around to see what was happening. It had occurred to him, in the final seconds of the dash across the moss, that there was one real possibility that he had refused to consider because it had final and fatal implications. What if the *Indulgence* had somehow been captured by the Zardalu, and they were waiting inside?

Breathe again. There were no signs of Zardalu—the cabin was empty except for the four new arrivals. "Kallik, bring us to a hover at three hundred meters. I want to look for Zardalu."

But the little Hymenopt was pointing at the control display where multiple lights were flashing. "Emergency signal, Captain Rebka. Not for this ship."

Rebka was across to the console in a couple of steps, scanning the panel. "It's the *Erebus*! In synchronous orbit. Take us right up there, Kallik. Graves should have stayed outside the singularities. What sort of trouble is he in now?"

The hover command was aborted, and the rapid ascent began. All eyes were on the display of the dark bulk of the *Erebus*, orbiting high above them. No one took any notice of the downward scope. No one saw the dwarfed image of Darya Lang, capering and screaming on the sunlit surface far below.

CHAPTER 20

DARYA WAS LEARNING the hard way. There was no way of knowing just how much discomfort and fatigue a person could stand, until she had no choicc.

The irritating little black bugs that crawled into her eyes, nose, and ears were nothing. Limbs that cried out with fatigue were nothing. Hunger and thirst were nothing. All that mattered was the disappearance of the *Indulgence,* the only escape from the surface of Genizee.

As the sun rose higher she sat down on a flat stone, filled with despair that changed little by little to annoyance and then at last to rage. Someone—someone of *her own party,* not a Zardalu—had stolen the ship, just a couple of minutes before she and Tally were ready to board it. Now they were hopelessly stranded.

Who could have done it? And finally, with that thought, Darya's head cleared. The answer was obvious: the survivors, whoever they were, of the first group that had flown down to the surface of Genizee. They had arrived on the seedship, but it had not been there when they wanted to leave. With that gone, they must have seen the *Indulgence* as their only way off the surface. But if that was so, once they realized that they had left people behind on Genizee, surely they would return. Hans Rebka would come for her. So would Louis Nenda. She was absolutely sure of it.

The problem—and it was a big one—was to be alive and free when that return took place. And one way that would certainly not work was to remain on the surface. When she peeked over the sheltering line of vegetation between her and the shore she could see the water bubbling with activity. Now and then a great blue head would break the surface. The Zardalu might not like the rocky, broken terrain where she and Tally were hiding as much as they liked the sea and shoreline, but by now they would have realized that the escaped prisoners had taken to the air ducts. It would surely not be more than another hour or two before a systematic examination of the surface vents began.

She rubbed flies from the corners of her eyes and crawled across to where E. C. Tally was sitting in front of a little bush bearing fat yellow leaves.

"E.C., we have to go back. Back into the ducts."

"Indeed? We went to considerable trouble to remove ourselves from them."

"The ship will come back for us"—she told herself she believed that, she *had* to believe it—"but we can't survive on the surface while we wait."

"I am inclined to disagree. May I speak?" Tally raised a bunch of the yellow leaves, each bloated at its extremity to a half-inch wrinkled sphere. "These are not good in taste to a human palate, but they will sustain life. They are high in water content, and they have some food value."

"They might be poisonous."

"But they are not—I already consumed a number." A considerable number, now that Darya's attention had been drawn to it. While she had been sitting and thinking, two or three bushes in the little depression had been denuded of foliage and berries.

"And although I am an embodied computer," Tally went on, "and not a true human, the immune system and toxin reactions of this body are no different from yours. I have suffered no adverse effects, and I am sure you will also feel none."

Logic told Darya that Tally could be quite wrong. He had direct control over elements of his immune system, where she did not, and the body used for his incorporation had been carefully chosen to have as few allergic reactions as possible. But while her mind was telling her that, her hands were grabbing for a branch of the bush and plucking off berries.

Tally was right. Too tart and astringent to be pleasant, but full of water. The juice trickled down her dry throat like nectar when she crunched a berry between her teeth. She did the same to a dozen more before she could force herself to stop and speak again. "I wasn't thinking of food when I said we couldn't stay here. I was thinking of Zardalu."

The embodied computer did not reply, but he raised himself slowly from a sitting position, until he was able to look out toward the shore. "I see nothing. If any are close-by, they are still in the water."

"Do you want to bet on their staying there? The air vent we came up is more than a mile from here and we don't know of a nearer one. If the Zardalu came out of the sea farther along the shore, between us and the vent, it would be all over. We have to get back there."

Tally was already pulling whole branches off the bushes. Darya began to do the same, eating more leaves and berries as she did so. Tally had the right idea. On the surface or under it, the two of them would still need nourishment. There might be bushes closer to the vent, but they could not take the risk. Collection had to be done now, even though it meant an added burden. She broke off branches until she had an armload. She would need the other arm free to help her over rough spots. She nodded to Tally. "Let's go."

The trip to the air-duct exit was surprisingly easy and quick—good light made all the difference over broken ground. And the light was more than good—it was blinding. Darya paused a few times to wipe sweat from her face and neck. Here was another reason why the surface might be intolerable. Genizee close to noon promised to be incredibly hot. She turned and went uphill, far enough to peer uneasily at the shore over the ragged line of plants. The water was calm. No towering forms of midnight blue rose to fill her with terror. Did the Zardalu keep fixed hours, for water and land living? She knew so little about them, or about this planet.

As they came close to the vent Darya noticed what she had not seen in the half-light of dawn: the whole region was covered with low bushes, similar to the ones whose branches they were carrying but with fruit of a slightly lighter shade of yellow. She broke off half-a-dozen more branches and added them to her load, popping berries into her mouth as she did so to quench her increasing thirst. These seemed a little sweeter, a little less inclined to fur her teeth and palate. Maybe the fruit was an acquired taste; or maybe these new berries were a fraction riper.

At the vent itself Darya hesitated. The aperture was dark and uninviting, heading off at a steep angle into the rocky ground. Its only virtue was its narrow width, barely enough for a human and far too small to admit an adult Zardalu. But it represented safety . . . if one were willing to accept an unconventional definition of that word.

"Come on, E.C. No point in hanging around." She led the way, wondering what to do next. They did not want to be too far below ground in case the ship came back. But they also had to reach a certain depth, to be sure that groping Zardalu tentacles could not pull them out.

What they *really* needed—the thought struck her as she took her first steps down—was a vent closer to the place where the *Indulgence* had rested. One of the only sure things in this whole mess was that anyone who came back for her would try to land at the same point where they had taken off.

"E.C., do you remember all the turns and twists we made on the way up?"

"Of course."

"Then I want you to review the last few branch points

before we came out on the surface, and see if any of the alternative paths that we didn't take might lead to an exit duct closer to where the *Indulgence* lay."

"I did that long ago. If the directions of the ducts at those branch points were to continue as we saw them, then a duct at an intersection before the final one would run to the surface about a hundred yards inland from where we watched the *Indulgence* take off. A little more than a mile from here."

Darya swore to herself. People could say what they liked about how smart embodied computers were, but something fundamental was missing. E. C. Tally must have had that information hours before; it had not occurred to him that it was important enough to pass on at once to Darya.

Well, use the resources you have. Don't waste time pining for ones denied to you. That was one of Hans Rebka's prime rules. And E. C. Tally's memory was, so far as Darya could tell, infallible. "Lead the way back to that intersection. Let's see where it takes us."

Tally nodded and went forward without a word. Darya followed, one arm full of laden branches, eating from them as they walked. The descent was far easier than their ascent. At this time of day the sun's rays lay close to the line of the entrance, so that the glassy walls of the tunnel served as a light trap, funneling sunlight deep below ground. Even a couple of hundred feet down, there was ample light to see by.

That was when they came to the first complication.

Tally paused and turned. "May I speak?"

But he did not need to. Darya saw the problem at once. The tunnel widened at that point to a substantial chamber, with one downward and three upward exits. Each would admit a human. But one of those upward corridors was more than wide enough for an adult Zardalu. If they went beyond this point and found no other exit, their one road back to the surface could be blocked.

"I think we have to take the risk," Darya started to say. And then the second complication arrived. She felt a spasm across her middle, as though someone had taken her intestines and pulled them into a tight, stretching knot. She gasped. Her legs would not support her weight, and she slid forward to sit down suddenly and hard on the chamber floor.

"Tally!" she said, and then could not get out another word. A second cramp, harder than the first, twisted her innards. Sweat burst out onto her forehead. She hung her head forward and panted, widemouthed.

E. C. Tally came to her side and lifted her head. He raised her eyelid with his finger, then moved her lips back to peer at her gums.

"Tally," she said again. It was the only sound she could make. The spasms inside her were great tidal waves of pain. As each one receded, it washed away more of her strength.

"Unfortunate," Tally said quietly. She struggled to focus her eyes and see what he was doing. The embodied computer had picked up a branch of the bush that she had dropped and was examining it closely. "It is *almost* the same as the first one, but almost certainly a different species." He squeezed a pale yellow berry in his fingers and touched it carefully to his tongue. After a moment he nodded. "I think so. Similar, but also different. A medium-strength emetic in this, plus an unfamiliar alkaloid. I do not believe that this is a fatal poison, but it would, I think, be a good idea if you were to vomit. Do you have any way of inducing yourself to do so?"

Darya was half-a-second ahead of him. Every berry that she had eaten came out in one awful, clenching spasm of her stomach and esophagus. And then, although the leaves and berries were surely all gone, her stomach did not know when to quit. She was racked by a continuing sequence of painful dry heaves, doubly unpleasant because there was nothing inside her for them to work on. She supported herself on the chamber floor with both hands and sat hunched in utter misery. Being so sick was bad enough. Being so *stupid* was even worse.

"May I speak?"

It was a few seconds before she could even nod, head down.

"You should not seek to continue at this time, even if you feel able to do so. And it is surely unnecessary. You can wait here, and I will proceed to explore the tunnel system. Upon my return, we can decide on the next best course of action. Do you agree?"

Darya was trying to throw up what was not there. She made another series of dreadful sounds, then produced a minuscule up-and-down motion of her head.

"Very good. And in case you become thirsty again while I am gone, I will leave these with you."

Tally placed the fronds of leaves and berries that he had carried down the tunnel on the floor beside Darya. She gave them a look of hatred. She would not bite one more of those berries to save her life. And it needed saving. As Tally went away across the wide chamber, she fought off another agonizing fit of retching.

She lay forward with her head on the cool glassy floor of the chamber, closed her eyes, and waited. If the Zardalu came along and caught her, that was just too bad. The way she was feeling, if she was killed now it would be a pleasant release.

And it was all her own fault, a consequence of her sheltered upbringing on the safe garden planet of Sentinel Gate. No one else on the whole expedition would have been stupid enough to eat—to *guzzle*—untested foods.

And no one else on the expedition would give up so easily. To come so far, and then to stop trying. It would not do. If somehow she survived this, she would never be able to look Hans Rebka in the eye again. Darya sighed and lifted her face away from the floor, straightening her arms to support her. She made a supreme effort and forced herself to crawl forward on hands and knees, until she was out of the chamber and ten yards into the narrowest of the ducts. Then she had to stop. The clenching agony in her stomach was fading, but her feet felt cold and her hands and forehead were damp and clammy.

She lay down again, on her back this time, chafed her cold hands together, and tucked them into her long sleeves. Before she knew it she was drifting away into a strange half-trance. She realized what was happening, but she could do nothing to prevent it. The alkaloid in the berries must have mild narcotic effects. Well, good for it. Maybe what she needed was a good shot of reality-suppressant.

Her mind, released from physical miseries, triggered and homed in on the single fact of the past forty-eight hours that most deeply disturbed her.

Not the capture by the Zardalu. Not the uncertain fate of Dulcimer. Not even the ascent of the *Indulgence,* when she and Tally had seemed so close to safety.

The big upset had been *the vanishing of J'merlia.* Everything else might be a misfortune, but to someone with Darya's scientific training and outlook, J'merlia's disappearance into air was a *disaster* and a flat impossibility. It upset her whole worldview. It was inexplicable in any rational way, inconsistent with any model of physical reality that she had ever encountered. The Torvil Anfract was a strange place, she knew that. But how strange? Even if the whole Anfract was a Builder artifact, as she was now convinced it must be, the only differences had to be in the local space-time anomalies. Surely the laws of physics here could be no different from those in the rest of the universe?

Darya drifted away into an uneasy half sleep. Her worries somehow reached beyond logic. E. C. Tally, totally logical, had seen J'merlia vanish, too, but the embodied computer did not seem to be affected by it as Darya was affected. All *he* knew was what was in his data bases. He accepted that there might be almost anything outside them. What Tally did not have—Darya struggled to force her tired brain to frame the concept—what he did not have were *expectations* about the behavior of the universe. Only organic intelligences had expectations. Just as only organic intelligences dreamed. If only she could make this *all* into a dream.

But she could not. This floor was too damned hard. Darya returned to wakefulness, sat up with a groan, and stared around her. The tunnel had grown much darker. She looked at her watch, wondering if somehow she had been unconscious for many hours. She found that only thirty minutes had passed. She crawled back to the main chamber and found that it, too, was darker. The sun had moved in the sky. Not very much, but now its rays no longer struck straight down the line of the tunnel that they had entered. It would become darker yet, as the day wore on.

Darya was within a few feet of the leaves and fruit that Tally had left behind. She had sworn never to touch another, but her thirst was so great and the taste in her mouth so sour and dreadful that she pulled a few berries and squeezed them between her teeth.

These were the right ones—they had that true bitter and horrible taste. But she was so thirsty that the juice felt as though it were being directly absorbed on the path down her throat. Her stomach insisted that it had not received anything.

She reached out to pull another handful. At that moment she heard a new sound from the wide corridor on the other side of the chamber.

It might be E. C. Tally, returning along a different path. But it was a softer, more diffuse sound than the ring of shoes on hard, glassy floor.

Darya slipped off her own shoes and quietly retreated to the narrow tunnel that she knew led back to the surface. Twenty yards along it she halted and peered back into the gloom. Her line of sight included only a small part of the chamber, but that would be enough for at least a snapshot of anything that crossed the room.

There was a soft swishing of leathery, grease-coated limbs. And then a dark torso, surrounded by a corset of lighter webbing, was gliding across the chamber. Another followed, and then another. As Darya watched and counted, at least a dozen mature Zardalu passed across her field of view. She heard the clicks and whistles of their speech. And then they were circling, moving around the room and talking to each other continuously. They must be seeing the unmistakable signs of Darya's presence—the leaves and berries, and the place where she had thrown up so painfully. For the first time since she and Tally had escaped, the Zardalu had been provided with a fix on their most recent location.

She counted carefully. It looked like fifteen of them, when one would be enough to handle two humans. If E. C. Tally chose to return at that moment . . .

She could do nothing to help him, nothing to warn him. If she called out it would announce her own location. The Zardalu must know enough about the air ducts to realize where she would emerge on the surface.

Five minutes. Ten. The Zardalu had settled into silence. The chance that Tally might return and find himself in their midst was increasing.

Darya was thinking of easing closer to the room, so that if she saw him coming she could at least shout a warning and take her chances on beating the Zardalu in the race back to the surface, when the whistles and clicks began again. There was a flurry of moving shapes.

She took four cautious steps forward. The Zardalu were leaving. She counted as they moved across the part of the room that she could see. Fifteen. All of them, unless she had made a mistake in their numbers when first they entered. To a human eye, one mature Zardalu was just like another, distinguished only by size and the subtle patterns on their corsets of webbing.

They were gone. Darya waited, until the room was once more totally silent. She crept back along the three-foot pipe of the air duct. Tally had to be warned, somehow. The only way she could do it was to assume that he would return along the same path by which he had left, and station herself in that duct. And if for some reason he favored a different return route, that would be just too bad.

The big room was filled with the faint ammoniac scent of the Zardalu. It reminded her of Louis Nenda's comment: "If you can smell them, bet that they can smell you." Her own recent misfortunes had swept the fate of the other party right out of her thoughts. Now she wondered who had escaped in the *Indulgence.* Who was alive, and who was dead? Were others, like her, still running like trapped rats through the service facilities of Genizee?

Out on the planetary surface, the long day must be wearing on. The sun would be approaching zenith, farther from the line of the air ducts. It was darker in the room than when she had left. She could barely distinguish the apertures of the ducting, over at the other side. She tiptoed across to the widest of them, peering along it for any sign of the Zardalu and ready to turn and flee.

Nothing. The corridor ran off, dark and silent, as far as she could see. She felt sure they would be back—they knew she had been here.

She moved on, heading for the third corridor, the right-hand one, which Tally had taken when he left. The second corridor, according to him, angled away in the wrong direction. If it led to the surface at all it would be farther from the place where the *Indulgence* had rested.

Darya hardly glanced at the round opening as she passed it. Any adult Zardalu would find it hard to squeeze more than a few feet along that narrowing tunnel.

She took one more step. In that same moment there was a rush of air from her left. She did not have time to turn her head. From the corner of her eye she saw a blur of motion. And then she was seized from behind, lifted, and pulled close to a body whose powerful muscles flexed beneath rubbery skin.

Darya gasped, convulsed, and tried to twist free. At the same moment she kicked at her captor's body, regretting that she had taken off her hard and heavy shoes.

There was a rewarding grunt of pain. It was followed by a creaking moan of surprise and complaint. Darya was suddenly dropped to the ground.

She stared up. Even as she realized that those were not tentacles that had held her, she recognized the voice.

"Dulcimer!"

The Chism Polypheme was crouching down next to her, all of his five little arms waving agitatedly in the air.

"Professor Lang. Save me!" He was shivering and weeping, and Darya felt teardrops the size of marbles falling onto her from his master eye. "I've run and run, but still they come after me. I'm exhausted. I've shouted to them and pleaded with them, promising I'll be the best and most loyal slave they ever had—and they won't listen!"

"You were wasting your time. They don't understand human speech."

"I know. But I thought I had nothing to lose by trying. Professor Lang, they want to *eat* me, I know they do. Please save me."

A tall order, when she could not save herself. Darya groped around on the floor until she found her shoes and put them on. She patted Dulcimer on his muscular body. "We'll be all right. I know a safe way to the surface. I realize that the Zardalu could be back here anytime, but we can't go yet. We have to wait for E. C. Tally."

"No, we don't. Leave him. He'll manage just fine on his own." Dulcimer was tugging at her, urging her to stand up. "He will. He doesn't need us. Let's get out of here before they come back."

"No. You go anywhere you like. But I stay here, and I wait." Darya did not like to be in the chamber any more than the Polypheme; but she was not about to abandon Tally.

Dulcimer produced a low, shivering moan. He made no attempt to leave and finally crouched back on the floor, tightly spiraled. Darya could not see his color in the dim light, but she was willing to bet that it was the dark cucumber green of a fully sober and nervous Polypheme.

"It will only be a little while," she said, in her most confident tone, and forced herself to remain seated calmly on the floor. Dulcimer hesitated, then moved close to her.

Darya took a deep breath and actually felt some of her nervousness evaporate. It helped to be forced to set a good example.

But it helped less and less as the minutes wore on. Where the blazes was Tally? He had had time to go to the surface and back three or four times. Unless *he* had been captured.

Dulcimer was becoming more restless. He was turning his head, peering around the room. "I can hear something!"

Darya stopped breathing for twenty seconds and listened. All she heard was her own heartbeat. "It's your imagination."

"No. It's coming from there." He pointed his upper two arms in different directions, one at the duct that Darya and Tally had used to reach the surface, the other at the narrow opening from which he himself had emerged.

"Which one?"

"Both."

Now Darya was convinced that it was Dulcimer's imagination. She would barely be able to squeeze into that second gap herself. He had gone across to peer into it, and his head was a pretty tight fit.

"That's impossible," Darya started to say. But then *she* could hear a sound herself—a clean, clear sound of hurrying footsteps, coming from the duct that Tally had left through. She recognized that sound.

"It's all right," she said. "It's E. C. Tally. At last! Now we can—thank heaven—get out of here."

"And I know a better way," Tally said. He had emerged crouching from the air duct just in time to catch Darya's final words, and now he was staring at the corkscrew tail of the Chism Polypheme, sticking out of the round opening to the other tube. "Why, you found him. That was very clever of you, Professor. Hello, Dulcimer."

The Polypheme was wriggling back out of the duct, but he took no notice of E. C. Tally. He was groaning and shaking worse than ever.

"I knew it," he said. "I just knew it. They're coming. I *told* you they were coming. Lots of them. Hundreds of them."

"But they *can't* be," Darya protested. "Look how small that duct is. You'd never get a great big Zardalu—"

"Not the *adults.*" Dulcimer's eye was rolling wildly in his head, and his blubbery mouth was grinning in terror. "*Worse* than that. The little ones, the Eaters, everything from tiny babies to half-grown. Small enough to go anywhere we can go. Those ducts are full of them. I saw them before, as I was running, and they're hungry all the time. They don't want slaves, they won't make deals. All they want is *food.* They want meat. They want *me.*"

CHAPTER 21

HANS REBKA GLARED at the image of the *Erebus* in the forward display screens. The appearance of the ship suggested a derelict hulk, abandoned for millennia. The vast hull was pitted by impact with interstellar dust grains. Observation ports, their transparent walls scuffed by the same microsand, bulged from the ship's sides like rheumy old eyes fogged by cataracts.

And for all the response to Rebka's signals, the *Erebus* might as well be dead! He had fired off a dozen urgent inquiries as the *Indulgence* rose to orbital rendezvous. Why was there an emergency distress signal? What was the nature of the problem? Was it safe for the *Indulgence* to dock and enter the cargo hold? No reply. The ship above them drifted alone in space like a great dead beast, silent and unresponsive to any stimulus.

"Take us in." Rebka hated to go into anything blind, but there was no choice.

Kallik nodded, and her paws skipped across the controls too fast to see. The rendezvous maneuver of scoutship and *Erebus* was executed at record speed and far more smoothly than Rebka could have done it himself. Within minutes they were at the entrance of the subsidiary cargo hold.

"Hold us there." As the *Indulgence* hovered stationary with respect to the other ship and the pumps filled the hold with air, Rebka scanned the screens. Still nothing. No sign of danger—but also no one awaiting their return and warping them into the dock. That was odd. Whatever had happened, the *Erebus,* everyone's way home, should not have been left deserted.

He turned to order the hatch opened, but others were ahead of him. Nenda and Atvar H'sial had given the command as soon as pressures equalized, and already they were floating out toward the corridor that led to the control room of the *Erebus.* Rebka followed, leaving Kallik to turn the scoutship in case they had to make a rapid departure.

The first corridors were deserted, but that meant nothing. The inside of the *Erebus* was so big that even with a thousand people on board it could appear empty. The key question was the state of the control room. That was the nerve center of the ship. It should always have someone on duty.

And in a manner of speaking it did. Louis Nenda and Atvar H'sial had hurried far ahead of Rebka. When he arrived at the control room he found them at the main console, leaning over the crouched figure of Julian Graves. The councilor was hunched far down with the palms of his hands covering his eyes. His long, skinny fingers reached up over his bulging forehead. Rebka assumed that Graves was unconscious, but then he realized that Louis Nenda was speaking softly to him. As Rebka approached, Graves slowly withdrew his hands and crossed them on his chest. The face revealed was in constant movement. The expression changed moment to moment from thought to fear to worry.

"We'll take care of you," Nenda was saying. "Just relax an' try an' tell me what's wrong. What happened?"

Julian Graves showed a flash of a smile, then his mouth opened. "I don't know. I—we—can't think. Too much to think."

His mouth snapped closed with a click of teeth. The head turned away, to gaze vaguely around the room.

"Too much what?" Nenda moved so that Graves could not avoid looking at him.

The misty gray eyes rolled. "Too much—too much *me.*"

Nenda stared at Hans Rebka. "That's what he said before. 'Too much me.' D'you know what he's gettin' at?"

"No idea. But I can see why the distress signal is going out. If he's on duty, he's certainly not able to control the ship. Look at him."

Graves had returned to his crouched position and was muttering to himself. "Go lower, survey landing site. No, must remain high, safe there. No, return through singularities, wait *there.* No, must leave Anfract." With every broken sentence his facial expressions changed, writhing from decision to uncertainty to mind-blanking worry.

Rebka had a sudden insight. Graves was torn by diverging thoughts—exactly as though the integration of Julius Graves and his interior mnemonic twin Steven to form the single personality of Julian Graves had failed. The old conflict of the two consciousnesses in one brain had returned.

But that idea was soon overwhelmed in Rebka's own mind by another and more pressing concern.

"Why is he on duty alone? It must be obvious to the others that he's not fit to make decisions." He bent over, took Julian Graves's head between his hands, and turned it so that he could stare right into the councilor's eyes. "Councilor Graves, listen to me. I have a very important question. *Where are the others?*"

"Others." Graves muttered the word. His eyes flickered and his lips trembled. He nodded. He understood, Rebka was sure he did, but he seemed unable to force an answer.

"The others," Rebka repeated. "Who else is on board the *Erebus*?"

Graves began to twitch, while the tendons stood out in his thin neck. He was gathering himself for some supreme effort. His lips pressed tightly together and then opened with a gasp.

"The only other—on board the *Erebus* is—is J'merlia."

Rebka, tensed to receive a disturbing answer, released

Graves's head and grunted in disappointment. Graves did not know it, but he had given the one reply that proved he was no longer rational. J'merlia was dead. Rebka had seen him die with his own eyes. Of all the people who had entered the Anfract, J'merlia was the only one who absolutely could not be on board the *Erebus.*

"That does it." Rebka moved to stand at Graves's side. "Poor devil. Let's get him where he can rest and give him a sedative. He needs medical help, but the only people who can give it are the ones who installed the interior mnemonic twin. They're back on Miranda, a thousand light-years away. I don't know what treatment to give him. As for the others on board, when I find 'em I'll skin them all. There's no way they should have left him here alone—even if he was nominally in command."

Rebka moved to one side of Graves and gestured to Louis Nenda to take the man's other arm. The councilor glanced from one to the other in bewilderment as they lifted him. He offered no resistance, but he could not have walked without them. His muscles had plenty of strength, but his legs did not seem to know in which direction they were supposed to move. Rebka and Nenda eased out of the door. Atvar H'sial stayed in the control room—first rule of space, *never* leave the ship's bridge with no one in charge.

They took Graves to the sick bay, where Rebka placed him under medium-level sedation—he already seemed only half-conscious—and swathed him in protective webbing.

"Won't help him much, but at least he can't get into trouble here," Rebka said. He tied the straps in a complex pattern. "And if he's together enough to figure out these knots, then he's thinking a whole lot better than he was when we brought him here."

The two men started back toward the bridge. They were at the final branch of the corridor when they heard the click of Kallik's steps from the other direction.

"Did you turn the *Indulgence*?" Rebka asked without looking at the Hymenopt. Instead of a reply in human speech, Kallik produced a high-pitched whistle and an unintelligible burst of Hymenopt clicks. Louis Nenda at once jumped to Kallik's side. He picked up the little Hymenopt and shook her.

"What are you up to?" Rebka backed away. One just did not *do* that to a Hymenopt! Anyone but Louis Nenda who tried it on Kallik would face rapid death. Kallik's short black fur—the hymantel, so prized by unwise bounty hunters—was bristling, and the yellow sting had involuntarily slipped out a couple of inches from the lower end of the stubby abdomen.

Nenda was unworried. "Hafta do it. She's in shock, see. Gotta bring her out of it." He banged the Hymenopt hard on top of her smooth round head with his clenched fist and unleashed a burst of clucking whistles. "I'm tellin' her to speak human—that oughta help. She don't know how to moan an' groan in that. Come on, Kallik, tell me. Whatsamatter?"

"I turned the s-sh-ship." Kallik spoke, but slowly and badly. She had regressed, back to the time when human speech had been new to her.

"Yeah. Then what?"

"I left the c-cargo hold. I began to move along the corridor. And then—then—"

"Get on with it!"

"Then—" The sting had retracted, but now the little body was shaking in Nenda's arms. "Then I saw *J'merlia.* S-standing in front of me. In the corridor that led to the control room."

"Kallik, you know that can't be. J'merlia's dead—you saw it happen." But Louis Nenda's eyes told a different story. He and Rebka exchanged looks. Impossible? Maybe. But from two quite independent sources?

"It was J'merlia. There could be no mistake. It was his voice, as well as his appearance." Kallik was steadying. She was a supremely logical being, and any offense to logic was especially troubling to her. But the explanation in human speech was restoring her natural modes of thought. "He was about twenty meters away from me, farther along this same corridor. He called out my name, and then he spoke to me. He told me that I must go at once to the control room, that Julian Graves was in need of help." Kallik paused and stared at Rebka. "That is true, isn't it? And then, while I was looking straight at J'merlia . . ."

She stopped speaking. Every eye in her whole black circle of eyes dimmed and seemed to go out of focus at once. Nenda banged her down hard on the floor.

"Don't you go brain-dead on me again. Spit it out, Kallik. Right now, or I'll scatter your guts all round the room."

Kallik shook her head. "I will say it, Master Nenda, as you command. But it is not possible. While I was staring at him, J'merlia vanished. He did not move, for I am faster than he and I would have seen and tracked any movement that he could make. I did not lose consciousness, either, not even for a moment, which was my first thought, because I was in midair, jumping toward him when he vanished. It could not be some trick of reflection, or some peculiar optical effect, because less than a second after he disappeared I stood in the spot where he had stood, and felt the difference in temperature of the floor where his legs had rested." Kallik slumped down, all her own legs wide. "It was truly he. My friend J'merlia."

Rebka and Nenda stared at each other.

"She's not lying, you know," Nenda muttered. He was talking more to himself than to Hans Rebka.

"I know. That's what I was afraid of. It would be a lot easier if she were." Rebka forced himself away from snarling impossibilities and back to things he knew how to handle. "You realize that's exactly what *he* said." He jerked his thumb back toward the sick bay where Julian Graves lay. "According to him, J'merlia was the only one with him on the *Erebus.*"

"Yeah. But we don't have to believe that. We can *check* who's here. At can sniff the central air supply, an' if there's anybody else on the ship she'll get a trace of 'em. Hold on a minute." Nenda hurried off, back toward the control room.

Neither man needed to spell out the rest: If no one but Graves and J'merlia had been on the ship, then where were Darya and the others? Almost certainly, on Genizee. Which meant that the ascent of the *Indulgence* had stranded them there.

Hans Rebka did not wait for Nenda's return. "Bring Master Nenda to the *Indulgence* as soon as he gets back from the control room," he said. He did not *ask* Kallik, who was still splayed on the floor—he *commanded* her. He hated to treat her as a slave, when he had argued so strongly that she was not; but this was a time, if ever, when the ends justified the means. The Hymenopt simply nodded obedience, and Rebka went hurrying back to the scoutship.

Kallik had done her job in the cargo hold. The *Indulgence* was waiting, power recharged and command sequences set, ready to return to space. Rebka went to the open hatch. He itched to fly straight out of the hold and back to the surface of Genizee, but first he had to be sure of the situation on board the *Erebus.*

When Louis Nenda returned he was not alone. Atvar H'sial was right behind him, gliding through the corridors in twenty-meter leaps.

"No worries," Nenda said, in answer to Rebka's unasked question. "Kallik's keeping an eye out on the bridge. She's actin' up some ways, but she'll be okay for a couple of minutes."

"What does Atvar H'sial say?"

"Agrees with Julian Graves, and with Kallik. Not a sniff of anyone else on board—*'cept* for J'merlia. An' that one's fading, At says, like he was here an' then just left. Downright spooky. If I were the worryin' kind, that'd be heavy on my mind." Nenda had moved past Rebka through the open hatch of the *Indulgence,* and was examining the controls. "You ready, then?"

"Ready?"

"Ready to head back down to Genizee."

"I am. But you're not going."

"You wanna bet on it? I'm goin', or you got a big fight on your hands."

Rebka opened his mouth to protest and then changed his mind. If Nenda wanted danger, why stop him? He was a liar and a self-serving crook, but he was also an extra brain and an extra pair of hands—and he was a proven survivor. "Fine. Get in, and hurry up. We're going now."

But the Karelian human was glancing over his shoulder to the hulking figure of Atvar H'sial, poised behind Hans Rebka at the hatch. "Uh-oh. Get set for takeoff, Captain, but before we go I gotta have a quick word with At there an' tell her what's what."

"Louis Nenda." The Cecropian's pheromonal message was strong as he approached her, the overtones full of suspicion and possible reproach. "I can read you clearly. We are safe in space, but you propose to return to the planet Genizee. Explain your actions . . . or lose a partner."

"*Explain.* There's nothin' *needs* explainin'." Nenda came close to the Cecropian and crouched under her dark-red body case. "Be reasonable, At. Rebka's goin', you see that, whether I do or not. We know there's all sorts of goodies down there, an' we know he's too dumb to take 'em even if he gets the chance. *Somebody* has to go with him, see what can be had."

"Then I will go, too."

"You wanna leave Kallik an' Graves in charge, without two ounces of sense between 'em? Somebody has to stay here an' keep things rollin' smooth."

"Then you can stay. I will go, in your place."

"Don't be crazy. You and Rebka can't say one word that the other understands. I *hafta* go."

"It is the human female, Darya Lang. You seek to succor her."

"Succor! No *way.* I don't know the meaning of the word. At, you're gettin' a real obsession about that woman."

"One of us surely is."

"Well, it ain't me." Nenda bobbed out from beneath the

carapace and started into the hatch. "At, you just gotta trust me."

The Cecropian moved slowly out of the way. "I see little choice. However, I have conditions. We have waited too long, and deviated far from our original objectives. I want a promise from you, Louis Nenda, here and now: that if I remain we will, as soon as possible after your return from Genizee, take possession of this ship for our own use. A safe path out of the Torvil Anfract is easy, according to Dulcimer—it is only the entry that is difficult and perilous. So you and I will leave the *Erebus* in this ship and return to Glister, where we will find your own ship, the *Have-It-All*. We have procrastinated long enough."

"Hey, I miss the *Have-It-All* as much as you do—more. You got a deal. Soon as I get back, we go."

"Just the two of us."

"Who else? Sure, just the two of us. Go pack your bags. I gotta be on my way, Rebka's all ready an' waitin'." He cut off pheromonal transmission to show that the conversation was over, and hurried back inside the *Indulgence*.

Hans Rebka was indeed waiting—but not for Louis Nenda. He was sitting at the controls and reentering an initializing sequence. His face showed total frustration. Nenda dropped into the seat next to him.

"What's the holdup? Let's get outa here."

"I'd love to. If *that* would let me." Rebka nodded to one of the displays. "I'm trying to open the connecting door to the outer hold. But the command set is being ignored."

"It shows the outer door won't cycle. That means the lock's in use."

"I know what it means—but that lock was *empty* when we came in through it." Rebka was switching to a camera that should provide a view of the lock area. "So how could it be in use now?"

Louis Nenda did not need to attempt an answer. While they watched, the air-pump sequence had ended. The outer lock now possessed a balancing atmosphere with the inner hold, and the door between the chambers could at last slide open. Both men stared at the scene shown on the displays.

"It's the *seedship,*" Nenda said. "How come it's arrivin' here now? Where's it been all this time?" Before Hans Rebka could do anything to stop him Nenda ran back to the hatch, flipped it open, and within a second was free-falling through the open interlock door toward the smaller vessel.

Rebka followed at a slower pace. He could fill in a line of logic, and it made almost complete sense. He and his party had gone to Genizee on the seedship, but on their return to their landing place it was not there. They had been forced to return on the *Indulgence.* Darya Lang's party had gone to Genizee on the *Indulgence,* but it had gone when they needed it. So they must have managed to locate the missing seedship on Genizee's surface, and were now returning in it.

Almost complete sense. The mystery component was again J'merlia. He had vanished into a column of incandescent blue plasma on Genizee, and reappeared on the *Erebus.* But how had he come here, if not on the seedship?

Louis Nenda was already over at the ship, cycling the lock. As soon as it was half-open he was squeezing through. Rebka followed, surprised at his own sense of foreboding.

"Darya?" he said, as he emerged from the lock. If she was not there . . . But Louis Nenda was turning to him, and one glance at his face said that he did not have the news that Hans Rebka wanted to hear.

"Not Darya," Nenda said. "Only one person on board. I hope you got an explanation, Captain, because I know I don't. Take a peek."

He moved to one side, so that Hans Rebka could see the seedship pilot's seat. Lolling there, breathing but unconscious, was the angular stick-thin figure of J'merlia.

CHAPTER 22

HANS REBKA COULD find no trace of a wound on J'merlia's body. He had watched the Lo'tfian fling himself into that roaring pillar of plasma so hot that it had instantly seared off the pursuing Kallik's leg. Now that wiry limb was just beginning to grow back, but on J'merlia's whole body there was no slightest trace of burn marks.

Rebka and Louis Nenda carried J'merlia back to the bridge of the *Erebus.* There Atvar H'sial was able to perform an ultrasonic scan of the unconscious Lo'tfian's body and confirm that his internal condition was apparently as intact as his exterior appearance. "And the brain seems to be no more damaged than the body," the Cecropian said to Nenda. "The source of his unconsciousness remains a mystery. One suspects that it arises more from psychological than physical causes. Let me pursue that approach."

She crouched by J'merlia and began to send powerful arousal stimuli to him in the form of pheromonal emissions. Rebka, to whom Atvar H'sial's message was nothing but a complicated sequence of odd and pungent odors, looked on for only a minute or two before he lost patience.

"She can do that all she wants to," he said to Louis Nenda, "but I'm not going to sit and sample the stinks. I've got to get down to the surface of Genizee. You come or stay, it's all one to me."

Nenda glared at him, but he did not hesitate. When Rebka headed back to the *Indulgence,* Nenda was hurrying at his side. "I'll tell you another thing," he said, as they prepared to soar free of the *Erebus* for the first phase of descent from orbit. "J'merlia may not want to wake up, but At says he *feels* better to her than he did last time she saw him. She says he's all there now."

"What does that mean?" Rebka was aiming the scoutship for exactly the same spot on Genizee's surface from which they had taken off, and only half his attention was on Louis Nenda. It was not just a question of navigation. At any moment he was half-expecting a saffron beam of light to spear out of the sky and carry them willy-nilly to some random place on the surface of Genizee. It had not happened so far, but they had a way to go before touchdown. He was losing height as fast as he dared.

"Beats me." Nenda could not hide his frustration. "I tried to get her to tell me what she meant, an' she said you don't *explain* things like that. If you don't feel the difference in J'merlia, she says, you won't know what she means even if she tells you." He rubbed his pitted and noduled chest. "She comes up with that, after all I went through gettin' this augment put in just so I could gab Cecropian!"

The *Indulgence* was finally at two thousand meters and still descending fast. Already the screens revealed the familiar curve of the shoreline, with the spit of land to the north jutting out into blue water. Inland, the dark scars in a carpet of gray-green moss showed Hans Rebka just where the seedship and Dulcimer's scoutship had landed. Those scars looked subtly different from when he had left. But how? He could not say. At seven hundred meters he took complete manual control and brought them in to hover over their previous landing site.

"See anything?" His own eyes moved to the cluster of buildings where their party had first been trapped. Nothing had changed there. No sign of disturbance in the calm waters. It was Louis Nenda, scanning the broken masses of rock and scrubby vegetation a couple of hundred yards farther inland, who grunted and pointed.

"There. Zardalu. Can't see what they're doin' from here."

There were scores of them, clustered in a circular pattern around a dark chasm in the surface. They were in constant motion. Rebka flew the *Indulgence* across to hover directly overhead, where the downward display screens under high magnification showed upward-turning heads of midnight blue and staring cerulean eyes.

"Full-size adults, most of that lot." Nenda moved to the *Indulgence*'s weapons console. "Let's give 'em somethin' to think about."

"Careful!" Rebka warned. "We don't know who else is down there in the middle of them."

"No worries. I'll just tickle 'em a bit." But Nenda selected a radiation frequency and intensity that would fatally burn a human in ten seconds. He projected it downward, choosing the spread so that it covered the whole group below them. There was an instant reaction. Zardalu jerked and jumped in pain, then fled in flurries of pale-blue tentacles across the shore, heading for the safety of the water.

Nenda followed them with the radiation weapon, pouring it onto the stragglers. "Don't die easy, do they?" he commented thoughtfully. He was burning them with a higher-intensity beam, yet every Zardalu managed to reach the water and swim strongly before plunging under. "Tough beggars, they eat up hard radiation. They'd be right at home with Dulcimer in the Sun Bar on Bridle Gap. Or maybe not. I guess they can take it, but they sure don't seem to like it."

The last Zardalu had vanished underwater. Hans Rebka hesitated. The easy piece was over, but what now? Was it safe to land the *Indulgence,* even with its sophisticated weapons system? He had learned the hard way an old Phemus Circle lesson: It's a poor civilization that can't learn to defend against *its own* weapons. The trouble starts when you have to defend against *somebody else's.*

The Zardalu Communion had at one time extended over

a thousand worlds. They could not have maintained their dominion without *something* to help them.

He brought the *Indulgence* to a hover thirty meters up, exactly above the scar in the moss left earlier by its mass. When all continued quiet, he cautiously lowered the ship to the surface. If Darya and any other survivors of her party were trying to escape from the surface of Genizee, there was no more logical place for them to seek. And if there were no survivors . . .

That was a thought that Hans Rebka did not care to pursue.

"Steady. Somethin's going on." Nenda's gruff voice interrupted his thoughts.

"What?"

"Dunno. But don't you *feel* it? In the ship?"

And Hans Rebka did. A minor tremor of the planetary surface, changing angles slightly and sometimes imparting a faint jitter to delicately balanced items of the ship's interior. Rebka instinctively lifted the ship to hover a couple of feet clear of the mossy ground cover, but further action on his part was overwhelmed by another input.

He had been watching the screens that displayed the seaward view, but now and again he switched his attention to one showing the land side. What he saw there filled him with strong and unfamiliar emotions.

It took a second to recognize them. They were relief and *joy*.

Running—staggering—across the uneven surface came Darya Lang. Right behind her was E. C. Tally, moving with the gait of a drunken sailor. And behind him, bounding along with a horde of dwarfed and apricot-colored young Zardalu snapping at his corkscrew tail, came a miserable, cucumber-green Dulcimer.

At the rate Darya and the others were moving they would be at the scoutship in less than thirty seconds. That was wonderful, but Rebka had two problems. The Zardalu were gaining—fast. They might catch Darya and the other two before they reached the safety of the ship.

And the shuddering of the *Indulgence* was growing. Accurate aiming of the weapons system to pick off the Zardalu was impossible.

Lift to safety, with Darya and the others just seconds away? Or wait for them, and risk the ship?

Hans Rebka placed his finger on the ascent control. Thirty yards to go, maybe ten seconds before they were inside the open hatch.

The ship lurched. He stopped breathing.

Those high-pitched, excited squeaks were the thing that had changed the Eaters from awful concept to Darya's worst reality.

The voices of the baby and adolescent Zardalu were quite different from the clicks and whistles of the parents. They had come echoing along the tunnel behind Dulcimer, rapidly increasing in volume. With those in her ears, decision-making had moved from difficult to trivial.

"Tally, are you sure you know a better way to the surface?"

"Certainly. I followed it all the way, and I even emerged onto the surface of Genizee itself. May I speak?"

"No. You may *move.* Get going."

For once, the embodied computer did not stop to give her an argument. He went scrambling up the steep incline of the duct, using the ribbed hoops of bracing material that supported the wall every few feet as a primitive set of steps.

Darya managed to stay close behind him for the first forty paces, but then she felt her legs beginning to tighten and tire. Even for someone in tip-top condition the steep ascent would be exhausting. But she had had no rest for days, no real food for almost as long, and she had spent a good part of the past few hours vomiting what little she had been able to eat. She had to stop. Her heart was ready to burst from her chest, and the muscles of her thighs were cramping into agonizing knots.

Except that the sound of the Eaters was louder. The young Zardalu were entering the duct that she was climbing.

Close on her heels came Dulcimer. He was sobbing for breath and gasping over and over again, "They'll eat me, they'll eat me. They'll eat me alive. Oh, what a terrible way to go. They'll eat me alive."

Not just *you,* Darya thought with irritation. They want to eat *me* as well. And then: Irritation is meant to be *used.* Build it to anger, to fury.

The Zardalu would not get a *living* Darya. Never. She would force herself upward along the lightening tunnel until she died of exhaustion. Then, if they liked, they could have her lifeless body.

She clenched her fists and moved faster, propelling herself up the narrow tunnel until suddenly she ran into the back of E. C. Tally. He had stopped a few feet from the end of the duct and was peering upward to the brightly lit surface.

"Keep going!" Darya's voice was a breathless croak. If Tally was going to stop now and start a discussion . . .

"But there may be Zardalu—above us—I thought I heard them."

Tally was as out of breath as she was. Darya did not have the strength to argue. She pushed right past him. Possible Zardalu on the surface could not compete with *certain* Zardalu ten yards behind them.

She scrambled the final few feet of the duct, pulled herself over the edge, and sat on skinned hands and knees. The sunlight was painfully bright after the tunnels.

She blinked around her. No Zardalu, not that she could see. But her nose crinkled with their ammoniac smell. Tally was right, they had been here. But where were they now?

She stood up and turned quickly to look at her surroundings.

Tally had been right about another thing. This was much closer to the place where they had landed the *Indulgence.* She glanced that way. And saw the most wonderful sight that she had ever seen.

The ship was there, just as though it had never left the surface of Genizee. It was no more than a couple of hundred yards away, and she could see that its main hatch was open.

A booby trap?

Who cared? No future danger could be worse than what they faced here and now. Tally and Dulcimer were out of the duct, and Tally was picking up big loose rocks and hurling them down the entrance. But it was not doing any good. The approaching high-pitched squeaks of immature Zardalu were louder and angrier than ever.

"Come on. We'll never stop them with rocks." Darya began to run toward the ship, across a broken terrain of stony fragments and low, ankle-snaring bushes. She thought that progress would be easier as soon as she came to the level stretch of moss, but when she reached it her desperate dash became a dreadful slow motion. She felt as if she were running through thick, viscous air; she was so tired that the whole shoreline and the sea seemed to tilt and roll in front of her. The sky darkened. She knew it had to be her own exhaustion and failing balance.

Just a little farther. Just a few more seconds, a few more steps. *Quickly.* The Zardalu were catching up with her. She dared not turn to look. She concentrated all her attention on the ship ahead. It must have weapons—so why didn't it fire them at the young Zardalu behind her, and to hell with Julian Graves and his pacifist views? *Fire, dammit, fire.* Or were the Zardalu so close that any shot would hit her, too?

And then she realized that there was something wrong with the ship itself. It had risen a few feet clear of the surface, but instead of hovering smoothly it was rocking and shuddering. There was something beneath it, something rising from the dark mud.

Tentacles. The pale-pink tentacles of gigantic subterranean Zardalu, curling up to grasp the whole forty-meter length of the ship.

And then, still staggering forward, Darya realized her mistake. Those were not Zardalu. They were not tentacles. They were the tiny perfumed flowers of the gray moss, on their delicate hair-thin stalks, as she had seen them when she first set foot on Genizee. But now they were enlarged to monstrous proportions and growing faster than anything could ever grow.

At last, and at the worst possible moment, the Zardalu were revealing their full mastery of biological science. In the time it took Darya to struggle five steps, the body-thick stalks had sprouted another three meters. They were curling up around the smooth convex hull of the *Indulgence.* The ship sank a fraction, tugged downward by the web of tendrils.

Louis Nenda was at the open hatch, four feet off the ground. He shouted to Darya and reached down past a thick pink growth that reached into the hatch itself. She held up her hand, felt it gripped in his, and was lifted into the air and into the lock in one arm-wrenching heave.

She lay flat on the solid floor. A moment later E. C. Tally was panting and grunting next to her. Darya lifted her head.

"Dulcimer!" she gasped. He was too heavy; Louis Nenda could never lift him in. She tried to struggle to her feet to help, but it was beyond her strength.

She heard a croaking scream from outside the ship. A dark-green body came soaring past her, the corkscrew tail fully uncoiled by one great leap. Dulcimer flew right across the hatch and on into the ship's interior, wailing as he went. She heard the bouncing-ball sound of rubbery Polypheme hide against metal bulkhead, and another anguished scream.

"All aboard. Take us up!" Nenda was kicking at the thick pink tendril. It was still growing.

"The hatch is still partway open." Rebka's voice came from the intercom at the same moment that Darya felt the ship rise and strain against its closing cage of vegetation.

"I know." Nenda had pulled out a wicked-looking knife and was stabbing at the tendril. The blade bounced right off it. "I can't close the damned thing. Give us maximum lift, and hope."

Darya suddenly understood Nenda's problem. The *Indulgence* had a powerful weapons system, but it was intended for longer-range use. The weapons had never been designed for anything that coiled around the ship itself.

The scoutship lifted a few more feet. There was a jerk, and the upward motion ceased. The whole hull groaned with sudden stresses. A few seconds later Darya felt another downward lurch.

"No good." Nenda was leaning dangerously far out of the hatch, stabbing at something out of sight. "We're at about ten meters, but we're bein' pulled down an' the Zardalu are comin' up. You hafta give it more stick."

"I hear you," Rebka's calm voice said over the intercom. "But we have a slight problem. We are already at full lift. And I don't think whatever's holding us is even trying yet."

The ship creaked all over, shivered, and descended another few inches.

"Wrong way, Captain," Nenda said. If he and Hans Rebka were in the same screaming panic as Darya, one would never have known it from their voices. "An' if we don't get out of here soon," he added, in the same conversational tone, "we're gonna have ourselves some visitors." He stamped on a pale-blue groping tentacle and booted it clear of the hatch.

Rebka's voice came again. "Get where you can grab something and hold on. And move away from the hatch."

Easy to say. But there was nothing within easy reach for anyone in the lock. Darya and E. C. Tally scrabbled across to the interior door of the lock itself and wedged themselves together in the opening.

"Hold on *now,*" Rebka said, while Darya wondered what he planned to do. If they were *already* at maximum lift, how could Hans hope to do better?

"I'm going to try to rock us out," Rebka continued, as though he had heard Darya's unvoiced question. "Might get rough."

The understatement of the century. The *Indulgence* began to roll from side to side. The floor beneath Darya's feet rose to the right until it was close to vertical, then before she could adjust to that it was swinging back, to roll as far the other way. Cascades of unsecured objects came bouncing past, everything from flashlights to clothes to frozen foods —the galley storage cupboards must have been shaken loose.

"Not working." Nenda had ignored Rebka's command to stay away from the hatch. By some impossible feat of strength and daring he had braced himself by one hand and one foot against its sides and was leaning far outside to hack and kick at the climbing Zardalu. He hauled himself back in to speak into the intercom. "We've been pulled another half-meter downward. Gotta do somethin' else, Captain—sharpish, I'd say."

"Only one thing left," Rebka said. "And I hate to try it. Away from the outer hatch, Nenda—and this time I mean it."

Louis Nenda cursed, threw himself across to the inner door, and braced his stocky body across Darya. "Hold onto your guts."

The ship moved. It dropped like a stone and hit the surface of Genizee with bone-jarring force as Hans Rebka canceled all lift. From below came the groan of buckled hull plates.

The cage of swathing pink tendrils was looser, opened at the bottom by the weight of the *Indulgence* and at the top by the ship's sudden fall. Before it could tighten again, Rebka had put the ship into maximum forward thrust. The pointed nose pushed aside the two stalks that were growing there, and the *Indulgence* shot forward across the gray moss.

Darya could see out the open hatch. The pink arm of vegetation whisked away out of sight. But then they were heading for the jagged inland fingers of rock, too fast to stop.

Spaceship hulls were not built for structural strength. Impact with one of those jutting rocks would split the ship wide open.

Hans Rebka had returned to maximum lift the moment they were free of the enfolding growths. The *Indulgence* flew toward the rocky outcrops, straining upward as it went.

Upward, but too slow. Darya watched in terrified fascination. Touch and go. They were heading right for one of the tallest rock columns.

There was a horrible sound of scraping metal and a glancing blow all the way along the bottom of the ship. Then Darya heard a strange noise. It was Louis Nenda. He was laughing.

He released his hold on the inner lock door and walked across to the still-open outer lock, balancing himself easily on the shifting floor. As Darya watched he leaned casually out to look far down at the receding surface, then slammed the lock shut with one heave of a muscular arm.

He came back to where Darya and E. C. Tally were still wedged in the doorway, clutching it—in Darya's case at least—with the unbreakable grip of pure terror. He lifted them, one in each hand, and set them on their feet.

"You two all right?"

Darya nodded, as a wail of anguish rose from beyond the lock. "I'm all right." It was the wrong time for it, but she had to ask the question. "You were *laughing*. What were you laughing at?"

He grinned. "To prove to myself I ain't dead." And then he shook his dark mop of hair. "Naw, that's not the real answer. I was laughin' at *myself*. See, when I come down here this time I told Atvar H'sial that I was fed up of gettin' close to the Zardalu, an' then comin' back without any blind thing to show they even existed. It happened on Serenity. It happened last time I was down on Genizee. An' damned if it didn't just happen again, though I swore to myself it wouldn't. I didn't collect even a tentacle-tip. Unless you wanna go right back down an' look for keepsakes?"

Darya shivered at the thought. She reached out and put her hand on Nenda's grimy, battered forearm. "I knew you'd come back to Genizee and save me."

"Not my idea," he said gruffly. He looked away, toward the interior of the ship where Dulcimer was still moaning and screaming. "Though it would have been," he added, so softly that Darya was not sure she heard him correctly, "if I were brighter."

He eased away from her in Dulcimer's direction. "I'd better go an' shut up that Polypheme, before he wakes up everybody on board who's tryin' to sleep. You'd think he was the only one anythin' ever happened to."

Darya followed him through to the main cabin of the *Indulgence,* E. C. Tally close behind her. Hans Rebka was sitting at the controls. Dulcimer was a few feet away, rolling around the floor in panic or agony.

"Shut him up, will you?" Rebka said to Louis Nenda. He gave Darya a wink and a grin of pure delight when she moved to stand next to him. "How did you like that take-off?"

"It was awful."

"I know. The only thing worse than a takeoff like that is no takeoff at all. My main worry now is the scrape on the hull, but I think we're fit for space." He glanced away from Darya to where Nenda and Tally were down on the floor next to the moaning Dulcimer. "You're not shutting him up, you know—he's making more noise than ever."

"He is. An' I don't see why, he looks just fine." Nenda grabbed hold of the Chism Polypheme, who appeared to be trying to form himself into a seamless blubbering sphere of dark green. "Hold still, you great streak of green funk. There's not a thing wrong with you."

"Agony," Dulcimer whimpered. "Oh, the sheer agony."

"Where do you say you're hurtin'?"

Five little arms waved in unison, pointing down toward Dulcimer's tail. Nenda followed the direction, probing down with his hands into the tight-coiled spiral.

"Nothing here," he muttered. And then he gave a sudden hoot of triumph. "Hold it. You're right, an' I'm wrong. Jackpot! Dulcimer, you're a marvel, bein' smart enough to grab this with your rear end. Relax, now, I've got to pull it off you."

"No! It's in my flesh." Dulcimer gave a whistling scream. "My own flesh. Don't do that."

"Already did. All over." Louis Nenda was bending low at the Polypheme's tail and chuckling with satisfaction. "Think of it this way, Dulcimer. You got a contract with us that gives you twelve percent of this. An' not only that, I think mebbe there's others will give you their share of it, too."

While Darya stared at him in total confusion, Louis Nenda slowly straightened up. He raised his right hand.

"Look-see. They're not gonna be able to say we made the whole thing up *this* time."

And finally the others could see it. Held firmly between Nenda's finger and thumb, wriggling furiously and trying to take a bite out of him with its tiny razor-sharp beak, was a pale apricot form: the unmistakable shape of an angry infant Zardalu.

CHAPTER 23

IF HANS REBKA had been asked—without giving him time to think about it—how long it was from leaving the *Erebus* to his return with Darya Lang and the rest, he might have guessed at fifteen to twenty hours. Certainly more than twelve. It was a shock to glance at the ship's log on the *Indulgence* as they docked, and learn that less than three hours had passed since they had floated free of the main ship.

Nothing on board the *Erebus* seemed to have changed. The ship was drifting along in the same high orbit, silent and apparently lifeless. No one greeted them as they emerged from the hold.

Rebka led the way to the bridge. Everyone followed him, not because they were needed there but because they were too drained to think of doing anything else. Dulcimer was the sole exception. The Polypheme went toward the nearest reactor with a single-minded fixity of intention that made him oblivious to everything else.

"Ah, let him have it," Nenda muttered, seeing Darya's questioning face. "Look at the color of him. He'll be good for nothin' anyway, till he gets a jolt of sun-juice. An' close that damned reactor door behind you," he called out to Dulcimer as they went past him.

The two of them had been walking last in the group, Darya drinking from every spigot until she felt like a rolling ball of water. They were both exhausted, drifting along and talking about nothing. Or rather, she was exhausted and Nenda was talking about *something,* but Darya was too tired to fathom what. He seemed to be trying to lead up to a definite statement, but then always he backed away from it. Finally she patted his arm and said, "Not just now, Louis. I'm too wiped out for hard thinking."

He grunted his disagreement. "We gotta talk now, Darya. This may be our only chance."

"Of course it won't be. We'll talk later."

"Can't do it later. Has to be now. Know what the Cecropians say? 'Delay is the deadliest form of denial.' "

"Never heard that saying before." Darya yawned. "Why don't you just wait and tell me about it tomorrow?" She moved on, vaguely aware that he did not seem pleased with her answer.

Nenda followed, the infant Zardalu tucked under one arm. It was peering around with bright, inquisitive eyes and trying to turn far enough to bite his chest. He sighed, gave the Zardalu a reproving swipe on the head, and increased his pace until he was again side by side with Darya. He put his free arm around her and hugged her shoulders, but he did not speak again on the way to the control room of the *Erebus.*

Hans Rebka had been there for a couple of minutes, staring into one of the alcoves of the huge room. His shoulders were bowed with fatigue—but he straightened up quickly enough when he saw Nenda's arm around Darya.

She knew that expression. To avoid an argument she pulled free and hurried across to the alcove herself—and received the biggest shock of all. Atvar H'sial was there, sitting crouched by J'merlia's limp and silent body.

J'merlia. Darya had seen him vanish, down on Genizee. He could not be here, lying on the floor of the control room.

"J'merlia . . ." she began, and then subsided. Her head was full of cotton. She didn't know where to begin.

"At says J'merlia's doin' all right," Nenda said. He had followed her over to the alcove. "She's in communication with him. She says he's not quite conscious yet, but his condition's improving. We just hafta be patient and wait a minute."

J'merlia was beginning to groan and mutter. Darya leaned closer. It was a language that she could not understand. She looked around the group. "Anyone recognize that?"

"Recognize, yes," E. C. Tally said. "Understand, no. That is J'merlia's native tongue; the language of an adult male Lo'tfian. Unfortunately there is no dictionary in the central data bank. I suspect that no one in this party speaks it."

"But that don't matter," Nenda added. "There's some sorta trauma in J'merlia for human speech, but everything'll come out anyway in the pheromones. Atvar H'sial can tell me what J'merlia's tryin' to say, and I can tell you. She says it might be a couple of minutes more before we get sense, but she wants us to be ready for it. Kallik, gimme a computer recording mode."

The Hymenopt nodded, and her paws flew across the console. She had apparently recovered from her earlier meeting with the vanishing J'merlia. Now she was perched on the rail of the console, staring intently down at the Lo'tfian and at Atvar H'sial hovering worriedly over him.

Darya noticed that Kallik was using her middle paws. One forelimb was missing. What had happened to it? No one bothered to mention it. Her eyes went on to Louis Nenda; his arms were covered with blister burns from contact with some hot or corrosive liquid. Those two were the worst off physically, but no one else was much better. Every face and body was lined with fatigue and covered with grime.

Darya must look as bad herself. And her inside was worse than her outside. She felt a thousand years old.

The ridiculous nature of the whole effort struck her. To

take this motley, wounded, and exhausted bunch of cripples, slaves, and misfits, and expect them to make progress in understanding *anything,* let alone the mysteries of Genizee and its shrouded belt of singularities . . .

That was some joke. Except that she could not laugh at it. She could not even feel angry anymore. And she had not faced up to the biggest mystery of all: J'merlia's very presence.

"How can he be here?" Darya found herself blurting out her question and pointing at the Lo'tfian. "He was on Genizee with me and Tally. And then he vanished—into the air."

They did not mock her statement, which would have been perfectly justified. "J'merlia was on the *Erebus* with Julian Graves, too," Hans Rebka said, a sigh in his voice. "He vanished here. He was with our party on Genizee. And he vanished *there.* And then a few hours ago he came back in the seedship—unconscious. Don't ask me, Darya. You're the one who's good at theories. What's *your* explanation?"

Optical illusion. Mirrors. Magic. Darya's thoughts were running out of control. "I don't have one. It's impossible."

"So wait another second, an' mebbe we'll hear J'merlia speak for himself." Louis Nenda pointed to Atvar H'sial. The Cecropian's pleated proboscis was trembling its way across J'merlia's body, touching his pale-lemon eyes on their short stalks, caressing the sensing antennas and the narrow head. J'merlia was jerking and mumbling in response to her touch. Darya and the other humans heard nothing intelligible, but suddenly Louis Nenda began to talk.

"Goin' to give it verbatim if I can." He placed the infant Zardalu on one of the control chairs, where it clamped itself firmly with multiple suckers and bit an experimental beakful of soft seat cushion. "At'll ask the questions, say what J'merlia says exact to me, I pass it on exact to you. Get ready, Kallik. Any second now."

The smell of complex pheromones was strong in the air of the cabin, their message tantalizingly hidden from most of the watchers.

"I, J'merlia, hear, and I reply," Nenda said, in a flat, unnatural voice. "It began with the seedship. I was left alone to repair that ship, whilst Dominatrix Atvar H'sial, Captain Rebka, and Master Nenda went to explore the shore buildings of the Zardalu. I completed the repair ahead of schedule and decided to test the seedship in flight. It performed perfectly. I therefore flew it back to the buildings, where I found that large numbers of Zardalu were emerging from the water . . ."

The room was totally silent except for J'merlia's harsh breathing and Nenda's gruff, emotionless voice. He might have been reading from a parts list when he spoke of the escape to space after the Zardalu had forced the others underground, of J'merlia's unplanned rendezvous with the amorphous singularity, of the agonies of physical distortion on the edge of that singularity, of the improbable rescue and transfer to Hollow-World. The description of J'merlia's awakening, and the meeting with Guardian, produced an irrepressible stir of interest and muttered comments.

"Sounds exactly like World-Keeper," Rebka said softly. "Nenda, can you ask Atvar H'sial to probe for a fuller physical description of that Builder construct?"

"I can ask her to try. I don't think she got good two-way talk yet, though."

The recital continued: of Guardian's message-probe survey of the spiral arm; of Guardian's increasing conviction of its own unique role as preserver and protector of Genizee for the return of the Builders. And finally—Atvar H'sial's proboscis writhed, and Louis Nenda's voice cracked as he spoke—J'merlia's own pain began. He had been split, his mind shattered to fragments, his body sent far away on multiple assignments.

He had been nowhere and everywhere, simultaneously; with Guardian on Hollow-World, with Julian Graves on the *Erebus,* and with both parties on and under the surface of Genizee. He had died in the roaring column of plasma, he had vanished from the grasp of the Zardalu, he had been cross-examined by Guardian, and later he in turn had asked his programmed questions of World-Keeper. And at the end, the worst agony: J'merlia's loss of selves and final collapse.

The Lo'tfian had been lying cradled in four of Atvar H'sial's limbs. As Nenda said the word "collapse" he sat up and stared around him. The pale-yellow eyes were puzzled, but they were rational.

"Collapse," he repeated in human speech. His tone was perplexed. "When that collapse was over, Guardian told me that my task was now complete. I was again on Hollow-World, but I was told that I must leave there. And now I am again on the *Erebus*. How did I come here?"

Darya glanced at each of the others in turn. They all seemed calm, even relaxed. Yet J'merlia's "explanation" of how he had been in many places at once, and vanished instantaneously from each of them, explained nothing.

Why weren't the rest as upset and confused as she was? Was she unique, in the way that things contrary to physical laws disturbed her? All her life she had sought rationality and shunned mysticism or magic. But now, faced with flagrant violation of what she believed possible . . . could she be seeing evidence of a whole new physics, radically different from everything that she had ever learned?

Darya rubbed her eyes. She could accept many things, but not that. But wasn't failure to accept itself unacceptable? Didn't she pride herself on her open-mindedness, her willingness to theorize based on *evidence* rather than prejudice?

Exhausted, Darya withdrew into her own unhappy trance of analysis and reassessment.

When J'merlia began to talk for himself, Louis Nenda ended his translation. With the attention of the group all on the Lo'tfian, he sidled across to Atvar H'sial and whispered a pheromonal question at a level that only the Cecropian could receive: "How is J'merlia? In the head, I mean. Can you tell?"

Atvar H'sial edged away from the group, leading Nenda

with her. "He is mystifyingly normal," she said softly. "Almost everything he has told us sounds impossible, yet there is no evidence that he is lying, or fabricating his own version of events."

"So he'll be able to talk for himself from now on? And answer questions when they have them?"

"I believe so."

"Then this is the best time, right now. The *Indulgence* is fueled and deserted. You made a flight plan for us to clear the Anfract. We could take off while everybody's sitting listenin' with their mouths open, and head back to Glister." He paused, a question mark in his pheromones. "If you still want to do it, I mean."

"I am not sure." Atvar H'sial was also oddly hesitant. "Perhaps such action is premature." The twin yellow horns in the middle of her head turned to the group clustered around J'merlia, then back to Nenda. "He *seems* normal, but that only means any derangement must be deep. It is a poor time to leave him."

"Are you tellin' me you wanna stick around awhile, to make sure your bug's all right? Because if you are, I guess I don't mind doing—"

"I did not say that. I realize that we made a deal before you left for Genizee. Cecropians do not renege on their commitments. But I *am* J'merlia's dominatrix, and have been since he was first postlarval. So if *you* wish to remain longer . . ."

"I agreed to that deal, too. If you want to change it, I'll be glad to. Just don't start tellin' me what *you'll* be leavin' behind if we go. I'm leavin' behind a helluva lot more." Nenda watched as Atvar H'sial's trumpet horns turned to focus on Darya Lang. "Don't get me wrong. What I mean is, I'm at least as close to *Kallik* as you are to J'merlia, and I'll be leavin' her behind." He sighed. "But a deal's a deal."

Atvar H'sial scanned Nenda, J'merlia, and Darya Lang for a long time before she nodded. "We will all suffer, but we cannot take them. And if we do not leave *now,* who knows when our chance will come? The separation with J'merlia and Kallik—or with anyone else—will surely be as brief as we can make it. But even so, if we are going, then I would prefer to go—at once."

Nenda nodded. The Cecropian and the Karelian human backed quietly away toward the exit of the control chamber. At the door they paused for a few seconds and stared back into the room. Finally, at some mutual decision point, they turned and hustled each other out of the chamber.

Their departure went unnoticed. Darya was still deep in her own brooding, and everybody else was focused on J'merlia.

"There are *many* sentient Builder constructs in the spiral arm," the Lo'tfian was saying. "Hundreds or thousands of them, according to Guardian, set in well-hidden locations where we have never dreamed of looking. They have intermittent contact with each other, as they have for millions of years. But Guardian and World-Keeper question the actions and even the sanity of most of the others. They are united in their view that this region, and this alone, will be the home of the Builders when they return to the spiral arm."

Darya had been fascinated by the Builders and their artifacts for all of her adult life; but at the moment other matters had higher priority.

"J'merlia!" She found a final pocket of energy and tried one last time. "You say you were *here,* at the same time as you were on Genizee. But that can't be right. Nothing can be in two places at once. How do you explain what happened to you?"

The pale-yellow eyes swiveled. J'merlia shook his head. "*Explain?* I cannot explain. I know only that it is so."

"And I know that it's *impossible.*"

"It cannot be impossible. Because it *happened.*"

It was the ultimate irrefutable argument. J'merlia was calm and immovable. Darya stared at him in frustration. The rest of the group looked on in silence, until E. C. Tally stirred and turned to Darya.

"May I speak?"

"Not unless it's *relevant,*" Darya snapped. She was so tired, so baffled—the last thing she could stand at the moment was some senseless digression from a witless embodied computer.

"It is, I believe, most relevant. May I speak?"

"Oh, get on with it."

"To a logical entity, such as myself, the behavior of organic intelligences, such as yourself, provides many anomalies. For example, the history of humanity, the species concerning which my data banks have most information, is replete with cases where humans, on little or no evidence, have believed in impossibilities. They have accepted the existence of a variety of improbable entities: of gods and demons, of fairies and elves, of 'good luck' charms, of magic potions, of curses and hexes and evil eyes."

"Tally, if you're going to blather about—"

"But at the same time, humans and other organic intelligences often seem unwilling to accept the implications and consequences of their own *legitimate scientific theories.*" Tally stared squarely at Darya. "For example, do you reject the basic concepts of quantum theory?"

"Of course I don't!"

"So you *accept* those ideas. But apparently only in some abstract sense. You reject them at a *practical* level."

"I do not." Darya's outrage was enough to burn away—temporarily—her lethargy.

"So you accept the central idea that a particle, or a system of particles, such as an electron or proton or atomic nucleus, can be in a 'mixed' quantum state. In essence, it can occupy several different possible conditions at once. An electron, for example, has two permitted orientations for its spin; but it cannot be said to have either one spin state or the other, until it is *observed.* Until that time, it may be partly in *both* possible spin states. Do you agree?"

"That's a standard element of the theory. It's well established by experiment, too. I certainly accept it. What *is* all this, E.C.? Get to the point."

"I am *at* the point. That is the point, the whole point. You were the one who told me that all researchers of the Torvil Anfract accepted the instantaneous interchange of pairs of Anfract lobes as evidence of quantum effects. The Anfract, you said, possesses *macroscopic quantum states,* of unprecedented size. You said that to me *before* we ever entered the Anfract.

"Then we flew in, with Dulcimer as pilot. Do you recall a time when the ship's motion became choppy and irregular?"

"Of course I do. I was scared. I thought for a moment that we were hitting small space-time singularities, but then I realized that made no sense."

"And you asked Captain Rebka what was happening. Since humans appear to have trouble recalling events exactly, let me repeat for you his exact words. 'Planck scale change,' he said. 'A big one. We're hitting the quantum level of the local continuum. If macroscopic quantum effects are common in the Anfract we're due for all sorts of trouble. Quantum phenomena in everyday life. Don't know what that would do.' You accepted his statements without question. Yet you apparently remain unwilling to face their implications. As I said, organic intelligences do not have *faith* in their own scientific theories.

"There *are* large-scale quantum phenomena inside the Anfract; and the Builder sentient constructs have learned how to utilize them." Tally pointed to J'merlia. "He, like you and me, consists of a system of particles. We are each described by a quantum-mechanical state vector—a very large and complex one, but still a single state vector. Isn't it obvious that J'merlia existed in a *mixed quantum state* when he was—simultaneously—here and on Hollow-World and in several places on Genizee? And isn't it clear that his total wave function did not resolve and 'collapse' back to a *single* state—to a single J'merlia—until he returned here on the seedship?"

Darya stared at the others—and saw no reaction at all. She found Tally's words mind-blowing. They appeared to accept what he was saying without question. "But if that happened to J'merlia, why didn't it happen to *all* of us?"

"I can only conjecture. Clearly, the actions of Guardian were of central importance. If the development of mixed quantum states in organic intelligences is a *borderline* event in the Anfract, something which occurs only rarely or under specially contrived circumstances, then a trigger action may be needed. Guardian knows how to provide that trigger. And perhaps J'merlia is by his nature unusually susceptible to accepting a mixed quantum state."

"Oh, my Lord." Hans Rebka had been lolling back in the pilot's chair as though he were half-asleep. Now he sat upright. "*Unusually susceptible to a mixed state.* Tally's right, I'm sure he is. That's what's been wrong with Julian Graves, ever since we got here. His two personalities were integrated back on Miranda, but we always knew it was a sensitive balance. They're still liable to disruption. He was *already* on the borderline, it wouldn't take much to push him over. No wonder he said he couldn't think any more! No wonder he sent out a distress signal. His mind was divided—*too much me.* Two parallel quantum states in one body, trying to make decisions and control the *Erebus.*"

"Those are my thoughts exactly." Since E. C. Tally lacked emotion or intellectual insecurity, his display of pleasure at Rebka's support was a tribute to simulation modeling. "And it means that it is not necessary to seek a treatment for the councilor's condition. He will *automatically* return to normal, as soon as we exit the Anfract and are again in a region of space-time where macroscopic quantum states cannot be sustained."

"So what are we waiting for?" Hans Rebka glanced around the group. "We can leave the Anfract at once. We've got the evidence of Zardalu we came for"—he nodded to where the infant land-cephalopod was systematically destroying the seat of the control chair—"the best evidence we could possibly have. The sooner we leave, the sooner Graves gets back to normal. Can anyone think of a reason why we shouldn't leave at once?"

With Julian Graves incapacitated, Rebka was in charge. He did not need approval from the others for a decision to leave the Anfract—except that he had learned, long before, that unanimous group decisions guaranteed a lot more cooperation.

He automatically looked for Louis Nenda, the most likely source of opposition. And he noticed his absence, and that of Atvar H'sial, just as Dulcimer came bouncing into the chamber.

This time the Polypheme had hit it exactly right. His skin was a clear, bright green, his master eye and scanning eye were alert and confident, and he was delicately balanced on his coiled tail. He was in fine physical shape.

He was also in an absolute fury.

"All right." He bobbed forward until he was in the middle of the group. "I've put up with a lot on this trip. I've been near-drowned and chased and starved and had my tail chewed half off—none of that in my contract. I put up with all of it, brave and patient. Only this is too much." The blubbery mouth scowled, and the great eye glared at each of them in turn. His voice rose to a squeak of rage. "Where's my ship? What have you done with the *Indulgence*? I want to know, and I want to know *right now.*"

Louis Nenda and Atvar H'sial were asking much the same question. They had carefully drifted the ship free of the *Erebus,* leaving the drive off so that no emergency telltales would flash on the bigger ship's control panels.

After a few minutes of floating powerless, Nenda again scanned his displays. The *Indulgence*'s complete trajectory for exit from the Torvil Anfract had already been set in the computer, needing only the flip of a switch to send the ship spiraling out. A few kilometers away on the right, steadily receding, the *Erebus* was a swollen, pimpled oblong, dark against the pink shimmer of the nested singularities. On Genizee, a hundred thousand kilometers below, it was night, and the high-magnification scopes showed no lights. If the Zardalu were active down there they had excellent nocturnal vision, or their own sources of bioluminescence. The only illumination striking the surface from outside would be the faint aurora of the singularities and the weak reflected light of the hollow moon, glimmering far above the *Indulgence* to Louis Nenda's left.

He turned to Atvar H'sial, crouched by his side. "We're far enough clear. Time to say good-bye to Genizee. There's a lot of valuable stuff down there, but if you're anythin' like me you'll be happy if you never see the place again. Ready to go?"

The Cecropian nodded.

"Okay. Glister, here we come." Louis Nenda flipped the switch that set in train the stored trajectory. For a few seconds they surged smoothly outward, heading for the constant shimmer of the nested singularities.

And then Nenda was cursing and grabbing at the control panel. The *Indulgence* had veered, and veered again. Atvar H'sial, blind to the display screens, clutched at the floor with all six legs and sent an urgent burst of pheromones.

"Louis! This is not right! It is not what I programmed."

"Damn right it's not! And it's not what's bein' displayed." Nenda had killed the program and was trying to assert manual control. It made no difference. The ship was ignoring him, still steadily changing direction. "We're goin' the wrong way, and I can't do one thing about it."

"Then turn off the drive!"

Nenda did not answer. He had *already* turned off the drive. He was staring at the left-hand display screen, where Hollow-Moon hung in the sky. A familiar saffron beam of light had speared out from it, impossibly visible all along its length, even in the vacuum of space. The *Indulgence* was caught in that beam and was being directed by it.

"Louis!" Atvar H'sial said again. "The drive!"

"It's *off*."

"But we are still accelerating. Do you know where we are going?"

Nenda pulled his hands away from the useless controls and leaned back in his seat. Genizee was visible in the forward screen, already perceptibly larger. The *Indulgence* was arrowing down, faster and faster.

"I'm pretty sure I know *exactly* where we're going, At." He sighed. "An' I'm pretty sure you're not gonna like it when I tell you."

CHAPTER 24

THE DEFINITION OF reality; the meaning of existence; the nature of the universe.

The philosophies of the spiral arm on these subjects were at least as numerous and diverse as the intelligences who populated it. They ranged from the Inverse Platonism of Teufel—*What you see is all there is, and maybe a bit more*—to the Radical Pragmatism of the Tristan free-space Manticore—*Reality is whatever I decide it should be*—all the way to the Dictum of Inseparability espoused by the hive-mind Decantil Myrmecons—*The Universe exists* as a whole, *but it is meaningless to speak of the function of individual components.*

Darya had no doubts about her own view: The universe was *real,* and anyone who believed otherwise needed a brain tune-up. There certainly was an objective reality.

But could that reality ever be comprehended by a living, organic being, one whose intelligence and logical faculties had to operate in the middle of a raging cauldron of glands and hormones and rampant neurotransmitters?

That was a far more subtle question. Darya herself was inclined to answer no. If one wanted a good example, all one had to do was examine recent events.

Look at yesterday. On her return to the *Erebus* from the surface of Genizee, the objective universe had been an old and worn-down and shabby place, a weary present grinding its way forward into a pointless future. She had been swept by the random tides of exhaustion from confusion to anger to total languid indifference.

And now, one day later? Twelve hours of forty-fathom slumber had pumped ichor into her veins. She had followed that with a meal big enough to stun a Bolingbroke giant, and discovered that the universe had been remade while she slept. It gleamed and glowed now like the lost fire-treasure of Jesteen.

And she glowed with it.

The *Erebus* was winding its way slowly and quietly out of the depths of the Torvil Anfract. Darya sat knee to knee in silent companionship with Hans Rebka, staring at the panorama beyond the hulk of the ship. He was more relaxed than she had ever seen him. The view from the observation bubble helped. It was never the same for two seconds: now it showed a lurid sea of smoky red, lit by the sputtering pinwheel fireworks of tiny spiral galaxies rotating a million billion times too fast to be real; a few moments later all was impenetrable blackness, darkness visible. But by then touch had substituted for vision. The ship moved through the abyss with a shuddering irregular slither that created a tremor in Darya from hips to navel. An invisible something caressed her skin—caressed her *inside* her skin, with the most delicate and knowing of sensual fingers.

"More macroscopic quantum states," Hans Rebka said lazily. He waved his hand at a Brownian-movement monitor. "But they're getting smaller. Another few minutes and we'll be back to normal scale."

"Mmmph." The intellectual part of Darya nodded and tried to look serious. The idiot rest of her grinned and drooled in sheer delight at the sybaritic pleasures of the world. Nothing ought to be *allowed* to feel so good. Wasn't *he* feeling it, the way that she was? Something wrong with the man, had to be.

"And according to Dulcimer's flight plan," Rebka continued, "it's the last time we'll meet macro-states. Another few minutes and Graves should flip right back to normal. He's feeling better already, just knowing what it is that's wrong with him."

"Ummm." If you were to run tourist ships out to this part of the Anfract, and keep them here for a few hours—assuming that anyone could stand such a wonderful feeling for so long—you could make your fortune. And maybe you could be on the ship *yourself,* for every trip.

"Hey." He was staring at her. "What are you looking so pleased about? I thought you'd feel down today, but you're wall-to-wall grin."

"Yeah." Darya gazed into his eyes and amended her last thought. He wasn't feeling it. You would run ships of *female* tourists out here.

But the tingle inside her was fading, and at last she could speak. "Why shouldn't I grin? We found the Zardalu, we all escaped from Genizee, we've got the live infant as evidence for the Council, and we're on the way home. Don't we have a right to smile?"

"*We* do. Graves and Tally and me do. You don't."

"Hans, if you're going to start that nonsense again about me and Louis Nenda . . . he was only trying to explain what they were going to do with the *Indulgence,* I'm sure he was. And then when I wouldn't listen to him, he put his hand on—"

"That's not a problem anymore. We know what happened to the *Indulgence.* While you were snoring your head off, Kallik located a flight plan in a locked file in the *Erebus*'s backup computer. Nenda and Atvar H'sial are heading for Glister and Nenda's old ship."

That stopped Darya for a moment. She had been hoping to return to Glister herself in the near future, but it was not the right time to mention it. "Well, if you think that I'm smiling because Nenda and I had been—"

"Haven't thought about that all day."

He had, though, Darya was sure of it—he had answered

much too fast. She was getting to know Hans Rebka better than she had ever known anyone.

"I'm not worrying about you and Nenda, or you and anyone." His face was no longer lazy or lacking emotion. "I'm worrying about *you,* and only you. You didn't come here to find the Zardalu, I know that."

"I came to be with you."

"Nuts. Maybe a little bit of that, and I'd like to think so. But mainly you came to find the Builders."

So she had! It was hard to remember it that way now, but he had pinpointed her original motives for leaving Sentinel Gate. Whether she liked it or not, he was getting to know her, too, better than anyone had ever known her. The flow through the empathy pipe ran both ways. It had been open for only a year. How well would they know each other in a *century*?

"And now," he was continuing, "you're going home without a thing."

"Nonsense! I have a new artifact to think about. An amazing one. The Torvil Anfract is a Builder creation, the strangest we've ever seen."

"Maybe. But can I quote what a certain professor told me, back on Sentinel Gate? 'There *was* nothing more interesting in my life than Builder artifacts—so long as the Builders remained hidden. But once you meet the Builders' sentient constructs, and think you have a chance to find the Builders themselves, why, the past is irrelevant. Artifacts can't compete.' Remember who said that?"

He was not expecting an answer. Darya had one, but she did not offer it. Instead she looked again out of the observation bubble. In the sky outside, the blackness was breaking to a scatter of faint light. A view of the spiral arm was coming into view; the *real* spiral arm, as it ought to look, undistorted by singularity sheets or quantum speckle or Torvil chimeras. They must be almost out of the Anfract.

"But you're no closer to the Builders now than you were a year ago," Hans went on. "Farther away, in some ways. When we were dealing with the Builder constructs on Glister and Serenity, you thought that The-One-Who-Waits and Speaker-Between held the key to the exact plans and intentions of the Builders. Now we find that Guardian and World-Keeper agree completely with each other—but they don't agree with the other constructs at all. It's a mess and it's a muddle, and you have to be disappointed and miserable."

Darya didn't feel the least bit miserable or disappointed. She had questions, scores of them, but that was what the world was all about.

She smiled fondly at Hans Rebka—or was she just smiling at the warm feeling inside her? Surely a bit of both. "Of course Guardian and World-Keeper agree with each other. You'd expect them to—because they are *the same entity*. They are one construct existing in a mixed quantum state, just the way J'merlia existed. But in their case, it's permanent." And then, while Hans jerked his head back and stared along his nose at her in astonishment, she went on. "Hans, I've learned more about Builders and constructs in the past year than anyone has *ever* known. And you know what? Every new piece of information has made things *more* puzzling. So here's the central question: If all the constructs are earnest and industrious and incapable of lying, and if they are all busy carrying out the agenda of their creators, then why is everything so confusing?"

She did not expect an answer. She would have been upset if Hans Rebka had tried to offer one. He was going to be the tryout audience for the paper she would write when she returned to Sentinel Gate. Their departure from the Research Institute had hardly been a triumph. She laughed to herself. Triumph? Their exit had been a *disaster*; Professor Merada, wringing his hands and moaning about the artifact catalog; Glenna Omar, her neck covered in burn ointment and bandages; Carmina Gold firing off outraged messages to the Alliance Council . . . The next paper that Darya produced had better be *really* good.

"I'll tell you why we've been confused, Hans. The Builder constructs have terrific physical powers, we know that by direct experience. And it's tempting to think that anything with that much power has to know what it's doing. But I don't believe it anymore. For one thing, they all have *different* ideas as to their purpose. How come? There's only one plausible answer: They contradict each other, *because each construct had to develop its ideas for itself.*

"Our assumption that the machines have been following a well-defined Builder program is nonsense. There's no such program—or if there is, the constructs don't know it.

"I'll tell you what I think happened. Five million years ago, the Builders upped and vanished. The machines were left behind. Like the other artifacts, they're *relics* left by the Builders. But there's one big difference: the constructs are *intelligent.* They sat and waited for the promised return—real or imaginary—of their creators; and while they waited, they invented agendas to justify their own existence. And each construct made up a Builder Grand Design in which it played the central role. Sound familiar?—just like humans?

"It wasn't the Builders who decided Genizee was a special place that one day they'd settle down in. They evolved on a *gas-giant* planet, for God's sake—what would they want with a funny little world like Genizee? It was *Guardian* who decided that its planet was special and set up a weird quarantine system to keep space around it free of anyone who failed the test of ethical behavior. Apparently we passed, and the Zardalu failed. Pretty weird, you might say, but the other constructs are just as bad. The-One-Who-Waits thought that Quake was uniquely special, and Speaker-Between knew that Serenity was the only important place."

Rebka was shaking his head. "I think you're wrong. I think the Builders are still around, but they don't want us *looking* for them. I think they tried to confine the Zardalu to Genizee, but the Zardalu escaped, and got out of control. The Great Rising took care of the Zardalu, they were no problem anymore. But now the Builders are worried about us. Maybe *we'll* get out of control, too. I think the Builders are *scared* of us."

Darya frowned at him. He did not seem to realize that one

was not supposed to interrupt the logical flow of a presented paper.

"Hans, you're as bad as the constructs! You're trying to make us *important.* You want the Builders to like us, or be afraid of us, or even hate us, but you can't accept the idea that they don't care about us or know we exist because on their scale of things we are *insignificant.*"

She paused for breath, and he squeezed in his question: "Well, if you're so smart and so sure you know what's going on, tell me this: Where are the Builders *now*?"

"I don't know. They could be anywhere—at the galactic center, out in free-space a billion light-years away, on a whole new plane of existence that we don't know about. It makes no difference to my argument."

"All right, suppose they are gone. What role *do* we play in their affairs?"

"I already told you." Darya grabbed his arm. One did not do *that* in a written paper, either, but no matter. "*None.* Not a thing. We're of no importance to the Builders whatsoever. They don't care what we do. They created their constructs, and they left. They have no interest in the artifacts, either—they're big deals to us, but just throwaway items to them, left-behind boxes in an empty house.

"The Builders have no interest in humans, Cecropians, or anyone else in the spiral arm. No interest in you. No interest in me. That's the hardest bit to swallow, the one that some people will never accept. The Builders are not our enemies. They are not our friends. We are not their children, or their feared successors; we are not being groomed to join them. The Builders are *indifferent* to us. They don't care if we chase after them or not."

"Darya, you don't mean that. If you don't chase after them you'll be giving up everything—abandoning your life-work."

"Hey, I didn't say I wouldn't chase them—only that *they don't care* if I do or I don't. Of course I'll chase them! Wherever the Builders went, their constructs couldn't go. But maybe *we* can go. We're not the types to wait for an invitation. Humans and Cecropians, even Zardalu, we're a pushy lot. Every year we learn a little bit more about one of the artifacts, or find a path that takes us farther into the interior of another. In time we'll understand it all. Then we'll find where the Builders went, and in time we'll go after them. They don't care what we do now, or what we are. But maybe they won't be indifferent to what we *will* be, when we learn to find and follow them."

As she spoke, Darya was running the sanity checks on her own ideas. Publishable as a provocative think piece? Probably—her reputation would help with that. Credible? No way. For people like Professor Merada there had to be supporting evidence. Proof. Documentation. References. Without them, her paper would be viewed as evidence that Darya Lang had gone over the edge. She would become one of the Institute's crackpots, banished to that outer darkness of the lunatic fringe from which there was no return.

Unless she did her homework.

And such homework.

She could summarize current progress in penetrating and understanding Builder artifacts. That was easy; she could have managed it without leaving Sentinel Gate. She could describe the Torvil Anfract, too, and offer persuasive evidence that it was an artifact of unprecedented size and complexity. She could and would organize another expedition to it. But for the rest . . .

She began to speak again, outlining the program to Hans Rebka. They would need more contact with Builder sentient constructs. On Glister, certainly, and on Serenity, too, once they found a way to make that jump thirty thousand light-years out of the galactic plane. Naturally they would have to return to the Anfract, and understand the mixed-quantum-state being, Guardian/World-Keeper. The use of macroscopic quantum states offered so much potential, it too could not be ignored. And of course they would have to hunt down other constructs, with help from Guardian, and interact with them long enough to detail their functions. Perhaps humans and Cecropians and the other organic intelligences would have to become new leaders for the constructs, defining a new agenda for them, one that corresponded to the reality of the Builders' departure. And they must return to Genizee, too, and learn how to handle the Zardalu. Julian Graves would insist on it, no matter what anyone else wanted.

Hans Rebka listened. After a while he took a deep breath. Darya did not seem to realize what she was proposing. She imagined that she was describing a research effort. It was nothing like that. It was a long-term development program for the whole spiral arm. It would involve all organic and inorganic intelligences in decades of work—centuries of work, *lifetimes* of work. Even if she was wrong about the Builders (Hans believed that she was) she was describing a monstrous project.

That did not faze her at all. He studied her intent face. She was *looking forward* to it.

Could it be done? He did not know. He knew it would not go as smoothly as Darya seemed to imagine—nothing in the real world ever did. But he knew he would never talk her out of trying. And she would need all the help that she could get.

Which left *him*—where?

Hans Rebka leaned forward and took Darya's hands in his. She did not seem to notice. She was still talking, shaping, formulating.

He sighed. He had been wrong. Trouble was not ending as the *Erebus* wound its leisurely and peaceful way out of the Torvil Anfract. Trouble was just beginning.

Epilogue

"—AND HERE THEY come."

Louis Nenda squinted gloomily across the open plain, a flat barren landscape broken in one place by a twisted thicket of the moss plants sprouted beyond gigantism. It was almost nightfall, and the *Indulgence,* in spite of all his efforts, had skidded to a halt within the elongated shadow of those same jutting sandstone towers where he had first run from the Zardalu.

"The weapons are ready." Either Atvar H'sial was totally calm, or she had a control of her pheromonal output that Nenda would never achieve. "However, the partial exposure of the target group makes complete success doubtful. With your concurrence I will withhold our fire until they pursue their usual strategy of a mass attack. At that time a more significant number of them will be within range."

"Okay—unless they try another one of their damn botany tricks. First sign of that you blast 'em—an' don't wait to talk it over with me."

The side ports of the *Indulgence* had been opened to permit Atvar H'sial a direct omnidirectional viewing of the area around the scoutship. Her vision unaffected by fading light, she sat at the weapons console. Louis Nenda was by her side in the pilot's chair. He had modified one of the displays to look directly down. At the first sign of sprouting life beneath them he would propel the *Indulgence* laterally across the surface. They might not be able to leave the surface of Genizee, but they could certainly try to skim around on it.

The Zardalu were rising from the sea, floating upward one by one to stand a few meters offshore with only their heads showing. Louis Nenda watched thirty of them emerge before he stopped counting. Numbers were not important. One would be more than enough if it reached the ship.

Evening sunlight glittered off bulbous heads of midnight blue. Judging from those same heads, the Zardalu included four of the biggest specimens that Nenda had ever seen. They were twice the size of the still-growing forms who had pursued them into the interior of Genizee. They must be part of the original fourteen, the Zardalu who had been held in stasis on Serenity. Nenda had fought them once and knew how tough they were.

"Get ready." The first one was wading ashore to stand spraddle-tentacled on the beach. It was close enough for Nenda to see the steady peristalsis of land-breathing in the thick body.

"I am ready, Louis. But I prefer a mass of them as target. One is not enough. And in addition . . . ????"

The pheromones trailed off into a prolonged question mark. Louis Nenda needed no explanation. An adult Zardalu in upright posture could glide the forty meters between shore and ship in a few seconds. But this Zardalu was not standing. While the rest stood motionless in the water, it had slumped forward like a flattened starfish, tentacles stretched wide and horizontal, head facing the ship. After a few seconds it drew its flexible limbs together into a tight group facing the sea and began to push itself slowly forward toward the *Indulgence.* The head was lifted just far enough for the huge cerulean eyes to stare at the ship.

"Twelve meters." Atvar H'sial was touching the button. "I think it is time."

"Hold just another tick." Louis Nenda leaned forward

to stare out the sea-facing port. "If that's what I think it is . . ."

The Zardalu had stopped moving. The long vertical slit below the beak had opened, to produce an odd series of sighs and clicking whistles.

"We request to speak." The language sounded like a clumsy attempt at Hymenopt. "We request that you listen."

"What is it saying, Louis?" Atvar H'sial could detect the sonic stream, but she could not interpret it. "I am ready to fire."

"Not yet. Keep your paw on the button, but hold it there till I say. Mebbe we're not dead yet. I think it wants to parley." Nenda switched to simple Hymenopt. "I hear you, Zardalu. What you wanna tell me? And keep it short an' simple."

"I speak for all Zardalu, new-born and old-born." Thick tentacles writhed to slap the mossy ground, while the main torso held its recumbent posture. "It is difficult to say . . . to say what must be said, and we beg your patience. But since we returned here, we have learned that before our reawakening we few survivors were held dormant for many millennia. While we slept, much changed. In times past, we in our travels around the spiral arm had little contact with humans, or with their great slaves." The blue eyes turned to regard Atvar H'sial.

Nenda had been giving the Cecropian a simultaneous pheromonal translation, but he kept the last phrase to himself. He did not want the envoy gone in a puff of steam.

The prone Zardalu inched closer. "But now we have met your kind in four separate encounters: one on Serenity, and three on this world. Each time, you seemed helpless. We were sure—we *knew*—that you could not escape death or slavery. Each time, you won free without effort, leaving us damaged. More than that, since our return to this world we have been unable to leave it. Yet you come and go from here as you choose."

"Damn right." Don't I wish! he added to himself. "We do anythin' we like, here or anywhere."

"Louis, what is it *saying*?" One more gram of pressure from Atvar H'sial's paw, and the Zardalu would go up in smoke. "It is moving still closer. Should I fire?"

"Relax, At. I think I'm startin' to enjoy this. Lookatit. It's gettin' ready to *grovel.*"

"Are you sure?"

"I'm sure. It's not talkin' regular Hymenopt, see, it's talkin' Zardalu Communion *slave-talk.* Anyway, I've done enough grovelin' myself in my time to recognize the signs. Look at that tongue!"

A long, thick organ of royal purple had emerged from the slit in the Zardalu's head and stretched four feet along the beach. Nenda took three paces forward, but he paused a few inches short of the tongue. He glared down into the wide blue eyes. "All right. You lot are finally learnin' what we knew all along. You're a pack of incompetent slimebags, an' we got you beat any day of the week. We know all that. But what are you proposin'?"

The tongue slid back in. "A—a *truce*?"

"Forget it."

"Then—a surrender. On any terms that you demand. Provided only that you will guide us, and teach us the way that you think and function. And help us to leave this planet when we wish to do so. And in return, we are willing to give you—"

"Don't worry your head about that. *We'll* decide what you'll give us in return. *We* got some ideas already." The slimy tongue had come out again. Nenda placed his right boot firmly on top of it. "If *we* decide to go along with your proposal."

"We?" With a tongue that could not move, the Zardalu garbled the word.

"Yeah. *We.* Naturally, I gotta consult my *partner* on a big decision like this." Nenda gestured to Atvar H'sial, and read the look of horror in the bulging cerulean eyes of the Zardalu. The great body wriggled, while a gargling sound of apology came from the mouth slit.

Nenda did not lift his foot a millimeter, but he nodded thoughtfully.

"I know. She may be so mad at bein' called a *slave* that she'll just decide to blast you all to vapor, an' that'll be that."

"Master—"

"But I'm a nice guy." Louis Nenda removed his foot from the Zardalu's tongue, turned, and headed casually back to the *Indulgence.*

"You stay right there, while I try to put in a good word for you," he said over his shoulder. "If you're real lucky, mebbe we can work somethin' out."

ABOUT THE AUTHOR

Born and educated in England, Charles Sheffield holds bachelor's and master's degrees in mathematics and a doctorate in theoretical physics from Cambridge University. He is past president of the American Astronautical Society and president of the American Astronautical Society and the Science Fiction Writers of America, and he was until recently, when he left to write full-time, Chief Scientist of Earth Satellite Corporation. He lives in Silver Spring, Maryland.